"No, Muhsin," she whispered, reading the intentions in his gaze.

He nodded his head slowly. "Yes," he said, curling one hand about her waist.

Duchess realized she hadn't the will to refuse further. Her body instantly arched into Muhsin's chiseled frame as she raised her lips to meet his. The kiss was as passionate as it had been earlier that day. Tiny moans escaped her mouth, she was so enthralled by the pleasure consuming her body. For the first time, it didn't matter that they were alone. That they were thoroughly involved with one another was all that mattered.

Muhsin ended the kiss by tugging Duchess's lower lip between his perfect teeth and soothing the surface with his tongue. He held her close for several moments, the wide plane of his palm stroking her back methodically.

"Will I be sorry I did that later?" he asked, pulling away to stare into her face.

Duchess smiled and shook her head. "You won't be sorry," she assured him, her fingers curling around the lapels of his jacket in an effort to stop their shaking.

AlTonya Washington

LOVE
Scheme

ARABESQUE
★BET
BOOKS™

BET Publications, LLC
http://www.bet.com
http://www.arabesquebooks.com

ARABESQUE BOOKS are published by

BET Publications, LLC
c/o BET BOOKS
One BET Plaza
1900 W Place NE
Washington, DC 20018-1211

All Kensington Titles, Imprints, and Distributed Lines are available at special quantity discounts for bulk purchases for sales promotions, premiums, fund-raising, and educational or institutional use. Special book excerpts or customized printings can also be created to fit specific needs. For details, write or phone the office of the Kensington special sales manager: Kensington Publishing Corp., 850 Third Avenue, New York, NY 10022, attn: Special Sales Department, Phone: 1-800-221-2647.

First Printing: April 2005

10 9 8 7 6 5 4 3 2 1

Printed in the United States of America

To my sister LaWanda Washington. Thanks, Wanda, for always listening to and supporting my ideas, and for being my best friend. I love you.

Acknowledgments

To the stores, libraries, and especially the readers who have welcomed my work into your establishments and homes. I thank you all so much.

Prologue

Philadelphia, Pennsylvania

Duchess Carver swore she'd never use the elaborate wall bar in her office. The company designers had decided to install the fixture when the headquarters was remodeled a few years earlier.

Shaking her head, Duchess sloshed a bit of vodka into a glass cooler and praised the design team's foresight. Known for her grace-under-fire demeanor, today she'd finally been pushed to the brink of losing all restraint. Several stiff drinks would be needed if she had any hopes of continuing the conversation with the CEO of Vuyani Enterprises in Chicago.

"Ms. Carver? Should I take your silence to mean you finally accept the fact that we can't do business?"

Duchess rolled her eyes, bristling at the raspy voice on the other end of the phone line. Though it was a voice she was sure would make most women's toes curl in delight, she was hoping the man would choke on his words and lose all ability to speak.

"Ms. Carver?" he repeated, the words colored with unmistakable impatience. "I'm a busy man, so if there's nothing else—"

"Why are you so against this?" Duchess blurted out, cursing the anxiety in her voice. She took a quick gulp of the vodka, hoping its relaxing powers would take effect. "Vuyani doesn't even use that building."

Toe-curling laughter sounded through the line. "True," he confessed, "but our conversations have got me to thinking that perhaps I may have a use for it after all."

Bastard, Duchess ranted silently. "Mr. Vuyani, you can't expect me to believe that all of a sudden you've developed a use for that building?"

"Maybe I have."

"But it's been sitting there unused for almost two years."

"Your point?"

Don't scream, Duchess willed herself.

Muhsin Vuyani rested his head against the Navigator's suede headrest and waited. Never had he so enjoyed a business call via cell phone in midday traffic. It was a shame this would be his last conversation with the dynamic Ms. Carver.

"Is this the way you usually do business, Mr. Vuyani? You can't have what you want so you refuse to negotiate? You just take your marbles and go home?"

Muhsin chuckled over the summation. "Negotiate, Ms. Carver? That unused building you're so interested in is worth five times what you're offering me for it. I feel my price is more than acceptable."

Duchess slammed her cooler to the oak bar. "Your *price* is controlling interest in my company."

"And with the state of your company, controlling interest wouldn't bring me much profit."

"I won't stand here and beg you for that dilapidated shack. Controlling interest at Carver is something you'll never have," Duchess said.

We'll see, Muhsin thought. "I'm sorry we couldn't come to an agreement, Ms. Carver. Good luck to you," he said, clicking off the phone just as he turned into the parking deck near the office building where his next meeting was scheduled. All offices in the building were accessible by private elevators only. Muhsin triggered the Navigator's alarm, then headed for the elevator to Isaiah Manfres's office.

Muhsin took a moment to recap his conversation with Duchess Carver. She was desperate to have that building; it was easy to hear in her voice. Unfortunately, he was desperate, too—well, he wasn't desperate. Still, controlling interest and having complete ownership of Carver Design Group was on the short list of future Vuyani acquisitions. One way or another, it was about to become a possession.

The elevator doors opened and Muhsin smiled when Isaiah walked toward him with an outstretched hand.

"Glad to see you found the place all right," Isaiah said.

"Impressive," Muhsin complimented, his deep-set brown eyes scanning the room.

Isaiah nodded his agreement. "Yeah, I got a bit more to do, a few more pictures to hang, but, yeah, it *is* impressive. Thanks for backin' me on this, man."

Muhsin strolled over to survey the glass entertainment center that occupied an entire wall. In addition to the state-of-the-art sound system and plasma-screen TV, the unit was stocked with awards, degrees and numerous photos.

One of those photos caught and held Muhsin's unwavering stare for several moments. His lips parted and his expression grew intent as he studied the framed photo of a laughing young woman with bright hazel eyes.

"Stop drooling, man," Isaiah teased, noticing the picture his friend now held.

"Who is she?" Muhsin asked, waving off the drink Isaiah offered.

"Duchess Carver," Isaiah said coolly, perching on the edge of his desk.

Muhsin shook his head. "Duchess," he whispered in disbelief.

Isaiah held his glass poised at his mouth. "What? You know her?"

Muhsin uttered a short, incredulous laugh. *Yeah, she's about to do business with Vuyani.*

Chapter 1

Philadelphia, Pennsylvania

Lee Robeson eyed the cloud of dust at the far end of the wide road. The blinding curves prevented him from determining the cause of the uproar. Still, being the dutiful security guard that he was, Lee continued to squint toward the edge of the driveway. The sight of a gleaming black SUV eased his curiosity a bit. With an annoyed grunt, he replaced his gray cap and adjusted the wire-rimmed spectacles that sat perched on the tip of his nose.

The intimidating SUV seemed to stop on a dime when the driver pulled to a halt before the security booth. After a second or two, a black tinted window rolled down.

"Can I help you?" Lee queried, eyeing the stranger closely.

The man behind the wheel looked down in his lap, then extended his arm out the window. "I'm Muhsin Vuyani," he said, passing the guard his identification. "Mr. Carver's assistant, Cicely Madison, called and asked me to come out."

"Right." Lee sighed, remembering the woman's urgent call to the guardhouse. "Sounds like there's quite a tussle goin' on in there."

Muhsin rubbed his index finger along the line of his brow. The security guard's words didn't surprise him at all. Anything from a "tussle" to a full-blown fight was sure to break out whenever Jerome Carver and Trent Vuyani crossed paths.

"Is it all right if I go on in?" Muhsin asked, eager to get his father out of the house and head back to Chicago.

Lee pushed a button and the red-and-white striped lever lifted high over the road. "Please do," he said, tipping his hat just slightly. "And please have Ms. Madison call if you people need help up there."

Muhsin stepped on the accelerator and continued his rapid journey toward the incredible mansion in his midst. When he reached the front of the stone house, a small, stout woman waited on the porch. Her hands were clasped tightly and the look on her plump, brown face went way past worried.

"Muhsin Vuyani?" the tiny lady called. Her childlike voice sounded close to breaking.

"That's right," Muhsin said, heading toward the porch.

Cicely forgot her unease as she gazed up at the tall, young man before her. The close-cut crop of flaming auburn hair and warm brown eyes held her speechless for a moment. "You look nothing like your father," she observed, enveloping one of Muhsin's hands in both of hers.

"I'll take that as a compliment," he said, unable to hide his one-dimpled smile.

Cicely turned toward the front door. "Please do," she mumbled.

"So what's goin' on in here?" Muhsin asked, pushing one hand into his tan trouser pocket.

Cicely massaged her neck. "The question is what *isn't* going on in here," she said, groaning. "Those two started five minutes after your father got here."

"Well, what's he doin' here, anyway?" Muhsin whispered, following Cicely through the mammoth-sized foyer and down the long, checkered hallway.

"Mr. Carver's daughter thought the meeting would turn out better if he and your father met away from the office."

"She was obviously mistaken."

"Well, we were expecting your father for dinner. I'm afraid he arrived ahead of schedule. Mr. Carver isn't big on surprises, I'm afraid."

"Especially when the surprise is Trent Vuyani," Muhsin acknowledged before his brows drew close. "Where is Ms. Carver?" he asked, hoping Cicely couldn't sense his interest.

"Taking a nap. Her father wouldn't let me wake her."

Muhsin's frown returned as he and Cicely neared a set of double mahogany doors at the end of the hall. "Is that them?"

"Mm-hmm," Cicely said, smoothing both hands over her round hips before pulling the doors open.

Inside, Jerome Carver and Trenton Vuyani stood across the desk in the spacious study. They resembled two dogs about to strike. The argument had elevated beyond a fevered pitch, giving Muhsin and Cicely a chance to walk inside without being noticed.

Jerome Carver leaned closer to his desk and braced both hands on its polished cherry-wood surface. "Shifty-eyed joker! I should've never agreed to this mess!"

"In all the years I've known your dumb ass, that's the smartest thing you've ever said!" Trent Vuyani retorted, his long, brown face contorted by a scowl.

Jerome's mouth curled into an ugly snarl beneath his neat mustache. "Negro, right now, I'm gonna put my foot so far up your—"

"Mr. Carver!"

Both men turned at the sound of Cicely's shrill voice. Unfortunately, the interruption did little to stifle the argument.

"What the hell is he doing in my house!" Jerome bellowed when he spotted Trent's son standing in the room.

Cicely smiled up at Muhsin. "I had hoped he could get you two to calm down. You are here to talk business," she reminded her boss softly.

"Forget that!" Jerome decided, waving his hand in angry disgust. "I got nothing more to say to this fool!"

"Likewise!" Trent spat, his expression murderous. "I wouldn't bail you out if my life depended on it."

Muhsin stepped a bit farther into the room. "Pop—"

"Bail me out!" Jerome interjected, moving from behind his desk. "Vuyani, what in the hell do I need you to bail me out for?"

Trent spread his arms wide. "That's why you wanted to meet me, isn't it? Things must be pretty bad if you had no choice but to call me."

"Pop—"

"Stay out of this, Blaze," Trent ordered his son.

Muhsin knew his father meant business whenever he used his nickname. Trent would hear nothing he had to say. Turning toward Cicely, he shrugged and shook his head.

"Sorry, Ms. Madison, this just isn't gonna work. These two jackasses got drama between them I can't even begin to understand."

Cicely's face dropped in defeat and she began to wring her hands. The door closed behind Muhsin, sounding muffled against Jerome and Trent's raised voices.

Muhsin decided to give the two enemies a bit more time to argue before he tried again to get his father to leave. He took a stroll around the grand, lower level of the home. The spacious floor plan allowed for long corridors between the huge rooms. The walls were decorated with paintings adapted from religious scenes of the Bible. The subjects were of African descent, drawing an observer's eye to the detail, richness and meaning of each piece.

Muhsin found himself enthralled with an incredible portrait of *The Last Supper*. Several minutes passed before he felt the desire to move on. At the end of the corridor, another room caught his attention. The area seemed to be gleaming with sunlight and beckoned him inside. Muhsin found himself standing at the threshold of a glass-encased sitting room.

Though he wasn't a huge fan of bright rooms, this one had a calming effect that surprised him. Slowly, he moved farther into the room, his vibrant brown eyes drawn to the immaculate back lawn. Again, time seemed to slip away as he enjoyed the spectacular view of the professionally manicured landscape. Some time later, a frown tugged his sleek brows. What sounded like a tiny whimper caught his ears. Muhsin's eyes narrowed when he turned to see a young woman curled on the overstuffed cream sofa.

Completely intrigued by her sleeping form, Muhsin took a step closer. Just then, the woman turned onto her back and uttered a soft sigh. He cast a quick glance across his shoulder before taking a seat on the edge of the sofa.

"Damn," he whispered, recognizing her from the picture in Isaiah Manfres's office.

Her flawless, cinnamon-brown skin appeared silken to the touch. He was entranced by her small nose and full, kissable lips. His gaze was trained on her exquisite features and he must have caressed every inch of her face with his eyes. He believed he could never tire of watching her. Suddenly, as though drawn by some invisible thread, he reached out to trace the smattering of fine hair at her temple. Just then, she fidgeted and the very long lashes brushing her cheeks fluttered open.

Duchess Carver gazed upon the blurry figure looming above her. Slowly, her sight cleared, but she was still in a dream state. A brief smile touched her lips before her lashes fluttered closed once more.

Muhsin could not move. He was too captivated by her unforgettable eyes. Such a striking shade of hazel, they were almost translucent in their appearance. Just one glance and he was entranced. Again, he reached out to touch her silken skin.

"What the hell are you doing?" an angry voice demanded.

Muhsin snatched back his hand and moved away from the sofa.

"What the hell are you doin' with my daughter?" Jerome Carver demanded again. This time he raised an index finger in Muhsin's direction.

"Don't start with my boy, Rome," Trent warned, heading toward his son.

Jerome forgot about Muhsin and focused on Trent. "Don't tell me what to do in my own house. I'll be damned if he gets his hands on Duchess the way you snatched Tarsha!"

Trent closed the distance between himself and his rival. "Son of a bitch!" he snarled, his hands a hair's breath from the collar of Jerome's casual gray shirt.

Luckily, Muhsin was there to restrain his father. He reached Trent just before the man could lunge at Jerome's neck.

"Get the hell out of my house. Both of you," Jerome ordered softly, though his voice was laced with steel.

"Come on, Pop." Muhsin urged his father, patting the man's shoulder. He couldn't resist casting another glance at Duchess. She hadn't stirred once amidst the deep voices in the room.

The easy look in his brown eyes vanished as quickly as it had appeared. Then, he turned and pushed his father from the sunroom.

Philadelphia, Pennsylvania—ten months later

Overcast skies hovered above DeMarcus Memorial Gardens. One corner of the huge graveyard seemed to be covered with people. Business associates, friends and family crowded the grave site where Jerome Carver's body was being committed to the ground. The church service itself had been an emotional event, but emotions ran even higher at the cemetery.

Duchess Carver was Jerome's only child. She sat staring straight ahead and tried to remain poised and cool, but failed miserably. Her large, unforgettable hazel eyes were blurred by tears and her wet cheeks soaked the handkerchief she clutched. Still, she conducted herself with the grace of a queen despite the sorrow claiming her heart.

Reverend Mitchell Simpkins wiped the sweat from behind his ears and raised his hands. "Now, if everyone would come forward and pay your respects," he instructed. The attendants began to move toward the casket. The front row was first to stand. Duchess held a single red rose in her black-gloved hand. When she stood next to the silver-gray coffin, her attempt at remaining reserved completely deserted her. Her long legs grew weak and she fell to her knees next to the grave.

"Come on, Dutch," Gretchen Caron whispered as she took her friend's upper arm in a firm hold.

"I'm sorry," Duchess said, her voice shaking as badly as the rest of her.

Jaliel Norris took hold of Duchess's other arm and held her close. "Shh . . . don't you dare apologize. Let's get you out of this crowd," he said.

Duchess allowed her closest friends and business associates to lead her away from the service. She sniffled profusely as her chest constricted against some unseen pressure. "I don't know how I'm gonna make it with everything going on," she admitted, her eyes now red from crying.

"Shh, sweetie," Gretchen murmured, patting her friend's hands as they stood beneath one of the huge elm trees lining the cemetery.

"You up for this trip to Chicago?" Jaliel asked, pulling Duchess back against his chest.

"I don't have another choice but to be ready," she said, her voice flat and lifeless. "This is my last chance to save my dad's business."

"Did you tell Mr. Vuyani you were burying your father today?" Gretchen asked, her attractive brown face clouded by concern.

Duchess nodded. "But I insisted on meeting him anyway."

"*You* insisted?" Gretchen asked.

"Something's got to be done. I'm desperate to have that building, and now that he's finally willing to negotiate . . . It could be the first step in turning the company around."

"But, sweetie, you just buried—"

"I know that!" Duchess snapped. "Daddy died sick over the state of his business. I'll do whatever it takes to get it back on track. If that means I have to go through Muhsin Vuyani, then so be it."

"Damn bastard," Jaliel whispered, his heavy northern accent adding a more hateful tone to the words.

Gretchen and Duchess both nodded, earning a rueful smile from the tall, molasses-complexioned man next to them.

"Bastard, indeed," Duchess said, wiping her runny nose with the handkerchief she still clutched. "When I insisted on keeping the appointment, he said if I wasn't at Vuyani headquarters by ten A.M. sharp, I could forget the deal."

The three old friends stood in silence for a while beneath the stately tree. They almost resembled a statue. Gretchen stood in front of Duchess, holding both her hands. Jaliel was standing behind, his arms around Duchess's waist in a reassuring embrace.

Suddenly, Duchess closed her eyes and took a deep breath. "Enough of this," she said, brushing her hand across the glossy, thick chignon she wore. "I need to get my emotions in order."

"Hey," Gretchen called, taking hold of Duchess's hands again, "get your emotions together tomorrow. Today you're saying good-bye to your father."

A black Mercedes limo sat across the cemetery yard. From behind the tinted black windows of the chauffered car, two men studied the trio of friends.

One of the men tapped the leather armrest with slow, methodic strokes. "Who's the guy holding her?" he asked after several moments of silence.

Roland Jasper cleared his throat when he heard the question. His friend's low, raspy voice held a tinge of something he couldn't quite identify. Roland shook his head, his brown eyes focusing on the threesome. "The guy is Jaliel Norris."

"So that's Norris?"

"Mmm . . . and his relationship is purely professional and platonic," Roland added.

"Good. Tell me about her."

Roland leaned back against the black leather seat and smiled. "Duchess Carver: only child of the successful entrepreneur Jerome Carver—self-made millionaire from menu designs and banners for gourmet restaurants and shops. They recently ventured into the very lucrative arena of Web design for their clients—Duchess's idea. Unfortunately, success does have its price, and the company has more orders than it can handle. They need more staffing and more space for minimum cost. One building you own would be perfect because it's right next to the Carver Design Group and would serve as an ideal annex. Vuyani's initial proposal was to sell the building at half its worth in exchange for controlling interest in the company. Mr. Carver was against that, of course. Duchess, however, is a savvy businesswoman. She's very respected in what she does. She wants to buy that building, but she hopes to change your mind about the conditions of the sale."

A soft chuckle rose from the man so interested in Duchess Carver. "This is all very impressive, Ro, and I've heard this already. I want to know about her. Just her."

Roland smiled. He wasn't at all surprised by his friend's request. "Well, she's a rarity on the singles scene, a bit of a workaholic. She does do a lot of charity work and such for the kids. People love her. They love to have her in their presence."

"I can understand that," Muhsin said.

Roland nodded, agreeing with his friend. "She's always involved with the big charity extravaganzas and fashion shows. Not surprising, considering how fine she is."

"But she doesn't have a man?"

"No, man," Roland confirmed, watching as his friend nodded satisfactorily. "You want to meet her?"

"Mmm-mmm, I'll wait until she comes to me."

Roland chuckled. "You'll try."

"Damnit," Duchess hissed as the taxicab trudged through the crowded slick streets. The cloudy overcast conditions earlier that day had given way to a severe rainstorm that night.

"Maybe your flight will be delayed, Miss," the driver called in an encouraging tone.

Duchess sent the man a thankful smile. "I hope so."

"Do you need help with your bags?" he asked as the taxi rolled toward the airport entrance.

"Thanks, I can handle it." Duchess passed the driver her fare, with a nice tip included. Since the trip was to be a short one, she packed light, taking only one carry-on bag.

Her hazel gaze was wide with anxiety as she raced toward the gate designated on her first-class ticket. "Please be there, please be there," she whispered, clutching the leather strap of the Louis Vuitton bag.

The airport seemed to be filled to capacity, despite the late hour. The closer Duchess came to her gate, the more the crowd seemed to thin out.

"Oh, no," she whispered, her steps slowing as she approached the gate lobby. The area was completely deserted. "Damn." Fiddling with the edge of the long, thick braid that swung high atop her head, she looked around for someone to talk to. "Excuse me," she called when an attendant appeared behind one of the booths.

"Yes, ma'am?" the attendant said, smiling as Duchess approached the counter.

"Flight seven ninety-three to Chicago: is it late . . . or has it left already?"

The attendant appeared apologetic. "Sorry, ma'am, that flight left twenty minutes ago."

"Damn," Duchess whispered for what had to be the tenth time that night.

The short, slender woman behind the counter smiled again. "Perhaps we could get you on another flight?"

Duchess slapped her chin with the end of her braid and gave the woman a rueful smile. "I don't suppose you have one that would get me to Chicago by eight A.M.?"

"Let's see," the attendant said as she typed on her computer. Her expression clouded when she viewed the information on the screen. "The next flight we have would get you there at ten-thirty tomorrow morning."

"Ten-thirty?" Duchess repeated in disbelief. Her extremely long lashes fluttered closed and she took a deep breath.

"Would you like to book that flight?" the attendant asked softly.

Duchess managed a smile for the attentive employee. "Thanks for your help, but ten-thirty would be too late."

"I'm sorry, ma'am."

"Thank you," Duchess said. She managed to keep the smile plastered on her lips until the woman was gone. Then, overcome by an already emotional day, she broke into tears. The sobs wracked her svelte, voluptuous frame. The tears were a mixture of frustration, sorrow and anger.

"Rhonda, I'll talk to you when I get in tomorrow morning, all right?"

"No problem, Muhsin. Everything's under control back here."

Muhsin smiled at his assistant's words. "I don't doubt that, Rhonda. Talk to you tomorrow." He clicked off the cellular phone he carried.

Muhsin passed the last few gates in that wing of the airport terminal. He was leaving Philadelphia for Chicago that evening. After all, he had a meeting with Duchess Carver in the morning. On his way to the hangar his jet occupied, he thought he heard a woman's sobs coming from one of the gates. Sure enough, he spotted a lady slumped against one of the reservation counters. One hand covered her face and her shoulders shook noticeably. It took Muhsin only a moment to re-alize who the woman was.

I hadn't planned on this, Ro, he thought, remembering his friend's teasing remark earlier that afternoon.

Duchess's soft crying had become harsh sobs that sent the tears rolling more steadily. She had no desire to con-trol her emotions. It felt as though she had just lost everything. She was so emotional at that point, she was oblivious to everything around her.

Two hands closed around her shoulders then, and she was pulled back into a firm embrace.

"Shh . . ."

The whispers brushed the soft tendrils of hair curling around Duchess's earlobes. It instantly calmed her and the tears eventually subsided. After a moment, she turned to tell the man she was sorry for the breakdown. When she looked up, her words deserted her.

Duchess found herself gazing up into the most gor-geous deep-set brown eyes she had ever seen. They had the same calming effect as his voice and appeared as though they could peer straight into a person's soul.

Duchess cleared her throat and hoped her words would resurface.

"I'm sorry," she managed.

Muhsin shook his head, a soft grin teasing his wide mouth. "You don't have to apologize to me."

Again, Duchess was speechless. This man's features had her entranced. He was very tall, with a broad physique—not massive, but blatantly powerful. He had a smooth, caramel complexion that only enhanced the richness of his brown eyes. Still, the most unique feature of the tall, sexy stranger had to be the wavy, auburn hair that was cropped into a close cut.

"Are you taking another flight?" Muhsin asked, noticing that the area was empty.

Duchess closed her eyes momentarily, then shook her head. "It won't get me there in time," she told him.

"Is that why you're crying?" he asked, using the pad of his thumb to brush a tear from her cheek.

Again, Duchess found that she could not speak. Her wide eyes were focused on the deep cleft in his chin. She had the strangest feeling she had seen him before.

Muhsin frowned a bit at the faraway look she sent him. He slid his index finger beneath her chin and tilted her head as he stared into her lovely face. "Hey, it's not the end of the world, you know?" he teased, in a meager attempt at taking his mind off how silken her skin felt against his fingers.

The innocent taunt sent Duchess crashing back to reality. "I feel like it's the end of the world," she argued, rubbing her hands across the oversize, red, button-down sweater she wore over a snug V-neck top and pants.

"Let's sit down," Muhsin suggested, curling his hand beneath her elbow.

Duchess allowed herself to be led. "I've got to make this meeting in the morning. All the flights that can get me to Chicago in time are gone. If I miss this meeting, that could signal the end of my father's business. I can't let that happen. Not when I just buried him today."

Muhsin listened as Duchess went on; he patted her knee in an absent, caring gesture. Vaguely, Duchess realized she was baring her soul to the tall god with the flame-colored hair. She couldn't seem to help it. Somehow it felt right. It felt easy.

"I'm sorry about your father," he whispered, after they had sat in silence for a few moments.

The kind words triggered Duchess's tears again. Muhsin cursed himself for making her cry and eased off his seat to kneel before her.

"Hey, stop this now. It's gonna be all right," he said, his large hands patting her knees in a reassuring manner.

Duchess shook her head. "You don't get it. If I don't make this meeting, I lose my chance to get this building. It's imperative we have it because I've got to hire several new people to accomodate all the new accounts we have. If I can't get the building, I can't hire the new staff and I forfeit all that new revenue. I'm already over-extended and I can't afford to lose that money."

"I have an idea," Muhsin said, a thoughtful frown coming to his face. "Why don't you fly with me?"

Duchess sniffled and wiped her eyes with the back of her hand. "I doubt they'll let me sit in your lap," she teased.

Muhsin smiled, a deep dimple appearing in one corner of his mouth. "That's interesting," he said, looking as though he were envisioning the idea. "What I meant was I can offer you a ride in my jet. I'm on my way to Chicago, too."

"Your jet?" Duchess whispered, her lovely eyes growing wider. "No, no, I couldn't," she said with a quick toss of her head. "I don't even know your name."

Muhsin thought for a moment. He decided it wouldn't be smart to reveal his identity just yet. "Call me Blaze," he told her.

"Is that your real name?" Duchess asked, her eyes narrowing slightly.

"Nickname. Can you guess why?" Muhsin challenged playfully.

Duchess smiled, looking at his extraordinary crop of hair. "I think I can." She joined in when he laughed.

"So, will you take me up on my offer?"

Duchess wanted to, needed to say yes, but still she hesitated. "I just don't know. . . . I'm sorry, you're very nice to offer, but—"

"Look, stop apologizing to me," Muhsin pleaded, waving one hand in the air. "You have every right to be suspicious of me. I am a stranger to you."

"I don't mean to insult you," Duchess told him, leaning forward in her seat.

Muhsin chuckled. "It's all right, you don't know me. Hell, I could be out to make you a part of my harem."

Duchess couldn't help but laugh at the assessment.

"What?" Muhsin replied, feigning confusion. "As lovely as you are, you have every right to be suspicious of strange men."

The subtle compliment rendered Duchess speechless. She barely managed a nod and a quick smile.

"Listen," Muhsin whispered as he covered both her hands with one of his, "I'm waiting for my pilot. He will register you in the passenger manifest so there would be a record of your travels."

Duchess began to fiddle with her long braid, her face a picture of guilt. "I am so sorry to be so suspicious. You've been so nice and sweet."

Muhsin realized he was the one who should've been calling her nice and sweet. Even after all he'd been told, he was still surprised to find she was so delightful. "Believe me, I understand."

"Thank you," Duchess said, the heavy fringe of lashes sweeping her cheeks when she lowered her eyes.

"So, may I tell the crew to prepare for two passengers instead of one?"

Duchess inhaled sharply. Blaze's persistence and the persuasive effect of his gorgeous brown eyes were an unbeatable combination. Finally, she nodded.

"This guy you're meeting in Chicago sounds like a real ass," Muhsin said, once the private Learjet was airborne. His eyes narrowed as they slid across Duchess's face.

"Hmph. 'Ass' is too polite a description for that jerk," Duchess replied, noticing his smile at her words.

"You wanna talk about it?"

Duchess grimaced. "Keeping this meeting is not something I'm looking forward to. My father is probably trying to turn cartwheels in his grave over what I'm doing. He hated the man and his father. I can't help but feel like I'm betraying him."

Muhsin shook his head. "You're trying to save his legacy. You should feel good about that."

Duchess smoothed the soft hair at her temple. "That may be true, but I could do without meeting Mr. Muhsin Vuyani. I tell you, just talking to the man tells me he takes himself too seriously."

"How so?"

"Well . . . he's got this tone," Duchess began, folding her legs Indian style on the sofa, "a tone that makes me think he looks down on everything and everyone."

"Do you meet him often?" Muhsin asked, knowing the answer.

"I've never met him. I've spoken with him by phone.

When I confirmed that I still planned to keep our meeting, he said if I wasn't there by ten A.M., I could forget the whole thing. The jackass."

Muhsin winced. "Ouch."

Duchess shook her head, spotting the cool smile teasing her host's mouth. "You must think I'm terrible."

"No, you sounded like you needed to get that out," Muhsin told her as he leaned back in the chair he occupied.

"Hmph, I did," Duchess admitted, smiling as she watched him get comfortable. "So tell me, what you do in Chicago?" She removed the leather ankle boots she sported.

Muhsin shrugged. "A little of this and that."

"Really?" Duchess drawled, taking in her plush surroundings. "It looks like a lot of this and that."

Muhsin chuckled, then began a long, yet vague description of his business dealings in Chicago. Duchess wasn't at all bored. The low, raspy voice was soothing and strangely familiar in its roughness. It wasn't long before his unhurried lazy brogue had lulled her to sleep.

Muhsin pushed himself out of the chair and moved over to Duchess. Gently, he eased her down to the sofa and pulled a gold-and-mocha-toned afghan across her. Then he knelt before her, his strong fingers toying with the abundance of fine hair along her temple. The soft look in his brown gaze slowly grew more pensive. A stab of regret pierced his heart. He wished he could erase his actions over the last several months. Unfortunately, he feared there would be no turning back now and he could only pray she wouldn't hate him forever once she learned the truth.

Duchess took a long stretch and grimaced when she discovered her braid had unraveled. She ran her fingers through the long, straight, glossy locks and sat up on the sofa. Though Blaze was asleep in his seat, Duchess still cursed herself for being such a heavy sleeper. Sure, he seemed nice enough, but he could've done anything while she slumbered.

Hmph, would I have cared? Duchess studied the man's magnificent features. She became engrossed with his strong bone structure, the slope of his nose, curve of his mouth, and that hair. . . .

Muhsin's lashes fluttered then and he looked directly into Duchess's eyes. She wasn't prepared for the tiny jolt that surged through her in response to his stare.

"Lord, I hadn't realized how tired I was," she whispered, trying to divert attention from her incessant staring.

"I know," Muhsin admitted, stretching as well. "But you should have plenty of time to sleep before your meeting in the morning.

Duchess tilted her head back to gather the silky black locks in both hands. "I can't tell you how much I appreciate you being so thoughtful," she said, missing the intensity of Muhsin's gaze as he watched her wind her hair into a loose ball atop her head.

Muhsin shook his head and looked away when she raised her eyes to him. "I can promise you I'm not that thoughtful. You best believe if some guy had been standing at the gate crying I would've kept walking," he teased, smiling when his words made her laugh.

Duchess sighed as she settled into the luxurious suede backseat of the limo that waited for them at the airport. The sleek, black vehicle housed almost every convenience: TV, DVD, minibar, fridge, CD player, phone and laptop.

"Everything you need for a trip up the road," Muhsin announced, crossing his long legs at the ankles as he reclined on his side of the seat.

"Blaze, thanks again. That flight was so relaxing. I really appreciate it," Duchess said as she turned to face him.

Muhsin nodded, his gaze lowering. "Can I get you something to eat before dropping you off at your hotel?"

Duchess was more than tempted by the sweet offer, but she shook her head. "I should go on to the hotel. That nap on the plane just teased me. I'm still really beat."

"No problem," Muhsin whispered, knowing they would have plenty of opportunities to dine together. "We've got a minute before we get there so feel free to doze off if you like," he suggested.

That was an offer Duchess couldn't refuse. It didn't take long before her lashes closed over her eyes. Meanwhile, Muhsin took pleasure in watching her as she slept. Chicago's city streets whizzed by as the car carried them from the airport to the other side of town.

Soon—too soon for Muhsin's liking—they'd reached their destination. "Duchess? . . . Duchess?" Muhsin called some fifteen minutes later as he attempted to rouse her from her nap.

After a second or two, Duchess opened her eyes and looked around. "Are we there?" she whispered.

"We're here," Muhsin said, nodding toward the window at the Raphael Hotel where Duchess would be staying.

Duchess saw the driver waiting to assist her outside the tinted window.

"You need any help?"

Duchess turned back to Muhsin and shook her head. "I'll be fine," she assured him. It was then that she realized this would be the last time she would see her handsome rescuer. On impulse, she leaned close to him and pressed a soft, quick kiss to his caramel-toned cheek.

Before Duchess could move away, Muhsin caught her hand. For the longest time, they simply stared into each other's eyes.

"Good night," Muhsin whispered, finally releasing her hand. He watched her leave the car and take the driver's hand. His eyes followed her until she disappeared past the hotel's revolving doors.

Duchess smiled at her rested, chic appearance as she studied her reflection in the mirrored panels of the elevator. Her thoughts traveled back to the previous evening and she inhaled deeply in remembrance of the beautiful stranger who came to her rescue. It wasn't until much later that she realized she'd never asked for his last name. "A gorgeous, sweet man I'll probably never see again. Just my luck." Duchess groaned, dismissing her warm thoughts of the brief friendship.

Again, she studied her reflection. For the meeting, she had chosen a lovely albeit severe black suit. The blazer sleeves fell past her wrists. Beneath it, she wore a pearl-gray silk blouse with cuffs that peeked out the suit jacket. The color was flattering. The hem of the tailored skirt stopped a few inches above her knee and carried a deep split on one side. Black leather pumps added several inches to her own stunning height. Though she wasn't looking forward to meeting the man who had been such a thorn in her side, the outfit spoke volumes. Muhsin Vuyani would know she was there for serious business.

Duchess recalled heated conversations she'd shared with her father over his adversity to dealing with the

Vuyanis. Now she realized why Jerome Carver wanted as little to do with Muhsin as he did with Trenton Vuyani. Muhsin was a shark, perhaps more of a shark than *his* late father.

The elevator doors opened and Duchess stepped out into the burgundy carpeted hallway. She drew scores of male stares when she walked by. The severe outfit and tight chignon couldn't diminish her startling beauty. Duchess cooly acknowledged the interested glances, but remained focused. In minutes, she was headed down the hall to the president's suite.

A lovely, dark-complexioned woman occupied the seat behind a long cherry-wood desk. Duchess was so taken by the stunning view of the harbor, it took her some time to speak to the president's assistant.

"I'm sorry," she whispered finally, offering the woman an apologetic smile.

Rhonda Cartwright waved one hand in the air. "Believe me, I understand. It took months before I stopped staring openmouthed when I walked by."

Duchess chuckled at the remark. "I'm glad you understand. I'm Duchess Carver. I have a ten A.M. appointment with Muhsin Vuyani."

Rhonda nodded, tucking a strand of her fine, shoulder-length, dark hair behind her ear. "Yes, Ms. Carver, he's expecting you. Please go right in." She gestured toward yet another long corridor.

Duchess smiled again before taking a deep breath and turning in the direction the woman instructed. Not wanting to be late, she had arrived almost fifteen minutes early and had expected to be kept waiting a while. Accepting the fact that the moment of truth had arrived, she squared her shoulders and began to walk forward.

The president's suite occupied the entire west side of

the top floor. Duchess covered the distance between the front desk and the foreboding cherry-wood doors. Following the assistant's instructions, she twisted the polished silver doorknob and stepped into the suite. The room was cooly lit as she'd expected. Still, the soft touch of the golden light cast a calm, mellow effect on the spacious office.

Artwork lined the painted cream walls of the office. Large, comfortable claw-foot armchairs sat before a covered but uncluttered desk. Mocha carpeting ran throughout the room, which also boasted an oversize living-room set to one side of an oak bar and a fully equipped entertainment center to the other.

Duchess's hazel eyes reflected surprise as well as interest. She never expected a man like Muhsin Vuyani to have an office that held such a soothing, artistic feel. Needless to say, she was instantly impressed and relaxed in the surroundings.

She studied the art and photos on the walls and was inspecting the seemingly endless stock of liquors behind the bar when she heard the soft squeak of a door opening. The sound seemed to come from the hallway past the entertainment center. Duchess turned and waited for the person to show himself. When he appeared, she wanted to faint.

"You . . ." Duchess breathed, raising one hand to clutch the gold-rimmed edge of the bar.

Muhsin "Blaze" Vuyani shrugged. His brown gaze was humorous and expectant. "Yes, it's me," he confirmed, pushing one hand into his black trousers when he leaned against the side of the doorway.

Duchess looked down and closed her eyes. "What are you doing here?"

"This is my office."

"What's your last name, Blaze?" Duchess asked, looking up at him with accusing eyes.

Muhsin chuckled, the single dimple instantly appearing. "Vuyani," he said, pushing himself from the entryway and heading farther into the office.

"Muhsin Vuyani," Duchess said, propping one hand on her hip.

Muhsin tapped his index finger to the deep cleft in his chin. "I prefer Blaze," he told her.

Duchess massaged her temples and turned away from the gorgeous man who watched her with such an amused look.

"Are you okay?" he asked, his long, slow strides bringing him closer to the bar.

"How could you do that to me?" Duchess whispered, her voice shaking terribly.

"Hey," Muhsin called, reaching out to pull her hands into his, "I never wanted to deceive you."

"You had all this planned, didn't you?"

Muhsin shook his head at the question. Confusion welled in the warm, bottomless depths of his eyes. "Planned?"

"Our conversation on the plane." Duchess reminded him, snatching her hands away from his. "You let me go on and on about how much I hated and despised you. What—do you get off on hearing that kind of stuff about yourself?"

"Duchess—"

"No, I know what it was. You did it so you'd have a very good reason for turning me down."

Muhsin's long brows rose as he decided to let her vent. He took a seat on the edge of his desk and just watched her.

"I mean, I could tell by our phone conversations that you weren't a nice man," Duchess argued, folding her arms over her chest as she followed him to the other side of the office. "I guess, aside from all that, I never expected you to be quite this cruel. It would have been just as effective if you'd turned me down over the phone, Mr. Vuyani."

Silence filled the room then and Muhsin decided it was safe to speak. "Duchess, turning you down is the last thing on my mind."

"Ha!" she spat. *Lord, please don't let me cry in front of this man again,* she prayed, remembering her behavior the day before.

Meanwhile, Muhsin continued to study her. He was entranced by how beautiful, exquisite and captivating she was. The tough, businesswoman demeanor was an added asset, but it was the emotional damsel-in-distress persona that truly had him hooked. The mix was an intoxicating combination.

After several minutes, Muhsin walked over to where Duchess stood in the middle of the room. His big hands closed around her upper arms and he gave her a gentle squeeze before turning her around to face him. "I didn't ask you here with intentions of turning you down, I swear."

Duchess's striking stare sparkled with unshed tears. "Even after what I said about you?" she asked, her eyes riveted to his white, even teeth as he chuckled.

"Believe me when I say I've heard worse."

Duchess shook her head. "I don't get it, then."

Muhsin's gaze was steady. "I asked you here to marry me."

Chapter 2

"What?" The lone word seemed to echo in the huge office. Duchess knew a befuddled expression was plastered on her face, but there was nothing she could do about it.

"Will you marry me, Duchess?"

No, she hadn't misheard him. Now she was outraged. "Jackass," she hissed, laying a loud slap to the side of his handsome face. "What the hell kind of game are you tryin' to play?" she demanded, wrenching herself out of his light grasp. "You're as sick as you are cruel. First, an all too coincidental plane trip, now a marriage proposal. Did you think I was a fool, Mr. Vuyani?"

Muhsin massaged his jaw, hoping to keep his amusement hidden. Though Duchess had delivered a powerful blow, it had left little more than a sting.

"Thank you for the plane ride and wasting my time," she spat, storming toward the main office door. Just as her hand curved around the knob, Muhsin stopped her by pressing one hand against the cherry-wood door.

"I'm not teasing you here and I don't think you're a fool," he whispered, curling one hand around her elbow. "I only want you to hear me out, please. If you still want to leave after that . . ." He left the statement unfinished because he knew he would not let her go.

"What is this?" Duchess bellowed, snatching her arms

out of his hold. She tried to dismiss the fantastic features on the face so close to her own. Instead, she concentrated on the fact that this man was taking her for an idiot.

"Would you please sit down so I can explain?" Muhsin requested politely.

Duchess set her full mouth in a thin line and refused to comply. Muhsin was maddeningly patient. He simply waved one hand before her and waited.

"You came to see me because you have no other choice but to accept my proposal," he said, once they were heading farther into the office.

Duchess stopped and turned to face him. "No, I'm here to buy that building from you at thirty percent below the listed price," she corrected, her gaze cool and challenging. "In return, I'll supply you with a comfortable piece of stock. I believe I agreed to your request for sixteen percent—an odd amount, but far more acceptable than controlling interest. If something's changed since we last spoke then I'll have to work on another solution to my company's problem. But, Mr. Vuyani, never think you're my last hope," she said, praying she sounded convincing enough.

Muhsin dipped his head in acknowledgment. "I'm sorry for assuming," he replied, and was more than impressed by her shrewd savvy.

Duchess rolled her eyes, her long lashes fluttering like a butterfly's wings. "*I'm* sorry for coming all the way to Chicago to play games."

Muhsin's expression hardened. "Will you just sit down and listen to what I have to say?"

The stiff tone of his words, combined with the raspiness of his deep voice, persuaded Duchess to abide. He waved her toward the sofa, but she chose a seat on one of his oversize matching armchairs instead.

Grinning lightly, Muhsin chose his place, sitting right

before her on the coffee table. "Your dad left you in quite a pinch, didn't he?"

"Don't you mention my father," Duchess warned, raising her round chin defiantly.

"I'm sorry," he said, lifting his hands. "But I do understand. My father did the same thing to me."

"Mmm . . ." she hummed, her dazzling gaze surveying the office. "I can see he left you starving."

Muhsin chuckled. "I promise you, I had to work my ass off for what you see before you."

Duchess offered a knowing smirk. "Please, this place has been growing steadily since your father started it."

"But when my mother died, he lost interest. I had to take over, and when I did the business was in danger of closing," Muhsin said.

"You took over before your father passed?" Duchess queried, watching him nod. "Then why weren't we dealing with you all along regarding the building?"

"My father wanted to deal with your father personally. Apparently, they were old friends or something."

"Old friends?" Duchess asked, her expression skeptical. "They were about as far from friends as you can get. Didn't you know anything about that?"

Muhsin knew everything, but this wasn't the time for revelations. "I knew a little," was all he said.

"Yeah," Duchess replied with a nod, "so did I, but I never got it. My dad had no enemies, business or otherwise. It must've been something pretty heavy to cause such a rift."

"Hmph. Well, at any rate, my father left this world at ease knowing that his business would survive."

A solemn expression crept across Duchess's cinnamon-complexioned, oval face. "That's good he died in peace. I tried to give that to my father, too . . . and would've been satisfied just knowing he was content."

Muhsin's eyes narrowed. His fingers ached to reach out and smooth the sadness from her face.

"So how'd you turn things around?" she asked.

"Well, money was going down the drain every month. Eventually I had to travel out to meet with clients that were considering cutting their ties with Vuyani. Many of the meetings were set so close that I had to drive. I spent a lot of nights in my car."

Duchess was impressed. "You did all that for your dad?"

Muhsin's smile was both serene and rueful. "I loved my pop, and this company was to be mine to run someday. But I'm afraid I had other reasons fueling my dedication."

"Such as?"

"Thirty million dollars in a trust fund."

"Excuse me?" Duchess asked, her tone of voice flat, though her eyes were wide and questioning. "Did you say—"

"Thirty million," Muhsin confirmed. "I almost passed out when I heard the amount myself."

Duchess leaned back in the armchair. "I'm surprised your dad didn't suggest it be used to save the company."

Muhsin shrugged. "Well, this fund was established after the company's problems were a thing of the past. Now I'm the only one who can touch it. Once the stipulations are met."

"Stipulations?"

"I had to keep the company in good standing; I've accomplished that. Now I've only got one more hurdle to cross and the loot is mine."

Duchess smiled as realization shone in the striking pools of her eyes. "The marriage proposal."

"My father was a real con man and he loved to con me," Muhsin said, resting his elbows on his knees while bracing his fingers together. "He called it makin' me strong and it did. He always said I was too much like him and if I kept on I would be a worthless playboy. He set up his last laugh to tie me down, so to speak."

"To get the money, you have to be married?"

"I have to be married," Muhsin said, with a slow nod.

Duchess recrossed her long legs, not noticing Muhsin's intense stare surveying the action. "But it's not like you need the money."

"But I want the money," Muhsin corrected, then shrugged. "I can't stand the thought of thirty million just sitting around going to waste." He shook his head as though the idea was ludicrous.

Duchess couldn't help but smile. "Well, it *is* thirty million. But . . . I still don't know why you're asking me. I mean, you must know tons of women who'd go for this."

"That's my problem. I don't need any greedy opportunists trying to take what I have."

"And you don't think I'm one of those greedy opportunists?" Duchess asked, her gaze cooly expectant.

"You want my building, not my money."

"Thirty million can be tempting."

"We'll have the agreement documented for both our sakes."

"And just what's in this for me?" Duchess asked, eagerly anticipating the response.

Muhsin braced his hands behind him on the desk and leaned back. "I'll give you the building flat out. In addition to the stock, you were going to pay me thirty percent below my asking price. I'll give that to you instead, up front, so you can begin reconstructing."

Duchess was speechless. Then, slowly, she began to shake her head. After a moment or two, she stood on shaky legs. Muhsin remained seated. His gaze was heated as it raked the graceful line of her body.

"I can't believe you," Duchess whispered, as though in a daze.

Muhsin stood as well. "I know this sounds outrageous."

"Ha!"

"That's why I want you to stay in town a few days and think about it."

Duchess slapped her hands against her thighs. "I only booked my hotel for one day."

"Consider it your suite until we make other arrangements," Muhsin assured her with a wave of his hand. He headed back to his desk.

Duchess paced the office, oblivious to the determined, possessive stare following her every move.

"Muhsin, why are you going to all this trouble when you could be wooing a woman you really love?"

The soft-spoken question brought a tiny smile to Muhsin's lips.

"Besides," Duchess added, turning to watch him closely, "you must be seeing someone special."

"I was," he admitted, rubbing his big hands together. "I was seeing several someones. But there's no one I can trust with this."

"How do you feel you can trust me?"

"Because you're a businesswoman," he replied promptly. "You'll have no false perceptions about anything I say . . . or do. And on top of that," he said, moving off the desk, "I'm not ready to jump into the marriage bowl yet."

"Amen," Duchess agreed. "But why not ask someone you work around, or even someone you've . . . hired?"

The deep, rough sound of Muhsin's chuckle filled the air. "I may be in this for the money, but I want a woman on my arm that I can be proud of."

Duchess opened her mouth to question his statement, but she never had the chance.

"You sound interested, Duchess. Does that mean you've made your decision?"

"I don't know yet," she replied curtly. Again, her eyes narrowed in suspicion. "Why don't you tell me how this plan is supposed to work? Do we just show up somewhere and pretend to be married? Have we been seeing each other long? What?"

Muhsin pulled one hand from his pocket and tugged on his earlobe. "The one thing you should know is that this marriage will be real."

"Wait a minute," Duchess breathed, her hands rising defensively. "You mean you actually expect me to marry you?" she asked, taking the set expression on his face as confirmation. "I always planned on marrying once—forever."

Muhsin studied her closely. His handsome features softened just slightly. "In order for the money to become mine, everything has to be thorough and real. That includes the courtship."

"The courtship? What do you—"

"I mean, this whole show has to be seen by everyone I know from beginning to end." Muhsin explained, strolling back to his desk with unhurried grace. "From the time we meet to the time we marry." *And beyond,* he added silently.

Duchess was in utter awe of the man's cunning mentality. "Tell me exactly what you're talking about, Mr. Vuyani," she said, propping both hands on her slim hips.

Muhsin resumed his place on the edge of his desk. "When we meet, it will be someplace public. A place where a good portion of my crowd will see us and witness the first day we begin to fall in love."

Duchess shook her head at the extent of his plan. "You are your father's son," she acknowledged.

Muhsin's smile triggered the deep dimple at the corner of his wide mouth. "Yes," he admitted, "and my pop taught me very well."

"So, then, what's next?"

"Before I get into that, I want you to go back to your hotel and think about what I've told you so far. Think hard, Duchess, because there's no going back once you accept," he warned.

The apprehension returned to her face as her gaze faltered. "What about my hotel room? I'm supposed to check out today, remember?"

Muhsin nodded, then stood and went behind his desk. He put the phone to his ear and waited a few seconds. "Rhonda, get me the manager at the Raphael," he instructed, leaning against the edge of the desk. "Gordon?" he said, once the connection was made. "Muhsin Vuyani, how are you? Glad to hear it. Listen, I have a favor to ask of you. I have a friend staying here in town at your hotel, room—what's your room number?" he asked Duchess, placing his hand across the mouthpiece when he spoke.

"Fourteen eighteen."

"She's in room fourteen eighteen. The problem is she's scheduled to check out today but she needs to stay in town a little longer than planned. I'd like to arrange for her to keep the room till she's ready to leave."

Duchess watched in wonder as Muhsin handled the call. When he replaced the receiver on its cradle, his expression was satisfaction personified.

"The room is yours until you make your decision," he announced.

"Thank you," Duchess replied in a hushed tone. Smoothing both hands across the tailored dark material of her suit, she turned to leave the office.

"I'll see you tonight at eight for dinner," Muhsin called.

Duchess left him with a quick nod, then exited the office. The easy expression on Muhsin's gorgeous face turned solemn and probing.

Duchess massaged her forehead and prayed the dull throb she felt there would not become a full-blown headache. Curling her fingers more tightly around the receiver, she braced herself for the answer to her next question.

"Does it look like they're jumping ship, Donnette?"

Donnette McGwire, VP of finance for the Carver Design Group, hesitated but a moment. "It looks that way, Duchess."

"Damn."

"Duchess, wait, now, they could just be worried because the company's been going through some tough times and they're just trying to protect themselves."

"And this is supposed to make me feel better? First you tell me stock ownership is changing hands at an alarming rate, and now—"

"Duchess, wait, let's just take it easy here—"

"Donnette, listen, thank you for calling. I'm not angry with you and I appreciate you keeping an eye on this situation in light of the fact that Jaliel should have been on top of it," Duchess said, not hearing the heavy sigh Donnette uttered when her boss's name was mentioned.

"What will you do next?" Donnette asked.

Duchess gave a muffled curse as the dull ache in her head transformed into sharp pains. "Whatever I do, Donnette, it's got to be fast. Listen, I'll be in touch, but if anything else happens, you call me that very moment, you hear?"

"I got it, Duchess," Donnette promised before hanging up.

Duchess tossed the phone aside, then flopped back on the sofa. Something "fast?" Muhsin Vuyani's offer was at the top of that list.

Duchess placed a call to Gretchen later that evening.

"I can't believe it all worked out so well," Gretchen said into the receiver.

Duchess checked her hosiery for any imperfections. "Thanks for your support," she retorted.

"Hush," Gretchen said. "You know I've got no doubts about your business savvy. It's just . . . I just had a real bad feeling about this trip."

"Hmph, a bad feeling." Duchess sighed, knowing exactly what her friend meant. Not wanting Gretchen to worry, she decided to keep the details of Muhsin Vuyani's offer to herself.

"Well, congratulations. Should we go on and cut the check or have the papers even been signed yet?"

Duchess eased off the bed and smoothed one hand over the figure-flattering burgundy frock. "You don't have to worry about cutting a check since Muhsin Vuyani is giving me the building."

"Say what?"

"He was very sorry for his behavior when I told him about Dad's funeral. He said this was his way of apologizing."

Gretchen whistled and leaned back in the high-back suede swivel chair behind her desk. "The man sure knows how to make up to a girl."

"That's the truth," Duchess agreed, taking a seat at the huge vanity in the master bath.

"So when are you coming home?"

Duchess switched the phone from one ear to another. "I was actually thinking about taking some time to myself. Maybe I'll stay in Chicago for a while and see the sights."

Gretchen nodded. "I'm impressed and shocked," she drawled, absently inspecting her professionally manicured nails. "The workaholic's finally taking a break. I hope you won't change your mind."

"Damn."

"What?"

Duchess heard the knocker hitting the suite's door. She couldn't believe it was eight already. "Gret, I gotta go. I'll call you tomorrow, all right?"

"No problem, girl. Just keep me posted on what's goin' on."

"Talk to you soon," Duchess said, sending a kiss through the line before hanging up.

The brass knocker rapped the white oak door again and Duchess hurried from the airy, cream and white bedroom. She stopped at the full-length hall mirror to give herself a closer look. The dress reached midthigh and hugged her slender figure adoringly. It's square bodice called attention to her firm, full bosom and figure-eight frame. Her only jewelry were a pair of diamond stud earrings and a delicate gold necklace.

What the hell am I doing? Duchess thought, frowning at her dazzling reflection. *This is not a date,* she reminded herself. Regardless of the surprising "proposal" she'd received earlier that day, she and Muhsin Vuyani were not a couple. There was no need for her to impress him.

Head held high, Duchess walked over to the door and pulled it open. Muhsin leaned against the doorjamb. His warm eyes caressed her lithe frame with intense appraisal.

"Come on in," Duchess invited, offering him a graceful smile.

"Do you have an answer for me?" Muhsin asked as he followed Duchess into the suite.

Duchess went to the center of the living room and turned to face him. "You've given me every reason to accept."

"But?" Muhsin prompted, a knowing smirk touching the sensuous curve of his mouth.

Duchess allowed her gaze to falter momentarily. "But there are some things I will not do. For any price."

Muhsin pulled his hands from his gray trouser pockets and folded his arms across the casual black herringbone jacket he wore over matching crew-neck shirt. He watched her closely for a long while. "Does that mean you're turning me down?" he asked finally.

Duchess shrugged. "I'd be a fool to do that now, wouldn't I?" she challenged, smoothing both hands across her thighs as she took a seat on the overstuffed sofa. "I've had my eye on that building since I found out it was empty. It's perfect for an annex to our current location. Not to mention the money you're giving me."

Muhsin took a seat on the sofa as well. "So?" he queried, propping one finger alongside his temple.

"So, before I make a decision, I want to know exactly what this show will show."

Muhsin's laughter matched his voice perfectly. It was more of a rumbling roar that was rough like his speaking voice. Duchess ordered herself not to stare, but the man was hard not to look at. The way his eyes crinkled, the striking appearance of the lone dimple and that gorgeous auburn hair. . . . She realized all she wanted was to run her fingers through his blazing, silky crop. Just once, maybe twice.

"What are you tryin' to ask me, Duchess?"

"I think it's obvious," she replied, forcing herself back to reality.

"I disagree."

"You should know what I'm asking."

Muhsin began to tap his index finger to the cleft in his chin. "Spell it out for me," he requested.

Duchess cleared her throat. "Look, Muhsin, your offer is very generous. I'd just hate to find out it's not gonna happen because I won't sleep with you. Now, is that spelled out enough for you? I could be more specific."

"You won't have to worry about anything like that."

"So you say."

"You'll have the building beforehand, remember?"

"A building you could easily snatch back."

"But you're forgetting the agreement we'll have between us."

Duchess's gaze lowered. "Right." She sighed, realizing she had no other excuses.

Muhsin's own probing gaze narrowed. "Duchess, if you don't want to do this, just say so. Just know that I've never forced myself on a woman. I wouldn't do anything you wouldn't want me to."

The subtle, suggestive meaning of the words brought a curious light to Duchess's eyes.

"So do you have an answer for me?" he queried before she could say a thing.

Duchess certainly couldn't deny the man's sex appeal. Being around him a few weeks wouldn't be a burden on her eyes at all.

"It's a deal," she said. "I'll marry you." She extended her hand for a shake.

Muhsin tipped his head just slightly. "You won't be sorry."

"I'll share that sentiment once the papers are signed, hmm?"

Muhsin's uproarious laughter filled the room again. "I can live with that!"

Duchess clasped her hands together and offered a refreshing smile. "So are you going to tell me what's expected of me now?"

"We'll talk about it over dinner."

"Oh. Where are we going?"

"Here."

"Here?"

Muhsin leaned forward to brace his elbows on his knees. "I don't want anyone to see me with you before tomorrow."

"What's tomorrow?" Duchess probed.

"Let's order first," Muhsin suggested, his brown eyes scanning the white oak coffee table before the sofa. "Have you got a menu from the hotel restaurant?"

"Um," Duchess gestured as she moved off the sofa. "The hotel has three restaurants, so we have a choice."

Muhsin leaned back to watch her search the living room for the menus. His soft gaze searched the lovely dress she wore as though he could see right beneath it.

"Here we are," Duchess breathed, returning to the sofa with three menus in hand. "I think one of these places is some type of steakhouse."

Muhsin forced his attention to the small booklet she held. "You can keep that one, since I don't eat beef."

Duchess's eyes snapped to his face as she smiled radiantly. "Neither do I."

"No kidding?"

"Nope," Duchess said with a definite shake of her head. "I let it go years ago. I indulge in seafood and chicken every now and then, but I mostly pig out on veggies and fruits."

Muhsin tapped his index finger to the cleft in his chin

and nodded. "I've got a recipe for stir-fry that uses a crushed herb marinade for seasoning."

Duchess's heavy lashes fluttered rapidly. "Mmm, that sounds wonderful. I could eat stir-fry all day."

While Duchess raved over a recipe she'd picked up, Muhsin let his attention stray to the elaborate upsweep of her hair. The classic French roll emphasized her high cheekbones. One long tendril lay outside the roll and curled against her neck. Again, he congratulated himself for making the perfect choice. His only hope was that he'd be able to remember she was not his to keep—not yet.

Duchess and Muhsin sat on opposite sides of the intimate round table and enjoyed a scrumptious vegetarian feast. There was spicy cabbage stew with broccoli and cheese cornbread, capped off by wine and a delicious cheesecake for dessert.

"So, uh, isn't it time you tell me how you plan to stage this scheme?" Duchess asked, when a lull rose in the conversation.

Muhsin's soft chuckle brought more of a sparkle to his warm gaze. "I'll send a car for you around one tomorrow afternoon," he explained. "It'll take you to the Now Eatery, which isn't far from my office. I spend a lot of time there and I know just about everyone who frequents the place. When you walk in, I'll have to approach you."

"What if someone else has already . . . approached?" Duchess asked, leaning back in her chair.

"Don't worry about that," Muhsin informed her pointedly and they shared a long laugh. "When I walk over and ask if I can sit down, you accept."

Duchess nodded. "What do we talk about?" she asked, waving one hand in the air.

Muhsin shrugged. "Anything in general. Our conversations won't be rehearsed. I want it real," he told her, taking in the obvious question in her eyes. "What?"

"It just seems like a big waste. You could be doing this with someone you really are interested in."

"I told you why I wouldn't do that," Muhsin sang, seeming to cringe at the idea.

Duchess raised both hands defensively. "So it starts tomorrow?"

"It starts tomorrow."

Muhsin was so cool, Duchess couldn't believe there wasn't something he was leaving out. "So what should I wear?"

Again, Muhsin's broad shoulders rose beneath the gray shirt. "I know anything you wear will be fine," he assured her, glancing toward her plate. "Are you done?" She nodded. "Let's take this in the living room," he suggested, referring to the coffee and unfinished cheesecake.

Duchess smiled at the idea and reached for the silver serving tray that had been set aside. Muhsin waited until she'd set the coffeepot and cake plate on the tray before he helped her from her chair. The looks passing between them were brief, but sweet.

Duchess cleared her throat as they strolled back to the living room. "So, is there anything I should know about you personally, or—"

"You won't know a thing. It's like we're meeting for the first time."

"Will you be sitting with me for the entire lunch?" she asked, when he gave no further explanations.

Muhsin only shook his head in response.

Duchess uttered a short, humorless laugh and set the tray to the coffee table with more force than necessary. "Well, let me tell you something about me, then," she snapped, drawing Muhsin's gaze to her face. "I'm not used to being a follower. I've never been one to sit back and let things happen to me. I don't intend to start doing that now—not for any price."

Muhsin took no offense to her firm stance. Surprisingly, he chuckled as his big hands rose. "Please don't get the idea that I expect you to blindly follow me anywhere. It's just that for this to be effective, you're gonna have to appear to be truly surprised and impressed by me," he explained, retrieving his coffee cup from the tray.

Duchess watched him suspiciously, scrutinizing his tall, lean frame. "Just don't get too creative, Muhsin."

"There is one thing you should know about me, though," he said, a tiny grimace curling his mouth. "I like being called by my nickname, Blaze."

A thoughtful frown came to Duchess's face. "Why don't you like your name?"

Muhsin shrugged. "Besides having everyone call me 'Moose' all my life?" he asked in an incredulous tone, grinning when she giggled. "Actually, I love my name. My mother gave me that name. One day I came home crying 'cause someone teased me about it. She sat me down and told me Muhsin is Arabic for 'sword.' It's a name associated with power and she said I'd be a strong, powerful man one day." He laughed and shook his head. "Every time I hear my name, I don't think about power. I think about that day with her and I feel like this little boy whose mother believes he's going to grow up to be the best kind of man."

"Well, haven't you?" Duchess asked, studying the sharp line of his profile.

"I don't think my mother cared how many material possessions I acquired during my life. I think she wanted me to be the best kind of man *inside*."

"And you don't think you've accomplished that?"

"No way."

"There's still time," she said, noticing the doubtful glint in his eyes. "Well, I happen to like the name and I think I'll use it to remind you that there's always time to be the best *inside*."

Muhsin shook his head, the lazy grin returning. He tossed back the remnants of the delicious hazelnut blend, then cleared his throat. "I better go now," he said, heading to the front of the suite.

Duchess followed. "So when do we sign the papers?"

"After lunch we'll take separate cars to my office and sign there," he said over his shoulder. "By Monday morning, construction can begin on your building annex."

Duchess prayed her expression was cool when Muhsin turned to her again. "Thank you," he whispered, the caress of his eyes across her face as soft as his words.

When the door closed behind him, Duchess paused a moment. Then she let out a yelp of happiness and twirled around the room.

Suddenly, as though she'd come in contact with a brick wall, she stopped. She was about to do something that would ensure her company's survival and prayed she would not live to regret it.

Chapter 3

"This'll have to do," Duchess murmured, snapping her tiny black compact closed and tucking the case inside her leather tote.

The chauffered car Muhsin had sent to her hotel was right on schedule. It zoomed through the ferocious midtown Chicago traffic and arrived at the Now Eatery in record time.

Duchess offered the driver a dazzling smile when she took his hand and stepped from the car's cushiony, dark interior. She was a vision in the sky-blue linen suit she'd chosen. The skirt fell around her shapely calves and carried deep slits on either side. The cut of the skirt offered scandalous glimpses of her toned thighs. The blazer was close-fitting and allowed no blouse beneath; it formed to her torso and emphasized the graceful line of her neck, full breasts and minute waist. She wore her glossy mane in a tight coil atop her head. A heavy lock fell to curtain the entire left side of her face.

"Just go right in through those double doors, Miss," the driver instructed.

Duchess nodded and pressed her hand against the older man's arm. "Thank you," she said, heading up the sidewalk toward the restaurant.

She drew the stares of several men as she passed, including one who actually stopped and turned to watch her.

"Duchess Carver?" he called.

Halting her purposeful steps, Duchess looked up. She frowned a bit at the tall, chocolate-skinned man who had called out to her on the crowded sidewalk.

Isaiah Manfres chuckled at the puzzled expression Duchess sent him. He approached her slowly, a gleaming white grin breaking through his handsome face.

"Isaiah?" Duchess cried, recognizing her old college classmate. "Boy," she whispered, when they embraced, "what are you doing here?"

Isaiah kept his hands closed around her elbows. "I'm meeting a friend for lunch, but I'd be glad to dump him for you."

Duchess laughed and slapped her hand against Isaiah's chest. "I meant what are you doing in Chicago, man?"

"I live here now."

"Well, now I know who to go to for a tour before I head back to Philly."

Isaiah bowed his head in a graceful gesture. "We could start after lunch. I already told you I don't mind getting out of my previous engagement."

Duchess couldn't help but laugh. "I can't let you do that," she said.

Isaiah held her close and began walking up the sidewalk again. "At least let me walk with you. Where are you headed?"

"Uh, the . . . Now Eatery?"

"Damn, small world. That's where I'm headed."

Duchess rolled her eyes. "Really?" she drawled, not believing him for a second.

"I swear, but what are you doing here?" Isaiah asked, curiosity tinging his onyx gaze.

Duchess hugged Isaiah's arm as they strolled along the sidewalk. "I had some business to handle and then I just decided to stay over a while longer and enjoy the city."

"Sounds like a good plan," Isaiah noted, nodding at her explanation. "You should be congratulated for having sense enough to take time out for yourself."

"Hmph, I wish I'd had sense enough to do it sooner."

"Better late than never, girl. Better late than never," Isaiah chanted, joining Duchess when she laughed.

The two friends strolled into the Now Eatery, laughing and conversing enthusiastically. Duchess already had a table reserved and Isaiah offered to escort her through the busy dining room.

"So, how's Mr. J. doin'?" Isaiah asked, as they followed the host to the table.

The laughter in Duchess's light eyes faded a bit. "He passed away. We had the funeral earlier this week."

"My God," Isaiah breathed, his dark eyes narrowing sharply. "Lord, girl, how can you handle business after going through somethin' like that?"

Duchess shrugged; her smile was solemn yet content. "I had no choice. The business was in pretty bad shape before Daddy died. I know he'd want me handling that instead of crying over him."

Isaiah shook his head. "Still strong and smart," he marveled, pulling her close for a tight hug. "Not to mention sexy as hell."

Duchess chuckled, her sadness dissipating like a light fog.

"Listen," Isaiah said, reaching into the deep pocket of his khaki pants, "I want you to give me a call so we can get together before you leave, all right?"

"You can count on it," Duchess said, taking the card before kissing Isaiah's cheek.

Across the dining room, Muhsin Vuyani watched the cozy scene through narrowed eyes. He'd seen Duchess the moment she'd entered the dining room, clinging to the arm of another man. Rubbing one hand across the back of his neck, he warned himself not to make anything of it. After all, he had no real claim to the woman. Of course, he knew he was fooling himself. He had wanted Duchess far too long and he would have her.

Isaiah walked across the room to Muhsin's table. "What's up, man?" he said.

Muhsin nodded toward the other side of the living room. "Who's your friend?" he inquired, pretending not to know Duchess.

Isaiah's thin brows drew close before he glanced across his shoulder. "Duchess Carver. Remember her from the photo?"

Muhsin smiled and sent his high school friend a quick wink. "Thanks," he said, standing from his chair.

Isaiah bowed his head, his grin far from humorous. "I should've known," he grumbled. As Muhsin walked away, the look in his dark eyes turned as cold as his smile.

"Thank you," Duchess told the waiter when he passed the menu. She scanned the list of appetizers for a moment, when she felt a soft squeeze against her shoulder. Seeing Muhsin towering above her, she offered him a cool smile.

"You mind?" he asked, waving toward the empty chair at the table.

"'Course not," she replied, the phrase tinged with a double meaning.

Muhsin tugged on the cuff of the loose-fitting, casual shirt he wore. "Saw you talkin' to Isaiah," he mentioned.

Duchess's lips parted in surprise. "I didn't know you knew him."

"How do you know him?" Muhsin probed, hoping he sounded cool enough.

Duchess took no offense to the questioning. "I've known Izzy since college. We've been friends ever since. He's crazy as hell. You know, he always said he'd never move back home. I was surprised to find him back out here."

"Mmm-hmm . . ." Muhsin sighed as his finger taps against the table grew harsher. The longer Duchess spoke of her cozy friendship with Isaiah, the more on edge he became. Muhsin didn't know whether it was luck or bad timing when they were interrupted.

"Well, hello, Blaze."

The two women standing next to the table had fought the curiosity nagging at them. It was a battle they lost. Like everyone else in the restaurant, they had to know more about the lovely young woman who had caught Muhsin Vuyani's roving eye.

"Roletta. Julie," Muhsin said, his wide mouth curled into a knowing smirk. "Duchess," he continued, acting as though he couldn't quite lock in on her name. "Duchess Carver, this is Roletta Franklin and Julianna Hembry."

Roletta had her hand extended before Muhsin completed the introductions. "Pleased to meet you, Ms. Carver."

"Call me Duchess, please."

"I love that name," Julianna interjected, shaking Duchess's hand as well.

"So, has Muhsin butted in on your lunch here, Duchess?" Roletta queried slyly.

"Oh, no, nothing like that," Duchess assured both

women, offering Muhsin an adoring smile for their benefit.

Julianna and Roletta exchanged glances with raised eyebrows.

"Well, we only wanted to stop and speak," Roletta explained, though it was obvious that both she and her friend were more than a little interested in the couple.

Julianna reached out to pat Duchess's shoulder. "It was nice meeting you. Blaze," she added, as though it were an afterthought.

Duchess was curious as well and studied the two women leaving the table. Before she could question Muhsin, the waiter returned.

"Mr. Vuyani, will you be joining the lady for lunch?" he asked, already prepared to pass out another menu.

Muhsin waved his hand while pushing the chair away from the table. "I better get back to my own table. I don't want to leave Isaiah hangin' too long."

Duchess gasped, her eyes filled with regret. "I didn't know it was you he was having lunch with. Why don't both of you join me over here?" she suggested.

"I don't think so," Muhsin said. "Denny, why don't you go on and take the lady's order."

"Miss?" Denny urged, stepping closer to the table.

Duchess forced her eyes back to the long, black, leather-bound menu and debated. The Now Eatery boasted fresh seafood caught daily, so she decided to indulge in a delicious shrimp fettuccine dish.

"When you're done here, the car will take you to my office," Muhsin told her, once Denny had walked away with the order.

"Is it safe to meet there?" Duchess asked, resting her chin against the back of her hand.

"Mmm-hmm," Muhsin replied with a slow nod. "Monroe, the driver who brought you here, he'll take you around to the private entrance."

"Sounds good." Duchess sighed, watching Muhsin come to his feet. When he offered his hand, she settled her fingers against his palm.

He leaned down as though about to kiss her cheek. "I'll see you later," he whispered.

Though Duchess thought she may have imagined it, she could have sworn she felt his lips brush her earlobe. Muhsin left her with a cool, easy smile as he rose to his full height and walked away. She ordered herself not to turn and watch him as he returned to his table.

"She turned you down, huh?" Isaiah asked, looking up from his hearty salad to pin Muhsin with a knowing glare.

"There was nothing for her to turn down."

Isaiah was mildly surprised. "You mean you didn't ask her out?"

"Not yet," Muhsin smugly replied. His brown eyes narrowed sharply when he spied the dark disapproval on Isaiah's face. "You care to say whatever's burnin' you up over there, man?"

Isaiah let his gaze slide back to his chef's salad. "She's a sweet one, Blaze. Too sweet for your bull."

Muhsin couldn't help but laugh. "I just met her, remember?"

"That's why I'm concerned. She don't know you," Isaiah returned, savagely forking a plump tomato slice into his mouth.

"What is this, man? Are y'all more than friends or somethin'?" Muhsin lightly queried, though his stare was probing.

Isaiah waved off the question. "Forget it, man. I don't have a thing to worry about. Dutch'll be goin' back to Philly soon, anyway."

Muhsin's easy mood vanished. "What the hell do you

mean you don't have anything to worry about?" he demanded, his voice sounding much rougher in light of his aggravation.

Isaiah remained unfrazzled. "Duchess Carver carries herself a lot differently from the money-grubbin' socialite wenches you're used to," he explained, leaning back to fold his arms across his knit top. "She's strong-minded, she's graceful and hardworking. She don't need her whole life messed up by a rich, conceited ladies' man."

Muhsin's laughter returned in an instant. "Damn, man, I only asked you her name."

Isaiah's expression remained solemn only a moment longer. Then his eyes closed as a wide grin spread across his face. He joined his old friend in a round of hearty laughter and lunch continued in ease.

At another table in the huge dining room, a group of five ladies sat discussing such shallow topics as the latest boutiques and spas to visit, the next big party and, of course, the latest gossip.

"So, who is she?" Monique Desmond asked, her false green eyes trained across the dining room.

Julianna Hembry glanced across her shoulder. "Duchess Carver. I think that's what Blaze said. Y'all know he didn't waste a bit of time zooming in on that one."

Silence surfaced at the table as each woman surveyed the young woman enjoying her lunch. Of course, Duchess had snagged the attention of almost everyone surrounding her. Each woman at the table grudgingly admitted that she was extremely beautiful.

"I wonder if she'll be his new love interest?" Roletta speculated.

"If she knows what's good for her, she'll stay the hell away from him."

The other four woman cleared their throats when the cold advice reached their ears.

Roletta leaned over to pat Tia Garrison's hand. "Girl, the man left her table too fast. Nothing will come of it," she said, trying to assure Muhsin's pouting ex-girlfriend.

Tia rolled her eyes and toyed with a lock of her cheek-length curly hair. She was far from convinced.

"Thanks, Monroe," Duchess said as the driver escorted her to the private rear entrance leading into Vuyani Tower.

One quick turn took her to the elevators and she allowed her cool facade to fade as the paneled doors closed. She pondered the decision she had made. Once the papers were signed, there would be no turning back. Sure, the company would be secure, but how would it affect her personally? She would be a divorcée!

"Hmph. A divorcée with money," she reminded herself, and waved off the last of her reservations.

The elevator opened right in the top-floor office. Muhsin, who was leaning against one of the deep, over-size armchairs in the office, was there to greet Duchess.

"Not too late to turn back," he cautioned when she stood before him.

Duchess's arched brows rose a notch. "I was just thinking the same thing," she admitted.

Muhsin folded his arms across his chest. "And?" he challenged, his rough voice barely audible.

"I really should say no," she began, rubbing her hands across the sky-blue sleeves of her suit, "but I can't." She sighed, sending him a cool stare.

"Glad to hear it."

Duchess walked away from Muhsin, enjoying the elegant comfort of the office. "Are the papers ready?"

"They're ready," he said and moved off the armchair. A few long strides carried him behind the desk, where he reached for the phone. "Come on over," he told the person that answered the line, then hung up and said to Duchess, "I want you to read everything."

Duchess folded her hands over her hips and offered him a gracious nod. "I intend to."

"Not that you can't trust me," he added in a quick teasing tone as he stepped toward her.

Duchess nodded. "'Course not."

"Listen to me," he whispered, the raspiness of his voice adding sincerity to the words, "I want to really thank you for doing this. You can't know what it means to me."

Duchess shrugged and tried to ward off the heaviness of the moment. "Well, it's not as though I'm not getting anything out of it, you know?"

Muhsin chuckled, triggering the gorgeous lone dimple. "I know where you're comin' from, but a building and money still don't equal what you're giving me."

"And just what am I giving you?" Duchess queried, her soft, clear voice laced with suspicion.

"You know what I mean," Muhsin said as he massaged her arms in a vaguely possessive manner. "Marriage is a serious thing."

"Exactly," Duchess acknowledged, her lashes briefly sweeping her cheeks. "Still, this is for a very good cause. Me."

"I like you, Duchess!" Muhsin bellowed over hearty laughter. Then his grasp around her arms tightened and he pulled her close to place a quick kiss against her mouth.

Duchess's laughter stopped abruptly and her eyes locked with Muhsin's. They seemed frozen where they stood and only pulled away when the office doors opened.

A short man entered the room. He wore an inviting smile on his attractive, round face.

"Roland Jasper, this is Duchess Carver," Muhsin announced, watching his best friend and attorney walk toward Duchess.

"Ms. Carver, it's a pleasure," Roland replied, extending his hand.

"Please, call me Duchess," she requested, taking Roland's hand in a firm shake. Though she had never met the man, something in the easy smile he offered made her like him instantly.

"Duchess, I'm glad to hear we were able to come up with an offer beneficial to you," Roland said as he held both her hands in his.

Duchess gave his hands a slight shake. "I'm just happy to know my business is on its way back on track."

"Well, then, let's get to it." Roland turned to retrieve the briefcase he'd set near the door when he entered the room. "I want you to take your time reading this document," he cautioned, extracting a long page from the case. "I'm in no hurry."

"Thanks," Duchess said, as she took the paper. Her eyes began to scan the wording as she let the strap of her purse slip from her shoulder. She strolled around the office, reading the agreement and oblivious to the two men watching her every move.

Roland had taken a seat next to Muhsin on the edge of the desk. "She's somethin' else, man."

"I know," Muhsin agreed, his deep brown eyes riveted by Duchess.

"Gonna be pretty hard agreeing to what you laid out in that contract," Roland predicted, his narrow green eyes twinkling with mischief.

"I got every intention of giving her that building," Muhsin argued, his handsome face marred by a frown.

Roland shook his head. "I'm not talkin' about the money or the building. Do you really think you'll be able to keep your hands off her?"

"Part of the deal, kid," Muhsin said smoothly.

"Mmm-hmm, and this is *you* we're talkin' about," Roland challenged, noticing the wolfish grin spreading across his friend's face.

"Everything looks good," Duchess announced when she finished reading the contract.

"Perfect," Roland replied, rubbing his palms together as he headed across the office. "When I leave here I'll get the ball rolling with the transfer of the title and there'll be a few more papers for you to sign regarding that. If you'll provide the account number, we can have the money wired by the end of the day. You can call your people in Philadelphia and get the ball rolling with the construction crew, architects and such."

Duchess felt her head spin from all the information Roland spouted. If she wasn't actually hearing it, she wouldn't have believed this was actually happening.

Roland pushed one hand into the trouser pocket of his gray, three-piece, pinstriped suit and smiled. "Any questions, Duchess?"

Slowly, her shoulders rose and she shook her head. "I know I should have some, but I can't think of a thing right now."

Roland nodded and turned to Muhsin. "Blaze, you got any questions?"

Muhsin trailed one hand through his hair and shook his head. "Duchess, you're sure you're all right with this?"

"I'm fine," Duchess assured both men, her hazel gaze sparkling with anticipation.

"Well, let's get these papers signed," Roland said, waving Muhsin and Duchess to the desk. He instructed them where to place their signatures, then placed his name on the witness line. "I'll get started on all the loose ends." He gathered the papers before turning to Duchess again. "Blaze has all my numbers, so you can contact me with any questions, you hear?"

"Thanks, Roland," she said, squeezing his wrist.

Roland sent another nod toward Muhsin, then headed out of the office.

"Well, what now?" Duchess asked when they were alone.

"Dinner, tonight. Did you pack any evening gowns?"

Duchess snapped her fingers. "I had no idea I'd need one for a two-day trip," she replied, a playful grimace animating her lovely face.

Muhsin waved his hands and strolled behind his desk. Duchess watched him lift the phone to his ear and punch one digit. "Monroe? Bring the car around, will you? Ms. Carver needs to go shopping."

As he set the phone down, he told Duchess, "We're eating at the Blackberry. It's a Japanese place, pretty formal."

Duchess smoothed both hands across her short skirt and closed the distance between them. "Anything in particular you'd like me to choose?"

"Get whatever you like," Muhsin instructed, pressing a silver credit card into her palm.

Duchess shook her head upon realizing what she held. "I can't take this. I have my own money."

"But you wouldn't need to buy a new dress if it weren't for me."

"I'm always in the market for new clothes," Duchess insisted and slipped the card back into his hand.

Muhsin caught her wrist and squeezed it. "Keep it, please."

"I don't feel right about it," Duchess said, pulling her bottom lip between her teeth.

"You're going to be my wife," Muhsin pointed out.

"But not really, right?" she challenged, smiling when he nodded slowly. "Besides, your wife is her own person and she has plenty of her own money. Thank you, though," she slipped the card between his strong fingers.

Muhsin shook his head as he watched her leave the room the way she came. He couldn't deny he was more than a little impressed.

Chapter 4

Duchess stood on the crowded downtown sidewalk and smiled. Chicago was indeed an incredible city and there was an exciting vibe that pulsed through the air like a living thing. Not to mention, the city itself was beautiful. Even if Muhsin had not made his magnanimous offer, she would've probably taken a few days to enjoy the place. Duchess could only hope she felt as amiable toward the town when this charade was over.

Get out of my head, she thought, shaking Muhsin's striking image from her mind.

The boutique was located right behind her, and once she passed through the tinted double glass doors, she knew she'd find the perfect gown. Immediately, she began to browse the pantsuits, already berating herself for becoming sidetracked. She'd been looking through the gorgeous outfits only a few moments when someone tapped her shoulder.

"Hello! We didn't expect to see you again today!"

Duchess offered a bright smile to the two women. Unfortunately, she couldn't remember who in the world they were.

"I suppose Muhsin finally let you finish your lunch in peace?" Roletta remarked lightly, though her brown gaze was unmistakably inquisitive.

"Oh, he wasn't so bad," Duchess assured them with a laugh as she remembered where she'd met the women.

"What'd you have to say to get him to leave you alone?" Julianna teased.

"He only asked my name and then sat around to make small talk," Duchess demured, turning back to the row of two-piece linen suits. "He was very nice," she added.

"Don't be fooled, girl," Roletta advised, exchanging glances with Julianna.

"Muhsin Vuyani is a shark," Julianna said.

Duchess chuckled inwardly at the remark. She remembered when she'd thought the same thing.

"Don't get me wrong," Julianna said as she became interested in one of the outfits, "the man is definitely sweet, attentive, interesting, sexy—oh, Lord is he sexy. But his darker side can completely overshadow all that goodness."

Roletta patted Duchess's shoulder. "Just be careful, girl," she warned.

Duchess pretended to be involved with the outfits until the women had walked on. Her hazel eyes narrowed as she watched them and wondered why they were such doubters of the man.

"Ma'am, are you finding everything okay?"

Duchess recognized the sales associate who had nodded at her when she'd walked into the boutique. "I'm supposed to be looking at evening gowns. You have a nice selection of everything, though."

The associate nodded as she and Duchess strolled toward the formal section. "Well, our evening gowns are just as incredible as the pantsuits you were looking at," she said, her eyes proudly surveying the elegant boutique. "What type of look are you going for?"

"Well," Duchess rubbed her hands together as the gowns appeared before her gaze, "it's just a dinner date, not a party or anything like that. I need something . . . cooly formal, not too severe, you know?"

The young woman nodded, sending a mass of microthin braids into her round, dark brown face. "Where will you be dining?"

Duchess brought one hand to her chin, her face a picture of consternation. "I knew I'd forget the name." She groaned, closing her eyes in the hopes of grasping the name. "The Grape? The um, Rasberry, Peach—"

"The Blackberry," the young associate supplied with a breathless giggle.

Duchess snapped her fingers and began to laugh as well. "Thank you. Have you ever eaten there?"

"Only once, but it was with my parents. They took me there for my birthday. It's more of a romantic place, though. I'd love to have my boyfriend splurge and take me there. This man must be pretty special?"

Duchess glanced across her shoulder. "I just met him today," she shared, fidgeting with the long lock that dangled along her face.

The associate shrugged as she began to shuffle through a few gowns on a glass rack. "You must've made quite an impression," she said. "No man takes a woman there unless he's tryin' to do some serious wooing."

"Well, what's it like?" Duchess asked, her clear, probing gaze showing just a trace of unease.

"The Blackberry is divided into private dining rooms. It was converted into a restaurant from an old Victorian home."

"Really?" Duchess replied, idly studying a gorgeous wine-colored gown on the wall.

"Patrons have the option of using the private dining rooms or eating alone at the personal tables in the small, main dining room," the associate explained, strolling farther into the forest of gowns. "Still, though,

a person really goes there for getting to know someone one-on-one."

"I see," Duchess said. *Maybe we're sharing a dining room
with a couple of his friends,* she hoped silently.

"You should try these on," the associate suggested,
having already selected three exquisite gowns.

Duchess sent her suspicions to the back of her mind
and took the dresses. She thanked the helpful salesper-
son and disappeared into the fitting rooms.

When the cream silk drapes swept closed behind
Duchess, Tia Garrison stepped from behind a wall of
wraps. Curiosity practically beamed from her dark face.

The sales associate smiled as she watched Duchess
twirl around before the mirrors just outside the dressing
room. "I wasn't sure about that one, but it looks like you
made a great choice."

"Thanks, I think so, too," Duchess remarked with a
light laugh.

"Let me just take this," the young woman whispered,
expertly removing the price tag from the dress, "and I'll
go on and ring everything up while you change."

"Thanks for all your help," Duchess replied, handing
the salesgirl a credit card before turning back to the
dressing rooms.

"Excuse me? Did you drop this?"

Duchess gasped when she turned to see the earring
her father had given her on her last birthday. "My God.
Thank you," she whispered, taking the gleaming diamond from the woman's hand. "I'm glad I didn't drop
this on the street in Philly."

"Is that where you're from?" Tia asked.

"Mmm-hmm," Duchess said as she removed her other

earring and placed both safely inside her purse. "I run my own business there."

"Oh," Tia replied. Her curiosity slowly turned into envy over the fact that the woman was an entrepreneur in addition to everything else.

"Thank you again for returning the earring. It was my father's last birthday gift to me. He just passed away recently."

"I'm so sorry," Tia said, genuinely saddened by Duchess's revelation. "My name is Tia Garrison."

Duchess extended her hand. "Duchess Carver."

"Nice to meet you."

"Same here."

"Ms. Carver, I can wrap that dress when you've changed," the salesgirl offered.

"I'm on my way," Duchess told the associate before patting Tia's hand. "Thanks again," she said, and then headed back into the dressing rooms.

The cunning smile returned to Tia's face as she tapped her finger against her chin. "So, he's taking you to the Blackberry, hmm?"

Duchess hissed when the sound of the door knocker reached her ears. She set the porcelain-handled brush aside and went to answer. Her waist-length mane followed her like a wild dark cloud as she sprinted to the front of the suite.

Muhsin's brown eyes crinkled a bit at the corners when he smiled. The look in his gaze was a cross between humor and desire. The silky black locks of Duchess's hair flew about her face in a wild disarray. He could never tire of watching her.

"You're early. What are you doing here?" she said,

more aggravated with herself than Muhsin. She could just imagine how awful she looked.

"Can I come in?"

With a shrug, Duchess stepped aside. "Maybe you can help me with something."

"With what?" he asked, his soft stare wandering over her hair when he turned to look at her. He hoped she would offer him the chance to put his hands in the silken mass.

"I went to that boutique with all intentions of getting one dress and getting out of there. I told Monroe to come back for me in one hour. Hmph, I spent close to three hours in that place," Duchess explained as she led the way to the bedroom. "I bought five evening gowns and a ton of other things. I don't know what to wear tonight."

Muhsin followed her words absently; he was completely focused on her hips swaying beneath the folds of the long, peach, satin robe. "Whatever you put on should be fine," he quickly assured her.

Duchess was pulling her hair away from her face and uttered a breathless laugh. "I just want to look right for your friends." She sighed, turning back to look at him— nearly slamming into the wall. Muhsin reached out and caught her elbow while his arm slid around her waist.

Duchess's gasp filled the short hallway when she realized how close she'd come to hitting the wall. "Thanks," she whispered, her eyes wide as she stared up into his handsome face.

"What friends?" he asked, savoring the feel of her body against him.

Duchess leaned back as far as he would allow. "Aren't we going out to fool your so-called friends?"

Muhsin's lashes lowered briefly and he offered a quick nod. He offered no response and slowly took inventory of their stance. Duchess cleared her throat softly and smiled when he finally released her.

"The sales associate told me how nice the Blackberry is," she relayed when they stepped into the posh bedroom suite. "It sounds like quite a place. She told me all the dining rooms are private."

"So?" Muhsin snapped, his eyes scanning the three gowns lying on top of the cream satin comforter covering the huge bed.

Duchess ignored the edge in his voice as she bowed her head between her knees and began brushing her hair forward. "It just seems like a very intimate place, that's all. Are your friends meeting us there, or what?"

"We'll see," Muhsin responded, having lost interest in the clothing on the bed. Again, he had grown captivated by her incredible hair. The room was silent with the exception of the brush stroking the silky tresses. When she tossed her head back, he couldn't stop the soft grunt from escaping his throat.

"Something wrong?" Duchess asked when he turned his back to her.

Muhsin cleared his throat and focused his attention on the gowns once more. "I like this one," he said, raising one hand at an empire-waisted satin gown. He rubbed the delicate, matching chiffon coat between his fingers and imagined how Duchess would look wearing it.

"Well, at least our tastes are the same," she called, turning back to the mirror.

As lovely as the gowns were, they didn't hold Muhsin's stare for long. Again, he had turned back to watch Duchess working on her hair. When her eyes met his through the mirror, he didn't look away.

She wasn't put on edge by the unwavering stare; instead, she chuckled as a knowing look crept into her eyes. "I assure you, it's all mine," she said, seeing his gaze follow every flip and swing of the healthy locks.

Muhsin's low, raspy laughter filled the room then. "I never doubted that," he said, stepping closer to the dresser. "You ever think about cutting it?"

Duchess's fingers shook just slightly at the question. "I used to think about it . . . every day," she admitted, growing thoughtful. "I did cut it once and Ma almost had a fit," she recalled, soft laughter tinging her words. "When she died . . . those thoughts died, too."

As he stepped closer, Muhsin could see emotion welling in her light gaze. He stopped just short of the dresser and listened.

"She used to run her fingers through it, massaging my scalp," Duchess said. "I think it relaxed her as much as it did me. No matter what type of aggravation I was going through, that always made me feel safe and calm." She stared blankly at her image in the mirror. After a moment, she shook herself back to reality. "I'm sorry," she said, pressing the back of her hand against her cheek.

Muhsin leaned against the dresser. "For what?"

Duchess grimaced. "I didn't mean to bore you with my life story. You're not interested in that."

Muhsin knelt before her, his large hands bracing against either side of the silk-covered bench she occupied. "Anytime you feel like talking about your parents, you do it. Hell, talk my ears off if you want to. I know how it is to lose both your folks," he reminded her.

"You're so sweet," Duchess whispered, smoothing her fingers across his flawless, caramel-toned cheek.

In response, Muhsin caught her hand. For a moment, he inhaled the soft, sweet scent of perfume against her wrist. Then he pressed a gentle kiss to the center of her palm.

Their eyes met and held amidst a flurry of emotion.

Duchess was first to look away, clearing her throat as she refocused on styling her hair.

"I'm going to the living room to fix a drink," Muhsin announced, rising to his full height. "I'll let you finish up in here."

Duchess remained involved with her grooming until the door closed behind him. Then she set the brush down and braced both her hands on the dresser top.

In the living room, Muhsin rushed to the brass bar cart near the balcony doors. He poured a cognac and tossed the drink back. *She's not yours to keep, man . . . not yet,* he thought, ruefully admitting he had to remind himself of that each time he saw her.

"Damn . . ." he growled. It was a mistake to go to her hotel room. He just had to see her and that was dangerous. Muhsin knew he had to stay focused on anything besides Duchess. Of course, there was the money, but nothing would stand in the way of him getting that. It was Duchess. He had to handle this situation carefully; there was too much at stake.

With that thought in mind, he began to stroll around the suite. He decided it was time for Duchess to leave the hotel. He wanted her someplace more permanent. He noticed a folded frame on the white oak coffee table— a picture of Duchess with her parents that he couldn't look away from. He was still entranced by the picture when she walked out into the living room.

Duchess found Muhsin on the sofa staring at the photo. She smiled at the soft look on his handsome face and waited a moment before stepping closer.

"We took that the day after I graduated high school," she explained, sitting next to him on the sofa. "We took pictures almost every day up until I went to college because Ma said she was gonna miss not seeing me every day." Duchess felt her eyes fill with tears, but she didn't try holding them back. "I thank God for her insight. We didn't take pictures much before that."

Muhsin watched as she spoke. His strong fingers brushed the baby-fine hair at her temples while he listened. Slowly, his warm brown eyes traveled across the elaborate hairstyle she wore. A thick braid snaked around her head like a regal crown. The cream gown flared around her ankles, but molded to her body like a sleek glove as the chiffon coat followed her like a fine mist.

"I'm sorry," Duchess whispered, waving one hand before her eyes. "I don't know what's making me talk so much."

Muhsin's fingers paused against the glistening gold stud in her ear and he smiled. "For the second time tonight: you're not talking me to death."

"You're just a good listener," Duchess countered, offering him a cool smile.

"Anytime," he replied, his deep, chocolate gaze unwavering.

Duchess sighed, eager to break the spell of Muhsin's warm stare. "I guess we better get going. We don't want to keep your friends waiting."

He made no comment and pushed himself from the sofa to follow Duchess out of the room. She was about to pull the door open when something stopped her. She turned quickly and bumped right into Muhsin. His huge hands rose immediately and caught both her arms.

Duchess fought the urge to knead the hard, chiseled wall of his chest. She thought she could just feel the unleashed power lying beneath the soft cotton of his cream shirt.

"I forgot my purse," she whispered, her gaze drifting up to his mouth.

Several seconds passed before Muhsin made one move. He released her arms and pushed his hands into the deep pockets of his stylish, dark brown trousers. Duchess stepped around him and grabbed her purse off the desk.

Lord, please don't let me make a fool of myself tonight, she prayed softly, before turning around.

Muhsin's hand closed around her elbow and he led her out of the suite.

The Blackberry was an exquisitely fashioned establishment. A mixture of old Victorian style combined with exotic Japanese artistry, it was a popular spot among the city's jazz and theater enthusiasts. The cozy, dim atmosphere past the red and gold double doors gave patrons a sense of stepping into another world.

"My . . ." Duchess whispered, awed as she studied the lavish paintings, masks and murals decorating the walls.

A soft, genuine smile teased Muhsin's lips as he watched the expressions cross her face. Though he had been to the Blackberry many times, he had a feeling that tonight would be quite different.

"Greetings, Muhsin."

Duchess turned at the sound of the childlike voice. A tiny, middle-aged woman approached them, her palms outstretched.

"Good evening, Mai," Muhsin replied, squeezing the dark lady's petite hands. The two of them spoke in Mai's native tongue for several moments. They exchanged a brief hug before the miniscule hostess walked off. Muhsin turned back to Duchess and patted her waist. "Our dining room is almost ready," he announced.

Duchess was awestruck. "Did you learn to speak Japanese in college?"

"Japan."

"Stop."

Muhsin's shoulders rose in a lazy shrug beneath the smooth, expensive fabric of his suit coat. "My father dragged me there one summer when he was closing a deal," he explained. "I was supposed to be taking 'formal lessons,' but I had more fun running the streets."

"Mmm, why am I not surprised?" Duchess drawled, her light eyes twinkling as they lingered on his handsome face.

Muhsin waved his hand and grinned devilishly. "I wasn't about to waste a trip to Japan sitting in some classroom. I made some very good friends running those streets. Besides, I was outnumbered in the language department. I had no choice but to learn Japanese."

Duchess folded her arms over her chest. "So you couldn't escape it after all," she mused.

"I never thought learning could be so much fun, and my pop didn't care where I learned the language as long as I learned it," Muhsin admitted, his soft chuckling triggering the dimple in his cheek.

For the next several minutes, the two of them stood talking and laughing like old friends. After an easy silence had settled between them, Duchess asked the question that had been on her mind all evening.

"So, um, when are your friends getting here?"

"My friends . . ." Muhsin replied, his brown gaze growing guarded for a brief moment before he decided to come clean. "My friends won't be joining us because we aren't here to meet them."

Duchess chewed her bottom lip. Her hands tightened on her arms as she fought to keep her calm.

Of course, Muhsin detected her unease. "Dinner tonight has nothing to do with our performance, Duchess."

"It doesn't?"

"No," he confirmed with a slight shake of his head. "I brought you here so I could thank you properly."

"There was no need for you to do all this. I mean, considering everything you've given me—"

"Duchess, listen," Muhsin interrupted, massaging the bridge of his nose as he spoke, "buildings and money are cool, don't get me wrong."

"Exactly," she agreed.

Muhsin's soft chuckle was as warm as the gleam in his incredible chocolate stare. "Duchess, believe me when I tell you I have better ways of saying thank you."

"Right," she breathed, her thick lashes fluttering in response to the subtly suggestive response. The intense moment was interrupted by someone calling Muhsin's name. Duchess recognized the slender, dark woman from the boutique she'd visited that day.

"What's goin' on, Tia?" Muhsin said, his tone cool, the look in his eyes becoming stony.

"Blaze," Tia replied, just as cooly.

"Duchess Carver," Muhsin said as his hand enclosed her elbow, "this is Tia Garrison." His raspy baritone voice held just a trace of irritation.

Duchess rested her hand across the place where Muhsin held her arm. Tia's eyes were instantly drawn to the gesture and she wondered how close her ex-lover was to the beauty standing next to him.

"I already met Tia earlier today," Duchess said.

Muhsin's eyes narrowed to the thinnest slits when the innocent revelation reached his ears. "Is that right?" he queried softly.

Tia swallowed, becoming shaken beneath her cool exterior. "Earlier today?" she replied, trying to appear confused.

"Mmm-hmm. Remember, you found my earring?" Duchess explained, missing the tension-filled looks.

Tia closed her eyes and smiled. "That's right. It's nice

to see you again," she gushed, hoping Muhsin believed
the act.

"Well, I'm on my way out, so I'll let y'all get to your
dinner," she added quickly before the conversation revealed anything more. A moment later, she was gone.

"She seems very nice," Duchess noted, watching Tia
rush out of the lobby. "In a quiet, sad sort of way," she
added.

Muhsin gnawed the inside of his jaw, causing the muscle there to twitch erratically. The relaxed expression on
his very handsome face had grown cold.

Just then, the hostess returned and announced the
dining room was prepared. Muhsin retained his grip
around Duchess's elbow as they ventured farther into
the establishment. Duchess was far too entranced by her
exquisite surroundings to notice how on edge he was.

They followed Mai upstairs, down a series of corridors
and finally reached a set of double black doors en-
crusted with a gold design of a dragon and clouds. The
doors opened and a rush of fragrances filled Duchess's
nostrils. Incense burned from the holders positioned on
small glass shelves lining the walls.

Duchess twirled around the room, which was designed
in a mixture of red, green, gold and black. There was a
square table, set for two, covered by a black and gold
tablecloth. Red velvet armchairs occupied either side of
the cozy table. Lush greenery filled every corner of the
room. Their leaves swayed beneath the gold ceiling fan,
causing the softest rustling to fill the air.

While Muhsin spoke with Mai, Duchess strolled across
the plush dining room. The heels of her wedge-heeled
cream pumps disappeared into the deep red carpet. She
let her fingers trail the green velvet love seat occupying
the farthest corner of the room. A short, clawfoot glass
coffee table sat before it.

Mai left the room after telling Muhsin they could place their dinner orders anytime. He thanked her and scanned the room for Duchess. She had already found her way to the window by the wide balcony that overlooked the waterfront.

"I could sit out here for hours," she marveled, laying her palms flat against the glass sheltering the space from the dining room.

Muhsin walked over to stand behind her. "We can have the table moved out here if you like," he offered, pushing his hands into his deep trouser pockets in hopes of keeping them off her.

She shook her head, the light sparkling against the gold studs she wore. "I was freezing in this dress when we stepped out of your truck. I can just imagine how cold I'd be eating outside."

"Here," Muhsin instructed, leaning around her to open the door to the balcony. "See? It's heated."

Duchess removed her chiffon coat and smoothed her hands across her arms. "Oooh," she cooed, relishing the warm air brushing her bare skin.

"Can I bring you a drink out here?" Muhsin asked, enjoying her enthusiasm.

"I'll have whatever you're having," Duchess replied absently, her gaze lingering on the lights twinkling in the distance. "You know, I think I'd come to this place all the time if I lived here."

Muhsin was seated on the love seat, fixing drinks from the small bar atop the glass coffee table. He smiled when he heard her remark. "I'll make a note of that," he said when he walked back onto the balcony carrying two mimosas.

"Thanks," Duchess said when he handed her the drink. "You really know how to thank a person."

"I appreciate that," he replied from his spot behind her.

Gradually Duchess became aware of how close they stood to one another. She could almost feel the strength radiating from Muhsin's tall, agile body. When she cleared her throat and worked up the nerve to face him, her heart raced from the strong emotion in his gaze. Before she lost her self-control, she walked back into the dining room.

"When are we eating?"

Muhsin took another sip of his drink and left the balcony as well. "Whenever you're ready," he said, stepping behind Duchess to help her into her seat.

Duchess held her breath when his hands touched her shoulders. The slight friction of his powerful hands against her skin sent tiny shivers racing down her spine.

"So, um, what's good here?" she asked when he moved away.

"Everything," he assured her firmly, his gaze hooded as he watched her from his seat. "Even the meat. Or so I hear," he added when she sent him a curious look across the table.

Duchess smiled before lowering her bright eyes to the huge red and white menu. "Hmm . . . stir-fry has been on my mind since we talked about it the other night," she said.

After Duchess made her decision, Mushin picked up the cordless phone and called the kitchen. They were dining in less than twenty minutes.

Duchess had done her best to concentrate on her delicious dish of crisp stir-fried vegetables. Unfortunately, Muhsin's incessant staring was making it difficult to enjoy the savory meal. For the past five minutes, he sat with his elbow resting along the arm of his chair and his face resting against his palm. His brown eyes followed her every move.

"Muhsin, is something wrong?" Duchess asked, letting her fork hit the plate with a clatter.

He shrugged, but his eyes never left her face. "How was your shopping trip?"

Duchess thought nothing of the question and turned her attention back to her food. "It wasn't anything special aside from the fact that I spent too long in the place and spent way too much money."

"You met Tia there?" he queried slyly.

"Mmm-hmm." Duchess nodded, crunching on a spicy mixture of onions, bell peppers, broccoli and snap beans. "I was so glad she happened to be there."

"Why's that?" Muhsin asked, crossing his long legs at the ankles as he reclined in his chair.

"I'd dropped one of the earrings my dad gave me on my last birthday. If it weren't for Tia, I probably wouldn't have realized I'd lost it."

Muhsin lowered his eyes to the table. "And that was it?"

"Mmm-hmm."

Muhsin nodded. Still, he couldn't believe Tia hadn't tried to get more out of Duchess. He'd spotted her at the Now Eatery that day and knew she'd find a way to probe his new "love interest."

"She asked where I was from, but that was about it."

Muhsin smiled at the innocent admission. The smile was far from humorous.

Duchess studied the set look on the face across from her. It was hard not to believe the man wasn't in some sort of dark mood, but she decided to ignore it. "So, how long are we going to, um, see each other before getting married?"

"Probably a few weeks."

Duchess's eyes widened at his cool reply. "A few weeks?

Muhsin, no one is gonna believe the marriage is real after a short courtship like that."

Muhsin stabbed several succulent morsels of shrimp and broccoli onto his fork. "Believe me, no one is gonna question the commitment."

"Will you please tell me what you have in mind?" Duchess almost whined as she leaned across the table.

"I don't think so," he said, though it was hard to refuse her anything with the little-girl excitement sparkling in her incredible eyes.

"I have a right to be prepared, you know?" she said, her full lips curving into a pout.

"But I want you to be surprised and swept away. Stuff like that."

"Why? This isn't real."

Muhsin's expression sharpened a bit at the simple truth. "I know that," he managed in a tight voice. "Are you done here?" he asked, before anything more could be said on the subject.

Duchess nodded and pushed her chair away from the table. "Are we going back to the hotel?"

Muhsin headed across the room and retrieved the chiffon coat from the love seat. "Not yet," he said with a smile.

"Thanks," she whispered, turning to slip her arms into the delicate sleeves.

Muhsin allowed his fingers to brush her satiny skin. Duchess took the arm he offered and let him lead her from the dining room.

Rudy Corrigan raved when Muhsin had introduced him to Duchess. "You are by far the finest thing that's walked past these doors tonight."

The short, robust man was the owner of On Notice.

The popular jazz club had a powerfully energetic atmosphere that seemed to affect every one of it patrons.

Duchess smiled at her rotund, albeit attractive host. "Thank you!" she replied over the music and conversation filling the air.

Though Rudy was captivated by Duchess, he couldn't have been more taken by her than the man escorting her. Muhsin was completely preoccupied by the excitement radiating from her face. She appeared even more dazzling than usual. Her fingers tapped his arm in tune with the thriving jazzy beats.

"Thanks, Rudy, man," Muhsin said with a quick wink and smile. He kept one hand around Duchess's elbow as they headed to one of the secluded back tables. His grin widened when he saw how absorbed Duchess was with the club. After a while, he shook his head and leaned close. "They have a big dance floor downstairs," he informed her, once they'd found a table to claim.

Duchess turned to gawk at him. Her expression was one of stunned disbelief. "Don't tell me you dance?"

"Is it so hard to believe?" Muhsin asked, his tone grim as he glared at her.

Duchess brushed her fingers against her chin and eyed him skeptically. "You just seemed too intense to, um, let loose on the dance floor."

"She already knows you, huh, Blaze?" someone teased.

Muhsin and Duchess looked up to see a small group gathered at their table. Two tall, dark-complexioned men were accompanied by three vanilla-toned beauties. The men grinned broadly, their arms linked around the waists of at least one of the scantily clad women.

Duchess watched Muhsin stand and shake hands with the two men. They were obviously friends, judging from the way they carried on with one another. When Muhsin greeted his friends' female companions, the three women practically beamed as they giggled and shook hands with the auburn-haired male.

"Lester Jessup and Tony Riles, this is Duchess Carver."

Lester and Tony's gazes narrowed as they surveyed the incredible beauty at Muhsin's side.

"It's nice to meet you all," Duchess said, trying hard not to laugh at the dumbfounded expressions on Lester and Tony's faces. Even the three glamourous companions seemed to lose some of their confidence as they coyly studied her.

"Duchess, are you new in town?" Tony asked.

"Yes, I've only been here a couple of days."

"You planning to move here?" Lester asked, trying to mask his interest.

Duchess's shrugged and held her hands clasped regally at her waist. "I was only in town on business. Beyond that, I don't know what my plans are," she told them, glancing up at Muhsin who nodded his satisfaction.

Lester stepped closer to brush her hand. "I hope to see you again before you leave us."

Muhsin chuckled then. "Smooth, Les," he interjected, while patting Duchess against her waist. "But right now Ms. Carver's laid down a challenge I have to answer. I think we got a spot on the dance floor," he whispered against her temple.

Duchess's vibrant smile signified her acceptance. The group they left behind watched with increasing curiosity.

Several couples jumped and gyrated to the up-tempo tune now pulsing through the club. Muhsin caught Duchess's hand in a tight grasp and twirled her out onto the hardwood floor. Her initial gasp turned into high-pitched breathless laughter as he handled her effortlessly.

A skilled dancer herself, Duchess was a complete vision as she moved against the sinfully handsome man holding her. Other dancers actually stepped aside to give the dazzling couple more room to work their magic. Muhsin's touch was as gentle as it was possessive. Duchess laughed the entire time, reveling in the skill of a strong partner. When Duchess turned her back toward Muhsin and shimmied down the length of his body, a round of applause and whistles filled the air. Taunts of "Go on, y'all!" and "Work it!" sounded from the other dancers. Duchess rose to her full height and felt Muhsin's hands close over her hips as he pulled her back against his chest. His handsome face settled to the crook of her neck, where he inhaled the soft, fresh scent of her perfume. Duchess's hand rose to caress his cheek before she twirled around to face him. Another round of applause filled the entire club. When the tempo finally changed to a slower, more sensual groove, Duchess and Muhsin caught their breaths.

"Surprised?" Muhsin asked as he held Duchess tight against his chest. A knowing grin tugged at the erotic curve of his mouth when he looked into her smiling face.

Duchess couldn't mask her guilt. "I must say I am," she admitted, her eyes lingering on the cleft in his chin.

Muhsin laced his fingers together at the small of her back. "Well, my father was Nigerian and my mother was Jamaican," he said, stroking her spine with both thumbs. "Everyone moved out of the way when they stepped on the floor," he added, with a devilish wink.

Duchess laughed, amused by his confidence. "So you're trying to tell me your rhythm is inherited?" she asked in a purely mocking tone.

Muhsin shrugged, his expression completely innocent. "What do you think?" he asked, smiling again when Duchess laughed louder and threw her head back.

"Your parents must've been somethin' else."

Muhsin's brown eyes took on a faraway look. "They were." He sighed.

Duchess tilted her head, bringing her gaze in line with his. "Hey? You wanna talk about it?"

"I just miss 'em," he admitted, taking a deep breath as he tried to control his emotions.

"I understand."

"My mother was . . . she was incredible."

Duchess's hazel eyes sparkled when she smiled. "I can tell you loved her a lot."

"She could make anybody laugh at anything," he recalled, shaking his head at the memories coming to mind. "She had so much energy, she outlasted me sometimes. When she died . . . no one could believe she was gone."

Duchess suppressed the urge to reach out and smooth the sadness from his face. She felt her emotions become more solemn as thoughts of her own mother and father grew prevalent. She chose not to dwell on the melancholy of the moment, though. Instead, she fiddled with the lapels of Muhsin's stylish chocolate suit coat and looked around the club. "So are all your hangouts this much fun?" she teased.

Muhsin's playfully arrogant grin returned. "I promise you, there are no stuffy dates when you're dealing with me. I'm known for being able to show a woman a good time."

"Mmm-hmm . . ." Duchess replied, a wicked gleam tinging her light eyes. "A good time in or out of the bedroom?"

Muhsin held Duchess tighter and brought his face closer to hers. "I guess you'll have to find that out for yourself."

Duchess trembled just a little. "This is business, remember?"

Muhsin felt her reaction. "I'll remember that as long as you do."

When the suggestive remarks had subsided, the soothing lilt of the music cast its hypnotic spell. Duchess
focused her eyes on Muhsin's clothes. The casual cut of
his cotton shirt called for no tie. She trailed the powerful line of his neck, stopping to rest at the base of his
throat where the pulse beat steadily against the gold
chain he sported. His grip at her waist tightened, forcing
a tiny moan past her lips. The embrace was comforting
in its subtle sensuality. Duchess realized she couldn't tell
if it was part of the act or something all too real.

Three melodies later, Muhsin escorted Duchess away
from the dance floor. They walked arm in arm and
Duchess let her head rest against his shoulder. She
looked content and very happy. Of course, Muhsin noticed and was more than pleased.

"You ready to go?" he asked, chuckling when she nodded against his shoulder.

Several curious spectators looked on as the couple exited the establishment. Just as planned, Muhsin Vuyani's
relationship with the mysterious Duchess Carver had instantly become the hottest topic in the club.

Chapter 5

"So, in other words, everything is going well with the annex?" Duchess asked the next morning during her conference call with Gretchen and Jaliel.

There was a brief silence on the other end of the line before Gretchen cleared her throat. "Um, things are goin' good, Dutch, but, um, we're—well, Jaliel is still concerned about Muhsin Vuyani suddenly turning the other cheek and just giving you that building."

"Concerned?" Duchess repeated, stirring her coffee with cream until it turned a cool shade of beige.

"We just want to make sure you're all right," Gretchen explained, her tone a bit uneasy.

"When are you comin' back?" Jaliel asked.

"Jaliel." Gretchen sighed. "The girl needs this time away, especially now. She needs to put that mess with Muhsin Vuyani behind and leave Chicago altogether. Visit some other places before coming back."

"Thanks, Gret. I promise, I'm fine," Duchess said, appreciating her friend's advice.

"Well, don't be gone too long," Jaliel added.

"Boy," Gretchen chastised, "Duchess ain't your mama. Let her have some fun. Goodness!"

"I'm gettin' off this line before y'all kill each other!" Duchess bellowed, laughing uncontrollably. "I'll talk to you sometime tomorrow."

After setting the phone aside, she took a tiny sip of delicious almond amaretto blend and relaxed on the sofa. For the second time that morning, her thoughts drifted back to her date the night before.

"Stop it, Dutch," she hissed, trailing both hands through her loose hair in hopes of warding off the warm memories. A moment later, she shrugged. What woman wouldn't be drawn to a man like Muhsin Vuyani, even if it was all pretend? Still, Duchess regretfully acknowledged she would have to be careful. This scheme could easily become more serious than she ever imagined.

The phone rang just then and she debated on whether to answer it. She had already decided to spend that morning alone, perhaps having breakfast in one of the hotel's restaurants.

You're not here on vacation, Dutch, she reminded herself, leaning off the sofa to grab the cordless phone from the coffee table. "Duchess Carver," she said.

"What took you so long to answer the phone?" Muhsin snapped, his raspy voice sounding that much rougher.

Duchess was startled, but only for an instant. "Well, it *is* eight-thirty A.M.! What the hell are you doin' callin' me so damned early?" she snapped right back.

Muhsin shook his head, his long lashes briefly shielding his eyes. "Duchess, I'm sorry for that. I didn't mean to come off that way."

"What's wrong?" she asked, curling her legs beneath her on the sofa.

"You got about five hours?" Muhsin retorted. "That's how long it'll take for me to tell you about all the crap I've had to deal with since I got to work this morning."

"Well, I guess you've just got a real crappy job."

"Hmph, funny," he replied drily, though a tiny chuckle did escape him.

"So, are you calling about our date tonight?" Duchess asked, leaning forward to reach for her coffee cup.

"Yes and no. Mostly no."

"Then . . . why are you calling?"

"I want to get together with you for breakfast this morning."

Duchess set her cup down and slapped her hand against her knee. "You must be reading my mind. I was just about to leave and get breakfast at Maurice's," she said, citing one of the hotel's restaurants.

"Good. I'll meet you there."

Duchess frowned a bit. "I'll probably be done by the time you get here," she cautioned.

"I doubt that, since I'm on my way right now."

"Cell phone?" Duchess guessed.

"You got it."

"Well, in that case, I'll see you when you get here."

"I'll meet you at the restaurant," Muhsin told her, before the phone clicked off.

When Duchess set her phone down she didn't realize she was smiling from ear to ear.

Duchess smiled up at the tall, lanky blond waiter at the table. "I think I'll wait until my friend gets here to order, if that's okay?"

The young man nodded while making a note on his pad. "That's no problem, ma'am. I'll be right back with your tea."

Duchess began to scan the menu and thought she heard her name being called in the distance. Sure enough, Isaiah Manfres was approaching her.

"You get around, don't you?" Duchess laughed as they hugged.

"That would be you."

"Sit down with me," Duchess ordered, resuming her place at the oval table. "What are you doin' here?"

Isaiah unbuttoned the tailored mocha suit coat and angled his tall frame into one of the gray armchairs. "I'm here to meet a client and I knew you were staying here. I didn't expect to find you, though."

Just then, the waiter returned. "Is this your breakfast partner, miss?" he asked, placing her tea on the table.

"Oh, no, but you're welcome to join us here, Isaiah."

"I'll take a cup of coffee," Isaiah replied. "But I'll decline the offer to join you," he told Duchess. "Besides, I don't think he'd appreciate havin' to share you with a friend, no matter how platonic we are."

Duchess giggled at the deduction. "I doubt we'll have to worry about that, since you happen to be friends with him."

Isaiah saw the waiter returning with his coffee and waited a moment before speaking. "Come again?" he requested, frowning for clarification.

"It's Muhsin Vuyani," she revealed, noticing the grimace cross Isaiah's handsome brown face. "What?"

Across the room, the host smiled when Muhsin approached the podium. "Table for one, sir?"

Muhsin spotted Duchess the moment he walked into the sparsely crowded dining room. When he saw Isaiah at the table as well, his eyes narrowed and his hand clenched into a fist inside his pocket.

"Sir?" the host inquired again.

"No," Muhsin responded, his gravelly voice as firm as the look in his eyes. "I see my date." He headed across the dining room with both hands clenched into fists.

Duchess was shaking her head at Isaiah. "I'm not going to stop asking until you tell me what that look was about," she persisted, ignoring the drawn expression Isaiah sent her.

"It was just a look that crossed my face, that's all."

"Uh-uh."

Isaiah took a sip of his coffee, then stared down into the black liquid a moment. "Just be careful," he advised, finally looking up.

Duchess was stumped. "Of what?"

"Blaze has his ways."

"Well . . . isn't that true of everyone?" Duchess pointed out, her gaze expectant.

Isaiah let his stare falter. "It's more true of some than others."

The grave reply sent a curious smile to Duchess's face. "I thought y'all were friends?"

"We are, so you know I know him. And speak of the devil now," Isaiah remarked suddenly, noticing the topic of the conversation approaching the table.

"Talkin' about me, eh?" Muhsin teased, though the glint in his gaze proved he felt far from humorous.

"Isaiah's got the idea you wouldn't appreciate him joining us for breakfast," Duchess said, hoping to lighten the subtle tension surrounding the table.

The hard look in Muhsin's eyes slowly took on an amused gleam. "You know me well, man," he said, tilting his head just slightly.

Isaiah held one hand in the air. "That's what I tried to tell her," he said, sending a pointed look to Duchess as he stood. "Call me," he ordered, leaning down to kiss her cheek.

Duchess shook her head. "You've got some strange friends, Muhsin," she declared when they were alone.

"I thought he was your friend, too?"

"That's not what I mean," she retorted, dismissing the inquisitive expression on his face. "All these friends you're trying to impress with your new love don't seem to like you very much. They seem more wary of you than anything else."

"Who else has given you that impression?" Muhsin asked, brushing an index finger across one of his sleek reddish-brown brows.

"Okay, in the boutique the other day, I ran into those two women we saw in the restaurant."

Muhsin thought back. "Yesterday?"

"Mmm-hmm," Duchess said. "Anyway, you should've heard them telling me to watch out for you and how cold you are."

"Duchess, lemme share something with you," he said, soft laughter just beneath the surface of his words. "I have no female friends. I have aquaintances."

"Meaning, all the women you know, you've slept with?"

"Meaning, many of the women I know, I've slept with. Not all," he corrected with a playful air of indignance.

Duchess reached for her menu. "So what about all the others? The ones you haven't slept with?"

"Bitter or jealous friends of the women I've slept with."

"Hmph. Very confident, Mr. Vuyani."

"I've got every reason to be."

Duchess couldn't help but burst into laughter.

"You don't seem offended," Muhsin noted, leaning back in his chair.

"Why should I be?" Duchess asked, tossing her head so that her high ponytail slapped her cheek. "It's not like we're in a real relationship. You're not really my man, are you?"

Muhsin was tapping his fingers against his temple. "You never know, Duchess. This whole thing might turn out a lot different than we expect."

Duchess's head snapped up, but Muhsin's attention was focused on his menu. It was then that the helpful advice of one of his aquaintances came to her mind. *Muhsin Vuyani is a shark.*

The blond waiter returned. "May I take your orders?" he offered, pen poised over his pad.

"Duchess?" Muhsin called, watching her a moment before leaning forward. "Duchess," he repeated, brushing his fingers against the back of her hand.

Duchess blinked and realized the two men were watching with expectant gazes. Quickly, she snapped to and placed her order.

"You all right?" Muhsin asked once the waiter left with both orders.

"I was just remembering someone telling me you were a shark."

"A shark, hmm?" Muhsin thought, smiling despite the insult. He actually seemed quite pleased by it. "But that doesn't matter to you, right? Because I'm not your man."

Duchess felt as though she were seeing a new man— the real man. Something about that unnerved her slightly. Against her better judgement, she kept her concerns silent. "So what are your plans after we eat?"

"My plans are with you. We're going to see your new place."

"My new place?" Duchess asked, pressing her hand against the front of the sylish bell-bottomed jumper she sported. "What new place?"

"Baby, I can't have you staying in this hotel indefinitely," Muhsin said, folding his arms over the purple T-shirt emblazoned with the emblem of his favorite Minnesota football team. "Besides, I know that room must be cramping you by now."

"Well . . ." Duchess couldn't help but agree. Still, she hadn't thought of changing her living arrangements in spite of the fact that they were pretty much "engaged." For Duchess, it would just make it seem too *real* for her peace of mind. "You know you shouldn't be going to all this trouble," she continued to argue.

"It was no trouble," he assured her, nodding when the waiter returned with the mug of coffee he ordered. "I have a place in the city. I stay there whenever I don't feel like driving home."

Duchess scratched the fine hair along her left temple. "You work in the city and hide out in the city. Not very ingenious."

Muhsin shrugged, adding about four spoonfuls of sugar to his coffee. "Sometimes it's best to hide out in plain view."

"I heard that."

"Besides, nobody knows about the place. Not even family."

"So are we leaving right after breakfast?"

"If that's all right with you?" Muhsin answered, grimacing at the still bitter taste of the coffee.

Duchess watched in amazement as he added even more sugar to the cup. "When's our next performance?" she asked when he caught her gawking.

"Tonight," he told her, this time smiling when he tasted the coffee. "We're meeting my uncle."

Duchess's hand fell to the table, causing her teacup and saucer to rattle. "You want me to meet your family already? Why?"

"Why not?"

"Muhsin, we both know this whole thing is fake, but still . . . people see each other a while before meeting each other's families."

Muhsin waved off the formality. "My uncle Q is more like my father than my own father was. I care a lot about his opinions and I really want you to meet him."

"Does he know what you're up to?"

"No," was the simple reply.

"Goodness. I'm gonna have to find something really nice to wear tonight," Duchess said.

"Don't do anything different. You're always just right," Muhsin complimented smoothly just as the waiter returned with two platters heaped with food.

"Oooh . . ." Duchess cooed when she eyed the delectable fruits filling Muhsin's plate.

"What?" he said, watching her suspiciously.

"Is that kiwi?" Duchess asked, using her fork to point.

"Mmm-hmm. Want some?" he asked, glancing down at the plate.

"Could I?" She scooted her chair closer as Muhsin did the same.

In addition to a mound of mouthwatering fruit, there were plump blueberry and apple-cinnamon muffins, along with a generous helping of fluffy scrambled eggs topped with cheddar. Duchess had ordered something a bit heartier, a four-cheese omelette topped with onions and green peppers, toasted English muffins smattered with jam and golden hash browns.

"How about some of that omelette?" Muhsin requested, eyeing the huge creation like a starving man.

"Oh, please," Duchess urged. "Take half."

"You're pretty slim to be such a big eater," Muhsin noted as he sliced the mammoth-sized omelette in half.

Duchess waved one hand in the air. "Please don't jinx me. Thank God for high metabolism."

"I know, right?" Muhsin agreed, adding some of the hash browns to his plate. "I should be at least four hundred pounds by now."

"Do you work out a lot?" Duchess asked, indulging in a few plump strawberries.

"Not as much as I used to. The most I do is maybe ball every weekend. Depends on my schedule," he explained.

"Mmm . . . I know. I generally go ballin' every other Saturday. Usually I just take a few laps in the pool."

Muhsin's fork paused over the eggs. "You play basketball?" he asked slowly.

Duchess nodded, still focused on her food. When Muhsin said nothing more, she looked up. "What?"

"I'm tryin' to imagine you on a basketball court."

"Why? That's not such an unusual thing these days."

Muhsin shrugged, a smirk playing around the sensuous curve of his mouth. "I know it's not unusual. You just . . ."

"'I just . . .'" Duchess prompted.

"Look, I'm sorry, all right?" Muhsin blurted amidst soft chuckles. "You just don't look like the type of sista who'd enjoy stuff like that."

"Oh, my goodness!" Duchess bellowed, not the least bit offended by Muhsin's admission. "Boy, lemme tell you somethin'," she drawled, pointing her fork in his direction. "I love all types of sports. I've even played football a time or two and it wasn't that powder-puff stuff, either."

Muhsin leaned back in his chair to watch her brag. His brown eyes narrowed as he studied the different expressions that crossed her face while she recited a list of her athletic interests.

"I even tried hockey once, but I admit that game scares me. Right now, my big interest is watching that pro wrestling on TV."

Muhsin let out a quick burst of laughter. "Wrestling?" he repeated in disbelief.

Duchess nodded before a wave of chuckles hit her as well. Soon she and Muhsin were in the midst of easy laughter. Several minutes passed before they realized how much fun they were really having.

Duchess cleared her throat and focused on her food. "So, um, what had you upset at work?"

Muhsin grimaced. "The same mess. You know, I try to be the kind of boss with an open-door policy. But it seems the more I try to be that way, the more excuses I hear. Sometimes I think my employees—some of them—believe an open door means that when they have a responsibility they don't care to follow through on, they can just go to the boss, complain a little and pass the buck."

Duchess nodded. "I know what you mean. And it's unfortunate that so many of the complaints and attempts to 'pass the buck' come from the top people."

"That's another thing," Muhsin added, reaching for the juice pitcher, "these fools have the staff to get the work done and still have complaints. I think I'd be embarrassed to go to the boss and tell him my staff can't cut it."

Duchess leaned forward to remove the slice of lemon from her tea. "That's one thing I am grateful for. I can honestly say that, for the most part, I have a very competent staff. Or at the very least, a loyal staff. They prefer to settle things among themselves. I rarely have to get involved unless it's something major."

"That's what I'm working toward." Muhsin groaned. "My problem is that I like to know everything."

Duchess giggled. "That's why I've got Gretchen and Jaliel."

Muhsin's expression turned a bit guarded. "Maybe I'm too suspicious to trust someone to tell me everything."

"Well, I'm sure your staff all love you."

Muhsin tried to hide his smile, but couldn't. "What can I say? 'Course, I wouldn't be surprised to find a bull's-eye with my face on it."

"Well, such is the nature of our business." Duchess sighed, taking a sip of her orange pekoe tea. "One day up. One day down. You'd be surprised how many people think we have it easy, that running a company is so dazzling and glamorous."

Muhsin was shaking his head. "I wouldn't be surprised. But you know, I wouldn't trade it for anything."

Duchess smiled. "Neither would I."

The two of them were quite a sight as they sat close and shared breakfast. Muhsin couldn't dismiss the incredible scent of the soft perfume clinging to Duchess's skin. Duchess was just as preoccupied by Muhsin's powerful hands curved over the delicate silverware. They were having the best time without realizing how close they were really becoming.

"Are you sure you want to turn this place over to me?"

A slow smirk began to tug at the curve of Muhsin's mouth. "Why?" he asked, slipping the keys to the penthouse into the back pocket of his baggy nylon jogging pants.

"Because you might not get it back when all this is over."

Muhsin laughed. "I'll take that to mean you like it?"

"Don't ask dumb questions," Duchess said, trailing her fingers along the edge of the sleek, silver suede sofa in the living room. Though the Lake Shore Drive residence was designed with blatant masculine overtones, it was still a gorgeous place. She wanted to kick herself for not accepting the offer to live there sooner.

"Feel free to change anything," Muhsin called, watching her stroll down the hall lined with framed photos of great basketball moments.

Duchess smoothed her hands across her bare arms. "This is only temporary, remember?" she sang.

"Right," Muhsin muttered, massaging the sudden tension creeping into his neck.

"So when can I move in?" Duchess said when she ventured into the spacious state-of-the-art kitchen decorated in black and gold.

Muhsin leaned against the doorjamb, crossing his sneaker-shod feet one over the other. "We can go get your stuff and you can move in today."

"Today?" Duchess sighed, her light eyes sparkling with excitement. "Oh, this is incredible."

"So glad I could please," he said, pushing both hands deep into the pockets of his forest-green jogging pants. He watched the contented look on her face change to a more uneasy expression. "What?"

Duchess propped both hands on her hips and bowed her head. "I'm just realizing how much of your time I'm taking up. You should be getting back to your office."

Muhsin spread his hands about him. "Do I look like I want to head back to the office?" he asked, glancing down at his casual athletic attire. "Unlike you, I'm not a workaholic."

Duchess leaned against the kitchen sink. "You know I don't believe that."

Muhsin shrugged and pushed himself away from the door. "I can prove I'm in no hurry to get back to the office."

"How?"

"We move your stuff in here and then it's a tour of my boat and then lunch," he replied, trying not to smile at the stunned look she sent him. "But if you'd rather I go back to work and forget about it—"

"Stop. No, don't you dare," she ordered, one hand poised in the air.

Grinning broadly, Muhsin closed the distance between them and pulled a set of keys from his pocket. "These are to the house. This one," he said, holding one key for clarification, "is to the front door and this one . . ."

Duchess listened absently as he rambled off each key and its use. She inhaled the clean fragrance of his cologne while her gaze stroked the powerful line of his neck and the outline of his wide chest beneath the T-shirt he wore. Her fingers ached to settle into the silky auburn crop of his hair and to caress the chiseled structure of his handsome caramel face.

"Duchess? You with me?" Muhsin whispered, his gorgeous eyes crinkling at the corners when he smiled at her.

"I'm sorry, what?" she muttered, blinking away the scandalous thoughts racing through her brain.

"These are yours," he said, slipping the brass key ring into her palm.

Duchess pressed her lips together and studied the way Muhsin's hand practically smothered her own. "Um, this is the only set?" she queried after a lengthy silence.

Muhsin answered the question with a soft chuckle that triggered the lone dimple in his cheek. *Blatant beauty and brains to match, what more could I want?* he asked himself. "The security office downstairs has the only other set," he assured her.

"Not that I don't trust you," Duchess explained quickly.

Muhsin shrugged. "Of course not," he said, his expression playfully skeptical, "but you should never take chances with a face and body like yours tempting a man."

"Are you tempted?" Duchess heard herself ask. Her lashes almost fluttered closed when she looked up at him.

"Hell, yes," Muhsin admitted in an instant.

Duchess smiled and stepped away. "We better go get my stuff," she suggested, massaging her fingers upon her forehead as she headed out the kitchen.

"Change in plans," Muhsin announced, after several moments of travel in his SUV.

Duchess watched him reach for the cell phone on the sun visor and punch in a few digits. He made arrangements for her things to be moved from the hotel to the condo. All she would need to do was sign out of the hotel.

Once that business was settled, they set off on a tour of the city. Chicago was incredible as autumn set in. The numerous parks were lined with trees vibrant with orange and golden leaves. There were musical groups on almost every corner. A trip to Navy Pier proved to be most enjoyable. They were like two little kids as they feasted on hot dogs, candy and other goodies while enjoying the numerous rides, shows and other attractions. Muhsin even treated Duchess to popcorn as they strolled the North Harbor. She couldn't remember the last time she'd had so much fun.

"My parents met here," Muhsin said as they looked out at the passing ferries.

Duchess smiled but didn't look up. "Tell me about it."

"She was in Chicago for the weekend. Her younger brother was opening a restaurant with some friends who lived here," he began, escorting her to one of the benches along the walkway. "Anyway, my dad was there at the opening. At the time, he was in his last year of grad school completing his master's in business. He was supposed to go back home to Nigeria afterward. When he met Mama, he forgot all about that."

Duchess was intrigued by the story. "So what were his plans when he got back to Nigeria?"

"Well," Muhsin began, picking through the bag for a few more choice pieces of popcorn, "he was going to go into business with his dad, who owned a small farmer's market."

Duchess was impressed. "You mean he was going to take a very valuable degree and use it to help his dad at home."

Muhsin nodded. "Yep, he had no plans to own a conglomerate and make multibillion dollar decisions. He was just a kid who wanted to make his pop proud. "

"I'll say he did that and then some," Duchess said. "So then what happened?"

Muhsin tossed a few kernels of popcorn to the gulls skirting the walkway. "Anyway, Ma was in school herself and was going back right after the opening. Afterward she had plans to go home to Jamaica."

"What happened?"

"Well, Pop didn't want to let her go."

"Uh-huh."

Muhsin's expression grew guarded then. "It was complicated," he explained slowly. "She, um, had a boyfriend at school."

"Ah," Duchess breathed, a knowing look coming to her face. "But the better man won out in the end?"

Muhsin grunted, then stood and sprinkled the remaining popcorn on the ground. "I'm gonna show you where they have all the races. If I remember correctly, you listed boating as one of your interests," he remarked in an overly amused tone.

Duchess began to laugh.

The delightful tour ended at the pier where Muhsin kept his boat.

"A yacht, I assume?" Duchess asked, her hazel stare bright as she looked out over all the gorgeous boats dotting the blue water. A view of the city skyline sat off in the distance.

"You don't approve?" Muhsin asked, his wide hand curling around her elbow as he guided her to the boat slip.

"Do you have a captain taking us out?" Duchess asked, tucking a loose strand of hair behind her ear when it flapped against the wind.

"I only have a captain on board when I'm throwing a

party. But don't worry, I'm capable of navigating myself. I won't have us shipwrecked," he said with a devilish grin.

Duchess rubbed her hands together. "Then the answer to your question is yes. I approve of people owning extravagant things if they understand them. There's nothing more pathetic than a man with twenty cars and no idea how to drive them."

Muhsin nodded, undoing the latch of the gate leading to the boat dock. "I know where you're coming from. You're an insightful lady, Duchess Carver."

"Thank you," she said, looking away from his gorgeous chocolate stare lest she become entranced again. "Can I have a tour?"

"No problem," Muhsin said, easily falling into the role of tour guide for the second time that day.

Duchess tried to concentrate on all the features aboard the grand *Red Storm*, but again she found herself admiring Muhsin. It was impossible not to. The man was incredible to look at and the rough raspy tone of his low voice sent tremors through her body. She could almost hear him whispering words of passion as he loved her.

"Duchess?"

Taking a deep breath, she looked away from his inquisitive gaze and strolled across the deck to lean against the polished maple railing. "Why don't you prove to me you can move this thing?" she challenged.

Some twenty minutes after he'd steered them out onto the bay, Muhsin turned to Duchess. "Satisfied?" he asked.

"I'm impressed," Duchess admitted, closing her eyes to enjoy the cool breeze hitting her face. She had loosened the high ponytail, allowing the thick tresses to bounce and whip in the air.

"Now it's your turn," he announced, leaving the wheel momentarily to grab her wrist.

"My turn for what?" Duchess demanded, frowning when he pulled her before the wheel.

"To impress me with your navigating."

"Ha! You'll be far from impressed, believe me!"

Muhsin shook his head. "I'm not havin' it. Here," he insisted, folding his hands over hers and curving them around the wheel.

"Muhsin, don't leave me here," she begged.

"I'm not going anywhere," he promised, the slow smile adding sincerity to his words. "Just relax." He stood close behind her as his large hands cupped her slender hips. "Okay, just keep it steady . . . easy . . . watch out for the other boats . . . you got it."

Muhsin's soothing tone instantly relaxed Duchess. She shocked herself at the ease with which she guided the mammoth-sized vessel.

"Lord . . ." she breathed, her brows rising in both excitement and pride.

"Congratulations," Muhsin said, relishing the opportunity to hold her so close. He bowed his head to inhale the soft, sweet smell clinging to her temple. His hands began to massage her hips, settling her even closer to his hard body.

Duchess couldn't ignore what was happening and indulged in the delicious sensations stemming from his touch. Muhsin's mouth was sliding down her temple, his hands smoothing across her thighs outlined against her light blue jumpsuit.

Somehow, Duchess managed to resist the demands of her body and she inched away. "Are we gonna have lunch on the boat?" she asked, grimacing at her breathless tone.

Muhsin was just as affected. He watched her bracing herself against the rail with her back toward him. "Um, no, I'm going to take us back in," he said, rubbing his eyes when he turned back to the wheel.

Duchess groaned when the waiter set the platter of food before her. She marveled over the delicious-looking feast and said grace before diving into the food. "I can't believe how hungry I am."

"That's why I took you to the boat first. To work up your appetite."

"Mmm-hmm, and yours," Duchess noted, her tone softly suggestive.

Muhsin added a mound of Parmesan cheese to the delectable vegetable lasagna and shook his head. "I never have problems workin' up an appetite," he said, sending her a meaningful look.

Duchess kept her eyes focused on her food. "I'll bet," she whispered.

Silence settled between them then. After a while, Duchess could feel Muhsin's brown gaze searing her skin. "So, tell me about your uncle," she said, hoping to ease the electric tension.

Although Muhsin knew what she was up to, he obliged. He never passed on an opportunity to discuss his uncle.

"Where do I begin?" Muhsin sighed as he smothered butter on the corner of a breadstick. "Quincy Fabusche can't be described with one word, or ten for that matter. He's the life of the party, creative, gregarious, crazy, intimidating, flirtatious; I could go on and on."

"I can tell you love him a lot."

"I do," Muhsin said, his gaze taking on a faraway look as he pictured the man. "Uncle Q was my mother's little brother, but I don't think the man was ever little."

Duchess almost choked on her lasagna as laughter

crept into her throat. "Does he live here in Chicago or in Jamaica?"

"He spends most of the year in Jamaica, but he could call just about anywhere home."

"He sounds like a fascinating man. I can't wait to meet him."

Muhsin's hearty chuckle turned the heads of several waitresses and female diners. "I warn you, he's a playa. A real flirt especially with younger women."

"Younger women, huh?" Duchess teased, cutting another chunk of the savory pasta. "I'm thirty-one. Does that still count?"

"Hmph. Quincy is almost fifty-five, so you could be fifty-three and still be in his target range," Muhsin assured her.

"Well, I still can't wait to meet him," Duchess said with a lazy shrug. "Maybe I'll find out where all that red hair comes from." She smiled when he winked. "Would you excuse me a minute?" she asked, rising from the table to go in search of a restroom.

Muhsin relaxed in his chair, his gaze soft as it followed her out of the dining room. He couldn't wait for her to meet Quincy either. Again, the tiny voice of his conscience rose to warn him that the time would soon arrive when Duchess would expect to be let out of the agreement. His jaw tensed, the look on his face going way past intimidating. Agreement or no, he had no intentions of letting Duchess go once he had her.

Duchess ordered herself to sit up, knowing Muhsin would be there any minute to pick her up. She had been lounging in the black claw-foot tub for almost an hour. She managed to push herself out from the disappearing bubbles and thought about what a whirlwind of a day she'd had.

"But it's been worth it," she admitted, smiling at her surroundings. Truth be told, she lingered in the tub so long because she dreaded leaving the gorgeous black and burgundy bathroom. Muhsin had given her permission to change anything in the penthouse. She told herself the place was too great to change, but the truth was it reminded her of its owner and she wanted to savor the effect.

"Stop it, Duchess," she hissed, suddenly agitated. She squeezed fistfuls of her hair in some attempt to prevent her thoughts from venturing into dangerous territory.

For a while, she stood in the middle of the bathroom and collected herself. This situation with Muhsin was slowly wearing down her defenses and that was dangerous. Especially when she was already so incredibly attracted to the man.

"Get dressed," she quickly ordered herself.

The outfit she'd chosen for the evening was lying on the bed. The sleeveless silver-gray jumpsuit had a scoop neck and dipped a bit low in the back. The pants formed to her curvaceous, slender frame and fell into a bootleg cut to show off the strappy, open-toed silver heels she sported. She had styled her hair casually with a row of tiny braids swept away from her forehead that cascaded into a riot of loose curls tumbling down her back. The doorbell rang just as she was sliding the backs onto her tiny diamond hoop earrings.

"Good, he can zip me up," she muttered, sprinting from the bedroom.

Muhsin waited on the wide front porch in a stylish three-piece, tan suit. He offered Duchess a cool smile before his cocoa stare drifted over her casual outfit.

"Could you zip this for me?" Duchess asked, missing the look in his unwavering stare as she pulled him inside.

"Where is it?" he asked, his eyes caressing the flawless skin of her arms and shoulders.

"Here," she replied, pulling her hair aside and motioning toward her back.

Muhsin studied the mole resting between her shoulder blades and resisted the urge to place his mouth against it. He closed one hand around her upper arm and pulled her close.

Duchess let out a soft breath and closed her eyes. She never dreamed something as simple as zipping could be so sensual. She prayed he could not feel her tremble in response to his fingers trailing her bare back when he eased the zipper up.

Once the task was complete, Muhsin brushed his hand against hers, instructing Duchess to let go of her hair. He watched the curled mass bounce to the middle of her back, then turned her around to face him.

"Thank you," she whispered, a tiny smile softening her lips as she gazed up at him.

Muhsin nodded. "Mmm-hmm," he muttered before tugging her into his tall, hard frame.

Duchess's lips parted instantly as his mouth slanted across hers. Their tongues met simultaneously, stroking tentatively at first, then with increased enthusiasm. Muhsin added more pressure, his tongue delving deeply as he groaned into her mouth.

Duchess grew more bold as well. She arched her shivering form closer to him. Her fingers curled into his hair. The soft gasp she uttered at its soothing texture allowed Muhsin to deepen his kiss with shocking intensity. His hands caressed her back, using brisk, sweeping strokes. He cupped the sides of her breasts, his thumbs grazing the rigid nipples under the bodice of her suit.

She could have kissed him all night, but Muhsin found the willpower to call an end to the devastating kiss.

He rose to his full height and smiled down at her. Duchess appeared as though she wanted to faint. Her lipstick was smudged and her mouth looked thoroughly kissed.

"Go fix this," Muhsin softly instructed, curving his index finger around her lips as he patted her waist.

Duchess was too shocked and breathless to say anything. She left the living room to do as he asked, and managed to make it upstairs to the bedroom, where her weak legs finally gave out beneath her.

She sat on the bed in a dazed manner. She could form no opinions about what had just happened; her mind was a complete blank. Absently, she brought shaking fingers to her mouth.

"Duchess, we need to hustle if we want to get there on time!" Muhsin called from the living room.

"Okay," she replied in a voice far too low for him to hear.

Chapter 6

Duchess felt more like herself by the time she and Muhsin arrived at the restaurant. He kept her close to his side from the moment he escorted her inside the establishment. She cursed herself for fidgeting when he traced her back while speaking with the hostess.

Muhsin was so in tune with Duchess's every move. He knew the kiss still had her on edge. He could feel her tremble beneath his touch.

The tall, brunet hostess began to laugh when she discovered who Muhsin was there to meet. "Mr. Fabusche is definitely here, Mr. Vuyani. The man has already made several of my waitresses blush during the ten minutes he's been here."

Muhsin shook his head. "Sounds like Uncle Q," he said with a chuckle before turning back to Duchess. "Ready?" he whispered, giving her waist a reassuring pat.

Duchess nodded, then tossed her hair over her shoulders. She and Muhsin followed the hostess into the dining room and spotted Quincy right away. The round table he occupied was surrounded by at least six giggling waitresses. The restaurant's other patrons should have been perturbed at their server's inattentiveness, but they were laughing just as hysterically.

"Quincy Fabusche!" Muhsin called over the melee as he approached the table.

The lively atmosphere quieted just a bit as Quincy frowned in the direction he'd heard his name. The wide, double-dimpled grin quickly returned when he spotted his nephew.

"Muhsin!" he bellowed, pushing his chair away from the table.

Duchess's eyes widened upon realizing Quincy's voice was deeper and even raspier than Muhsin's. Though the man was well into his fifties, he was incredibly handsome and very well built. Duchess felt as though she were looking into the future and seeing what Muhsin Vuyani would become in future years. The picture was very impressive indeed.

Uncle and nephew were locked in a hearty embrace. The waitresses had dispersed to check on their customers, but laughter was still in the air.

"I was getting lonely, boy! You took your time about showing up!" Quincy chastised playfully.

Muhsin's lopsided grin added a boyish element to his gorgeous looks. "Mmm-hmm. I saw how lonely you were over here by yourself."

"The ladies love me, Muhsin."

"Blaze, Uncle Q."

Quincy rolled his eyes. "Your mama named you Muhsin. And who is this?" He pushed his nephew aside. "Goodness," he whispered, his brown eyes focusing on the beauty standing nearby.

Muhsin smiled at the expression on his uncle's face. "Quincy Fabusche, this is Duchess Carver." He uttered a soft grunt when Quincy pushed him farther away and took Duchess's hands in his.

"You are lovely," Quincy told her, his warm gaze caressing her face with flattering intensity.

"You're very nice to say so, Mr. Fabusche," Duchess

replied, taking in the smattering of freckles across the man's nose.

"Nice? Hell, it's true. You'll sit next to me," he declared firmly, pulling her away from Muhsin's side. "Please call me Quincy."

The waitress arrived while they were all getting settled at the large round table. Quincy's roving eyes were already appraising the young woman's shapely legs beneath the short skirt of her uniform.

"What would you all like to drink?"

Muhsin and Duchess scanned their drink menu while Quincy shook his nearly empty glass in the air.

"I'll take a refill on this Scotch, honey."

"Very good, sir," the young woman replied as she scribbled the notation on her pad.

"Call me Quincy," the man urged, grinning broadly when the waitress smiled wider.

"And for you, ma'am?"

Duchess pressed her fingers against her chin and debated. "I'll just have a white wine."

"So, where have you been hiding all night?" Quincy asked the waitress.

"I just came on duty, sir."

"I'll have a cognac," Muhsin interjected over his uncle's flirting.

Quincy never lost a beat. "I'll have to make sure I stay a little longer so we can get to know each other," he said, his deep chuckle mingling with the blushing waitress's giggles.

Duchess brushed her fingers across the back of Muhsin's hand and leaned close to him. "Now I know where you get that red hair."

"The whole side of our family has it," Quincy said, having heard the whispered comment. "Muhsin's mother, Tarsha, had a head full of the stuff," he continued, leaning back to fold his hands across his wide chest. "Have you seen any pictures of my sister?"

Duchess shook her head, offering a tiny smile. "We haven't been seeing each other that long," she explained, glancing at Muhsin.

Quincy waved his hands in the air. "Doesn't matter. I have a feeling you'll be around for a long time," he said, the lilting Jamaican accent adding more certainty to his words. "I see a lot of my sister in you."

Duchess was intrigued. "How so?" she asked, her light eyes widening.

Quincy pondered the question for a moment. His long, reddish-brown brows drew closer. "It's something unspoken. I can't quite put my finger on it. There's a gracefulness. You know what I mean, boy?" he said to his nephew.

Muhsin was reclined in his seat and his eyes never left Duchess's face. "I see it," he assured Quincy.

Duchess didn't need to look at Muhsin to realize the intensity of his demeanor as he watched her.

Quincy, on the other hand, watched his sister's child closely. It was as though he was awed by what he saw.

"So tell me where you're from, love," Quincy asked Duchess, once the waitress had returned with their drinks and taken the dinner orders.

"I live in Philadelphia where I run my father's business."

Quincy's raised brows proved how impressed he was. "What type of business is it?"

Duchess took a sip of the delicious white wine and pondered her response. "Jerome Carver had his hand in some of everything."

"Jerome Carver?" Quincy repeated, surprise and something else appearing in his chocolate gaze.

Muhsin shot a quick glance toward his uncle, his expression revealing nothing.

"That name sounds familiar," Quincy said.

"Well, if you visit restaurants frequently, you've probably seen or held a product of his company," Duchess explained, always eager to discuss business. "We consult with restaurateurs, helping them produce everything from menus and napkin designs to banners and advertisements."

"Jerome Carver," Quincy repeated. This time realization dawned and he sent his nephew a pointed glare.

After a while, Duchess became aware of the thick silence surrounding her and decided to move the conversation elsewhere. "Tell me about your work, Quincy. Muhsin's told me you've lived all over the world."

"My business is hotels, dear," he replied, the suspicions set aside for the moment. "I have several here in the States and in Jamaica, but I have dabbled around with restaurants," he added with a soft chuckle.

"It's so strange that we've never crossed paths," Duchess said.

"Well, my mark in the field isn't that extensive. I've mostly worked on joint ventures with friends in the business."

Duchess recrossed her legs and rested her elbows on the table. "Anyone I might know?"

Quincy rubbed his jaw and concentrated. "Let's see, there's Mitchell Quells from—"

"Horizon Foods," Duchess supplied, already nodding. "They own a chain of sports bars in the northeast."

"Mmm-hmm. We're trying to get him to expand, but—"

"He's so stubborn. It took me and my design team an entire month to convince him how lucrative setting up a Web site would be."

Quincy burst into laughter. "Yes, my dear, that definitely sounds like Mitch!"

"So you say you've only dabbled in the restaurant business. Any plans for more involvement?" Duchess questioned, taking a sip of her drink as she awaited his response.

"Funny you should ask. I'm working on a venture now with hopes of constructing a new hotel in South Africa."

"South Africa?" Duchess breathed, enthralled by the man's business acumen.

"Mmm-hmm, and you know, I wouldn't mind having your input on the project if you're available. It'd be an added coup having a restaurant consultant on the team."

"Oh, Quincy, I'm so flattered, but I don't have the time. Right now I'm tied up in restructuring my business. I'm afraid it'll be some time before I'm able to take on any new projects."

Quincy covered Duchess's small hand with his larger one. "My dear, that is certainly not a problem. No definites are pending at this time because we're still discussing financing for the whole thing. And nothing takes longer than convincing a bunch of old fools to part with a little cash!"

"Well, you certainly sound like a man who's not afraid of risks," Duchess commented once the laughter had settled.

"Sweetness, without a little risk, how do you know you're alive?"

Duchess nodded. "Amen. So tell me what it's been like living in so many places?" she asked, sounding like an inquisitive, eager student.

Of course, Quincy didn't mind speaking of his struggles or accomplishments. Amid the conversation, the soups arrived and they dined on a delicious egg-noodle creation. Quincy spoke of his travels abroad and also how difficult a time he'd had as a young black man trying to make it with no real assets to his name.

"You must love what you do." Duchess remarked, halfway through her soup.

Quincy pulled away the large navy-blue napkin that covered the front of his black, three-piece, pinstriped suit. "I love the freedom its afforded me, love. I have homes in places I could only dream about as a boy. I never would've expected to own a cabin in the Canadian mountains."

"The Canadian mountains?" Duchess said, a faraway look in her eyes. "I've always wanted a snowy cabin in the mountains. What's it like?"

Quincy chuckled, charmed by Duchess's excitement. "You should have Muhsin take you up there. After you two progress to that level, of course."

Muhsin and Duchess exchanged quick glances and cleared their throats simultaneously. "If you two will excuse me, I'm going to the ladies' room," Duchess said, deciding it was the perfect moment to make an exit. Her heart leaped to her throat when she caught Muhsin's unwavering stare. She managed a soft smile before heading out of the dining room.

"What?" Muhsin asked, not long after Duchess left. He could feel his uncle watching him without even looking at the man.

"Jerome Carver's daughter," Quincy simply stated as he signaled for another drink. "What are you up to, boy?"

Muhsin shrugged. "We were doing business together and we hit it off."

"Bull," Quincy retorted, toying with the thick mustache above his lips. "Carver hated your father. He never would've allowed it."

"The man is dead. So is my father," Muhsin cooly reminded his uncle, a smug smirk coming to his mouth. "Duchess is dealing with me."

"And let's talk about that. In business, Jerome Carver was no more fond of you than he was of Trent. Now I know those feelings had to carry over as far as his baby girl is concerned."

Muhsin massaged his eyes. "Let's not talk about it, all right, Q?"

"Does she know about it?"

"No."

"Muhsin—"

"Uncle, please."

Quincy ran one massive hand across his curly red Afro. "I knew Trent's conniving genes would show in you one day," he muttered with a slow shake of his head. "Let me tell you something, boy," he pointed his huge pinkie finger at Muhsin, "whatever you're trying to get started with that lovely lady will fizzle if you're not straight with her."

"Duchess knows where things stand between us," Muhsin declared.

"I hope she does, because she's too beautiful to lose, man."

Muhsin rubbed his temples. *I know that,* he silently agreed.

Quincy chastised Muhsin and Duchess as he eyed their heaping platters of broccoli, spinach and three-cheese fettuccine. "I never heard of such nonsense. You're both too young not to eat meat. It's good for you."

"We eat seafood sometimes," Duchess assured him, looking to Muhsin for confirmation.

Quincy waved them off. "You should come to my inn in Jamaica. You haven't had seafood until you've been there," he said. "Muhsin can tell you about the times we spent on the beach with a case of crabs between us."

Muhsin smiled as those memories flooded his mind. "We used to eat for hours. When it got dark we would build a fire and keep on eatin'."

"Gee-whiz, I almost forgot!" Quincy bellowed, bringing his palm down flat on the table. "I'll be having a masquerade ball there in a few months. You bring this girl down there, boy!" he demanded, missing the meaningful looks pass between Duchess and Muhsin.

Later, when they all enjoyed flavored coffee and cheesecake, Quincy was still remarking on their dining choices. "Well, it pleases me to see that your finicky tastes don't apply to sweets."

Duchess reached across the table and covered Quincy's hand with her own. "This was so nice. I hope we get to see each other again," she said.

Quincy kissed the back of her hand. "I'm sure we will, love."

Muhsin rubbed his hands together and pushed his chair away from the table. "I think it's time we say good night, Uncle."

"Are we going to be able to get together again before you leave town?" Duchess asked Quincy, not wanting to go until that was settled.

Quincy leaned close and cupped her face in his huge hands. "You are too sweet. I'll be leaving town in a week, so it's up to Mr. Vuyani, here."

Duchess looked up at Muhsin, her gaze expectant.

"We'll go out to dinner the night before Uncle Q leaves. I'll take us out on the boat," Muhsin said.

Duchess clapped her lovely face that was bright with excitement. The expression only made her appear more beautiful to the two men watching her. Muhsin moved behind her chair, brushing her shoulder to urge her to stand.

Duchess walked to Quincy and hugged him tightly. "I enjoyed this," she whispered, pressing a kiss to his cheek.

"I hope to see you again, my dear," Quincy whispered back.

Muhsin was next to say his good-byes. He stepped close and extended his hand. Instead, Quincy pulled him into a bear hug and kissed his cheek. Everyone shared a long laugh over the gesture, and then said their parting words.

"Will he be all right by himself?" Duchess asked Muhsin when he escorted her from the dining room. "He's been drinking quite a lot." A frown marred her cinnamon-brown face when Muhsin began to chuckle.

"Q hasn't driven a car since he graduated college," he informed her.

"Mmm . . . he takes full advantage of his success, doesn't he?" Duchess murmured as she tried to ease into a black cotton jacket.

"You need any help?" Muhsin asked, his gaze twinkling as he watched her struggle.

Duchess's expression turned a bit uneasy as she pulled her bottom lip between her teeth. "I got it," she declined softly and walked on ahead of him.

Muhsin rubbed his jaw and grimaced. He had an idea why she was on edge but did not confront her. He could only hope she would come to him.

The ride back to the town house was silent, with the exception of Duchess humming to the soft old-school groove vibrating through the speakers of the high-quality sound system.

"I didn't knew you could sing," Muhsin remarked as he weaved the sleek BMW SUV in and out of the light downtown traffic.

Duchess smiled. "I can hum," she corrected, leaning back against the leather headrest. "Mama used to hum away whenever she massaged my scalp." She closed her eyes and thought of the soothing feel of her mother's fingers in her hair.

Muhsin glanced over and noticed how affected she

was by the memory. "You okay?" he asked, patting her knee as she smiled and nodded.

The trip back to the condo soon reached its end. Muhsin parked his SUV, then walked around to help Duchess from the passenger side. She hesitated, staring down at his wide palm for a moment before accepting his help.

"I'll see you in the morning," he whispered when they stood before the door.

"Why don't you come in?" Duchess asked, staring at her fingers interlaced with his.

Muhsin toyed with the diamond thumb ring she wore. "I better not."

"Please," she insisted, already turning to unlock the front door.

"You okay, Duchess?" Muhsin asked as he followed her inside and closed the door.

Duchess tossed her jacket aside and gestured toward the sofa. "Sit down," she requested, pacing the living room as he made himself comfortable against the silver, suede sofa cushions.

"Happy?" he asked, his long brows rising in playful challenge.

"What are you up to?" Duchess replied, facing him squarely.

Muhsin leaned to one side and propped his elbow along the arm of the sofa. "You know what I'm up to."

"You know what I'm talking about," Duchess accused, her eyes narrowing dangerously.

"Maybe I don't."

"Muhsin, we kissed tonight."

He nodded, unable to hide the confident smirk teasing his mouth. "People kiss," he said.

Duchess folded her arms across her chest and focused

on her strappy heels. "We don't. Not unless there's an audience."

"Is that so important?"

"It's supposed to be."

"Why?" he taunted.

"Muhsin." Duchess groaned, bringing her hands to her forehead. "I can't handle it."

Still playing the innocent role, Muhsin watched her with concern. "What can't you handle?"

"Do I have to spell it out for you?" She sighed, turning her back on him.

Muhsin toyed with the soft, red curls atop his head and smiled. He delighted in studying her figure-eight frame, the line of her back, tiny waist, full round bottom and long legs. It was all he could do not to pull her into his arms again. Finally, he cleared his throat and leaned forward on the sofa. "Uh, Duchess, I think the answer to your question is yes."

After a moment, Duchess turned to glare at him. Her thick curls bounced against her back when she did so.

"You do need to spell it out for me," Muhsin said, answering her questioning glare.

"Kissing me without an audience wasn't part of the deal," she retorted without hesitation.

"You kissed me back, Duchess." The soothing tone of his rough voice made her name sound more like an endearment.

"I know that," Duchess admitted, closing her eyes as the kiss filled her memory. "This is what I mean about not being able to handle it."

"Do you really expect me to be around you and not touch you?" he asked, the question holding just a tinge of disbelief.

Duchess propped her hands on her hips. "That's what we agreed to."

"A piece of paper doesn't control human nature. You know that."

There was a lengthy silence, then she asked, "Are you going to stick to your part of the agreement?"

"Haven't you asked me that already?"

"I'm asking again. Will you answer me?"

Muhsin appeared irritated for the first time. "If you're asking whether I'll snatch back what I already turned over to you if you don't give in to me, the answer is no. I won't do that, but you can't ask me not to respond to you. I'm a man with a healthy appetite for the opposite sex."

Duchess didn't want to appear uneasy but she couldn't help it. She had the feeling she was getting in way over her head and powerless to stop it. "Maybe you should go," she told him, walking over to lean against the oak bar in the corner of the room.

"You're not afraid of me, are you?" he asked while pushing himself off the sofa.

Duchess's chin rose a bit. "I'm not afraid of anyone."

"Good. Then you won't mind having breakfast with me in my office tomorrow morning."

Duchess knew he was daring her to refuse. "So you're finally going into the office, hmm?"

"I'll be there for a while," he said, sliding one hand into his trouser pocket as he approached her. "After that we'll get out and do some stuff together."

"Together for show?"

"If that makes you feel better."

Duchess wanted to hide her smile, but Muhsin stood too close to miss it. He also noticed when it left her face and was replaced by a frown.

"What?" he asked, placing one hand on the bar, trapping her there.

"I'm supposed to have lunch with Isaiah tomorrow," she said, suddenly remembering the date.

"Isaiah?" Muhsin muttered, his expression stony.

Duchess instantly noticed the change in his mood. "Yeah, I'll need to give him a call," she replied slowly, her expression wary.

"Sneaky jackass," Muhsin growled.

Duchess had had every intention of canceling with Isaiah, but before she could say anything to that affect, Muhsin said "This thing won't work if you start traipsing around town with Isaiah Manfres."

"Muhsin, we're not traipsing. I've known him forever and he's just a friend."

"Friend, my ass. That fool knows what he's doing."

Duchess couldn't help but wince at Muhsin's mood. She had never seen him angry. He seemed to be a completely different person.

"I expect you to cancel this," he ordered.

"Hold it," Duchess snapped, irritated and quite surprised by how seriously Muhsin had taken Isaiah's platonic position in her life. "Now, I hope you're not *telling* me to cancel."

Muhsin's cocoa stare was steady and guarded. "Take it any way you like, but you can forget going out with him."

"Oh, this is good," Duchess muttered, pushing herself away from the bar. "We aren't even in a relationship and you're flippin' over my having lunch with a friend. Someone I knew before I ever met you!" Her eyes blazed with intense aggravation.

Muhsin followed her across the living room. He offered no verbal response to her tirade, but the anger on his handsome face was unmistakable.

"Who in hell do you think you are, standing up in here acting like you own me?" she demanded, hands propped on her waist as she struggled to control her rapid breathing.

By this time, Muhsin was standing before Duchess. He reached out, curving one hand about the soft flesh of her upper arm. "Until I get what I want out of this thing, I do own you."

Duchess tightened her lips, refusing to let him see her tremble. He let her go after a while and left the house as cooly as he had entered.

After tasting the delicious spiced tea, Duchess leaned back and smiled. Since Muhsin's departure, she'd been a bundle of nervous energy. The long bath she'd taken was supposed to calm her enough to allow sleep to take its toll, but it hadn't helped so she'd prepared tea and settled down in the living room with Billie Holiday to keep her company. The tea and music finally helped her relax, but then she thought back over what had ruined their evening.

She balled her fist beneath the long sleeve of the red satin robe as memories of the heated moments replayed themselves. Duchess's eyes slid over to the phone and she cursed herself for even thinking about calling Isaiah to cancel. Unfortunately, she couldn't risk doing anything to give Muhsin reason to renege on his deal. The papers were signed and he had given her his word that he wouldn't take back the building. Still, she was really beginning to believe the man could be as ruthless as everyone said.

"Damnit," Duchess whispered for the tenth time that night. She leaned across the back of the sofa and snatched the black cordless phone from its round cradle; she hoped to get the answering machine, but the line was answered on the second ring.

"Hello?"

"Hey, Isaiah," she responded after a moment's silence.

"Duchess!" Isaiah said, sounding quite pleased to hear from her. "You're the last person I expected to get a call from tonight."

"Yeah, I'm sorry to be calling so late."

This time, Isaiah hesitated. He could hear the strain in her soft voice. "What's up, Dutch?"

Duchess bit her lip, feeling ashamed and cowardly for allowing Muhsin to command her actions. "Isaiah, I'm gonna have to cancel our lunch for tomorrow," she finally managed to say.

"Mmm . . ." Isaiah replied, wondering if he'd ever be wrong about Muhsin Vuyani. "Is anything wrong?"

"I, um, I'd forgotten I already made plans."

"Mmm-hmm," Isaiah replied again.

"I'm sorry about this. I was really looking forward to it."

"Did Blaze have a problem with it?"

Duchess closed her eyes, thankful that Isaiah had put his finger on the trouble without her help. "How did you know?" she blurted out, and then cursed herself for the question.

Isaiah laughed. "I know my friend very well."

"What's that tone about?" Duchess asked, snuggling deeper into the sleek sofa.

"What tone?"

"The tone you always get when we discuss *your friend.*"

Isaiah sighed. "You're not lettin' up on this, are you?"

"You know better than that."

"Blaze and me have, um, butted heads before over the same woman."

Duchess appeared skeptical. "Butted heads so many times you've managed to remain friends?"

Isaiah massaged his neck. "It was only once before."

We'd probably be married by now if it weren't for him, he thought.

The solemn tone of Isaiah's voice told Duchess that whatever happened in the past still pained him to discuss. "Listen, Izzy, we'll talk later on and try a more spur-of-the-moment get-together."

Isaiah cast his morose thoughts aside and chuckled softly. "I'll look forward to it."

"Good night," Duchess whispered.

Isaiah's attempt at lightheartedness fled with the end of the call. He tapped the receiver to his thigh, his handsome dark face twisted into a sinister glare.

Duchess silently congratulated herself on arriving on time for breakfast at Muhsin's office. Her attempts to unwind had not produced the desired results. Now it seemed the need for sleep was commanding her mind and body. Despite that, she was still dazzling. The simple cotton turquoise dress hugged her slim body, emphasizing every curve while the scoop neckline accented her bosom.

"Please don't let me fall asleep in front of his friends," Duchess whispered, fluffing out her silky tresses that had been tightly curled so they bounced just past her shoulders and framed her face.

"Good morning, Ms. Carver," Rhonda Cartwright said, her round face brightened by a wide smile. "Go right in, Muhsin's expecting you."

Duchess returned Rhonda's smile and nodded. Then she headed down the corridor leading to the office. She tapped on the door while twisting the silver lever and stepped inside.

"There she is," Muhsin announced as he eased off the corner of his desk.

Duchess took a deep breath and smiled. Her lashes

fluttered constantly as she watched Muhsin approach her with open arms. He seemed totally changed from the night before as he pulled her against his chest and pressed a soft kiss to her temple. Duchess wouldn't allow herself to melt into the sweet gesture and stepped back after a moment.

Their gazes held for a while before Muhsin slipped his arm around her waist and turned to the other couple. He was about to make introductions when Duchess's eyes connected with the tiny dark woman across the room. The blackberry-complexioned woman emitted a soft scream as she, too, focused on Duchess. Seconds later, both were rushing across the office to envelope the other in a tight embrace.

A tall, handsome Asian man looked over at Muhsin. Both men exchanged shrugs.

"I guess I don't have to introduce your wife, huh, Tan?"

Duchess pulled away from Ophelia Dayton and fixed her old college roommate with stunned eyes. "I can't believe I'm standing looking at you," she said.

"You can't believe it?" Ophelia cried, her huge, dark eyes wider than usual. "Blaze told us we were meeting the new lady in his life, but I never would've expected to see you, girl."

Muhsin took that moment to interrupt the happy reunion. "Duchess, this is Tan Kioto. He and Ophelia are married," he said, grinning broadly as Tan stepped forward with his hand outstretched. "Tan, this is Duchess Carver."

"So nice to meet you," Duchess replied, shaking hands with her friend's handsome husband. "Married?" she teased Ophelia, who offered a smug smile in return.

"Not everyone's as slow as you," Ophelia admonished playfully when another round of hugs ensued.

"It's a pleasure to meet you, Duchess," Tan said as they all headed to the round table near the tall office windows. "I've met my in-laws, but living in Tokyo, I haven't had the chance to meet any of Oph's friends. I was beginning to think she hadn't any," he said, grinning when everyone laughed over the jibe.

"Well, what I want to know is how you guys met," Duchess said to Tan, who held her chair.

Ophelia provided the reply. "I got a job here at Vuyani a few years after college. The company sponsored something along the lines of an exchange program a couple of years after I'd been working here. Tan was one of the newest executives and was assigned to be my mentor."

Tan chuckled. "One thing led to another, we started to date and—"

"Your mentoring skills paid off," Muhsin interrupted, drawing another chorus of laughter from his guests.

"Paid off in the best way," Tan agreed, once the laughter died down. He reached across the table for his wife's hand.

Ophelia shook her head at the sensuality she saw in Tan's slanting onyx gaze. She returned her attention to their breakfast partners before his staring got the better of her.

"So we've told you our love story, Dutch. I wanna know how you and Blaze happened," Ophelia asked, her dark eyes darting back and forth between the couple.

Duchess's brows rose as she added cream to her cup of amaretto roast. "Well, we haven't been seeing each other that long," she said, sending her friend a cooly wicked look. "A, uh, business trip turned more . . . personal than I had expected and . . . let's just say I haven't gone back to Philly yet."

The group was still laughing when the office doors opened and two cafeteria workers wheeled in a large cart. The breakfast included everything from bagels and flavored cream cheese to hash browns and eggs topped with a sautéed onion, green pepper and herb mixture. Everyone filled their plates and ate heartily while enjoying the breathtaking view from the top floor.

"I can't believe you both work for Muhsin," Duchess said when they were halfway through the meal.

Ophelia nodded and tapped the corner of her mouth with the gray napkin from her lap. "Well, I'm more of a housewife now. Tan and I live in Tokyo, where he runs Vuyani's overseas offices."

Ophelia, with Tan's assistance, launched into an enthusiastic discussion about her husband's homeland. The delicious breakfast was made even more enjoyable and memorable by the delightful conversation. Duchess was ecstatic when she learned the couple would be in Chicago for several months. She couldn't wait to spend more time with them.

When breakfast reached its end and the couple was preparing to leave, Duchess hugged Tan and whispered, "It was so nice to meet you," before turning to Ophelia. They made plans to get together again soon.

Alone again, Duchess turned to Muhsin and threw her arms around his neck. He savored the hug, though he knew it was prompted by Duchess's happiness over seeing her friend.

"Did I do something right?" he asked, his very long lashes sweeping his cheeks as he inhaled the scent of her perfume.

Duchess arched farther into his hard frame, unconscious of the affect she was having on Muhsin's hormones. "You did something very right," she whispered, rubbing her fingers into his auburn hair.

"Duchess?" he said as his hands formed to the dip of her back and curve of her hips.

"Hmm?"

"About last night," he continued, "I'm sorry for the way I acted. You're right, I don't own you and I shouldn't have come off like I did."

Duchess looked up into his incredible brown eyes and saw the sincerity there. "It's over now," she said, reluctantly withdrawing her fingers from his luxurious hair.

Muhsin cleared his throat softly, his gaze faltering briefly. "Um, listen, I need to make a few calls and get some stuff cleared up. Then we can head out, all right?"

"Take your time," Duchess whispered, closing her eyes for a short moment before she smiled. "I'm gonna rest here on the couch while you handle your business." She turned toward the office living room area.

Muhsin watched her remove her pumps and relax on the sofa. Her eyes closed and, in seconds, she appeared to be sleeping. *Snap out of it, man,* he grudgingly ordered himself, realizing he had been staring at her for several seconds. The sooner he tied up business, the sooner they could leave.

His first call was to the Rogers Inn, a cozy spot located along the outskirts of the Chicago suburbs. Muhsin confirmed the reservations he'd made and talked briefly with the inn's owner. The second call was to Rhonda, right outside the office.

"Yes, Muhsin?"

"Rhonda, are the tickets for the Will Downing show here yet?"

Rhonda chuckled and pulled the envelope from her top drawer. "They're here, they arrived this morning."

Muhsin sighed, not wanting anything to upset his plans. "Thank you."

"You know, out of all the women I've seen you with, I can't ever remember you going to such lengths for one you just met," Rhonda said.

Muhsin scratched the line of his brow and smiled. "What does that tell you?"

Again, Rhonda laughed. "I'll just wait and see."

After the conversation with his assistant, Muhsin stood behind his desk and nodded to the cafeteria workers who were clearing the breakfast items.

"Thanks, fellas," he called and then headed back to the sofa to indulge in one of his favorite activities, watching Duchess sleep. His stare was unwavering as it swept the arch of her eyebrows and the long, thick lashes brushing her cheeks. With a quick shake of his head, he reached for the blanket draped over the back of the sofa and placed it across her prone form.

The phone buzzed then, intruding on the serene moment. Muhsin ignored the ring, taking a seat on the edge of the sofa. He watched Duchess closely before placing the softest kiss to her temple. Then he left her side.

Duchess and Muhsin spent the day together. They embarked upon more sightseeing and visited various Vuyani holdings throughout the greater Chicago area. That evening, the couple met with Quincy for dinner. "Thank you," Duchess whispered when she accepted the glass of white wine from Muhsin. "I was surprised to find out we were having dinner in your suite, Quincy. I thought you'd want to spend the entire night partying away."

Quincy took the brandy snifter from his nephew. "I never go out on my last night in a city," he said.

Duchess set her glass on the coffee table and leaned back. "Why is that?" she asked, folding her arms across the bodice of her empire-waisted fuchsia dress.

"I prefer to be well rested when I flirt with the flight attendants," he explained cooly.

Duchess giggled. "So many women. Has one ever caught your eye?"

"Yes," Quincy admitted, his warm gaze becoming serious. "But, I couldn't very well marry my own kindergarten teacher."

Laughter erupted and filled the dimly lit living room suite for several minutes.

"Well, I'm surprised you'd let a little thing like that stop you," Duchess teased.

Quincy feigned aggravation. "Oh, it wasn't that. It was her husband!" he bellowed, slapping his hand to one trouser-clad knee.

Everyone was still laughing when dinner arrived via room service.

"I'll take care of it," Muhsin announced and headed toward the front of the room.

Quincy moved from his armchair to sit next to Duchess on the sofa. "I have to tell you, love, I have never seen my nephew more attentive or captivated by any woman. This thing between the two of you must be pretty special."

Duchess blinked. She didn't know how to respond. "Um, is it that obvious?" she asked finally.

"It most certainly is," Quincy assured her, pressing his hand against her forearm. "I may not have a special woman in my life, but I'm old enough to know what love looks like when I see it."

Dinner soon arrived and the four-cheese lasagna and steamed asparagus dinner was scrumptious. The conversation was even better. Soon Quincy was yawning and preparing to retire for the evening.

"You can't possibly be tired!" Duchess taunted.

Quincy pulled her close. "I got a lot of attendants to flirt with, young lady," he jested. "Anyway, Muhsin, you two finish up your drinks. The door will lock behind you, so take your time. As for you, lovely, I hope to see you again. Don't let my nephew keep you away."

Duchess giggled. "I won't," she promised and kissed his cheek.

"Come here, boy," Quincy called and they shared a long hug.

"Does anything ever get that man down?" Duchess wondered once Quincy had adjourned to his bedroom.

"Don't let him fool you," Muhsin said as he set the used glasses on the dinner table. "There was someone very special in his life a long time ago."

"Really?" Duchess asked, smoothing her hands across her bare arms.

"She was an island girl," he explained, taking a seat on the arm of the sofa. "Uncle Q adored her. She was killed in a shark attack. There wasn't even enough of her body left to bury."

"Lord," Duchess breathed, her hand going to her throat.

"If you visit any of Q's hotels, you'll notice they're all right on the water." Muhsin shrugged. "I guess he thinks it brings him closer to her."

A troubled expression marred Duchess's oval face. "I hope I didn't bring up any bad memories."

Muhsin waved off her concerns. "He thinks about Umenja all the time. Believe me, he'll have sweet dreams. You ready?" He moved from the arm of the couch.

Duchess gathered her things, then walked over to Muhsin. "Thank you for sharing this, for including me in your family. I know it's all for show, but it's still very sweet." With those words, she stood on the tips of her open-toed heels and kissed his cheek.

Muhsin watched her walk to the front door. He touched the spot where her lips had brushed his skin and smiled.

* * *

Muhsin and Tan decided to treat the ladies to a week-end on the yacht. The *Red Storm* had been washed and stocked with all the trimmings. Duchess and Ophelia couldn't have been more excited. Not only were they sailing with two gorgeous men, they would also have the chance to catch up.

"Okay," Ophelia said as she looked into the freezer chest, "we've got everything from steaks and chicken to fish and crab legs."

"Steaks? I thought Mr. Vuyani didn't eat beef?" Duchess said.

Ophelia sent her friend a playful, haughty look. "Well, Mr. Kioto does."

Duchess hooked her thumbs between the belt loops on her dark blue denim jeans. "I think we can work with some fish," she said.

"Cool," Ophelia replied, digging out four salmon steaks.

Duchess watched Ophelia set out the fish and begin checking for seasonings. She hoisted herself on the edge of the galley island and traced the pattern swirling through the emerald marble countertop. "So, um, girl, what's it like? You and your husband working for *his* best friend?"

Ophelia chuckled. "It's surprisingly wonderful. Muhsin's a great boss. He's very fair and manages to remain firm and objective without losing the adoration of his employees. Hey, what's that look?" she asked, catching Duchess's raised brow.

She shrugged. "It's just that you're the first person to have a truly friendly word to say about the man."

Ophelia nodded, folding her arms across her snug yellow T-shirt as she leaned against the stove. "I know. Lots of people perceive Blaze as a very intimidating, unlikable person. Now, he's been known to have an overabundance of women, but that's the only negative—he's never been mean to me or any of his employees, that I know of. And in case you're wondering, I felt this way about him before I married one of his best friends!"

Duchess couldn't help but laugh. Her conversation with Ophelia moved on to other topics by the time the guys announced they were ready to set sail.

The red sun setting against the late-evening yellow-orange skies was more than beautiful. Tan and Ophelia cuddled at the bow while Muhsin and Duchess enjoyed the view from the wheel.

"Having fun?" Muhsin leaned down and whispered in her ear.

Duchess nodded as her head rested back against his chest. "Despite the fact that it's all fake, I'm having the best time," she replied.

Laughter rumbled in Muhsin's chest. "You think you could try to forget that this weekend?" he requested and pressed a kiss to the shell of her ear.

Snuggling deeper into his embrace, Duchess closed her eyes and nodded. "Right about now, I'm ready to forget everything."

"Guys, this has been lovely, but we've gotta head back to the galley if we want to eat tonight!" Ophelia called as she eased out of her husband's arms and waved to her cooking partner.

Muhsin and Tan followed the women below deck, where they opted to have a few beers in the living area.

"Oh, this smells so good!" Duchess said when she checked the salmon steaks on the indoor grill. When she turned, Ophelia was smiling. "What?"

Ophelia toyed with a curl from her high ponytail and

stepped closer. "There's something I've been wanting to say for a while."

Duchess shrugged and reached for a cracker to nibble on. "Spill it."

"It's about Muhsin. Girl, I have never seen that man behave this way around any woman. I mean, he's always charming and respectful, but I've never seen him so attentive. He's almost doting."

Duchess looked away. "Maybe it's just for show," she replied in a fake, airy tone.

"No," Ophelia corrected, "I can't believe that. What I see in that man's eyes when he looks at you can't be faked."

After dinner and dessert, the two couples headed off to bed. Since there were only two cabins, Muhsin and Duchess were forced to share. Inside the room, Duchess decided not to make a big deal of the sleeping arrangements. The bed was quite spacious and she was determined to keep to her side. She only hoped Muhsin would do the same.

By the time Muhsin exited the private bathroom, Duchess had changed into what she thought to be conservative sleepwear. Unfortunately, the snug T-shirt emblazoned with the word *Babydoll* across her bosom and the comfortable gray cotton sleep pants were murder on Muhsin's hormones. When she left to use the bathroom, he got beneath the covers and prayed sleep would visit before she ventured to bed.

However, the instant Duchess slipped between the crisp, navy-blue sheets, Muhsin was wide awake. He kept his back turned until he was certain she was asleep. He turned over then, resting on his elbow. He watched her sleep, his fingers aching to touch her flawless, silken skin. His brown eyes were trained on the slow, rhythmic rise and fall of her breasts. When his gaze traveled upward, he was staring directly into her hazel eyes.

"What's wrong?" she whispered, watching him with an uneasy stare.

Muhsin surveyed the distance between them in the bed. "Everything," he replied pointedly.

Duchess read the desire in his eyes and knew it was mirrored in her own. "I'll leave," she said, sitting up in bed.

"No," Muhsin said, his fingers brushing her arm, feeling her tremble. Their gazes connected and he leaned close to slide his mouth along her temple and the side of her face.

Duchess turned into the sweet caress. Her eyes were closed and she let touch be her guide. Her lips met Muhsin's briefly before moving to his cheek and jaw. Again, their mouths touched. This time, their tongues played a slow, sensuous game of hide-and-seek. Muhsin groaned and brought his hand to Duchess's neck. He held her still and deepened the kiss. Low, ragged groans rose between them. The kiss grew increasingly lusty until it was deep, hot and wet. Muhsin's tongue stroked every recess of her mouth. Soft, helpless moans sounded in his throat in response to the overwhelming satisfaction he experienced.

Duchess turned to slip her arms around his neck. She was an eager participant in the steamy kiss, arching her breasts high against his chest and rubbing them next to his unyielding pecs.

"Duchess . . ." Muhsin whispered, his hands rising to cup the sides of her breasts. Slowly, his thumbs brushed the nipples, which stiffened in response to his attention. He broke the kiss to slide his mouth across the full, firm globes. Without lifting the snug T-shirt, he simply rooted his lips to her rigid nipples, sucking them madly until that area of the shirt was wet. Now fierce determination raced through him. The need to see what he touched overruled all other thought.

Duchess gasped when Muhsin hauled her against him and effortlessly placed her beneath him on the bed. She wriggled out of the T-shirt when he eased it over her head. When her breasts were bared to his seductive brown gaze, she shivered from the intensity of his eyes upon her body. Muhsin caught a tendril of the long hair that lay against her chest. For a moment he studied the manner in which the lock curled around her breast. Then his head lowered, his mouth smoothing over the mound. Duchess threaded her fingers throughout his luxurious crop of hair. She sighed at the feel of its thickness and silky texture. She could hear Muhsin's soft, raspy voice chanting her name as his lips and tongue tasted her skin.

"Mmm . . ." she moaned when he encircled one nipple before suckling it. His hands were on her back, his fingers massaging her spine while lifting her closer to his mouth.

He ended the caress and an arrogant smirk came to his face when he heard her disappointed sigh. He found his way beneath her breast, tasting the silken area before trailing down the flat plane of her stomach to tongue her navel.

She cried his name, her fingers tightening in his hair.

He covered her body with his, bringing his lips back to her own. His hands curved around her thighs and spread them apart. Duchess's hands slid over his rock-hard chest, her fingers tracing the perfectly defined abdominal muscles that flexed beneath her touch. Muhsin settled between her legs, and though they both still wore their sleep pants, that did not diminish the effect of the friction when they rubbed against one another.

Duchess was in complete bliss, especially when Muhsin's hand slipped inside her pants. She broke the kiss and tugged her bottom lip between her teeth, her hips arching and rotating with a mind of their own in response to Muhsin's thrusting fingers.

His face rested in the crook of her neck. Muhsin closed his eyes and made a mental image of everything that was happening. He had dreamed of touching Duchess that way for far too long. His fingers played in the dark area of curls at the junction of her thighs. Then they stroked the silken petals guarding her feminity. He could feel the moisture there, but ignored it for the moment.

Duchess was so weakened by desire, she barely had strength in her hands. She felt his fingers entering her body and gasped at the astonishing skill with which he delivered the caress.

Muhsin teased her womanhood with shocking thoroughness. Finally, his middle finger began a devastating assault, thrusting with such sweet tortuous expertise, she wanted to scream. In the far recesses of her mind, a faint, yet persistent voice cried, *This has to end. This shouldn't be happening now. It shouldn't be happening at all!* Unconsciously, Duchess began to press against Muhsin's chest. She knew she would hate herself in the morning, but she had to tell him to stop.

Muhsin frowned and told himself the quick, insistent shoves against his chest were not acts of refusal. Finally, he had to acknowledge that they were just that. He forced the frown from his face and looked down at Duchess. What he saw in her eyes brought him back to earth. He ran one hand through his close-cut hair and caught his breath. Then he left the bed and walked out of the cabin.

Muhsin was up preparing breakfast early the next morning. Tan woke and the two of them had the meal finished by the time Ophelia and Duchess arrived in the galley.

"We should take this up on deck," Ophelia suggested.

"What's the weather like?" Tan asked.

Duchess pulled a loose string from her black tennis dress and headed to the stairway leading up to the deck. "I'll go check." She returned less than a minute later. "Forget eating outside. It's freezing out there."

"Freezing?" Muhsin said. He wiped his hand, then went to check out the weather himself. He returned, frowning. "Damn."

Ophelia rubbed her hands together. "Oh, well, I guess we better set the breakfast nook."

The foursome worked together easily. Duchess and Ophelia set the small, square booth table while Muhsin and Tan brought flapjacks, sliced fruit, squeezed juice and fresh ground coffee from the galley area.

"Guys, this looks great," Ophelia said, pouring blueberry syrup on her flapjacks.

"We know," Tan boasted shamelessly, shaking hands with his cooking partner.

For a while only the clink of silverware against the plates penetrated the otherwise silent atmosphere. Several times Duchess looked up to find Muhsin watching her. His expression revealed nothing, yet it unnerved her just the same. When he focused on his food, she allowed her gaze to linger on his hands and mouth. Vivid memories of the night before filled her head. She could almost feel the flame his touch ignited.

"Um, would y'all excuse me, please?" Duchess practically whispered as she gathered her mug of coffee.

Muhsin watched her leave. A few moments passed before he left behind her.

Duchess had taken solace on the deck. In spite of the chilly temperatures, she enjoyed the feel of the sea air against her face. The cry of the gulls overhead added a more enticing allure to the atmosphere.

"Duchess?"

She closed her eyes against the sound of Muhsin's voice. It held the same raspy quality as it had the night before. She grimaced at the recollection of the previous evening.

"Duchess—"

"I made a fool of myself," she blurted out.

Muhsin's heavy brows drew close. "How?" he whispered, complete confusion coloring his voice.

Duchess was shaking her head. "I practically threw myself at you," she said, averting her face when he sat next to her on a deck chair.

"Hmph, I think I could be accused of doing the same," he said softly.

"But it was me who insisted on keeping this strictly professional."

"Mmm." Muhsin said. "Strictly professional. Duchess, it would be impossible for me to have 'strictly professional' thoughts about you," he said, hoping to make her laugh.

It didn't work and Duchess appeared even more distressed.

Muhsin knew it would be pointless to make any further attempts to cheer her up. He stood. "Enjoy your coffee," he whispered and pressed a kiss to her temple.

Duchess remained on deck at least an hour. Tan and Ophelia must have sensed her mood, for they did not disturb her. The climate continued to grow cooler as the day progressed. Over a quiet dinner that evening, the group decided to cut short the trip and head back to port.

Gretchen placed a check mark next to the final item on the agenda for her meeting with Jaliel. "Guess that's it." She sighed, preparing to leave the chair facing his desk. Suddenly she snapped her fingers and uttered a soft curse. "Did Donnette talk with you about something going on with the shareholders?" she asked.

"Isn't human resources your department?"

Gretchen blinked at Jaliel's snappy rebuttal. "I only asked because Donnette mentioned it to me. With all that's going on, I forgot to run it past you and—"

Jaliel slammed down the page he'd been scanning and rolled his eyes. "The finance department would run a lot smoother if my subordinates would keep department business in the department."

"'Department' business?" Gretchen retorted. "Jaliel this sounds like *company* business if I'm not mistaken."

"Damnit. Gret, you know what I mean."

"Jaliel, what the hell is going on with you?" Gretchen hissed, standing from the chair she'd occupied.

Jaliel's face was the picture of agitation. "What's happening with the shareholders is a finance matter and we've got our eye on it."

"So I can take that to mean you've contacted the shareholders and you've urged their loyalty through this time?"

"I know my business, Gret."

"*Duchess's* business, love. She's out there in Chicago trying to save this place and we can't afford to have any oversights risking her losing it."

Jaliel, who hadn't reviewed one of the many reports Donnette had forwarded regarding the shareholder issue, tugged at the navy-blue tie that threatened to cut off his air supply. Slowly he rose from his chair and braced both hands on the surface of his cluttered desk. "For the last time, we have it under control. The finance department has just as much on its plate as everyone else."

Gretchen raised her hand. "I know that."

"Then get off my back!"

Jaliel's roar caused Gretchen to unconsciously step

back. She was about to agree that it was a stressful time for everyone when her eyes narrowed on his face.

"Jaliel? Your nose is bleeding."

The anger drained from Jaliel's face as his hand rose. He sniffed several times on his way to the washroom in the corner of his office. The door slammed shut behind him and the concern in Gretchen's gaze turned to suspicion.

A week had passed since the boat trip. In that time, Duchess had questioned her actions, or, rather, her lack of actions. Why did she stay? Why not return to Philadelphia? All of Muhsin's associates knew she had a business there. It wouldn't have appeared at all strange if she left for a while. Besides, she'd already breached the decision of "hands-off" with Muhsin. Better to put major distance between them now before anything more intimate occurred between them.

Unfortunately, knowing what she had to do was far more easy to handle than *doing* what she had to do. The simple truth: she wanted to be around him, close by where she could see him frequently. They had only spoken by phone during the past week and even those simple conversations were enough to make her want to scream in frustration. Still, she could sense that he'd wanted to give her time alone and she was grateful for his concern.

Duchess had hoped Muhsin would decide against attending that evening's Will Downing concert. That morning, he'd called to confirm the date, thus sealing her fate. Now they were in the parking lot outside the Rhythm and Grooves Club where the show would be held. Duchess watched him shut down the SUV's engine before he turned to face her.

"Duchess, about the boat—"

"Muhsin—"

"I'm sorry for getting carried away," he interjected.

Duchess shook her head and fiddled with the stylish butterfly collar of her red pantsuit. "You don't have to say anything. I'm not upset with you. You didn't force anything, I just . . . I just don't want to talk about it, okay?" she pleaded, unable to admit that just the mention of the encounter was making her cheeks burn.

Muhsin watched her closely and then decided to drop the subject. He reached into the inside pocket of his casual olive-green suit coat and checked for the tickets. His hand paused on the door handle, but he didn't look her way as he spoke. "Just so you know, I've been thinking of doing that since I met you. Daydreams have nothin' on reality."

Duchess closed her eyes when Muhsin left the SUV. She willed her heart to stop racing.

Chapter 7

The next several weeks had Duchess feeling as though she were caught up in a whirlwind. Muhsin was like a prince as he treated her to the best of Chicago culture. They enjoyed several jazz and theater shows, ate at all his favorite restaurants. They quickly became one of the most well-known couples in Chicago's black society.

Everything would have been perfect had Duchess not let her softer side cloud her view of the real scene. Muhsin's attentiveness, gentleness and sweet persona had truly won her over. She had undoubtedly fallen for him. Hard.

"Stop it, Dutch!" she whispered, clutching fistfuls of hair. They only had a while longer to play this game—she hoped. The scheme was taking far longer than she had expected and Muhsin hadn't even mentioned marriage. It was almost as though they were really seeing each other.

The chiming doorbell sounded throughout the house, jerking Duchess from her deep thoughts. She looked down at herself and grimaced at the flimsy cream nightie she wore.

"What the hell?" she grumbled, pushing herself away from the kitchen table to answer the insistent ring.

A delighted scream flew past Duchess's lips when she whipped the door open and found Gretchen standing in the hallway. "Girl," she breathed. "So a visit *was* on your mind when you called and asked for the address," she said, happy to see her best friend as she pulled her inside and hugged her tightly.

Unfortunately, Gretchen was far from happy. She pushed Duchess away and pinned her with a look of disdain. "What are you still doin' here? What the hell is going on?"

Duchess offered a tiny shrug and appeared to be confused. "I thought y'all wanted me to get away?"

"Don't play with me, Dutch," Gretchen ordered, her onyx stare ablaze as she brushed past her friend. "You know what I'm getting at. Does your staying here have anything to do with Muhsin Vuyani?"

"Muhsin Vuyani?" Duchess asked and turned away, lest Gretchen see how shaken she was. "After everything I've been through with the man, why would you think that?"

"Mmm-hmm," Gretchen replied, folding her arms across the front of her tailored tan cotton blazer. "Talk."

Duchess knew she had no choice and turned to head back into the kitchen. "How about some coffee, Gret?"

Gretchen followed her friend through the incredible town house. An awed look shone on her chocolate face as she scanned the exquisite artistry lining the earth-toned walls.

"I found all these delicious brews at one of the local markets," Duchess said as she retrieved another mug from the windowpane cabinets above the sink.

Gretchen's frown returned. "Girl, I don't care what we drink. I want an explanation," she demanded, slamming her palm to the table for emphasis.

Duchess remained calm as she prepared a mug of aromatic coffee for Gretchen and freshened her own cup. "We can take this in the den," she whispered, knowing her friend was becoming increasingly impatient.

Gretchen carried on as she stormed into the den behind her friend. "I hope you're not gonna try to shoot the breeze for twenty minutes before telling me what's up!"

Duchess placed her mug on the glass end table and got comfortable on the sofa. "My being in Chicago has everything to do with Muhsin Vuyani."

"How?" Gretchen asked, her thick curls bobbing into her face when she shook her head.

"He wants me to marry him."

"Huh?"

"Well, he hasn't asked me yet, but that's what it's leading to."

Gretchen waved her hand and sat on one of the plaid armchairs facing the sofa. "Dutch, do you think I could get this story from the beginning?"

Duchess reached for her mug and took a sip of the delicious chocolate-macadamia-nut roast. Then she gave Gretchen what she asked for. She told the girl exactly how the building was aquired and what Muhsin's offer entailed.

"You're crazy," Gretchen breathed, more than a little stunned.

Duchess grimaced, expecting the reaction. "Girl, do you remember the shape Daddy's business was in? Now I've been able to hire more people and expand the building."

Gretchen was not impressed. "This is foolish."

"That may be true," Duchess agreed with a nod, "but I have to think about what's best for Daddy's business."

"There has to be another way."

"I couldn't find it at the time."

"I can't believe you're really gonna do this," Gretchen said in a hushed tone. "So what's Mr. Vuyani getting out of this? I mean, surely he's capable of finding his own women."

"He's more than capable," Duchess assured her

friend, "but he's trying to aquire a huge stash his father allotted for him only when he marries."

"Mmm . . . cunning," Gretchen said. "Will you be partaking in the reward as well as the building?"

Duchess pushed a loose tendril back into the chignon she wore atop her head. "Well, he's already giving me the building plus a very pretty amount to handle construction, renovation, decorating—"

"And he's asking you to marry him," Gretchen coolly interjected. "*Marriage*, Dutch."

"The benefits, Gret."

"Forget the benefits. You don't love this man."

Something flickered in Duchess's eyes before her gaze faltered. "I know that." She sighed, pushing herself off the sofa.

Gretchen's dark eyes narrowed as she leaned back in the armchair. "Oh, Lord," she breathed, pressing all ten fingers to her forehead.

"What?" Duchess squeaked, knowing what her friend had discovered.

"Don't tell me you're in love with him."

"'Course I'm not."

"But you are falling for him?"

"'Falling for him?'" Duchess repeated with a sigh followed by a long groan. "Oh, Gret," she said, flopping back onto the sofa, "I told him no funny stuff. I told him this was strictly business, and look at me now."

Gretchen couldn't help but laugh. "Baby girl, that's hard for women to do with their feelings. Especially if the man is a god."

Duchess looked over at Gretchen and smiled. "The man *is* a god," she assured her, envisioning Muhsin in her mind.

"So what are you gonna do?"

"I know what I'm not gonna do," Duchess said, bracing herself on her elbows. "I'm not gonna sit here moaning all day. I'm gonna get out, maybe take a walk along the pier."

"Oh, goody. Sightseeing," Gretchen said, clasping her hands in a mockingly happy gesture.

Duchess moved off the sofa, throwing a pillow in Gretchen's face when she passed.

Muhsin and Roland Jasper occupied a table at the Now Eatery for lunch. They had just wrapped up their review of that afternoon's agenda when the waiter returned to ask if the meal was satisfactory.

"So, is it my imagination, man, or are you eating more lately?" Roland asked when their server walked away.

"Blame Duchess," Muhsin replied, soft laughter following his words. "Girl eats like a linebacker."

Roland's sleek, dark brows rose in disbelief. "Hard to tell, considering how fine she is, how tiny," he noted.

"Mmm," Muhsin agreed, closing his eyes as Duchess's image filled his mind.

Roland smiled. "You remember, this is all just for the money, right, man?" he asked, focused on the pasta before his eyes.

Muhsin grimaced, realizing then how he wished he'd informed Roland of his true intentions. "What are you saying?"

"It'd be hard for any man to let go of a beauty like that," Roland said with a shrug. "Whether it was preplanned or not."

"I won't have a problem letting her go," Muhsin said, his expression closed.

Roland's contagious laughter turned several heads. "I hope you don't expect me to believe that bullshit!"

Muhsin gritted his teeth. The muscle in his square jaw

danced wickedly as he struggled to contain his laughter. He failed miserably.

"Well, well, this is a surprise."

Roland and Muhsin looked up to see two lovely women standing by their table.

"We're here all the time. Where have y'all been?" Roland teased.

Brenda Sagan tugged on the cuff of the quarter-length maroon blazer she sported. "You know Sarita and I are busy with our business. We don't have time for three-hour lunches like you and Blaze."

"Don't even try it, Bren," Muhsin warned when everyone stopped laughing. "I just saw you up in here last week."

"Why didn't you come talk?" Brenda challenged, running her slender fingers through the shoulder-length microbraids she sported.

"I got a business to run!" Muhsin cried, mocking Brenda overenthusiastically.

"Well, since we're all having such a hard time getting together, why don't we all have dinner?" Sarita Hodges suggested, nudging her hip against Roland's shoulder.

"Sounds good to me," Roland whispered, his narrow green gaze sliding along the line of Sarita's exposed thigh.

"And depending on how good a time we have at dinner, we could also have breakfast together," Brenda told Muhsin, her fingers caressing her bright hair.

"How 'bout it, Blaze?" Roland asked, eager to take full advantage of the suggestive offer. "We could all go somewhere tomorrow night."

Muhsin briefly closed his eyes as one corner of his mouth tilted upward into a lazy smile. "Sounds like a very good offer, but I'm gonna have to decline."

Sarita and Brenda exchanged knowing glances as their smiles grew even wider.

"I heard you had a steady lady in your life," Brenda said, toying with Muhsin's earlobe. "Now I know for sure." Her disappointment was apparent in her low, husky voice. "Still," she whispered, bending to speak into his ear, "if you do grow bored with your friend, you know my number."

"I could never forget it," Muhsin whispered back, pressing a sweet kiss to Brenda's jaw.

The cozy group dispersed a few moments later. Brenda sauntered off while Roland left the table, discussing plans with his dinner date. Muhsin remained seated, tapping his fingers against the table as he recalled Roland's earlier words. The man was right, it would be impossible letting go of someone as lovely as Duchess Carver. Again, she was at the center of his thoughts. So much so, it took some time for him to realize he was being spoken to.

"What's up?" he said, a tight smile coming to his face when he looked up at Tia Garrison.

"Did I just witness you turn down a date with one of the wenches you messed with behind my back?"

"Damn, do you spend all your time scoping my every move?" Muhsin snapped, his stare ablaze.

Tia placed one hand on her hip and practically snarled down at him. "I don't have to scope to know how tight you are with your latest piece of ass."

"Don't call her that," Muhsin warned, the tone of his voice close to a growl.

Tia's professionally arched brows rose. She took a seat at the table, smiling when Muhsin grimaced in distaste as her flowing scarf settled against his hand. "Well, well, could that be why you're still hanging on to her?" Tia queried, her wide brown eyes glazed with wicked certainty. "She hasn't given you the panties?"

Muhsin did an admirable job of keeping his cool, despite visions of his hands tight around Tia's neck.

"So what is it about her that has you so taken?" Tia rambled on, oblivious to how enraged Muhsin was.

"Well, it's like this," he said, lacing his fingers together atop the green tablecloth, "she's a lady, first and foremost. I mean, I've known tons of females, but she's the first one who carries herself like a lady. As lovely as she is, knowing she could snag any man out there, she's not running around with her skirt up and her legs open." He watched Tia wince. "She's got her own money and ain't in my pockets twenty-four-seven, shopping and cackling with her friends about her man's bank account or cock size."

Tia wanted to mask the hurt Muhsin's words inflicted, but she knew her eyes were shining with tears. "Cold bastard," she breathed.

"Why?" Muhsin asked, his face a picture of faux bewilderment. "I'm only telling the truth."

Tia leaned forward, her hand drawn into a tight fist. "Truth? You've got no idea what truth is. The way you dogged me out before, during and after we split up. Please!"

Duchess had decided to treat Gretchen to lunch at the Now Eatery after their walk. They followed the host, both staring straight ahead as they caught the eyes of every man there—including Muhsin's, who focused on Duchess the moment he spotted her.

"So, when is the wedding?" Gretchen asked once they were seated.

Duchess placed her brown leather tote on an empty chair. "I can't be sure. He says he wants to surprise me."

Gretchen set her teal sweater and purse on the same

chair. "Girl, it sounds like that man is really tryin' to woo you."

"Please don't say that, Gret," Duchess begged, raising both hands. "This whole thing has done more of a number on me than I care to admit."

"Has he given you any reason, any physical reason to think he wants more?" Gretchen asked, fiddling with the scoop neckline of her T-shirt as she watched her friend closely.

"He kissed me," Duchess said, and refusing to say more about their encounters, her fingers settled across her lips.

Gretchen nodded. "How'd that make you feel?"

"Damnit, Gret, how do you think!" Duchess snapped, realizing how on edge she was. "I need a drink," she said just as the waiter approached.

"And what can I get you, Miss?" the tall, young man asked, smiling when both women looked up.

Duchess and Gretchen placed their drink orders and accepted menus from the waiter. For a while, conversation settled on the food possibilities.

"Damn."

"What?"

Duchess had just spotted Muhsin across the dining room. She cursed softly, her fingers curling more tightly around the menu.

"What's the problem, Duchess?" Gretchen tried again, only to have Duchess shake her head.

"It's nothing," she replied, relieved when her friend shrugged and turned her attention back to the menu. Duchess pretended to ponder her lunch order as well, but couldn't stop her exquisite stare from straying across the dining room. She saw Muhsin seated with the woman from the boutique, the same one they'd seen in the restaurant that first night out. Whatever they were discussing appeared to be intense. Duchess shook her head and told herself she had no reason to be interested. Unfortunately, she couldn't stop the twinge of disapproval she felt at seeing them together.

Gretchen had been calling Duchess with no luck at gaining her attention. Finally she turned and followed her friend's gaze.

"What are you looking at?" Duchess snapped, noticing the action.

"What are *you* looking at?" Gretchen retorted, a frown marring her dark face.

"Let's just order." Duchess sighed, hiding her face behind the menu.

Back at Muhsin's table, Tia was watching Muhsin as though she could have killed him. "Well? Are you going to answer my question?" she spat.

"What question?" Muhsin remarked absently.

Tia pounded her fist on the table. "Damnit, Blaze, do you love her or something?" she hissed, hating herself for sounding so frantic.

The question regained Muhsin's attention. Roland returned to the table then and Muhsin stood. "Why don't you ask Roland?" he suggested, patting the man's back. "You both seem interested in the same thing today." On that note, he left the table.

No longer watching Muhsin, Duchess looked at Gretchen. "So, how's Jaliel?" she asked, smiling when Gretchen gave her another aggravated glare.

"That boy is gonna drive me crazy, D," she said. "There's no way we can cohead that company. Jaliel is way too domineering."

"I think you've just met your match," Duchess teased, tugging on the flaring sleeves of the brown, cotton V-neck sweater she wore.

Gretchen was not so amused. "I'm not exaggerating."

Something in Gretchen's tone concerned Duchess. Before she could inquire, she heard a familiar rough voice calling her name. Though she was on edge seeing him talking with Tia, she still melted when he spoke.

"Hey, Muhsin," she whispered, offering a sweet smile when she looked up into his soft brown eyes.

He leaned down to place a kiss against her cheek. "Hello," he replied against her ear, smiling when he felt her shiver.

Duchess spotted the knowing look in Gretchen's dark eyes and cleared her throat. "Uh, Muhsin, this is Gretchen Caron, my best friend and business associate. Gret, Muhsin Vuyani."

Muhsin extended one of his huge hands and nodded. "Gretchen, it's a pleasure," he replied, offering her his gorgeous dimpled smile.

"Yes," Gretchen breathed, her eyes wide as she studied his flaming, silky hair, deep-set eyes and handsome features. "Nice to meet you."

"I hope you'll be in town a while," Muhsin said as he resumed his stance next to Duchess, placing one hand along the back of her chair. "Your friend here can tell you there's plenty to see and do here."

"Well, yes, I had planned to stay a while," Gretchen replied, her smile growing brighter by the moment.

Muhsin caressed Duchess's back as he spoke. "Glad to hear it. Maybe we can all go out for dinner soon."

"Well, why don't you join us now?" Gretchen suggested, already charmed by the man.

"I appreciate it, but I'm having lunch with my business lawyer," Muhsin informed her and risked glancing down at Duchess. He knew she'd seen him at the table with Tia, but he would have to wait for his chance to explain. "I better let you ladies get back to your lunch. Gretchen,

I'd like it if you had dinner with me and Duchess tonight at my home."

"Oh, that sounds wonderful!" Gretchen accepted eagerly.

Duchess uttered a low sigh. She had already contemplated telling Muhsin she couldn't make it that evening.

"I'll be sure to tell my staff there will be four for dinner."

"Four?" Duchess asked.

"Roland," Muhsin said. "I'll see you tonight, Gretchen. Duchess," he added, leaving her with a lingering stare before walking away.

Meanwhile, Tia had begun grilling Roland at the other table. She was determined to extract more information about Muhsin's new love interest before leaving.

"I only want to know what's going on. I mean, this woman came out of nowhere," Tia said, still trying to reason with Muhsin's sudden interest in monogamy.

Roland scratched the line of his brow and shook his shaved his head. "Damn, Tia, what is it with you?" he said, watching the woman in disbelief. "Ain't you tired of worryin' about Blaze after the way he treated you? That's why he let you go, 'cause you were too nosey."

Tia flinched as though she'd been slapped. "I've got my reasons for asking."

"What reasons?"

"You leave that to me."

Muhsin returned to the table just then. His cool expression darkened when he realized Tia was still there. "Don't you have somebody else to get gossip out of?" he snapped.

Tia stood so quickly her chair wobbled a bit. "Don't have a fit, Blaze. I'm leaving," she grumbled, leaving the two men watching her.

"What the hell is she up to?" Roland queried.

Muhsin reclaimed his seat. "Something she'll be sorry for."

"Who's that with Duchess?" Roland asked as he picked up his glass.

The knowing smile on Muhsin's lips triggered the dimple. When it came to beautiful women, Roland was almost as scandalous as he was.

"Gretchen Caron. Her best friend and business partner. I'm surprised you don't remember her from the funeral."

"Right, right," Roland whispered, stroking the light goatee shadowing his chin.

"Well, any more questions about her will have to wait until tonight when she comes to dinner with Duchess," Muhsin said before his friend could probe him further.

Roland leaned back in his chair and smiled.

On the other side of the dining room, Gretchen and Duchess were preparing to leave.

"Girl, I need to stop by the ladies' room," Gretchen said after the lunch tab was paid.

Duchess was already heading toward the lobby. "All right, I'll just wait out here," she called, finding a secluded corner near the pay phones. She was searching her purse for a compact when a hand curled around her elbow. Before she could say anything, Muhsin pulled her farther into the private corner.

"I know you want to ask me about Tia being at my table," he said, trapping her against the wall as he watched her.

Duchess's brows rose a notch as she shrugged. "Actually, no—I mean, it's not any of my business."

"Mmm-hmm," Muhsin replied, not believing a word of her statement. "She was over there trying to find out what was up with us and upset because I wouldn't tell her what she wanted to know."

"Why does she have all these questions?" Duchess asked, propping one hand on her hip. "Is she still pining for you or something?"

Muhsin tapped his hand against the waistband of the form-fitting cream pants Duchess wore. He debated the question, gnawing the inside of his jaw before replying. "I really don't know if she's pining for me. Would you be?"

Duchess let her stare narrow seductively as she rested her head against the wall. "Fishing for compliments, Mr. Vuyani?"

"Never."

"Mmm-hmm. Well, to answer your question, I'd only be pining for you if I were in love with you," she replied coolly. She was about to move away when Muhsin's hand tightened at her waist.

He pulled her into a deep kiss, growling low when he heard a gasp escape her lips. Slowly his tongue caressed the even ridge of her teeth before delving deeper into the sweet recesses of her mouth. He moved closer, drawing her slender form more snuggly against his body. Duchess's response was instant. Eagerly she arched herself into his hard frame. Her fingers kneaded the broad shoulders beneath the expensive fabric of his suit coat before sliding into his silky hair. She returned the lusty kiss with equal passion, emitting soft moans as her tongue stroked over, under and around his.

They were still locked in the devastating embrace when Gretchen walked out of the ladies' room.

"Not in love with him?" she whispered, smiling at the scene she witnessed. "Yeah, right."

"Both of you just up and go! I wasn't surprised when you left, but with Gretchen gone, too, it's just too much," Jaliel complained into the receiver.

Duchess rolled her eyes toward the ceiling. She cursed herself for even thinking of calling to check on her business affairs in Philadelphia. She sighed. "Can't you handle it?"

"You know I can handle it."

"That's what I heard, so why are you giving us the third degree when you're obviously basking in power?"

"When are you coming back?" Jaliel asked, curtly dismissing the question.

Duchess shrugged, toying with her loose hair as she relaxed on the sofa. "If everything's fine back there, we'll probably stay away a few more weeks."

"Hmph. Must be nice," Jaliel muttered.

"Look, Jaliel, we're here and you're there," Duchess snapped, losing her patience with the man. "Now when Gret and I get back, you can take time off for as long as you like, go wherever you want."

"Thanks for permission, Dutch." Jaliel sighed, unimpressed by the offer. "I guess I'll just see you whenever," he added before breaking the connection.

Duchess stared at the receiver after the click sounded firmly in her ear. After a moment, she shook her head and set the phone back on its cradle.

"Told you," Gretchen replied with a shrug when Duchess looked at her.

"What's gotten into him?"

"Your guess is as good as mine, hon."

"You think he really could be upset because we left him there to handle everything?" Duchess asked, curling her legs beneath her on the sofa.

Gretchen shook her head. "I doubt that's it. I mean, he almost seemed happy when I told him I was coming out here. It was like he was pretending to be upset because I was expecting it."

"I may need to take a trip home," Duchess said, massaging her tired eyes.

"Mmm," Gretchen agreed. "We should surprise him."

"I'll have to talk to Muhsin about it."

Gretchen chuckled, gathering the bags from their shopping trip earlier that day. "Yeah, you should definitely check with your man before you go anywhere."

Duchess shot her friend a murderous glare. "Muhsin Vuyani is not my man."

"That's not what it looked like today at the restaurant," Gretchen sang on her way out of the living room. "The kiss I saw didn't look like it was for the crowd."

"Whatever." Duchess groaned, pushing herself off the sofa. "On that note, I'm going to take a nap before dinner."

"Oh, I can't wait!" Gretchen shrieked as they made their way upstairs. "I can imagine what the man's house must look like."

"Yeah, it is a vision," Duchess admitted, having been there a few times already. "I don't plan on becoming too content there, though. Nothing's permanent, you know?" She left Gretchen with a lazy wave before disappearing into her bedroom.

Gretchen found herself unable to sleep or relax, she was so excited about the evening. Luckily the hours until dinner passed quickly. She was putting the final touches to her coiffure when the doorbell rang.

"I got it, Dutch!" she called, racing down the plush, carpeted stairway. The ankle-length linen coat that matched her silver-gray pantsuit flowed behind her.

Muhsin's heavenly smile appeared when the door opened. "Hello, Gretchen."

"Muhsin please come in," Gretchen said softly, stepping

aside to wave him into the town house. "Can I get you anything?" she asked, following him into the living room.

"No, thanks. Where's Duchess?" he asked, sliding one hand into the pocket of the maroon trousers he wore.

"Still getting dressed, and I'm not quite ready myself, so I better move it!" she called, already jogging from the room.

Muhsin managed to entertain himself for a while, but curiosity get the better of him. He headed upstairs to the master bedroom he knew Duchess occupied. The oak door was open just a crack and he could hear her soft humming. Gently, he pushed the door open with the tip of his finger. Leaning against the doorjamb, he watched her contentedly. She wore olive-green silk tap pants with a matching bra and pumps of the same color.

Duchess was pulling her outfit from the closet when she turned and glanced toward the doorway. "Muhsin," she whispered, clutching the ankle-length, fitted, spaghetti-strapped gown to her chest. "Is anything wrong?" she asked as he stood there watching her.

Several moments seemed to pass before he shook his head. "No, everything's fine."

Clearing her throat, Duchess focused her attention on the outfit she held. "I didn't think you were coming to pick us up yourself. I think Gretchen expected you to send a hot-air balloon or something," she teased.

Muhsin smiled, but did not reply.

"Is this okay?" Duchess asked, hoping to prompt conversation when she shook the olive-green dress on the hanger.

Muhsin nodded. "Mmm-hmm," he assured her, pushing the door closed and locking it before walking farther into the room.

Duchess had already turned to place her outfit on the bed. When she looked up, Muhsin was right next to her.

The deep-set brown eyes held her entranced as he pulled the dress from her fingers and set it aside.

"No, Muhsin," she whispered, reading the intentions in his gaze.

He shook his head slowly. "Yes," he said, curling one hand about her tiny waist.

Duchess realized she hadn't the will to refuse further. Her body instantly arched into Muhsin's chiseled frame as she raised her lips to meet his. The kiss was as passionate as it had been earlier that day. Tiny moans escaped her mouth, she was so enthralled by the pleasure consuming her body. For the first time, it didn't matter that they were alone. They were thoroughly involved with one another, that was what mattered.

Muhsin ended the kiss by tugging Duchess's lower lip between his perfect teeth and soothing the surface with his tongue. He held her close for several moments, the wide plane of his palm stroking her back methodically.

"Will I be sorry I did that later?" he asked, pulling away to stare into her face.

Duchess smiled and shook her head. "You won't be sorry," she assured him, her fingers curled around the lapels of his jacket to stop their shaking.

Muhsin returned her smile and nodded. "Hurry up," he whispered, giving her waist a soft proprietary pat before he turned and left the room.

Alone, Duchess propped both hands on her hips and stared down at the floor. "Oh, Dutch, what are you doing, girl?"

"Goodness," Gretchen breathed, her wide black eyes stretching to their greatest extent. Slowly she stepped from the back of the BMW SUV and gazed upon Muhsin's mammoth-sized estate.

The mansion sat several acres off the main road. It was shielded by tall trees that sheltered a curving dirt road leading to the house. The white, brick, three-story home sat on a vibrant green lawn. Spotlights were situated in an oval pattern surrounding the house, illuminating its lovely elegance. From the top of the level roof, several fireplace vents were seen and each window was filled with a flickering white candle.

"Muhsin, this is incredible. Did you grow up here?" Gretchen asked, accepting the arm he offered.

"Thanks, and, yes, I did grow up here," he replied, his gaze soft as he too enjoyed the sight of his home. "It's changed a lot, though, since I was little, and I hardly come here to stay except when I'm throwing a party or planning something special."

The grand tour began the moment Muhsin escorted Duchess and Gretchen past the oak windowpane-lined doors. Though quite extravagant in its furnishings, the house held on to a warm, inviting aura. Each room was thickly carpeted and decorated with paintings and photographs.

"Hello, Mr. Vuyani."

"Serena," Muhsin replied, smiling at the pretty housemaid who nodded before she disappeared down the corridor.

"A maid," Gretchen noted.

Muhsin raised both hands defensively. "Serena's only here for tonight," he explained.

Duchess had remained silent, observing Muhsin and all the trouble he'd gone to that evening. When Gretchen walked ahead of them to the living room, Duchess moved closer to Muhsin's side.

"So did you plan all this before or after you found out Gretchen was coming?"

Muhsin shrugged, his dimple appearing though he

tried to hide the telling smile. "Does it matter, Duchess?" he whispered, easing his arm around her waist.

Duchess cleared her throat, unable to answer. Her heart thudded wildly at the sound of Muhsin's soft chuckle.

Inside the living room, Roland had already approached Gretchen. Muhsin shook his head over his friend's weakness for the opposite sex.

"Dinner should be ready in twenty minutes," Muhsin announced once everyone held a drink.

"Sounds good," Roland said while rubbing his palms together. "How about a tour, Gretchen?" he asked and offered her his arm.

Gretchen eagerly accepted. "Thanks. I knew it'd take more than one look to see all of this place."

Duchess had visited Muhsin's home on several occasions. She strolled out to the living room balcony as she often did and took in the fresh air. Muhsin watched her for a moment before setting his glass aside and following. He stepped behind her, sliding his strong arms about her waist as he pulled her back.

"Marry me," he whispered, brushing his lips against her temple.

"That's the plan," Duchess said, under the impression that he was teasing.

Muhsin chuckled briefly before cupping her hips and whirling her around to face him. His mouth fell upon hers in a wave of intense need. His tongue invaded her mouth, drawing stunned gasps from her lips. Of course, Duchess was an eager participant in the impromptu kiss. She moaned shamelessly, delving her fingers into Muhsin's bright hair as he stroked the bare skin beneath the straps of her dress.

"Marry me?" he asked this time, slipping a dazzling marquis-cut diamond ring onto her finger.

Duchess's bosom heaved rapidly against Muhsin's

chest as she stared at the incredible piece of jewelry. For an engagement and marriage that were supposed to be phony, the man was pulling out all the stops.

"Should we be doing this without an audience?" she asked, her uneasy expression matching her shaking voice perfectly.

Muhsin stroked the lush curve of her bottom lip with the tip of his thumb. "We'll have a party later," he told her.

The response did nothing to soothe Duchess's curiosity. Muhsin noticed her unease, but overlooked it. Instead, he lowered his gaze and pressed his forehead against hers.

"Do I get an answer?" he whispered.

Duchess's smile triggered the sparkle in her hazel eyes. "Why do you need an answer when you already know I will?"

"I want to hear you say it."

Closing her eyes briefly, Duchess prayed Muhsin couldn't feel her heart racing. "I'll marry you," she said, gasping when he pressed a quick kiss to the corner of her mouth and enveloped her in a tight hug.

Duchess pressed her nose against Muhsin's shoulder and inhaled the crisp scent of Nautica cologne clinging to the fabric of his maroon jacket. She did an admirable job of not quivering in his arms like a mass of jelly. Her lashes fluttered rapidly as she was caught between twin emotions of happiness and confusion.

Chapter 8

"It's all right, Roland. You and Muhsin can talk around Gretchen. She knows everything."

"So what have you got planned for the wedding, Muhsin?" Gretchen asked.

"I want to surprise your friend so I better not speak about it," Muhsin replied smugly, his gaze focused on his huge salad.

Gretchen's long, arched brows rose a notch. "Sounds like you're wooing her for real," she said, missing the look exchanged between Duchess and Muhsin.

"So, Gretchen, who's watching the business while you're playing hooky with the boss?" Roland asked.

Gretchen cleared her throat. "Well, we have another partner, Jaliel Norris. He's back in Philly taking care of things," she explained, adding more peppercorn dressing to her salad.

"You guys been working together long?" Roland asked, tugging on the cuff of the dark blue cotton sweater he wore.

"I went to school with Gretchen and Jaliel. My dad offered them jobs afterward," Duchess explained, a little smile playing around her full mouth as she remembered. "We've had our ups and downs, but we've always been close despite working together."

Conversation continued over the tasty meal. Though

Roland and Gretchen weren't vegetarians, they de-voured the delicious vegetable quiche and seafood salad. When Muhsin suggested they all have champagne and dessert in the living room, no one thought they had room for anything else.

Duchess was surprised by how much she'd enjoyed herself that evening. She'd even managed to set her sus-picions aside regarding Muhsin's motives. Meanwhile, Roland and Gretchen hit it off so well, they decided to take a drive together after dinner.

"Roland said he'd bring Gretchen home," Muhsin an-nounced when he found Duchess in the den fiddling with the piano.

She looked up at him, her eyes wide as small moons. "They already left?" she asked, mentally kicking herself for not cautioning her friend on riding with a man she barely knew.

Muhsin appeared to be reading her thoughts. "He can be trusted, I promise."

Duchess nodded. "Mmm," she replied, adding a brief smile.

"Come sit next to me," he requested, gesturing to the gold love seat. His gorgeous gaze narrowed as he watched her leave the piano bench and walk across the room. The enchanting olive-green gown hugged her slender frame adoringly.

"What's got you upset?" he asked, as though speaking to a child.

Bursting to relay her concerns, Duchess managed to su-press them. Besides, she was so tired of sounding like a broken record on the subject. On top of that, the several glasses of champagne she had indulged in were weighing heavily on her eyelids. She massaged her forehead, then leaned back against the sofa and closed her eyes.

Muhsin curled his arm around Duchess's shoulders

An Important Message From The ARABESQUE Publisher

Dear Arabesque Reader,

I invite you to join the club! The Arabesque book club delivers four novels each month right to your front door! It's easy, and you will never miss a romance by one of our award-winning authors!

With upcoming novels featuring strong, sexy women, and African-American heroes that are charming, loving and true… you won't want to miss a single release. Our authors fill each page with exceptional dialogue, exciting plot twists, and enough sizzling romance to keep you riveted until the satisfying end! To receive novels by bestselling authors such as Gwynne Forster, Janice Sims, Angela Winters and others, I encourage you to join now!

Read about the men we love… in the pages of Arabesque!

Linda Gill
PUBLISHER, ARABESQUE ROMANCE NOVELS

*P.S. Watch out for the next Summer Series **"Ports Of Call"** that will take you to the exotic locales of Venice, Fiji, the Caribbean and Ghana! You won't need a passport to travel, just collect all four novels to enjoy romance around the world! For more details, visit us at www.BET.com.*

SPECIAL OFFER! 4 BOOKS FREE!

www.BET.com

A SPECIAL "THANK YOU"
FROM ARABESQUE JUST FOR YOU!

Send this card back and you'll receive 4 FREE Arabesque Novels—a $25.96 value—absolutely FREE!

The introductory 4 Arabesque Romance books are yours FREE (plus $1.99 shipping & handling). If you wish to continue to receive 4 books every month, do nothing. Each month, we will send you 4 New Arabesque Romance Novels for your free examination. If you wish to keep them, pay just $18* (plus, $1.99 shipping & handling). If you decide not to continue, you owe nothing!

- Send no money now.
- Never an obligation.
- Books delivered to your door!

We hope that after receiving your FREE books you'll want to remain an Arabesque subscriber, but the choice is yours! So why not take advantage of this Arabesque offer, with no risk of any kind. You'll be glad you did!

In fact, we're so sure you will love your Arabesque novels, that we will send you an Arabesque Tote Bag FREE with your first paid shipment.

* PRICES SUBJECT TO CHANGE.

YOU'LL GET 4 SELECT ROMANCES PLUS THIS FABULOUS TOTE BAG!

ARABESQUE

Visit us at:
www.BET.com

THE "THANK YOU" GIFT INCLUDES:

- 4 books absolutely FREE (plus $1.99 for shipping and handling).
- A FREE newsletter, *Arabesque Romance News*, filled with author interviews, book previews, special offers, and more!
- No risks or obligations. You're free to cancel whenever you wish with no questions asked.

FREE TOTE BAG CERTIFICATE

Yes! Please send me 4 FREE Arabesque novels (plus $1.99 for shipping & handling). I understand I am under no obligation to purchase any books, as explained on the back of this card. Send my free tote bag after my first regular paid shipment.

NAME _____

ADDRESS _____ APT. _____

CITY _____ STATE _____ ZIP _____

TELEPHONE ( ) _____

E-MAIL _____

SIGNATURE _____

Offer limited to one per household and not valid to current subscribers. All orders subject to approval. Terms, offer, & price subject to change. Tote bags available while supplies last.

Thank You!

AN045A

ARABESQUE

Accepting the four introductory books for FREE (plus $1.99 to offset the cost of shipping & handling) places you under no obligation to buy anything. You may keep the books and return the shipping statement marked "cancelled". If you do not cancel, about a month later we will send 4 additional Arabesque novels, and you will be billed the preferred subscriber's price of just $4.50 per title. That's $18.00* for all 4 books for a savings of almost 30% off the cover price (Plus $1.99 for shipping and handling). You may cancel at any time, but if you choose to continue, every month we'll send you 4 more books, which you may either purchase at the preferred discount price. . . or return to us and cancel your subscription.

* PRICES SUBJECT TO CHANGE

THE ARABESQUE ROMANCE BOOK CLUB
P.O. BOX 5214
CLIFTON NJ 07015-5214

THE ARABESQUE ROMANCE CLUB: HERE'S HOW IT WORKS

PLACE
STAMP
HERE

Duchess smiled but didn't look up. "I should be waiting up—you should've come back with Muhsin and me. You don't know Roland Jasper well enough to be riding off in the night with him."

"Yes, Mommy," Gretchen teased, raising her hands defensively.

"I'm serious, Gret."

"Aw, come on, Dutch, he's a nice man. You can't deny that," Gretchen argued, strolling to the stove to prepare a cup of the fragrant tea for herself.

"Yeah, he is." Duchess sighed, staring absently into the burgundy liquid.

"So if you weren't waiting up for me, what were you doin'? Couldn't sleep?" she taunted, sliding her friend a saucy stare. "I'd understand," she added, turning back to the stove. "With a fine thing like Muhsin givin' you a rock like that tonight, I probably couldn't sleep either."

Duchess finally looked up at her friend. "Yeah, that did blow me away. But something else got me up."

Gretchen kicked off her shoes and took a seat at the table. "Spill it," she ordered.

"Donnette called me an hour ago."

"Why?" Gretchen mumbled, focusing on sweetening her tea.

"It looks as though all thirty percent in shares have changed hands. Donnette's been working so hard on this, but I've yet to talk with Jaliel."

"Does Donnette feel there's something to be really worried about?"

Duchess set her cup aside. "Could be, but it's Jaliel who really has me concerned," she said, fiddling with a loose string dangling from the sleeve of the blue chenille robe she wore. "Have you noticed anything, Gret?"

Gretchen left the table to check the refrigerator. "I haven't really spent a lot of time inside the office since we acquired the annex. I've been handling the supervision over there, remember?" she said, adding lemon juice to her tea.

Duchess tucked her long legs beneath her on the ladder-back maple chair. "Remember how aggravated Jaliel was when we talked to him?"

"Hmph. Girl, Jaliel is in his element back there."

"Well, what about you?" Duchess asked, resting her chin against her palm. "You had something on your mind regarding Jaliel, too."

Gretchen pushed her fingers through her thick curls and smiled. "I think I was just smarting over the fact that he doesn't need me back there."

Duchess's hazel eyes narrowed. "That all?"

"I swear that's it," Gretchen declared, raising her hands defensively. "Listen, you can sit here tryin' to play psychic if you want to, but I'm hittin' the sheets." She took her mug and left the kitchen.

The sound of the phone ringing woke Duchess the next morning. Eyes closed, she fumbled for the receiver on the gray marble nightstand. "Duchess, um, Duchess Carver," she managed.

"Good morning." Muhsin's soft, sexy response eased through the line like warm syrup.

"I hope I didn't do anything scandalous in my drunken state," Duchess remarked, trying to push herself up as she grew more lucid.

Muhsin chuckled. "Unfortunately not."

"Well, thanks for putting me to bed anyway."

"Hungry?"

"Ha! I think I'm still full from dinner last night."

"I thought you might want to eat while we discuss the party."

"The party?" Duchess asked, now sitting straight up in bed.

"The engagement party?"

Duchess's lashes fluttered closed. "Right," she breathed. The concerns from the night before came flooding back like a tidal wave. She couldn't tell Muhsin that the situation had become too much to handle because she had fallen in love with him. Knowing he still viewed this as a scheme was making it impossible for her to continue the lie. Of course, she knew that she would.

"Duchess?"

"Can you just come over here for breakfast?"

"I'll be over soon," he promised.

The connection broke and Duchess fell back against the bed. She debated on whether to prepare a big breakfast when she remembered the call to Philadelphia.

"The Carver Design Group, Marlissa Shields," Donnette's assistant answered.

Duchess smiled, hearing the familiar voice on the line. "Hi, Marlissa, it's Duchess. Is she in?"

"Hi!" Marlissa said, the wide smile on her face coming through in her voice. "She's not here right now. I don't expect her until three."

"All right, well, I'll just try later."

"Should I tell her you called?"

"Uh, no, no, thanks, Marlissa, don't bother. You take care."

"Same to you. Bye-bye."

Duchess returned the phone back to the cradle and tapped her long nails against the black receiver. Before her suspicions could run away with her, she reached for the phone and dialed a different number at the office.

"The Carver Design Group."

"Hey, Lorrell, it's Duchess. Could I speak with Jaliel if he's in?"

"Oh, sure, Duchess, just a sec."

Duchess expelled the deep breath she'd been holding and prayed she and Jaliel wouldn't argue.

"Duchess?"

"Hi."

"When are you coming home? What the hell is going on out there?" he demanded.

Duchess closed her eyes. "Jaliel, please. Let's not do this again, all right? Now, why don't you tell me what's going on with the business?"

"Everything's . . . all right," Jaliel replied after a brief hesitation.

"Jaliel, I really need you on top of this thing with the shareholders. Donnette's doing a lot, but I'd feel better knowing you were on top of this as well."

Jaliel sighed heavily on the other end. "I know, Dutch, don't worry. Everything's fine, but I really just need you to get back here."

"Well, if everything's . . . being handled, what's the rush for me to get back there?"

"Screw it," he suddenly snapped. "I don't even feel like goin' into it."

Duchess could make no sense out of Jaliel's behavior. She had always known him to be a very patient and giving person. Since she'd been away, it was as though he'd turned into a different man.

"Listen, Jaliel, I only wanted to check in. Maybe it'd be best if we just went ahead and ended this call."

"Fine," he replied promptly and slammed the phone down.

Duchess sat up in bed, her mouth hanging open at Jaliel's actions. *What the hell is happening back there?*

* * *

The phone rang just as Muhsin entered the living room.

"Vuyani," he answered in a brisk tone.

"Hey, did the messenger get there already?" Roland inquired.

Muhsin smiled at Roland's question. "Mmm-hmm. I got the keys in my hand right now."

"When do you plan to take her out there?"

"After the engagement party," Muhsin said.

"How are you going to get her to go?"

Muhsin chuckled, rubbing the set of brass keys between his thumb and forefinger. "She'll go anywhere with me after that party."

"I like your optimism, man," Roland said with an easy sigh. "So when are you going to tell her everything? You are gonna tell her, right?" he added when his friend offered no response.

"I'll tell her. I just can't say when."

Those words did not ease Roland's curiosity. "I'll hand it to you, Blaze, you planned this love scheme of yours to a tee. But even the best plans have a way of backfiring."

Muhsin rubbed one hand across his bright hair and grimaced. "I don't plan on losing her if that's what you're concerned about," he said, beginning to regret he had come clean with Roland about his true motives. "By the time I tell her, she'll be all mine with no thoughts of leaving me."

"Like I said, I like your optimism."

"Mmm-hmm. I'll talk to you later," Muhsin said, setting the phone aside on the way out of the living room.

Duchess was sprinkling more pepper on the golden crust of her cheese omelettes, when Gretchen waltzed into the kitchen.

"Mmm-mmm, something smells good!"

Duchess laughed softly and nodded toward the cabinets. "Grab a plate."

"Please, I know you're not going to town in here just for the two of us. Muhsin must be coming," Gretchen teased, taking a glass from the cabinet instead.

"Hush," Duchess whispered, removing the fluffy egg creations from the frying pan.

"Besides, I'm meeting Roland."

"Mmm, Mr. Jasper's getting a lot of play."

"Whatever," Gretchen said with a flippant wave. "I don't have time for a long-distance fling. Especially now with Jaliel and all his crap."

Duchess set the pan aside and turned. "What does that mean?"

"I'm just talking, girl," Gretchen said, her head disappearing into the refrigerator, where she searched for juice.

"Gret, if there's something I need to know . . ."

"There's nothing, Dutch," Gretchen assured her, deciding against the juice as she slammed the refrigerator door shut. "Anyway, I gotta get going." She brushed her hands across the stylish pink bell-bottoms and gray silk shirt she wore.

Duchess watched her friend sprint from the kitchen.

She was removing golden blueberry muffins from the oven when the doorbell rang. Duchess hadn't been hungry when she began to cook, but preparing the delicious meal had whetted her appetite. She set the hearty muffin pan on the counter and rushed out of the kitchen. On the way to the door, she glanced down and noticed she hadn't taken time to change out of the spaghetti-strapped T-shirt and matching blue-and-white-striped sleep pants. Her hair was loose and followed her like a glossy, jet-black cloud. Her stomach growled and she realized this was no time for being cute.

Muhsin cleared his throat the instant the door opened. His sweet, chocolate stare surveyed the tousled vision before him.

"I'm sorry for looking such a mess, but I started cooking soon after you called," Duchess explained, waving him inside the house. "I haven't had time to change."

"No problem," Muhsin replied softly. He pushed the door closed and followed her inside.

Duchess was on her way to the kitchen. "We're having cheese omelettes, toast with jam, hash browns with a sour-cream sauce and blueberry muffins."

Muhsin tried to pay attention to her words, but couldn't stop himself from focusing on her full bottom and the healthy length of her hair brushing against it.

"Are you all right?" Duchess asked when she heard what sounded like a low grunt.

"Yeah, did you, um, fix any coffee?" he asked in a hurried tone.

"Sit down, I'll get it for you," she offered.

Muhsin chose his spot at the table and watched Duchess move around the kitchen. "I can't believe you went to all this trouble cooking for me," he said as she brought things to the table.

Duchess's soft laughter filled the kitchen. "It has been a long time since I fixed breakfast for anyone other than myself. When I start cooking, I just can't stop." The innocent admission launched a humorous discussion about the meals she used to prepare for her father. Within minutes, the huge breakfast was set out on the table. Of course, Muhsin was surprised and impressed by her culinary skills.

"I guess you expected me to be no good in the kitchen, huh?" Duchess asked, her fork poised over her plate as she leered across the table.

Muhsin's shoulders rose beneath his metallic-blue

sweatshirt. "Well, the truth is, most women who look the way you do usually don't know a spoon from a spatula."

Duchess laughed. "I should be offended, but I feel flattered. I hope you're complimenting me."

"Most definitely."

Desperate for conversation after their gazes held for several seconds, Duchess asked, "So, um, what about our engagement party?"

"Right." Muhsin sighed, delving into his food like a starving man. Soon he began to discuss his ideas for the gathering that would be held at his home. A jazz band and caterers would also be hired for the event.

Duchess knew her mouth was hanging open, but she couldn't help it. "Muhsin . . . this isn't . . . It isn't real and you're going all out like this. . . . "

"Baby, it has to look real, remember?"

"Still. . . ." Duchess sighed, staring blankly into her plate.

"What's up? You getting cold feet?" Muhsin asked, taking a few more bites of his food.

Duchess didn't want to seem wary so she managed a smile to brush off the question. "What do you want me to do?"

"All you need to do is show up looking as fine as you always do."

"How long after the party until the . . . wedding?" she asked, pushing her plate aside.

Muhsin stroked the cleft in his chin and pondered the question. "I figure about a few weeks," he replied and noticed when she relaxed. "What?"

"Well, such a short time until the big day obviously means you're not planning some big throw-down," she said.

Deciding not to confirm her remark, Muhsin concentrated on his breakfast. There was no need to reveal his plans about the wedding until the time arrived.

Duchess told herself there was nothing wrong with a huge fancy party and began to relax a bit. She left the table to transfer the muffins from the baking pan to a straw basket. "So who's coming to this thing?"

Muhsin wiped his mouth with the purple napkin near his plate and leaned back. "That's where I need your help. The guest list and the menu."

"I don't have a lot of people who'll be able to travel to Chicago for a party," she said, setting the muffins on the table. "I know I'd like for Gretchen and Jaliel to be there; they'll help it look more real."

Muhsin smiled. "So what about the menu?"

Duchess shook her head. "I don't think I need any part of the menu. I've been eating so much lately, by the time I leave here I'll be twenty pounds heavier."

Hours later, Muhsin and Duchess had discussed and confirmed plans about the party. The morning passed so swiftly, Duchess barely noticed. Planning parties had never been a favorite task of hers, but with Muhsin she found it more enjoyable. They had the best time teasing each other on musical tastes and themes. Finally they decided on an elegant, catered gathering at Muhsin's estate. They made plans to visit a few local jazz clubs in the hopes of snagging a live band for the party.

"Hungry?" he asked, tossing the pad he'd carried onto the living room coffee table.

Duchess looked at him from her spot on the sofa they shared. "Haven't I told you that food is fast becoming my enemy?" she retorted playfully. "I'll be so fat I won't want to go back to Philly."

"That's the idea," Muhsin replied in the softest tone, though his gaze was steady and intense.

Duchess felt the urge to leave the sofa, but never had the chance. Muhsin's hand closed over hers where it rested along the back of the sofa. He pulled her across the space separating them and into his lap.

"I can't," she whispered.

His handsome face was buried against her neck. "Yes, you can," he said, his big hands cupping the sides of her breasts as he caressed the nipples through the thin fabric of her T-shirt.

"This isn't fair." She moaned even as she arched into his hard frame.

"Shhh . . ." he urged, sliding his mouth down the column of her neck. He held her slender body straddled across his lap and settled her closer to the arousal straining against the zipper of his jeans.

Duchess's soft whimpers added fuel to the need raging inside Muhsin. He slipped the straps of the T-shirt from her shoulders and farther down until her breasts were bared to his cocoa eyes. He lost himself in the sweet smell of her skin and the luscious hair that shielded her breasts with its length.

Muhsin's tongue swirled around the curve of her breasts several times before favoring the nipples with the lightest kisses. Then he was pressing her back into the sofa, his mouth filled with her soft flesh.

Duchess cupped the back of his head, her fingers buried in his gorgeous hair. She moved against him in a sensuous fashion, moaning as his lips and tongue pleasured her shamelessly. He pulled away, bringing his mouth to hers. Duchess's soft moans caught in her throat when they kissed. The friction of her nipples against the smooth fabric of his sweatshirt only increased the sweet sensations running through her.

Muhsin's hands curved around her hips to hold her in place. Again he was drawn to her rigid nipples. His tongue flicked against one before his teeth grazed it gently again and again. Duchess wanted to feel his skin next to hers and pulled her fingers from his hair to venture beneath his shirt. She shivered upon feeling the taut muscles of his back and abdomen as they rippled and flexed against his every move.

Hushed sounds of need filled the room. Neither wanted the moment to end, but it was interrupted by the phone's ring. Duchess ignored it easily, not realizing how desperate she was for Muhsin's touch.

Muhsin couldn't ignore the insistent ring for long and soon raised his head to send a murderous glare in its direction.

"Damn, I need to get you an answering machine in here," he growled before releasing her.

Duchess pushed herself up and tried to catch her breath before turning to answer the phone.

"Dutch? It's me. Look, I'm on my way home. How about we go shopping for that engagement party today?"

"Um, yeah, yeah, Gret," Duchess replied, wincing against her friend's loud, upbeat voice.

"Great! We'll head out soon as I get there, all right?"

Duchess didn't care what they did as long as she was away from Muhsin with time to think.

"Dutch?"

"Yeah, yes, Gret, I'll be ready to go when you get here," Duchess promised, then clicked off the phone. She pushed both hands through her hair and set about fixing her clothes. When she turned to tell Muhsin about the call, she realized he was already gone.

The look on the sales associate's face reflected disappointment and mild aggravation when Duchess was unimpressed by another outfit.

"Girl, what is the matter with you?" Gretchen asked, leaning across the short, black, claw-foot sofa when the associate walked away. "That dress was as fierce as the last seven you sent back."

Duchess squeezed her eyes shut and sighed. "I guess I'm not as into this as I thought I'd be."

"Well, what's wrong? What's going on?" Gretchen whispered, her dark eyes narrowed in concern.

"Muhsin," Duchess whispered, her lashes fluttering slightly. "He . . . we kissed again."

Everything fell into place for Gretchen then. "And we're here looking at outfits for the party. So that only means this whole engagement thing is—"

"Tearing me apart. I'm in love with him," Duchess admitted, her hazel eyes welling with tears.

Gretchen leaned back against the arm of the sofa. "Are you going to tell him?"

"Hell, no."

"Why?"

"Gretchen, after all my big warnings to him that this was business and he had to give me his word that he wouldn't try anything, now I'm supposed to walk up to him and say 'I'm in love with you'?"

Gretchen nodded, her arched brows rising in challenge. "Yes, Dutch. He just might feel the same."

"Hmph," Duchess grunted, leaning forward to hold her head in her hands. "What time is it?"

"Past four, why?"

"That's good enough for me. I need a drink," Duchess said, pushing herself off the sofa. "Join me?" she asked Gretchen, who had no complaints.

Jaliel's heart raced as he massaged the ache in his neck. Donnette's report involving the situation with the shareholders had him more than concerned—he was downright terrified. The annoying buzz of the phone easily succeeded in snapping his last thin nerve. Muttering a vicious curse, he snatched up the phone.

"Lorrell, didn't I say no interruptions!"

"I realized that, Jaliel, but the, um, gentleman waiting says you're expecting him."

"Who is it?"

"A Mr. Shaunnessy Wright."

Jaliel stood behind his desk so quickly that the high-backed leather chair almost teetered to the floor. "Show him in," he ordered quickly, his demeanor changing into one of a humble, nervous man.

Shaunnessy's facial expression was a permanent scowl. He was very dark with cold, black eyes as calculating as they were suspicious.

"I don't care for coming to people's places of business," he told Jaliel, shaking hands as Lorrell left the office.

Jaliel's nervousness eased a little. "It's no problem. I got the run of the place," he announced, sharing a laugh with his associate.

"What can I do for you, man?" Shaunnessy asked, removing his leather jacket and perching his tall frame along the edge of the desk.

Jaliel wasted no time. "I'm in the market to purchase some coke for a party."

Shaunnessy's guarded expression registered surprise. "A party? It'll cost you. What's the occasion?"

"I'm entertaining some clients who like to dabble and I want to close this deal."

Shaunnessy nodded. "When do you need it?"

"They'll be in town Saturday."

"You'll have it tomorrow."

Jaliel winked. "That's what I like to hear," he said, shaking hands with Shaunnessy again.

"Anything more I can do?" the man asked, a knowing grin coming to his long, oval face.

Jaliel didn't pretend to misunderstand. "I could use a lil' somethin'-somethin' myself."

Shaunnessy chuckled as he pulled a neat square pocket of white powder from the pocket of his gray trousers. Jaliel passed him a few bills and took his product. He cleared a space on his desk and unabashedly enjoyed the merchandise right there.

"This is the quality of stuff I'm looking for," Jaliel remarked after he'd sniffed a few lines of the cocaine.

"You know I always deliver the good stuff," Shaunnessy unnecessarily reminded one of his best customers.

A quick knock sounded on the door and Donnette walked in, rambling about some paperwork Jaliel wanted. She looked up just in time to see her boss wiping traces of powder from his desk and face.

Donnette stood in speechless surprise. Her lively light brown eyes darted from the desk to Shaunnessy Wright. Several seconds passed before she tuned into Jaliel barking at her.

"What is it, Donnette?" he asked for the third time.

"Oh, um, these figures. You—you said you wanted them right after lunch."

"Fine. Leave 'em on the desk and I'll get back to you," he ordered, watching the young woman do as she was told.

"She cool?" Shaunnessy asked once the door closed behind Donnette.

Jaliel waved off the question. "Nothin' to worry about. She knows where her bread's buttered. All of 'em do."

"That include your lady boss?" Shaunnessy asked, a small smile coming to his face.

Jaliel tensed, but only briefly. "Duchess knows I'm single-handedly keepin' this place afloat while she's off jet-settin'. I'm the last person she wants to rile."

Outside Jaliel's office, Donnette and Lorrell spoke in

hushed voices. Jaliel's unsettling visitor was the topic of discussion.

"Well, who is he?"

"Shaunnessy Wright. That's all I know."

Donnette chewed her bottom lip while tapping her nails against Lorrell's desk. "Is he a business associate?"

"No, I'm sure he's not. But Jaliel gave me specific orders not to disturb him. He practically bit my head off when I did, but when he heard this man was here to see him, his attitude quickly changed."

Before Donnette could question Lorrell further, Jaliel's office door opened. Shaunnessy offered a faint smile to the two women as he passed on his way down the hall.

"Donnette," Jaliel called when he noticed the woman turning to walk away.

Donnette sent Lorrell an expressionless glance. Then she reluctantly followed Jaliel into his office and closed the door.

Jaliel was walking back to his desk. "Donnette, about what you saw—"

"Hold it, Jaliel. Now, I hope you're not gonna try changing my mind about what was going on in here," Donnette challenged, folding her arms across her chest.

Jaliel's jaw tightened and he held one finger poised in Donnette's direction. "Now, you hold it. I'd think twice about coming in here with my ass on my shoulders if I were you."

Donnette smoothed one hand across the sleek French roll that pulled her hair away from her face. "Are you threatening me, Jaliel?"

"'Course not," he replied with an easy shrug. "But then again, I'm not tryin' to raise two kids with no man. You have a good thing going here. I really don't think you want to be out there pounding the pavement."

Donnette blinked the tears away from her eyes, refusing to let Jaliel see how much he had rattled her. "You did say you weren't threatening me, right?" she queried in her most sarcastic tone.

"What I'm saying is that you should be smart before you go blabbing about what you thought you saw."

Duchess tightened the belt around her short, white, terry robe and ran to the front door. Muhsin waited outside. It had been days since they'd seen each other, but Duchess could barely look at the man who stood watching her with intense eyes.

"I see you bought an answering machine. I get it every time I call, so you must be avoiding me," he said, pushing himself away from the doorjamb. "May I come in?"

Duchess smoothed both hands across her bare thighs and retreated into the house.

"Did I wake you?" Muhsin asked, his gaze sliding over the short robe and her tousled hair.

"I was out late with Gret."

"Mmm, how is she?" he asked, following Duchess and pushing both of his hands deep into the pockets of his saggy light blue jeans.

"She's good."

"Why haven't you called me?"

It was obvious that Muhsin was very hurt and Duchess didn't know what to make of it.

"Why haven't you called me?" he asked again, his gravelly voice sounding soft as mist.

"There's just been a lot going on, Muhsin. I'm sorry," she whispered.

Muhsin knew exactly what Duchess meant, but pretended to be confused. "We have a contract between us, remember? This thing between us won't last forever."

That was something Duchess didn't need to be reminded of. She rolled her eyes and headed for the kitchen. Muhsin followed.

"Did you find an outfit for the party?" he asked, attempting small talk to dispel the tension in the air.

Duchess nodded and strolled to the sink. "I found something. Party's in a couple of days, right?" A long sigh followed the question.

Muhsin stepped behind her and smoothed his hands across her arms. "What's wrong?" he murmured against her hair.

Duchess only shook her head.

"Talk to me," he coaxed, nudging her hair aside to press his mouth next to her ear.

"Don't." She gasped when his teeth tugged against her lobe.

"Why?"

"Muhsin . . ." she began, losing strength in her legs when his fingers disappeared beneath the short hem of the robe. He caressed her inner thigh with fleeting strokes that skirted the edge of her panties before moving away. "Don't," she begged again.

"I want to take you to bed," he moaned into her neck, "and I think you want me, too." This time his fingers slipped inside her underwear to discover the damp middle.

"Damnit, Muhsin, would you please go? Please!" she urged, turning to glare up at him.

Muhsin could see she was close to tears, but he ignored that. Instead, his hands curled about her soft upper arms and he jerked her close. "Do you want me to?" he asked, watching her striking gaze lower to his mouth. Taking that as an answer, his lips fell upon her own with tremendous force.

Duchess's entire body shook when Muhsin's tongue invaded her mouth. Amidst the explosive kiss, he effortlessly placed her on the wood countertop. He loosened the robe's belt and pushed the material from her shoulders. His eyes narrowed sharply when he realized she wore nothing but the wispy lace panties beneath.

Duchess tossed her head back and cherished the possessive kisses trailing her body. Muhsin's mouth and hands were everywhere. He suckled her nipples until they stood firm, then focused his attention on the deep valley between them. His strong hands caressed her back while his mouth trailed lower to favor her flat stomach and navel with his touch.

"Muhsin . . ." Duchess cried when she felt his mouth against the crotch of her underwear. His nose nudged the damp middle as his fingers curled around the thin waistband.

"Wait," she whispered, pressing her hands against his shoulders. "Wait," she called with more force, this time taking fistfuls of his denim shirt and urging him to move away.

Muhsin complied after a while. He rested his cheek against her satiny thigh before looking up into her lovely cinnamon-brown face.

"I—"

"Shhh . . ." he commanded, pressing his lips against hers. *After the party,* he promised himself, then left the apartment.

Duchess eased herself off the counter and relaxed against it, too weak to move any farther. She covered her face in her hands and admitted that the situation had become intolerable. She couldn't handle it and turned to go after him and say the deal was off. Her very next thought was the business. It was the only thing she should have been concerned with, not some schoolgirl feelings.

The rationalization calmed her somewhat and she found the strength to leave the kitchen. "Speaking of my business . . ." She headed to the phone on the desk in the living room and dialed Jaliel's direct number.

He answered the phone in a relaxed, almost jovial tone.

"Hello, Jaliel."

He cleared his throat. "Duchess? Um, hello. Anything wrong?"

"Should there be?"

Jaliel was more than a little suspicious. He prayed Donnette had not called his bluff or that someone else had revealed his secret.

"Jaliel?"

"I'm sorry, Dutch. What was that?"

"Listen, I called to let you know I'm thinking of coming back home soon."

"Coming back, why?"

Duchess laughed. "Because it's where I live and I have a business to run, as you keep reminding me."

"Well, I have everything under control. There's no need for you to rush back," he reassured her quickly.

"This is quite a change, Jaliel."

Smoothing both hands across his close-cut fade, Jaliel ordered himself to remain calm. "Dutch, listen, I know I've been showing my ass here the last few weeks and I'm sorry. You deserve to get away more than anyone. Especially after everything you've been through. I never should have come down on you about that."

Jaliel's attempt at sincerity did nothing to ease Duchess's mind. Though going back to Philadelphia anytime soon was out of the question, she let him think her arrival would be swift. Now she was certain her friend was going through something. Something terrible.

Chapter 9

"I can't believe one of my best friends is about to marry one of my husband's best friends," Ophelia squealed.

Duchess raised her water glass in a mock toast. "Yeah, I can hardly believe it myself," she said.

Ophelia was all too delighted by the news. With Gretchen leaving town earlier that week, Duchess had no one to confide in and toyed with the idea of telling Ophelia everything. Common sense won out and she decided against that. The charade would come to an end soon, she hoped.

Duchess refused to let those thoughts cast a cloud over her lunch date with Ophelia. Soon the two young women had resumed their wonderful conversation. They were laughing hysterically over old times when Isaiah approached the table.

"Won't you please join us?" Ophelia offered after Duchess reminded her who Isaiah was.

"Well, you two look like you're having too much fun over here to be disturbed," he noted.

"Don't be crazy. Sit down," Duchess ordered, pushing back one of the chairs at the table.

The waitress stopped by the table then and Isaiah asked her to change his to-go order, deciding to take the offer made by the two ladies.

The three of them were talking and laughing loudly

when Muhsin and Tan Kioto walked into the dining room. The two spotted their ladies immediately and headed to the table. Tan smiled while Muhsin's expression was a hard mask.

"Baby," Ophelia said when she saw her husband.

Duchess managed a smile, though she knew Muhsin was not pleased to see Isaiah there. Luckily, Tan and Ophelia were there to keep things lively.

"Surprised to see you here, man," Muhsin said when there was a moment of silence.

Isaiah brushed a crumb from his blue silk shirt and grinned. "I stopped to place a to-go order and saw Dutch. Since we hadn't been able to get together for lunch . . ."

"Mmm-hmm," Muhsin replied stonily, turning his attention back to the conversation at hand.

Isaiah grew silent as he leaned back in his chair to study Duchess. She was always radiant and today was no exception. A few curly tendrils framed her face while the rest of her hair was pulled back into a thick French braid. The peach dress with its scooped neckline and capped sleeves complimented her flawless skin. Still, beneath the radiance she didn't appear to be as glowing as a new bride should be. Isaiah knew he should ask about it, but decided to keep his comments quiet for the time being. He had survived the cut list and received an invitation to the party. He would play it cool until he got there. Not wanting to agitate the situation any further, Isaiah excused himself from the table. He promised to see the happy couple at the party.

In spite of Isaiah's departure, Duchess had a feeling Muhsin would soon explode over the man having been there at all. To her surprise, she realized whether he exploded or not didn't faze her. In a way, it pleased her to know he felt so strongly about another man infringing on their time together. Then again, she thought, why should she want Muhsin to experience such feelings? It would only make things harder.

"Duchess, how about you and Blaze joining us tonight for dinner and a show?"

Duchess hesitated over Ophelia's invitation. She never knew what Muhsin's mood would be.

"It sounds good to me, Ophelia. Unless Duchess has other plans?" Muhsin said, before favoring Duchess with his soft stare. When she shook her head, he turned back to Ophelia and sent the woman a dimpled smile.

Of course, Ophelia was delighted and began to discuss her plans for their evening. The foursome parted company after a while.

Duchess aimed the keyless-entry remote toward the rented hunter-green Mercedes waiting in the restaurant parking lot. She closed her eyes and prayed Muhsin would just let her go quietly. Her prayer went unanswered.

"Duchess—"

"Muhsin, please. I didn't know Isaiah would be there today," she began to explain, quickening her steps to the car. "It happened just like he said. I was there with Ophelia, not to see him."

The explanation forced a smile to Muhsin's lips. Truth be told, Isaiah was the last person on his mind. True, at first he'd been a little perturbed at finding the man there, but the feeling had been fleeting, he was pleased to admit.

Duchess braced her hand against the hood of the car before turning around. She could detect nothing angry in his easy expression or in the casual stance as he leaned back on his long legs with one hand pushed deep into his burgundy trouser pockets.

"I believe you. I believed Isaiah, too," he said, watching as she visibly relaxed. "Actually, I was about to ask if you'd stay with me at the house on the day of the party."

"Stay with you?" Duchess asked, cringing at the defensive tone in her voice.

Muhsin pulled his hand from his pocket and stepped closer. "I only want to make sure you're satisfied with everything beforehand and I'd like you to be there when everybody starts to arrive."

Duchess searched every inch of his handsome face. She found nothing there that said he wasn't being honest. Besides, his reasons sounded harmless enough. Unfortunately, she was still uneasy and didn't trust herself alone with him for a minute. Of course, she would feel silly arguing about it now.

"I'll be there," she finally agreed. The reply was whisper-soft.

Muhsin nodded, taking yet another step closer. "I guess I'll see you tonight, then," he said, glancing toward the ground as though suddenly developing a case of shyness. He looked up and cupped her face in his wide hands. A deep kiss followed.

Duchess whimpered at the instantaneous rush of sensation. Eagerly, she responded, thrusting her tongue slowly into his mouth as her fingers curled around the open collar of the black shirt he wore beneath his jacket.

"Duchess . . ." Muhsin groaned, moving his hands from her face to cup her hips. He pressed her back against the car, the force of his kiss increasing every second. He knew he was dangerously close to allowing his hormones complete control over his actions. Commanding willpower from someplace deep inside, he forced himself to let her go.

Duchess's long lashes fluttered and she looked up at him. Muhsin brushed her swollen lips and leaned forward again to treat himself to one last taste.

"I'll see you later," he whispered against her mouth. Then he was gone.

Donnette was both surprised and overjoyed to hear that Gretchen had returned. So much so that when Gretchen stepped into the office, Donnette rushed across the room to hug her.

"Now, did you miss me that much or are things that bad around here?"

"Both, girl," Donnette instantly admitted.

Gretchen pulled away and turned to push the office door shut. "Talk to me," she said, tossing her gray leather purse and coordinating scarf to the brown suede sofa.

"I walked in on Jaliel sniffing cocaine in his office. How's that for starters?" Donnette retorted, needing no further persuasion to reveal the events that had been driving her mad.

"Damn," Gretchen cursed, smoothing her hands across the sleeves of her purple silk blouse. "That's why I came back earlier than I planned. When Dutch told me you'd called . . . Did you tell her anything?"

Donnette shook her head, fingering a loose strand of her wavy hair. "I was going to but . . . Jaliel threatened I'd lose my job. We only spoke briefly about what's going on with the stockholders. Gretchen, that mess has turned him completely crazy!"

"Tell me about it," Gretchen agreed, remembering her nasty argument with Jaliel before she left for Chicago.

"How is Duchess?"

Gretchen slapped her hands against the sides of her black skirt. "She's engaged. It was a sudden thing," she added, smiling at the shock on Donnette's face. "Don't mention it to anyone just yet, all right?"

Donnette nodded, slipping her black dress beneath

her as she took a seat behind her neat mahogany desk. "Are you going to tell her what's going on here?"

Gretchen would have preferred to do anything but that, knowing what her best friend was going through with Muhsin Vuyani for the sake of the business. Despite that, she knew there was no way she could keep Jaliel's drug use—a thing that could quite possibly ruin the business—a secret.

"Is this okay?" Muhsin asked when he escorted Duchess to her bedroom suite on the afternoon of the party.

"It's incredible," Duchess whispered, her eyes wide as they spanned the spectacular room with its bay windows overlooking the back garden.

"I'm sorry Gretchen can't be here," Muhsin said as he set the small overnight bag on the maple comforter covering the king-size bed.

Duchess smiled and turned away from the windows. "It's okay. They needed her back in Philly. Besides, Oph will be here and Gret has my cell number, so she'll probably call later."

Muhsin tugged on the tassles dangling from his Grambling State sweatshirt and glanced around the room. "Is there anything else you need in here?"

Duchess waved her hand. "I'll be fine. I'm gonna take a nap before I get dressed."

"Well, I'll be back to check on you, all right?" he said, sending her a smile before he left her alone.

When the door closed, Duchess folded her arms across her snug yellow T-shirt and gave her surroundings a closer inspection. A girl could get used to this, she told herself, loving everything from the room's high ceilings to the plush cocoa carpet running throughout. A delighted gasp passed her lips when she stepped into the private bath.

The plush peach and cream room, with its sunken tub in the far corner, pushed all thoughts of sleep from her mind. She opted for a nice, long soak instead.

Muhsin's head was covered with a thick green towel when he heard the phone ring. Tossing the towel aside, he pulled the black cordless from the nightstand. "Yeah?" he answered.

"Mr. Vuyani, we have Ms. Carver's rental car down here. Should we leave it with the other guests' cars or have it parked in the garage?"

Muhsin toyed with his wet, curly auburn locks and debated. "Mike, I'll go get her keys and have them sent down. You can put the car in the garage. She won't be leaving after the party," he said. When the call ended, he pulled on a robe and left the room.

Duchess was enjoying her bath and drifting in and out of sleep when Muhsin approached her bedroom door. He knocked lightly, then twisted the brass knob and stepped inside.

"Duchess?" he called, then closed the door and walked farther into the room. "Duchess?" This time the sound of splashing water reached his ears and he turned toward the bathroom.

The sight of her lounging in the bubble-filled tub practically robbed him of his breath. For several minutes he stood watching her. His brown eyes followed every movement, sliding along the length of her long legs when she raised one, then the other, from the bubbles.

Duchess opened her eyes and found Muhsin standing just inside the bathroom. She didn't appear surprised by his presence, however. Her vibrant gaze beckoned him closer and when he knelt beside the

tub, her eyes fell to his mouth. Muhsin accepted the
silent invitation without hesitation.

Water sloshed outside the tub when Duchess threw
her arms around his wide shoulders and brought her
lips to his. Muhsin caught a fistful of her hair and pulled
her head back as he indulged in the sweet taste of her
mouth. She massaged his shoulders, before pushing her
hands beneath his navy terry-cloth robe. The feel of his
smooth skin stretched over taut muscles sent a gasp past
her lips. Muhsin uttered soft, almost inaudible groans
when he broke the kiss to trail his mouth down her neck
and chest. His tall, athletic body lay sprawled half in, half
out of the tub. His fingers disappeared into the water in
search of what he most yearned for. Duchess arched toward him again, her legs parting farther for his probing
fingers.

"I won't let you leave me tonight," he growled into the
valley between her breasts.

Duchess could only shiver in response. Her fingers
went to the belt around his waist, eager to have him
nude beside her in the tub.

"No . . ."

One of them moaned the word when the shrill ring of
a cellular phone pierced the air.

"It's probably Gretchen," she whispered, breathless as
she stared up at Muhsin.

"Don't take too long," he whispered, squeezing water
from his robe before standing. "Where are your car keys?"

Duchess couldn't take her eyes off the powerful
length of his legs outlined beneath his damp robe.

"Duchess?"

"I'm sorry, what?" she whispered, quickly shaking
her head.

Muhsin smiled down at her. "Your keys? I'm having
your car moved to the garage."

"Oh, they're on the dresser," she replied slowly, leaning back against the tub.

"I'll be back to get you," he promised before strolling from the bathroom.

The cell phone's ringing had ceased only to resume the moment Duchess stepped from the tub. She wrapped herself in a bath sheet, then rushed to grab the phone off the bed.

"You must be with Muhsin," Gretchen guessed when the connection was made.

"It's not what you think."

"Oh, I bet it is."

Duchess pushed her wet hair behind her shoulders and went back to the bathroom. "What do you want?" she asked, faking an angry tone of voice.

Gretchen giggled. "I just wanted to wish you luck tonight, girl."

"And?" Duchess prompted as she knelt to pull the water stopper from the tub.

"And what?"

"You know what. How are things going?"

"They're fine," Gretchen said before clearing her throat.

Duchess stopped in the middle of the bathroom. "'They're fine,'" she mocked.

"Mmm-hmm. Listen, you need to be concentrating on this party tonight, so I'll just—"

"Damnit, Gret, you're as bad as Jaliel with all this quick talk. He's got it down pat."

"Hmph, I'll bet."

"What?"

"Nothing, Dutch, damn."

Duchess sighed and reached for a small towel to dry her hair. "You know, when I don't answer my cell, the answering service clicks on. You could've left your congratulations there. Now, it's obvious you wanted to talk to me. So talk."

"Damn you," Gretchen hissed, hating how well her friend knew her. "I just hate tellin' you this mess over the phone, you know?"

"Well, I'm tired of getting the runaround, so this'll have to do," Duchess said. "Does this have to do with Jaliel?"

"You know he hasn't been himself."

"That's understating it."

"I've, um, I've suspected for a while about what was wrong with him." Gretchen sighed over the line. "It wasn't until I talked to Donnette that I knew for sure."

"Knew what for sure?" Duchess asked, setting the towel on the counter.

"Dutch, Jaliel's . . . using drugs. Donnette saw him with her own eyes. Cocaine. She walked into his office and found him with his . . . distributor."

"What?" Duchess whispered, taking a seat on the porcelain toilet. Never would she have imagined anything like that.

"Are you coming back?"

"I need to, but . . . my obligations here . . . No, no, I'll be home soon. Gret, you can count on it. Even if I have to come back to Chicago and finish this."

"Are you sure?"

"I have to be. I'm not about to go through all this with Muhsin only to have Jaliel run my business into the ground."

Forty-five minutes later, Duchess opened her bedroom door to Muhsin. She resisted the urge to gawk at his appearance. The stylish three-piece black suit had been tailored for his broad shoulders and lean, muscular frame. The gray silk shirt under his black vest required no tie.

"Ready?" he asked, pushing himself from the doorjamb.

Duchess managed a nod and forced herself to look into his eyes. The intensity of his gaze brought a frown to her face. "Is everything okay?"

"More than okay," he assured her, his soft stare as flattering as the tone of his voice.

The couple made their way down the wide, spiral staircase. Muhsin kept his hand at Duchess's waist. His thumb brushed her spine, left bare by the V-cut of the ankle-length black gown that dipped equally low in front. The soft strokes of his fingers seemed innocent enough, but they produced the same sensuous results.

"You all right?" He felt her shiver.

"I need a drink," she said, groaning.

Muhsin's hearty laughter burst forth. "My fiancée says she needs a drink!" he bellowed to announce their arrival at the party.

The party was a catered affair that boasted a guest list of at least seventy-five people. Muhsin and Duchess had opted for something simple, yet elegant. There was an elaborate buffet, full bar and live jazz band that most of the partygoers knew from the group's local performances. The lively crowd grew even livelier as best wishes were bestowed. Amid it all, the engaged couple was separated. Duchess was mingling with a couple she recognized when someone took her by the arm.

"Isaiah," she said, pulling the man into a bear hug.

"I'm taking you for that drink," he said, escorting her to the bar in the rear of the living room.

"Where have you been hiding?" Duchess asked, once they'd chosen two stools and ordered from the bar.

"Didn't want to cause any waves between you and your

fiancé," he teased, watching her smile fade a bit. "Speaking of which, why don't you look as happy as you should?"

"What?" Duchess replied, surprised laughter following the word.

Isaiah's dark eyes narrowed. "Something's not quite right with you."

"I'm fine," she assured him, leaning forward to pat his arm through the sleeve of his tuxedo.

"You should be better than fine," he argued.

Duchess tapped her fingers to the glass bar and pressed her lips together. "It's my business," she admitted finally. "I have a friend running it and he's going through something serious. So serious, it could affect my business for the worst. I can't afford that."

Isaiah covered her hand with his. "I'm sorry."

"I'll handle it."

"So none of this has anything to do with Blaze?"

"No, he's been great."

"Good."

The simple reply told Duchess it wasn't meant in good faith. Before she could ask, Isaiah kissed her cheek, grabbed his drink and told her he'd speak to her later. Pleased by the moment's solitude, she thought back to her conversation with Gretchen. Jaliel and drugs were a combination she never would've guessed upon. Unfortunately, it was a reality and would have to be dealt with. The sooner, the better.

Duchess noticed hands resting against the bar, one on either side of her. She turned to find Muhsin behind her.

"Let's dance," he suggested. His hands closed around her arms to pull her from the stool.

The touch took Duchess right back to the earlier scene upstairs and she trembled a little. That trembling went into overdrive when Muhsin held her in a warm embrace and nuzzled her ear with the tip of his nose.

"I'm not letting you go," he whispered.

Duchess giggled and looked into his handsome face. "I hope not, since you just asked me to marry you."

Muhsin wasn't as amused. "I'm not letting you go home tonight," he clarified, oblivious to all the interested glances directed toward the two of them.

Duchess trembled again, this time from sheer excitement and anticipation. Instinctively, she arched closer to Muhsin, moaning an instant before his lips met hers. The kiss was lusty and deep and lasted a long while. By the time they drew apart, shouts, clapping and laughter drowned the music filling the room.

The newly engaged couple danced nonstop, never realizing how happy they were. Muhsin was completely enchanted by his fiancée and it showed. He kept Duchess by his side for the better part of the evening. When she all but insisted on visiting the ladies' room, he reluctantly allowed it.

Duchess promised to hurry, as eager to return to Muhsin's side as he was to have her there. She made quick use of the washroom and was checking her updo for any loose strands when Tia Garrison stepped inside.

"Congratulations," she called.

"Thanks," Duchess replied, but initiated no further conversation.

Tia hadn't been invited. She managed to attend thanks to an unescorted male friend who had made the guest list. She bowed her head briefly and then checked her makeup in the lit mirror. About to leave, Tia then changed her mind. "I'm truly happy for you, you know? Even though it could've been me in your shoes enjoying all the glory."

"I'm not sure I know what you mean," Duchess whispered, turning away from the mirror.

Tia folded her arms across the snug bodice of the sleek, short, blue, spaghetti-strapped dress she wore. "Duchess, by now you must know Muhsin and I used to have a thing going."

"And it didn't work out," Duchess finished.

Tia fluffed her short curls and smiled. "Muhsin can be ruthless when it comes to getting what he wants."

"I haven't seen that side of him yet," Duchess said, though silently she admitted that she had.

"Well, that's because he has you. There isn't anyone or anything standing in his way. Everything's going just the way he wants it."

"Look, Tia, if you have something unfinished with Muhsin, you should take it up with him. It's none of my business, you know?"

"I'd have to disagree. Especially if Blaze is the man you're going to marry."

"What are you getting at?" Duchess snapped, finally losing patience with the woman.

Tia went to the bathroom door and twisted the lock. "Let me tell you something I'm sure you don't know, Duchess. When I met Muhsin, I was in a serious relationship with Isaiah Manfres. I think you know him?" she asked, pausing when Duchess appeared surprised. "Anyway, Muhsin didn't know we were a couple when he approached me at a party Isaiah threw. In fact, Izzy had asked me to marry him and was waiting for an answer."

"Marriage?" Duchess whispered.

Tia nodded. "Blaze found out, but instead of backing off, he went after me even more aggressively. I tried to be true to Isaiah. I wanted to be. As you know, Muhsin Vuyani is not a man you can deny for long."

Duchess looked away. She steeled herself against wanting to nod.

"Isaiah, with his sweet self," Tia reminisced, as she paced the small confines of the washroom, "he wouldn't give up on us and we would've made it had it not been for the phone calls and the women."

"He cheated on you?" Duchess asked, disbelief clinging to the words.

Tia leaned against the door. "I thought he cheated on me."

"Meaning?"

"Muhsin devised the entire thing. He had women calling Izzy's house, stopping by. I even walked in and found two of the bitches in his bed."

"Tia, how do you know—"

"That it was Muhsin? I didn't at first. Isaiah and I broke up and Muhsin had me," she replied, her brown eyes beginning to gloss with tears. "After a while, I guess he got his fill of me or I got too needy or I wasn't enough of a challenge for him anymore. He cut me off, just like, that and it hurt. It almost killed me and I hate that bastard."

"Tia," Duchess whispered, pressing her fingers against her temples, "this story . . ."

"It's incredible, I know. I had to tell you because you seem smart and you seem to be a good person. I can sense that."

"Tia, if all this is true, how can you and Isaiah remain friends, remain civil even, with Muhsin?"

Tia shrugged, casting her gaze toward the black tiled floor. "I guess I'm civil to a point because I know what he's capable of. With Isaiah, it's purely financial. He depends on Muhsin's backing for certain aspects of his business."

"Right. . . ." Duchess sighed, finally understanding Isaiah's strange mood whenever they discussed Muhsin.

"Listen Duchess, I'm sorry I upset you. You didn't deserve that. Not tonight, anyway. Who knows? Maybe Muhsin's changed and maybe he'd never do the same things to you," Tia said. "Despite everything, I get the strangest feeling that man really loves you. But if you should ever feel threatened, just remember I told you so."

Duchess leaned against the counter and watched Tia leave the washroom. Then she realized she had been holding her breath.

"Oh, I can't wait for the wedding!" Ophelia cried hours later. She had marveled over every aspect of the evening. "Have y'all set a date yet?"

"Hopefully in a few weeks," Muhsin answered.

As he spoke, Duchess never took her eyes off him. When he caught her staring, she looked away.

"Well, keep us posted and let me know if I can do anything to help," Ophelia told Duchess, pulling her into a tight hug.

"I will," Duchess promised, managing a smile for her friend.

"We're going to say good night now," Tan announced, shaking hands with Muhsin before pressing a kiss to Duchess's cheek.

When the good-byes were said, the Kiotos headed for the front entrance. Duchess prepared to show them out, but Muhsin caught her arm and stopped her.

"Is everything all right?" he asked, his brown eyes narrowed.

Duchess blinked after a moment and finally managed a nod. "Yeah," she whispered, then left his side.

The inquisitive expression remained on Muhsin's face as he watched her. Slowly he followed her out to the foyer, where they said good night to their friends. Soon, other guests began to follow suit, and after a while everyone had left.

Duchess hugged herself and retreated to the living room. The place was practically silent with the exception of the crystal goblets and glass plates clinking together as the caterers cleaned up.

Muhsin followed Duchess into the room and stood watching her for a while. He closed the distance between them and pulled her back against his chest, squeezing her upper arms gently. When Duchess moved away, he pushed one hand into his pocket and massaged his forehead with the other.

"What the hell is wrong with you?"

"What?" Duchess asked, turning to watch him with wide eyes.

"Why are you so distant all of a sudden?"

"Things have been pretty wild lately," she reminded him, smoothing her hands across her dress as she paced the room. "Besides, I do have a business to think about."

"Is something wrong back in Philly?"

"That's putting it mildly."

"Talk to me," Muhsin said, leaning against the corner of the sofa, his arms folded across his chest.

Duchess confided about Jaliel going through "some type of ordeal," omitting the part about the drugs. Muhsin appeared concerned, but his expression grew drawn when she mentioned having to go home soon. Duchess noticed and waited to see how he would react.

"Just tell me about your plans before you leave," was all he said.

Duchess nodded. "I need to get my stuff and get out of here," she mumbled, brushing past him on her way out of the room. She made it to the stairway when he caught her elbow and pulled her back next to him.

"I told you I wasn't letting you leave me tonight," he murmured into her ear.

"Are you going to force me to stay?" she asked, straining against his hold.

Muhsin buried his handsome face against her neck. "I would never force you. Besides, I don't think that'd be necessary." He smiled when she shivered.

Duchess closed her eyes and cursed her weakness. Surrendering to the need raging inside her was the last thing she should do.

"Don't leave," Muhsin whispered. This time his hand dipped inside the front of her dress and he cupped her breast. "Please," he added, giving a light squeeze.

Duchess held on to the polished oak bannister and leaned against it for support. Muhsin manipulated the nipple of one breast between his thumb and index finger. His other hand folded over her hip and pulled her closer to his powerful arousal. Sensing the strength about to leave her legs, he caught her in his arms and carried her to his bedroom.

All the way, Muhsin whispered the sweetest words as his lips feathered her temple with soft kisses. Duchess was too engrossed with his touch to pay attention to her surroundings.

The desire pulsing through him demanded he not waste time with niceties, but he was determined not to rush what was taking place. He had waited too long to have her. Inside the room, his shoulder brushed the light switch and the room was bathed in dim light. He had to see her.

Duchess massaged his silky, auburn hair as her lips teased the strong line of his jaw. They slid to his neck and she nibbled the spot where his pulse pounded. Tiny gasps rose from her mouth as his fingers caressed her breast with more intensity. She pushed herself higher

against his chest, seeking his mouth as though she were
dying for the taste of him.

Muhsin didn't disappoint her. His perfect teeth
tugged her bottom lip. He kissed her slowly, lowering
her to the center of the mammoth-sized bed. Duchess
reached for him when he moved away, but Muhsin
kissed her flexing fingers before pressing her hands to
the bed. He focused on taking her out of the gown,
pulling at the long sleeves to expose her round breasts
and, lower still, over her flat stomach and the curve of
her hips.

Duchess's lashes fluttered open and she watched the
expression on his face. No man had ever made her feel
so beautiful simply by gazing at her. In response, she
arched herself toward him, fingers trailing her bare skin
and the edge of her wispy black silk panties.

"Duchess . . ." Muhsin groaned, his mouth replacing
her fingers along the waistband of the lingerie. His
hands curved around her hips to hold her in place as his
lips traced the outline of her womanhood. Expertly, he
eased the panties from her body. His tongue followed
the path down her thighs, calves and tiny feet still en-
cased in the strappy black heels.

"Muhsin, please." Duchess moaned, eager to feel him
next to her. Soon she was covered by the weight of his
body. A shudder ripped through her from the friction of
his clothes against her. His hands massaged her back as
he kissed her deeply.

Duchess grunted as she pushed the jacket from his
shoulders and then went to work on the vest. She wasted
no time with the buttons on his shirt and simply ripped
them off, desperate to feel his bare skin beneath her fingers.

Muhsin didn't mind, he was just as eager to be rid of
the clothes. He deepened the kiss, squeezing his eyes

shut as he savored the taste of her mouth and the sweet scent clinging to her body. His hands moved to his belt and slid it, his trousers and boxers from his waist along with his shoes and socks.

"Damn . . ." he groaned when their unclothed bodies touched. His last ounce of control had deserted him and he began to favor her body with harsh, wet kisses. Duchess snuggled deep into the bed and let him have his way. Her fingers delved into his hair as his lips and tongue pleasured her shamelessly.

The breathless cries reaching Muhsin's ears brought a smile to his face. Unable to deny the ultimate pleasure of her body any longer, he pulled a condom from the nightstand drawer.

Duchess tensed briefly when she felt him invade her body. His huge hands rested against her thighs as he thrust forward. His brown gaze was narrowed as it studied every expression that crossed her face. Her chest heaved and her entire body quivered incessantly.

Muhsin's thick lashes closed over his eyes when his length was fully sheathed inside her warmth. He nibbled her earlobe and chanted her name almost reverently as he stroked her deeply.

Duchess moved against him, matching his fire with flames of her own. Her nails raked his glistening back before cupping his firm buttocks and drawing him deeper inside. They made love the rest of the night.

Around five A.M., only a couple of hours after sleep claimed her, Duchess woke to see Muhsin fully clothed and watching her steadily. His expression was soft and grew softer still when she looked up at him and smiled.

"Get up and get showered so I can take you home."

Feeling completely relaxed for the first time in weeks, Duchess snuggled into the warm bed. "Are you going to make love to me there, too?" she asked, her gaze past naughty.

Muhsin shook his head. Unable to resist a taste of her, he leaned close. Duchess was delighted, cupping his face in her hands as she wantonly returned the kiss.

"You need to get home and pack," Muhsin said after he'd managed to end the kiss and pull away.

"Pack? For what?" Duchess asked, a tiny frown marring her features.

Muhsin pressed a kiss to her nose. "It's a surprise that'll take all weekend to show you."

"All weekend? Muhsin—"

"Hey," he cut in, tapping his index finger beneath her chin, "now that I have the taste of you, literally, I'm not letting you go yet. I plan on making love to you many times before this weekend is over."

The sultry promise brought the naughty smile back to Duchess's lips. "Can we start now?" she asked, curling her fingers into the neckline of his cream sweatshirt.

Muhsin chuckled, granting her another kiss. Duchess pushed the sheet away and arched her nude body against him. Muhsin moaned and ached to pull the clothes from his back, but he resisted. Duchess was so lost in the kiss, she didn't realize Muhsin had lifted her from the bed and carried her to the master bathroom.

"Take a bath," he ordered, slapping her bottom and running out before she could find something to throw at him.

"When did you find time to plan this?" Duchess asked, as Muhsin's SUV rounded the curving cobblestone drive of the Rogers Inn.

The rustic, three-story, brick Victorian home looked like something right out of a bedtime story. It offered an

unforgettable view of the still lakefront with leafless trees
and gray skies that signaled the approach of winter.

When Muhsin parked the truck and escorted Duchess
out, the inn's proprietor, Matilda Rogers, was on her way
past the establishment's tall maple doors to greet them.
The short, round Irish lady had been close friends with
Trent and Tarsha Vuyani. She was more than delighted
to have their son and his fiancée in her midst. Matilda
repeatedly complimented Duchess and was prepared to
pamper them both. She had a staff member escort them
to their suite right away. Since the inn was located so
close to the lake, the air was extremely chilly; Duchess
said she couldn't wait to snuggle into bed and, of course,
Muhsin agreed. The moment their bags were tucked
away, the door was closed and Muhsin had Duchess in
his arms.

"Sleepy?" Muhsin teased when they were seated at a
cozy back table in the inn's restaurant.

Duchess smiled, pulling her eyes from the bowl of
creamy, thick clam chowder. "Relaxed," she told him.

"Glad you came?"

"Mmm . . . in more ways than one."

"Stop," Muhsin warned in response to her wicked
reply. "I'll take you to bed and forget about dinner."

Duchess raised both hands. "Please don't. I'm too
starved for that!" she cried. Sobering, she cleared her
throat and watched him closely. "Thank you."

"For what?"

"I feel really good. Being here has a lot to do with it."

"Being here or being with me?"

"Both."

Muhsin smiled and looked down at the table. He
seemed to have more to say, but kept quiet.

Duchess kept the conversation flowing by asking how he'd located the inn. Muhsin told her how far back the owner went with his parents. Dinner arrived during the discussion and they couldn't wait to dig in. The delicious feast consisted of fresh-baked breads, aged cheeses, broiled and steamed shrimp, Cajun-fried trout and succulent lobster tail.

Duchess waited until they were enjoying coffee to ask something that had been nagging her since she had known him.

"Can I ask you a question?"

"What's up?" Muhsin prompted.

"Well, do you have any friends? Any real friends? Besides Tan and Roland?" she blurted out.

"What?" Muhsin asked, surprised by the question.

"It's just that everyone I've met, all your so-called friends, seem so . . . wary. Intimidated, even."

Muhsin tapped his fingers to the tablecloth and nodded. "You're very perceptive, Duchess."

"Comes from running my own business, I guess," she said. For the first time, she noticed Muhsin's easy expression grow vulnerable. She could almost see the remorse behind his soft brown eyes.

"I've done things in my past, in my youth, that I'm not proud of," he said, confiding in her.

"Things?" Duchess prodded, bracing her elbows on the table.

Muhsin pulled the sleeves of his sweatshirt over his muscular forearms and grimaced. "I prefer not to go into details, but they've affected a lot of my friendships. I burned a lot of bridges once."

"And now?"

"Now I'm scared I'll never really change."

"Are you trying to change?"

Muhsin's brows rose and he waved his hand before him. "I want to, but I don't think I try hard enough."

"Is something holding you back?"

"I don't know, but it's like a safety net. The . . . meanness keeps me secure."

"Secure?" Duchess asked. She never would've guessed a man like Muhsin Vuyani would be concerned with not feeling secure. "Maybe it's all in your mind," she said, her expression hopeful.

Muhsin chuckled. "I hope you're right."

A few minutes later, Matilda approached the table. "How are things over here, you two?"

"It's incredible. You have a lovely place here," Duchess complimented, smiling into the woman's kind face.

"Well, I'm glad you're pleased, dear," Matilda replied, clasping both hands to her chest. "But you haven't seen the half of it. It's rather nippy out, but the inn has some beautiful paths that run all over the property. Very nice for those long, romantic walks," she suggested in a sly tone. She patted Muhsin's shoulder before she sauntered away.

Muhsin tapped his hand to the table, regaining Duchess's attention. "I'm not tryin' to take any long, romantic walks unless it's back upstairs."

She chuckled and rubbed her arms through the sleeves of the heavy black knit sweater. "You read my mind, Mr. Vuyani."

The next two days were like something right out of a dream. Muhsin and Duchess spent most of their time in bed, though they did take some time to enjoy the outdoor activities at the inn. Through it all, Duchess longed to tell Muhsin how she really felt. His actions and the things they'd shared gave her hope that he could possibly feel the same way.

Duchess and Muhsin decided to take Matilda's advice

and enjoy the gorgeous views. They enjoyed a carriage ride around the large property; an unexpected snowfall turned the landscape into a picture-perfect wonderland. A small cottage sat nestled beneath towering snow-capped trees and tiny bushes. Duchess was delighted to discover that it was a small coffee shop owned by the inn.

When the driver stopped, Muhsin turned to Duchess and motioned toward the cottage. "We can keep going or—"

"Oh, please, let's go in!" Duchess cried. She was like a little child, eager to see the inside of the adorable house.

"Come back for us, Jerry," Muhsin instructed as he whipped back the thick checkerboard blanket covering their legs. He jumped to the ground, then walked around to help Duchess from the carriage.

Their boots crunched against the pristine snow until they reached the cleared walkway to the coffeehouse. Inside, Duchess closed her eyes when a wave of warmth hit her face.

"This is lovely," she breathed, her hazel stare scanning the cozy surroundings.

There were small tables and cushiony armchairs situated throughout the room. Framed black and white photos of winters long past decorated the brick walls and a roaring blaze crackled in a huge stone fireplace.

"This is absolutely incredible," Duchess continued to marvel, once the hostess seated them. "Did you know this was here?"

Muhsin nodded while shrugging out of his brown, leather, wool-lined jacket. "My parents have been bringing me here since I was little."

Duchess shook her head as she unfastened her own three-quarter-length, fur-lined leather coat. "Boy, you must've had some childhood," she said, smoothing her hands against her gray cashmere sweater.

"It was good," Muhsin said, his low voice sounding un-characteristically light as he remembered. "My folks were big on exposing me to lots of things. So I got to travel a lot. I think I was the first kid at my elementary school to go out of the country."

"Hmph. That must've been quite overwhelming as a child," Duchess said.

Muhsin's shoulders rose in a lazy shrug. "I guess, but there were a lot of things about growin' up I would've changed."

"Such as?"

"I spent a lot of time around adults," he explained, shifting his tall frame in the deep burgundy armchair. "Too much time, if you ask me. I think I learned too much too soon and grew up way too fast."

Duchess nodded as she scanned the menu of coffees, cocoas, teas and cappuccinos. "I can relate to that. I was about seven or eight when my father really got his business off the ground. From then on, it was business dinners, dinner parties, cocktail parties and weekend visits to clients' homes. For me, hangin' around grown folks was tons more fun than playing with my dolls."

Muhsin propped his chin against his fist and smiled. "It has its good and bad effects, I guess."

For the next hour, they shared childhood memories over several cups of the delicious, hot beverages served at the coffee shop. It was approaching dusk when they finally returned to the inn.

They decided to continue the conversation back in their suite. They undressed and settled onto the furry beige carpet in front of the strong, crackling fire that cast the only light upon the room. Muhsin rested on his stomach while Duchess straddled his lean body and massaged his back.

"You ever think about having kids?" he asked.

Duchess's hands slowed momentarily against his wide back. "Sure," she replied finally. "Some day."

"More than one?"

"I don't know," she admitted, reaching for the musk-scented massage oil. "My parents never let me feel like I was alone. Besides, I had a lot of family and even more friends."

"But?" he queried, catching the hesitation in her voice.

"I don't know. There were times I felt lonely. Lots of times I wished I had someone my size to share my room and my toys."

"And break your toys and mess up your room," Muhsin teased.

Duchess couldn't help but laugh. "We escaped that, huh?"

"Luckily."

The wood popping from the fireplace was the only sound in the room for a very long time. When Duchess sighed, Muhsin shifted his weight beneath her.

"What?" he asked.

Duchess shook her long hair from her face and grimaced. "Our parents were such great people. It makes me wonder why our fathers hated each other so much."

"Business brings out the worst in people," Muhsin said, tensing a bit at the turn in the conversation.

"Yeah, I guess. . . . I always got the feeling it was about more than that."

"Who knows?" Muhsin groaned, turning over beneath her. "Right now, I think we should use this romantic atmosphere for something more fun than talking about our pops."

Duchess smiled and leaned forward. "I agree," she whispered, her long hair curtaining their faces as her lips touched his.

Duchess woke up to find herself smothered beneath Muhsin's heavy body. Her cell phone was ringing nearby and she tried to inch across the bed to grab her purse.

"No, you don't," Muhsin growled, his hands closing over her hips to pull her back beneath him.

A long kiss ensued and they were both eager to see where it would lead, but the insistent ring of the phone could not be ignored.

"Shut that damned thing off," Muhsin ordered, as he gnawed the side of her neck.

"Let me get it. It'll only take a second," Duchess said, patting both hands against his chest, before reaching for the phone. "Yeah?" she said breathlessly into the phone.

"Dutch? I'm sorry to bother you."

Duchess flinched at the sound of Gretchen's voice. "What's wrong?"

"Jaliel was arrested last night."

"What?" Duchess gasped, sitting up in bed. "What? How? What happened?"

Gretchen sighed. "There was some party. Drugs everywhere, prostitutes . . . It seems that he was entertaining some potential clients."

"Oh, no." Duchess groaned, covering her face with one hand. "Where is he now?"

"I bailed him out this morning."

"Jesus, thanks Gret. I'll be home soon, all right?"

"I'll talk to you later," Gretchen replied before the connection broke.

Muhsin had propped himself on his elbow and was

tracing invisible patterns in the sheet. "When are you going?" he asked when she'd set the phone aside.

"I'll have to get out of here today."

"Wanna talk about it?" he asked, rubbing her back with reassuring strokes.

Duchess turned and pressed a kiss to the palm of his hand. "Mmm-mmm," she said.

Muhsin sat up and nuzzled her ear. "How about a walk? You can clear your head, then we can have breakfast and get you out of here."

Duchess turned grateful eyes on him. "That's the best thing I've heard today."

Gretchen tapped her nails on the receiver and shook her head. She hated to call Duchess, but it had to be done. A sound like shattering glass reached her ears then and she hurried to the living room. She had bailed Jaliel out and driven him back to his condo.

"What the hell are you doing?"

Jaliel didn't bother to respond. He simply sent Gretchen a nasty glare and returned to his activities.

"Jaliel!" Gretchen bellowed, hands propped on her hips. She'd walked into the living room and found that he'd knocked a glass ashtray streaked with white powder off the glass coffee table. "I don't believe you're in here gettin' high when I just bailed your ass out of jail because of this!"

"Get the hell off my back, Gret!"

"Fine," she said. "Let's see you tell Duchess that when she gets here."

"Where the hell do you get off spillin' my business to her!" Jaliel raged, brushing against the table when he stood.

"She employs you, fool, and you were doin' this crap

with possible clients for her business. There was no way I'd keep this from her! You need to shape up, man. This mess is tired!"

"Well, why don't you just do me a favor and ship out. Get the hell out of my house!"

Gretchen eyed Jaliel as though she didn't recognize him. He had changed as much mentally as he had physically. He hadn't brushed his hair or shaved, he reeked of musk and liquor and his eyes were bloodshot and fringed with morning crust. Finally she rolled her eyes and stormed out of the room. "I'm through with you, Jaliel!"

"Good!" he spat, returning to his coffee-table project.

"Feel better?" Muhsin asked as he and Duchess strolled through the lovely grounds of the inn. Obviously, she was still preoccupied by Gretchen's call. "Baby, maybe you'd feel better if you told me what Gretchen said. You're scaring me here, you know?"

Duchess curled her fingers into the crook of Muhsin's arm and massaged the soft tan suede of his jacket. "It's Jaliel. He's been watching the company while I've been away. Now, he's, um, goin' through something like I told you before. But it's very heavy and could possibly ruin his life. We're too close for me to let him go through it alone."

Muhsin nodded, but the muscle in his jaw twitched wickedly at the explanation. He wondered if Jaliel was just a "friend" or if Roland had missed something when he profiled the people in Duchess's life. He managed to push his suspicions aside and took her back toward the inn.

"How long do you think you'll be gone?" Muhsin asked as they strolled along the leaf-cluttered walkway.

Duchess's hands curved into fists. "I'm not sure," she said, nestling her hands into the pockets of her hooded sweater.

"Well, don't be gone too long. I'll miss you."

Duchess stopped walking and turned to face him. "Muhsin, why did you do this?" she whispered.

He gave a quick shake of his head. "Do what?"

"The inn. Everything," she said, praying he would tell her what she longed to hear.

Muhsin reached out and brushed his thumb across her chin. "I've wanted you since I met you. Having you so close and not being able to touch you was driving me crazy."

The response left Duchess cold. It told her Muhsin's feelings were more sexual than emotional and her heart broke a little at the fact. The rest of their walk passed in silence.

Chapter 10

"What do you mean, you're through with him?" Duchess asked Gretchen, who had just told her about the fight. Duchess had returned to Philadelphia and was unpacking at her home.

Gretchen punched her fist into one of the overstuffed pillows on the bed. "I mean, I can't handle Jaliel. The way he spoke to me, girl, I was this close," she said, positioning her index and thumb inches apart.

"Save it, Gret," Duchess ordered with a wave of her hand. "The three of us have had some terrible fights over the years."

"Yeah, but none of them were ever drug-induced."

"How do you know his habit is something new?" Duchess asked, her hands pausing over the suitcase.

Gretchen pondered the question, then shook her head. "I don't know if it is or not," she admitted, watching Duchess shake her head and resume unpacking. "So how was the inn? And Muhsin?"

"It was incredible." Duchess sighed without a moment's hesitation. "We made love and . . . we talked. It was so nice. Unfortunately, I made the age-old mistake of trying to find out where things really stood between us."

"And he didn't say what you wanted to hear?"

"Bingo." Duchess groaned and flopped down on her bed. "I was so upset when I heard about Jaliel, but I am

so glad to be back home. This scheme is harder on me
than I thought it would be."

Gretchen folded her hands across the top of her
denim overalls and fixed her friend with a skeptical look.
"So how are you gonna handle Jaliel? After all, you got
into this with Muhsin to save your company. You can't afford to have Jaliel's mess ruin it."

"I wish I knew what to do about this."

"I take it you're not gonna fire him?"

Duchess pushed both hands through her loose hair. "I
won't know that until I see him, talk to him. Find out
where his head is."

Gretchen rolled her eyes toward the bedroom's carved
ceiling. "Jaliel's head is in a table full of coke."

The remark was crude. Still Duchess had to admit it
may have been true.

"I don't have time for these damn excuses! Just get it
to me now!" Muhsin barked into the speaker, the gravel
tone of his voice adding more fire to the demand.

Roland walked into the office and heard his friend's
outburst. "Duchess is gone, I guess?" he teased when
Muhsin slammed down the phone.

Muhsin shrugged. "Yeah, and?"

Roland laughed, unfazed by his friend's mood. "Don't
even try it. You're goin' crazy without her here. How long
is she gonna be away?"

"Until she handles her business, I guess."

Roland smoothed his hand across his beige silk tie and
took a seat on the arm of the sofa. "Did she tell you what
was going on?"

Muhsin massaged his eyes. "It was something about
one of her friends in Philly. He's been watching the busi-

ness, but there was some trouble she had to go back to take care of."

"And you're all right with her being gone indefinitely?"

"I have to be, don't I?"

Roland eased off the arm of the sofa. "Blaze, man, this is me you're talking to."

"And I got work to do," Muhsin retorted, tugging on the cuff of his navy suit coat as he picked up a folder. When the door closed behind Roland, he tossed the folder aside and leaned back in his chair.

Duchess felt completely rejuvenated, despite her business woes. She stopped by the construction site to check on the annex and was pleased to discover how well it was coming along. Inside the offices of the Carver Design Group, everyone was overjoyed to see their boss had returned. When Duchess made it to the hall of executive offices, she bypassed her own and headed straight for Jaliel's. She stepped inside without knocking and slammed the door shut.

Jaliel whirled around in his leather chair. His dark eyes grew wider when he saw Duchess.

"You've been busy," she noted softly, stepping into the spacious corner office.

"Should I take that as a compliment?" he asked, standing behind his desk.

Duchess pushed her hands into the deep pockets of her black pinstriped trousers. "I wouldn't."

Jaliel nodded. "I guess you're here to jump down my throat about what happened?"

"Could you blame me?"

"It's passed, Dutch."

"Is it?"

"What do you want from me!" Jaliel snapped, his deep voice rising several octaves.

Duchess was determined to remain cool. One of them had to. "I want to know about the drugs. When, why and why here?"

Jaliel tilted his head and seemed confused. "Why where?"

"Jaliel, I know about the visits your dealer makes here."

"That damned Donnette. I told that bitch—"

"Hey, hey," Duchess interjected, stepping closer to the desk. "This has got nothing to do with Donnette. It's about *you* and this foolish habit."

Jaliel pulled the olive-green suit coat from his broad shoulders. "It's none of your business," he grumbled, tossing the coat to an armchair across the room.

Duchess massaged the bridge of her nose. "It damned well is my business if it affects your career here."

"You firing me, Dutch?" he asked, his voice going soft.

"I'd like you to take a leave of absence," she replied after a moment's silence. "I think it'd do you good."

"I disagree."

"You have no choice."

Jaliel uttered a muffled curse. "I can't believe you're in here taking everybody's word over mine. Pushing my back against a wall, forcing me to take a leave of absence."

Duchess's eyes blazed with anger. "I could've fired you. So I suggest you take what I'm offering."

At last, Jaliel realized he was about to get burned and stepped away from the fire. He mumbled below his breath, but took it no further. Duchess stormed out of the office, leaving the door swinging open behind her.

A ringing phone greeted Duchess when she walked into her office for the first time in months. Still steamed from her conversation with Jaliel, she stomped to her desk and snatched the receiver from its cradle.

"What?"

Silence, then a low chuckle met the fierce greeting. "I thought *I* was in a foul mood today."

Duchess shivered when the familiar voice came through the line.

"I miss you. When are you coming back?" Muhsin asked.

Duchess forced herself to remain unaffected by the sweet sincerity in his voice. "I'll be back in time for the wedding," she assured him.

"I don't care about that. I want you with me."

This time Duchess groped for her chair and sat down. "Well, there's a lot going on here and it's only day one. So, I don't really know how long—"

"I'm tempted to come over there."

"You miss me that much?"

"Are you serious?" Muhsin whispered, a soft chuckle following the question. "After what just happened between us, you expect me to leave you alone now?"

Although the question was delivered in a playful tone, Duchess was still saddened by it. "Uh, Muhsin, listen, I really need to go now, so—"

"Hold on a minute. I'll call you later, all right?"

"Mmm-hmm. That's fine," she said tiredly before hanging up the phone.

Starting that day, Duchess buried herself in work, becoming reacquainted with her business and staff. She stayed with Gretchen the night after Muhsin's call in order to avoid speaking with him again. Afterward, she simply hid behind her voice mail.

After two weeks, he stopped calling.

A tiny voice warned her that she should at least make an effort to maintain communication. After all, the last thing she needed was for him to have any doubts about her commitment to their deal. Sadly, an uncharacteristic bout of cowardice set in as her agitation over their situation began to interfere with her better judgement. Finally, she made a mental note to contact Muhsin only about the progress of construction on the annex. Unprofessional? Probably. Cowardly? Definitely. Unfortunately, she could bring herself to do no more.

Thankfully, Duchess's uncertainty over how best to communicate with Muhsin did not extend to her involvement with the annex preparation. The executive staff met at Duchess's penthouse condo to discuss several important details pertaining to the new building.

"So, it looks as though we'll be able to begin operating out of the annex before next spring."

Duchess's announcement was followed by roaring applause. Because everyone was ecstatic to have Duchess back, the business dinner quickly turned into yet another welcome-back party.

Of course Gretchen was in attendance and she lingered behind in order to help with the cleanup when guests began to leave.

"Whew!" Duchess said, dropping to the sofa with one arm shielding her eyes. "Thank God nobody brought up Jaliel."

"I don't think anybody really misses him," Gretchen muttered, stacking round glass saucers atop the coffee table. "When did you talk to him last?"

"Not since the day I suggested he take a leave of absence," Duchess recalled, her face marred by concern. "I hate the way things are, but I think the space is best right now."

"Girl, Jaliel can be one stubborn brotha, not to mention the fact that his habit is breaking him financially. How long can you keep up the silent act?"

Duchess toyed with the gold chain belt around her casual teal linen slacks. "I'll let him pout a while longer, and then I'll go to him," she said. "Men. . . ."

Gretchen's arched brows rose as she agreed with her friend's brief complaint. "Speaking of men, Dutch, have you, um, talked to Muhsin?"

"It's been weeks since I spoke with him."

"What does that mean?"

Duchess shrugged and pushed herself off the sofa. "I don't have time to dwell on it now. There's too much going on."

"And what about the deal?" Gretchen asked as she carried the last of the empty saucers into the kitchen.

"I won't renege. Don't worry," Duchess answered, just before Gretchen disappeared up the short stairway leading to the kitchen.

"Well, you know best," Gretchen said, when she returned to the living room. "And on that note, I'll be saying good night to ya."

"All right, girl," Duchess whispered, pulling her friend into a quick hug. When the door closed behind Gretchen, Duchess loaded the dishwasher then headed upstairs for a shower.

Brian McKnight's softly seductive voice filled the condo an hour later. Duchess relaxed on the living room sofa, combing her wet hair and enjoying the compilation CD she never tired of listening to. After a while, she set the comb aside and leaned back on the sofa. Moments after she closed her eyes, the doorbell rang.

She walked barefoot to the door, decked out in a pair of comfortable gray drawstring pajama bottoms and a snug white T-shirt.

Jaliel waited in the hall, his handsome dark face

clouded by a guarded look. For a moment, he and Duchess simply watched each other. Then, as though the coldness were melting away, he stepped forward and pulled her close. They shared a tight, warm hug that lasted several seconds.

Afterward, Duchess took Jaliel by the hand and pulled him inside. No words were spoken as they stepped through the soft-lit foyer and living room. Each took a seat on the sofa, where the silence continued.

Finally, they spoke in unison.

"Jaliel—"

"Dutch—"

"Go on," Duchess urged, waving her hand.

"I'm sorry, Duchess. So sorry. The things I said . . . forgive me," Jaliel whispered, his dark stare gleaming with sincerity.

"You know I do," Duchess whispered back, leaning across the sofa to pat his knee. "But you know I have to ask how you got caught up in this."

"It's been goin' on for years," Jaliel admitted, knowing the time had passed for keeping secrets. "Like many addicts, I started off with the 'simple' stuff, weed. Somehow, and don't ask me how, Dutch, but somehow I graduated to the most heinous crap."

"Did you ever want to quit?"

Jaliel laughed. "I want to quit now. More than ever, I want to quit. Being in jail . . . if only for a night—I tell ya, it opened my eyes."

"Have you ever thought about rehab?" Duchess asked, folding her legs beneath her on the sofa.

Jaliel smiled at her innocence. "I've done it before, but the trick is staying clean after you get out."

"So you don't want to try it again?"

"I want to try it on my own."

Duchess frowned. "Isn't that dangerous?" she asked,

pushing a lock of hair behind her ear and leaning forward.

"Dutch, after trying rehab, which has failed me more than I care to admit, this may be my only choice. I have got to beat this mess somehow," he said, desperation clear in his deep voice. "I need support." He watched her steadily. "I can understand if you want no part of it. Lord knows, I've already stepped on so many toes, I wouldn't be surprised or upset if you didn't want to be bothered."

Duchess pushed herself to her knees and reached for both Jaliel's hands. "Boy, if you think I'd turn my back on you now, you're crazy."

Jaliel studied Duchess's clear eyes, and what he saw there sent tremendous relief rushing through his body. "Thank you." He sighed, pulling her into another tight hug.

Later, Duchess refilled two tea mugs in the kitchen. Her conversation with Jaliel was still thriving after two hours. The doorbell rang just as she set the tray on the coffee table.

"I got it," she whispered, waving her hand toward Jaliel when he made a move to stand. After brushing her hands over her T-shirt and pj's, she pulled the door open.

Muhsin leaned against the doorjamb. His luscious chocolate gaze narrowed as he took in her surprised expression and the glossy onyx mane that surrounded her slender form. "You wouldn't return my calls, so I had no choice," he explained.

Duchess was speechless. Her eyes widened with each passing second as she stood there with her hand clutched around the door.

Muhsin could barely contain his laughter and leaned close. "You gonna let me in?" he whispered against her ear.

Duchess managed a jerky nod as she moved aside.

Muhsin brushed past her and in a daze she followed him. The man strolled with a natural air of confidence. His steps slowed, however, when he found Jaliel preparing tea in the living room.

"Um, Jaliel?" Duchess called, finally recapturing her voice. "Jaliel Norris, this is Muhsin Vuyani. Muhsin, Jaliel is Carver's president of finance," she announced, fidgeting when she viewed the suspicion on each man's face. "Uh, Muhsin can I get you some tea?"

His expression remained guarded. "No, thanks."

Jaliel, who by now was standing, tilted his head slightly. "I'm surprised to be meeting you in person, Mr. Vuyani."

"The feeling's mutual," Muhsin replied, perching his tall frame on the arm of the chair that was closest to where Duchess stood.

Jaliel began to nod. "I'm glad we were able to work something out with the building annex."

Muhsin's smile was purely wicked when he looked at Duchess. "Yeah, well, I couldn't refuse my fiancée something so important, could I?"

Jaliel could not mask his shock. "Fiancée?" he repeated, looking at Duchess, who wriggled her fingers in the air.

"We didn't get around to talking about it tonight," she stated timidly.

"Obviously," Jaliel said, though there was much more he wanted to say. Instead, he reached into the pockets of his baggy blue jeans and pulled out his keys. "I need to be going anyway, but I'll talk to you tomorrow, Dutch."

"Sounds good," she whispered, rubbing her hands together.

"I'll show myself out," he told her, when she prepared to follow him.

Duchess prayed that not sharing the news of the engagement wouldn't put her and Jaliel back at odds with one another. She jumped when the door shut heavily behind him. Silence settled for a few moments.

"He seemed surprised."

Duchess rolled her eyes away from Muhsin and raked her fingers through her hair. "We didn't have time to discuss it."

"It's been over two weeks."

"Muhsin, things have been so crazy around here. Jaliel's going through a lot."

"That explains it then." He sighed, pulling the sandstone suede jacket from his shoulders.

Duchess folded her arms across her chest. "What?"

Muhsin claimed a vacant armchair. "That explains why you haven't returned my calls."

"I just haven't had time."

"Not even to speak?"

Duchess slammed her hands to her sides. "Muhsin, what? What is it? Why are you here?"

The tiny muscle twitched frantically in Muhsin's jaw as he clenched his hand into a fist. "I guess you don't know when you're coming back?"

"Everything's up in the air."

"And?"

"Look, I'll be back in time to help you pull off your big charade, all right?"

"So, how's Gretchen?" Muhsin asked, determined not to have the discussion turn into an argument. He leaned forward, bracing his elbows on his jean-clad legs.

Duchess smoothed her hands over her arms to ward off the chill touching her skin. "She's fine."

"And the annex? Everything on schedule?"

"Yes, um, actually I just had a meeting about it with my executive staff," Duchess explained, her mood beginning to improve as business became the topic of conversation.

When she moved the tea back into the kitchen, Muhsin

followed. He watched her rinse out the teapot and mugs before wiping down the paneled countertop. After a while, he closed the distance between them.

"So, why haven't you returned my calls?" he asked, his mouth brushing her ear as he spoke.

The familiar chill returned and Duchess shut her eyes tight. "Don't. . . ." she said, inching closer to the sink.

"I missed you," he whispered, this time against the nape of her neck. His hands closed over her hips to settle her back against him.

"I can't handle this right now," she said, even as she arched into his body.

Muhsin wasted no more time with words. He turned her to face him, his soft cocoa eyes caressing her face as though he was trying to memorize it. His wide hand curved beneath her chin to hold her in place for his kiss.

Duchess let her lashes flutter closed over her eyes as his mouth found hers. His tongue followed the lush outline of her mouth before delving past her parted lips. Duchess held on to the edge of his sweatshirt while standing on her toes. Eagerly, she responded to the kiss, emitting tiny moans each time he stroked her mouth.

An instant later, Muhsin had scooped her into his arms. His intention was to find the nearest bedroom. He carried her as far as the living room, where they made love on the sofa.

Hours later, when they lounged in bed, Muhsin questioned her about Jaliel.

Duchess pulled the gray silk sheets beneath her chin and averted her gaze. "I really don't like discussing people's personal problems."

Muhsin smoothed one hand across his bright hair and gnawed the inside of his jaw. "I'd like it if you told me anyway."

"Muhsin—"

"Whatever this is, it's weighing on you. Heavy. I could see that before you left Chicago. Now that you're back here . . ."

Duchess steeled herself against telling Muhsin how much she was in love with him. His concern was obvious and seemed real enough—so much so, she let down her guard and confided everything about Jaliel. When her emotions got the better of her, Muhsin leaned closer and brushed her tears away with the tip of his thumb.

"You shouldn't let this weigh you down. It's not good for you," Muhsin advised, cupping the side of her face in his hand.

Duchess shook her head. "I can't worry about that now. I've known Jaliel too long."

Tiring of the conversation, Muhsin's eyes began to roam her face. His fingers followed a seductive trail beneath the covers. When they stroked the warm area between her

thighs, Duchess gasped and forced her breathing to calm when he ended the caress. He pulled her into the protection of a spooning embrace and she offered no resistance. Sleep visited quickly.

Muhsin reached across the bed for Duchess, wanting her close. When he touched cold sheets, his eyes snapped open. There was no note, but he knew she'd left for the office. Settling back against his side of the bed, his brown eyes studied the patterns in the ceiling and the elegant, feminine warmth of the room. He had been in town more than a week, and in that time Duchess had spent more hours tending to Jaliel or her business than to him. He thought it was admirable, her wanting to help a friend, but he didn't like it. Before any conniving thoughts could enter his head, he rolled across the bed and reached for the phone to make a call.

"Huh?" a groggy voice said when the connection was made.

Muhsin chuckled at Roland's response. "Wake up, man," he ordered playfully.

"What's up, kid?" Roland managed to ask after a while.

"Not much." Muhsin sighed, lying back in bed.

"That can't be true. You've been there more than a week and this is the first call I've gotten."

"Hmph. It's goin' well," Muhsin admitted, smoothing his hand across his bare chest. "Duchess is here, so . . ."

"Man, that in itself makes for a successful trip."

"Damn right."

"So why do I get the feeling you still have complaints?"

Muhsin pressed his hand against his forehead and smiled at Roland's keen perception. "Her friend Jaliel Norris—I could do without him being around."

Roland grunted, familiar with the aggravation in his friend's voice. He was well aware how the man could react to competition of any kind. "So, what are you planning?"

"Not a damn thing," Muhsin assured his lawyer. "I pulled my last scheme with Duchess." *But I'll be damned if I lose her over some sorry bastard's drug problem.*

Duchess made another notation on the questionnaire she'd prepared for her afternoon meeting with the designers and architects. "So, based on the amount of staff and the space at hand, is this layout realistic?" she asked chief architect Cammy Schwartz.

"It's very realistic, Duchess," Cammy answered. "The annex has a dome shape that's going to allow us more working space with its oval design."

The phone buzzed just as they were wrapping up the meeting.

"Yeah, Farris?"

"Duchess, I have Muhsin Vuyani here to see you."

Duchess's hand weakened at her assistant's announcement. She shouldn't have been surprised to hear his name. After all, she had tried to avoid talking with him that week. Her workload and Jaliel had greatly infringed on their time. She knew he had to be upset about that.

"I'll be right out, Farris," Duchess said.

Farris replaced the receiver, then nodded toward Muhsin, who stood looking out of the east window. The tall window on the twenty-second floor offered a fantastic view of the annex.

Duchess showed the group out of her office, then headed to the lobby. She smoothed both hands across her chic pea-green skirt and slowly approached her visitor.

Muhsin smiled when the scent of Duchess's perfume drifted beneath his nose. He glanced her way when she peeked around his arm and studied the construction site.

"It's comin' along," he noted.

Duchess chuckled. "Thanks to you," she reminded him unnecessarily.

Muhsin shook his head. "I never thought the place had so much potential."

"Would you like a tour?"

"Later," he said, his low rough voice carrying just a trace of aggravation. "Right now, I want to know why you left this morning without telling me."

Duchess decided not to continue the conversation there in the lobby. Instead, she curved her hand around his arm and pulled him in step with her. She dismissed the tiny electric jolt that surged through her when she felt the hard bicep beneath the expensive, three-piece, pearl-gray suit. "This way," she whispered, leading him toward her office.

"You looked so peaceful, I didn't have the heart to wake you," she told him once the door was shut. "I left very early," she added, retreating behind her white oak desk.

Muhsin caressed his jaw, tapping his finger against the cleft in his chin. "But that isn't really it, is it?" he asked, looking up when silence met the question.

Duchess cleared her throat and tapped her nails against the polished surface of the desk. She would not answer him.

Muhsin's deep eyes narrowed as his temper reached its breaking point. He slammed one fist against his palm before pinning Duchess with an angry glare.

"What is it with you?" he demanded softly. "One day you respond to me like you can't get enough of me. The next, you act as though you can't stand to be around me. What the hell are you tryin' to tell me? I don't read minds, Duchess." He stopped his tirade when he saw she was crying. A low curse passed his lips.

"I'm in love with you," she whispered, her eyes downcast.

Muhsin looked as though he had been hit. Hard. "What?" he replied, pressing one hand against his chest.

Duchess turned away, allowing her hair to slip from behind her shoulder. She had worn it straight that day. The simple part down the middle allowed the hair to curtain her face. She was grateful for the shield against Muhsin's probing stare.

"I've, um . . . I've known for a while now. I guess I wasn't as good as I thought at keeping my personal and professional feelings separate. I couldn't tell you how I felt," she explained, her words slow and ragged as she held her fist against her mouth. "I couldn't tell you after I insisted we keep this business only. Now it—it's hard.

Too hard." She sniffled loudly as her eyes blurred with tears. Suddenly, she tilted her head back. "But don't worry," she continued, blinking water from her eyes, "I plan to see our agreement through. The sooner, the better and then I'll be out of your life for good."

Muhsin was speechless. His heart practically soared when he heard her admit to her feelings. It had been killing him to think that she may never feel the same way he did. Would she believe him now if he told her he felt the same? Would he want her to believe him? After everything he'd done to bring her into his life, did he deserve her? How could she love him once those deeds were brought to light?

Duchess had finished baring her soul. The heavy silence that followed almost unleashed another round of tears. Obviously he didn't want to hurt her feelings by telling her he didn't feel the same, she thought. Taking a deep breath, she focused on a couple of folders lying on the desk.

"I've got a lot of work here, so . . ." She left the statement unfinished, hoping he would take the hint and leave.

Muhsin knew he had upset her by remaining silent. Still, he was reluctant to change her state of mind. He turned and left the office without another word.

Duchess waited for the door to close. Then she dropped to her chair and cried.

Chapter 11

"Hey, Raphael, any messages?" Duchess asked the evening security guard when she returned home around seven P.M. that night.

"No, but there is a young man waiting to see you," Raphael announced, his lilting Mexican accent clinging to every word.

"A young man?" Duchess whispered, glancing around the huge candlelit lobby. "Where?"

Raphael tilted his head to the left. "The lounge," he replied, smiling when Duchess patted his hand and headed in that direction.

Duchess closed her eyes as she headed to the lounge. The area, complete with a full-service bar, had been designed at the behest of the numerous businesspeople who resided in the building. Of course Duchess knew it was no business associate waiting to speak with her. It had to be Muhsin and she was in no mood to continue the heavy conversation from earlier that day. She knew he'd follow her upstairs if she didn't meet him. Tonight, that would be too much.

Her olive-green pumps ceased their clicking upon the floor when she stepped onto the lounge's thick black carpeting. Duchess let her eyes adjust to the dark atmosphere before heading farther inside the half-empty room. She found Muhsin toward the back and strolled over.

"Glad you came," he whispered, not bothering to stand when she stood before him.

"Did I have a choice?"

"Sit down."

"I really don't want to rehash this," Duchess told him as she settled into the chair across from him.

Muhsin pretended to be confused. "Rehash what?"

Duchess smarted as though he'd slapped her. She couldn't believe he had forgotten what she'd told him. It hurt her more than she cared to admit. "What do you want?" she whispered after several seconds of silence.

"The wedding," he replied, toying with the ice in his glass. "It can take place as soon as we get back to Chicago."

"Right," Duchess agreed through clenched teeth. She prayed her expression was guarded enough.

Muhsin stole glances at her through his thick lashes. He knew his attitude was killing her, but she would never believe him if he told her he had loved her far longer than she'd known him.

"If that's all you needed to tell me, I'm gonna say good night." Duchess sighed, sliding her chair away from the table.

Muhsin stood and dropped a few bills next to his glass. "I'll take you up."

Duchess fiddled with one of the buttons on the three-quarter-length blazer. "I'd prefer if you just left," she told him.

"I insist," he said, taking her upper arm in a gentle hold as he escorted her from the lounge.

Tired and weary, Duchess could offer no further arguments. She allowed Muhsin to guide her to the elevators and to her top-floor apartment. Inside, she headed into the living room and right to the sofa. With a contented sigh, she lay down and closed her eyes. Muhsin walked over to the couch and sat down. He placed her head in his lap. His fingers traced her temples before they slid into the sleek tresses.

Duchess relaxed into his lap and became lost in the sensation of the relaxing scalp massage. When she turned and looked up at him, the emotion in her eyes was unmistakable. Muhsin's fingers tightened in her hair when he bowed his head. Duchess's lips parted instantly for his kiss. She gasped, allowing him deeper access to her mouth. Her fingers inched up to the back of neck to hold him close. Muhsin unbuttoned the blazer she wore, then went to work on the cream silk blouse underneath. Soon he had reached inside to cup one breast in his wide palm. Duchess arched closer when his middle finger slid beneath the lacy bra cup to fondle a hard nipple. The low, ragged sounds he uttered during the kiss sent delicious shivers throughout her body. She wanted him so desperately, but realized she would only be setting herself up for more heartache. Eventually, she found the will to push him away.

Muhsin's magnificent features twisted into something sinister. His expression was murderous as he watched her hurry from the sofa.

"You have to go," she announced, unmindful of her blouse gaping open as she looked down at him.

Muhsin leaned back against the sofa and showed no signs of leaving. "Just like that, you want me to leave?"

Duchess nodded. Her gaze remained steady. "Just like that. I can't handle this," she said, pressing her lips together when his eyes narrowed.

"We are getting married."

"In name only, remember?"

Muhsin braced his elbow on the arm of the sofa and traced the line of his brow. "You expect me to honor that now?"

"Damn right."

"You're crazy."

"It's what we agreed to."

"Well, it seems we've made a lot of agreements that have been broken," he pointed out, his soft cocoa gaze daring her to argue.

Duchess sent him a hateful look, then stomped out of the living room and upstairs. She stormed into her private master bathroom and braced her hands against the lavender marble countertop. She stood there, for several seconds, inhaling deep gulps of air, when she heard the door slam.

"Muhsin, I'm not in the mood to argue," she said. Suddenly she felt him right behind her. He hauled her back against him and she watched him through the huge lit, square mirror. The set look on his handsome face sent a flash of fear through her. He bent her slightly over the sink and unzipped the skirt she wore. It fell with a whisper and pooled around her pumps.

Duchess was speechless. She was unable to offer any verbal or physical resistance. Muhsin was like a man possessed. In fact, he could think of nothing more than having her, having her until he could burn her out of his mind, out of his heart. He knew he didn't deserve her. He'd taken from her the one thing she had to hold on to after her father's death: the company. He'd done it to avenge some decades-old vendetta of his father's. He had allowed that hatred to rule his own actions. But somewhere, somehow it had happened: he had fallen in love with her. She was everything he thought he'd never find.

His hands spanned the supple skin above the lacy edges of her stockings. Duchess's fear was soon replaced by a mixture of excitement and arousal. She let her head fall back against Muhsin's shoulder when his fingers slid past the edge of her panties to invade her body. He winced in satisfaction as a wealth of moisture covered his skin. Duchess ground her bottom into the powerful hardness pressed against his trousers. Her legs parted a bit more when his fingers thrust and rotated inside her.

Muhsin buried his face in Duchess's hair and ordered his desire to cool. This was not the way, he told himself, knowing his frustration had fueled his actions. She'd been confused, and was hurt and angered by his silence when she'd admitted her love. Muhsin was angry with himself as well and the last thing he wanted was to take those emotions out on her. Pulling away, he patted his hand against her hip.

"I'm sorry," he whispered, pressing a kiss to her ear before leaving the bathroom.

Almost half an hour passed before Duchess left the bathroom. Muhsin appeared to be asleep in her bed and she sat next to his prone form. Studying his handsome features relaxed in sleep, she couldn't believe how strong her feelings had become. Unfortunately for her, the gorgeous, auburn-haired playboy wasn't interested in a serious relationship. The phone rang, bringing a shattering end to her thoughts. She had it off the receiver before it could ring again.

"Yes?" she whispered, kneeling next to the nightstand.

"Duchess?"

"Jaliel? Why are you whispering? I can barely hear you."

"I couldn't call anyone else."

"What's wrong?" Duchess asked, fearing she already knew.

"I'm in trouble," he told her, his voice not only soft but frantic as well.

Duchess pushed her hair from her face. "Is this about the drugs, Jaliel?"

"I'm at this club. I ran into my old dealer."

"I take it he's not happy about losing you as a customer?"

Jaliel laughed shortly. "I wish that was all, Dutch. I owe him money. A lot. From the stash he hooked me up with for the party I threw."

"Jaliel!" Duchess gasped, suddenly angry.

"Dutch, listen! The only thing saving my ass is I told Shaunnessy I was calling someone who could front me the money."

Duchess nodded. Obviously that *someone* was her. Of course she had no intentions of paying any money to a drug dealer. "Where are you?" she asked Jaliel, who gave her the name of the club and the address. Duchess repeated the information, then told him she would be there shortly. She dressed in her suit from earlier that day and left the room.

Jaliel, what the hell were you thinking coming here? Duchess asked herself. She angled her black Mercedes into a parking spot, then left the car's comforting interior and inspected her surroundings. The establishment sat on a corner well known for drugs and prostitution. Duchess activated the car alarm and boldly headed toward the club.

Inside, she drew stares from everyone. Clearly she didn't belong there. Still, she carried an air of confidence and no-nonsense that was undeniable. She seemed totally unfazed by the club's hard-looking patrons.

Jaliel sat cowering at a small round table just off the dance floor. Duchess's face was hardened by anger and disgust. She stormed over to him, slamming her hand down on the table.

"Did you bring the money?" he asked, his eyes bright with hope.

"You're already broke because of this. And it's one

debt I won't pay!" Duchess retorted, tempted to laugh at his nerve.

Jaliel's eyes grew wide. "Well, what the hell are you doin' here, then? That's why I called you. I need that money, Dutch."

"We're gettin' the hell out of here," Duchess ordered, daring him to refuse. When she turned, Shaunnessy Wright was standing behind her. Though she had never met Jaliel's infamous drug dealer, she knew it had to be him. She also knew this was a man she didn't care to be around.

Shaunnessy's long face was softened momentarily by a brief smile. "I like the way you repay your debts, man," he told Jaliel, though his dark eyes were sliding over Duchess. There was no mistaking the meaning behind his leering gaze.

"He's not paying any debt," Duchess corrected cooly, propping a fist against her hip. "Not to you," she added.

Shaunnessy took a step forward and folded his arms over the gawdy red silk shirt he sported. "A debt is a debt, Miss. No matter who it's owed to."

Duchess's cold smile was a perfect match to the look in her hazel eyes. "I disagree, especially when that debt is owed to a sorry excuse for a man. One who pushes poison to his own people regardless of their age. You'd probably threaten your own grandmama if she got behind in a payment."

Shaunnessy's easy mood vanished from the tongue-lashing. "Jaliel," he said in a warning tone.

"Look, man," Jaliel whispered, stepping around the table with his hands raised defensively, "she's got no idea what she's sayin'. It's just gonna take a little while longer to get the money and—"

"Forget that! I been waitin' for weeks!" Shaunnessy yelled, his chest heaving rapidly. "I never deal on credit, man. You knew that, but I did you a favor anyway. Now you bring this polished sista up in here to come down on me? You must be crazy!"

Duchess, full of courage and still a bit unaware of how serious the situation was, turned her scathing glare from Shaunnessy to Jaliel. "Let's get the hell out of here," she said, brushing past Shaunnessy.

When Shaunnessy caught her arm, terror shot through her for the first time. She stifled herself from showing it, though her heart raced frantically.

"Obviously you don't know who I am, Miss," Shaunnessy growled, his face inches from hers. "When someone, anyone, owes me money and they give me the run around instead of what they owe, two things can happen. They can either get beat or they can get dead. Which do you prefer?"

Jaliel stepped in then. "Hold it, Shaunnessy, man, she ain't got nothin' to do with this shit!"

"Shut up!" Shaunnessy roared, laying a vicious backhand blow to the side of Jaliel's face.

Duchess screamed, watching her friend reel backward and crash into the table behind them. She moved toward him, but Shaunnessy held her fast.

"Now, I want my money," he whispered against her ear. "Or would you prefer to try me again?"

Duchess closed her eyes, fearing she would share Jaliel's fate. Before her worries could reduce her to a trembling heap, Shaunnessy was jerked backward. Shaunnessy's crew jumped to their feet at once, but found themselves completely helpless. Muhsin stood behind the man, one of his huge hands wrapped around Shaunnessy's neck. The bodyguards knew one move would mean death to their boss.

Muhsin's eyes were narrowed to the thinnest slits as he spoke close to Shaunnessy's ear. "Did I just hear you threaten my fiancée?" he growled.

Shaunnessy's eyes grew wide. Immediately, he began to shake his head. "Man, it was nothin' personal. Just business."

"Business?" Muhsin whispered, his tone losing none of its raspy fierceness. "Does she look like she'd have business with you? Does she?"

"Nah, nah, man."

"Then why the hell are you threatening her?"

"Her boy, her boy Jaliel owes me, man."

Muhsin's hold tightened around Shaunnessy's neck. "So you should be talking to him, right?" he asked, watching the man nod frantically. "Right?" he repeated, insisting on a verbal response.

"Right, right man." Shaunnessy gasped, closing his eyes as though he were praying.

Muhsin wasn't done yet. "So I guess that means you owe her an apology?"

"What?" Shaunnessy cried, shrieking when the vicelike hold beneath his jaw tightened more. "Yeah, yeah, man, I'm sorry, sorry."

"Not to me!" Muhsin bellowed, directing the man's face toward Duchess.

Shaunnessy's eyes were full of tears. "I'm sorry. Very sorry, Miss. Very sorry," he chanted.

Duchess managed a nod, though the rest of her body was tightly clenched.

"Good," Muhsin muttered. Unfortunately, he was still dissatisfied.

The club's speechless patrons looked on in amazement as the tall auburn-haired man released Shaunnessy. Then, in one lithe maneuver, he took Shaunnessy's arm and twisted it behind the man's back. The awkward position resulted in a loud snap that sent a resounding gasp throughout the crowd.

Duchess almost cried out when she heard the bone

break. Horror and fascination shone in her hazel eyes as she watched Muhsin step over Shaunnessy, who writhed on the floor.

Everyone watched the tall stranger with the blazing hair. They retreated a step when he walked past them to pull the beautiful lady close to his side and guide her swiftly to the nearest exit.

Duchess glanced over her shoulder. "Jaliel!" she called, breathing a relieved sigh when he emerged from the crowd and ran toward them.

"Man, thanks for what you did back there," Jaliel rambled on breathlessly as he followed Duchess and Muhsin out to the parking lot. "That brotha's always been crazy."

Muhsin's grip tightened on Duchess's arm and he halted his steps. He turned to Jaliel and watched the man rave a few moments longer. "Listen," he finally interrupted, leaning close to Jaliel. "I suggest you get out of my sight. Now. The way I feel at this moment, I'm apt to snap another arm." With that, he pulled Duchess close and walked away.

Duchess was too weary to say anything and allowed Muhsin to bundle her in his truck. Jaliel stood in the parking lot and watched them drive away.

"Drink it all. Then get some sleep," Muhsin ordered.

Duchess smiled and accepted the big cup of chicken broth he pushed between her hands. "Thank you," she whispered, savoring the warmth from the pink and blue ceramic cup. "Will you be here when I wake up?"

Muhsin tapped her chin with his index finger. "I'm not goin' anywhere. In the morning I'm helping you pack and we're going back to Chicago."

Duchess closed her eyes. She was content with the

idea and desperately in need of time away from Philly and the drama with Jaliel.

Muhsin sat on the edge of the bed and watched Duchess intently. He smiled at her beauty even as his fists clenched in memory of how close he could have come to losing her earlier. Realizing how much he truly loved this woman sent more than a few jolts of fear throughout his body.

Duchess noticed him staring and set the mug aside. "Thank you again," she whispered, her eyes lowering to his mouth when he cupped her face. He leaned close and pressed a soft kiss to her lips. Duchess watched him leave her side and head out of the room. When the door closed, she snuggled beneath the covers.

Muhsin decided he needed a drink, he was so wound up from earlier events. But before he could head to the bar, the doorbell rang and he uttered a muffled curse.

Jaliel waited in the hallway. His expression grew uneasy when Muhsin, instead of Duchess, answered the door.

"I'm not in the mood, Norris," Muhsin informed him wearily.

"I just want to know if she's all right," Jaliel said, pressing his hands against the door before it was closed in his face.

Muhsin watched him for a moment. "She's fine," he replied finally.

"Can I see her?"

"Man, do you know what could've happened to her? How could you ask her to meet you in a joint like that?"

"I wasn't thinking."

The soft-spoken excuse set Muhsin's temper to boil and he clenched his fists. Knowing he was seconds away from attacking Jaliel, he walked away from the door.

Bravely, Jaliel decided to enter. "Listen, man, I love

that woman like she was my own sister! I never expected what happened out there tonight!"

"Well, you should've expected it, fool. That bastard could've killed her!" Muhsin roared, more outraged than he could ever remember being.

Duchess woke amid the raised voices and decided to investigate. She didn't want to see Jaliel, but prayed Muhsin wouldn't take his anger out on her friend.

Jaliel decided it was in his best interest not to argue further. He had no desire to witness the man's wrath again. Still, he didn't want Muhsin to think he took no responsibility for what happened that night.

"Listen, man, you don't have to believe me. I probably wouldn't believe me either, but I do care about Duchess. This mess has got me so crazy, I almost let her get hurt because of it. I swear it won't happen again."

Muhsin propped his elbows against the bar and covered his head with his hands. "I can't lose her, not now. I've wanted her too long," he said with a short laugh. He turned and pinned Jaliel with cold eyes. "If you think I'll let some sorry dope fiend ruin all that, you're very mistaken. Now get out of my sight."

Jaliel knew there was nothing more to be said and quickly left the apartment. When the door closed, Muhsin massaged the back of his neck and closed his eyes. Then, he walked over to the desk and traced the glossy white phone. He debated for a moment before pressing the receiver to his ear and dialing the necessary digits.

A groggy voice answered after three rings. "Yeah?"

"Roland, man, it's me."

"Blaze? What's up?" he asked, frowning when silence met the question. "Duchess?"

"I'm ready for this mess to be over. I'm ready for the whole thing to end," he said, perching on the corner of the desk in the room.

"You ready to tell her everything?" Roland asked once Muhsin had relayed the heated events of the evening. "Blaze?"

"I didn't say that."

"But, you know you have to, right?"

"Roland . . ."

"Look, why do you think you're so stressed over this crap? You say she loves you, so tell her the truth."

Muhsin's striking features hardened. "That's right, Ro. She loves me. She loves me, because I planned it that way. I arranged all this, every aspect of our meeting, because I had to have her. I've done too much to have her and I feel I've also done too much to make her want to stay."

Roland sighed. He prayed his friend would see how close he was to losing everything if he sustained the lie.

"Listen, Ro, I'm gonna hang up now. I just needed somebody to talk to. I, um, I'll talk to you later," he said, hanging up before Roland could say another word.

"What did you mean by that?"

The question was whispered across the spacious living room, but Muhsin heard it clearly. He turned to find Duchess on the stairway and knew she had overheard the conversation.

"Go back to bed," he urged.

"What did you mean?" Duchess insisted, slowly descending the stairway.

"I meant what I said. I care about you too much to lose you."

Duchess was standing in the middle of the living room now. "You said you had done too much to get me. That you'd arranged every aspect of our meeting. I'm asking you to be straight with me here," she said. Her tone was close to pleading. Her light eyes were filling with tears.

Muhsin couldn't stand the sight of her so upset and turned to fix a drink at the bar. Duchess waited silently in the middle of the room. She twisted the beige silk belt on her ankle-length robe and watched him.

"The first time I saw you," Muhsin began, his back toward her, "it was on a photo Isaiah had on his wall, then it was at your father's house," he said, grimacing as he realized how cold and calculating the explanation would sound to her. He had no choice but to continue. "He and my father had been meeting. They began to argue and your dad's secretary called me out there to see if I could calm them down."

Duchess frowned and looked as though she was remembering as well. "I arranged that meeting. My father arrived earlier than we expected."

Muhsin tossed back a shot of gin and poured another before turning to look at her. "It wouldn't have mattered when or where they met. Those two couldn't talk anywhere. Didn't your father ever tell you why he hated mine so much?"

"I never knew he hated him until I came up with the idea for the annex," Duchess said, suddenly growing very cold. She took a seat on the sofa and rubbed her hands over her arms. "I'd never seen him like that. Why?"

"My mother," he replied. "He had plans to marry my mother long before he ever met yours. Trouble was, my father wanted her, too, and he wasn't known for playing fair in business or pleasure. Your father had his revenge, though."

Duchess absorbed what she had been told. Suddenly, she shook her head. "What does all this have to do with us?"

Muhsin tossed back the gin, then poured a third shot. "They wouldn't listen to me, so I left. I, um, wound up in your sunroom," he recalled, taking a seat on one of the armchairs. "That's where I saw you. Asleep. I couldn't move, but I knew I had to talk to you. Your dad found me in there with you and he went completely off. Told me and Pop to get the hell out, but I promised myself I'd see you again."

"So this whole story about the money was a lie?" Duchess whispered, amazed by the intricacy of his plan.

Muhsin waved his hand. "The money is there. Mine when I'm married. My hands weren't burnin' to have it, though. The business is more than enough."

"My God," Duchess whispered, her eyes narrowed in disbelief. "You were never trying to scam your friends, were you? You were trying to scam me."

"Duchess . . ." Muhsin tried to think of something to excuse himself, but he couldn't.

"I came to you, desperate because my business was in jeopardy and I needed your help, but to you . . . to you, my misfortune just helped you plan your scheme more effectively."

Muhsin stood and reached out to her. "Duchess—"

She evaded his grasp, her mind processing what he'd just admitted. She didn't know what to say. Muhsin realized her silence frightened him more than any outburst she could have conjured. He'd hoped she would order him to get out—out of her life. Then he wouldn't have to tell her the whole story and see the hate that was sure to fill her eyes.

"What time to do we leave tomorrow?"

Her question, asked in the calmest of voices, rendered Muhsin speechless for a moment. "Leave?"

"Chicago?" she reminded him, never looking his way as she spoke. "We have to complete the charade. There's a lot at stake."

Muhsin hated the lifeless tone to her voice, but took solace in the fact that she was still willing to return to Chicago. Perhaps he could find a way to correct all that had gone wrong between them. Perhaps there he could find the courage to be completely honest with her. There was no hope for them if he couldn't find a way to do that.

"We leave tomorrow afternoon," he informed her softly, watching her nod once before turning to leave the room as quietly as she'd entered.

Muhsin and Duchess had returned to his Chicago apartment late the next afternoon. Her indifference to him was still in tact, but he knew it would be a grave mistake to try and bully her out of the mood. She'd disappeared to her room, saying she needed a nap before they headed for dinner that night.

Muhsin decided to place a call to his uncle; he wanted to hear the man's advice and prepared himself for a healthy dose of reprimand.

"You were a real fool, boy. I knew you had too much of Trent in you to keep a woman like that."

Muhsin groaned and held his head in his hands. He'd been listening to his uncle berate him for the last forty-five minutes regarding his treatment of Duchess. "I only called for some advice, Uncle Q, I could do without so much of the third degree."

"Well, the third degree is what you deserve," Quincy snapped. "You deserve a hell of a lot more. Besides, I think it's too late for advice. I hope she slapped your face and told you to get the hell out of her life."

"Hmph. She did everything but slap my face."

"Good for her."

"Q, if it makes you feel any better, I've already beat myself up over this enough."

"Not enough for me."

Muhsin rubbed his fingers through his auburn hair. "She told me she loves me, Uncle Q. I have to know if she'll say it again once she knows the entire story."

"Hmph."

"I mean it."

"You love her?"

"I do."

"Funny way of showin' it, boy."

Muhsin sighed and flopped back on his bed. "Just tell me what to do, Uncle."

"I'm not helping you trick that child into staying."

"I want her, Q. Honestly, with no plans, no tricks," Muhsin said, his hand tightening around the receiver. "I love her and I don't know what I'll do if I lose her."

In her room several doors down from Muhsin's, Duchess lounged on her bed. She rested on her stomach, her long hair spread about her like a cape, and talked on the phone to Gretchen.

"I can't believe he dragged you out to a club like that," Gretchen cried, then cursed Jaliel below her breath.

Duchess closed her eyes. "I went on my own, Gret."

"Hmph. Whatever."

"Would you just check on him, please?"

"Ha! You must be crazy," Gretchen said. "I don't have some knight in shining armor to come save me."

Duchess barely managed to stifle another groan. Gretchen had been raving over Muhsin ever since she'd heard about his heroic efforts at the club. The fact that he'd saved their friend put him tops in Gretchen's book. Duchess had decided not to share the rest of the evening's events.

"Jaliel needs someone in his corner, Gret. I'm only asking you not to forget how close we all used to be."

Gretchen was silent several moments. "I'll see what I can do," she replied finally.

"Thank you."

"So, moving on to happier topics, when's the wedding? You better not jump the broom without calling me."

"It's all fake, remember, Gret?"

Gretchen sucked her teeth. "Hmph. You love that man, Dutch. I think he feels the same about you."

"Muhsin Vuyani is all about control. I don't think he has a clue about love."

The remark spouted another one of Gretchen's speeches praising the man. The two young women spoke a while longer before ending the call.

Duchess set the phone aside, then turned onto her back. Her hair was tousled, covering her face and torso. Through the strands, she could see Muhsin leaning against the doorway.

"What?" she said.

Muhsin shook his head. "Nothing," he said in a low voice, his deep-set gaze strikingly intense.

Minutes passed. The two of them stared at each other and longed to indulge in the ecstasy they'd shared.

Finally Muhsin straightened and pushed himself from the doorjamb. "We leave for dinner in two hours."

The waiter seemed to sense the tension between Duchess and Muhsin. He waited patiently for their orders, then asked them to let him know if there was anything he could do to make the evening more enjoyable.

Muhsin tapped his fingers against the cream-and-burgundy-striped damask tablecloth. "Are you going to give me the silent treatment all night?" he asked Duchess, who sat tracing invisible patterns on the cloth.

"What do you expect?" she whispered without bothering to look up.

"I'm trying to make this up to you," he said and then grimaced at how weak the words sounded.

"Spare me the apologies," Duchess said coldly, rolling

her eyes at him. "I only want to know how long it is until the wedding."

"We can have it after we get back," he told her, leaning back to judge her reaction.

"Get back?"

"We leave for Jamaica in two days."

"Jamaica. Jamaica?" she screeched, both shocked and angered by his nerve. "You expect me to go to Jamaica with you, after—"

"Duchess, please. Uncle Q wants to see you. Remember, he invited us to that fish fry? It's this weekend."

In spite of her mood, Duchess couldn't resist smiling when she heard Quincy's name. She couldn't deny the man's charm or the fact that she had really come to like him.

Muhsin cleared his throat and focused on his cognac. "You'll have to call Quincy yourself if you want to decline the invite."

Duchess pursed her lips and reclined in her chair. She studied Muhsin in the stylish tailored suit that highlighted the rich color of his hair. "You always have it figured out, don't you?" she said, her eyes holding no trace of admiration.

Muhsin shook his head, realizing how he had come across. Duchess rolled her eyes and took a sip of her merlot. She turned her attention toward the other diners enjoying the food and atmosphere of the elegant establishment. When she spotted Isaiah and Tia, a delighted gasp left her lips.

"Well, well," she whispered.

Muhsin watched Duchess push her chair away from the table and stand. His eyes clung to the strapless ice-blue dress she wore. When she slapped her napkin on the table and walked away, a frown clouded his face.

"Isaiah," Tia said when she saw Duchess walking toward them.

"Am I witnessing a reconciliation, here?" Duchess asked. She smiled when the couple looked at each other and took each other's hands.

Isaiah's dark eyes twinkled as he watched Tia. "We're workin' on it."

Duchess stepped closer and pressed her fingers to the table. "I'm sorry for what Muhsin put you both through. No one deserves that."

Tia's brown eyes slid across the dining room. "Seems that you two are still an item?"

Duchess shrugged. "It's a long story," she said, trying to hide her grimace.

"Well, maybe we can all get together for lunch and you can tell us about it," Tia suggested, her eyes narrowing when she saw the knowing look pass between Duchess and Isaiah. "What?"

"We've been trying to go out for lunch since this girl's been here," Isaiah mused, a soft chuckle following his words.

Duchess laughed as well. "Maybe the help of a third party will get us together."

The three of them were still laughing when Muhsin joined them at the table. Duchess stiffened when she felt his hand against the small of her back. She missed the hurt look flash in his brown eyes.

"What's up, Isaiah? Tia?" he said, not surprised by their unenthusiastic responses.

Again Duchess brushed her fingers against the table. "I'm gonna say good night, guys. We'll get together for lunch this time," she promised before walking away with Muhsin right behind her.

"What do you think?" Isaiah asked Tia when they were alone at the table.

"They're in love with each other."

Isaiah sighed. "And trying hard to deny it."

"Heaven help that sweet girl," Tia said.

"What was that about?" Muhsin asked as he and Duchess returned to their table.

"I guess even your manipulating can't stop true love," she retorted, digging into her chicken Caesar salad.

The dig brought a smile to Muhsin's lips. *I'm counting on it,* he replied silently.

After dinner, Muhsin headed right back to his condo. When he offered to help Duchess from the SUV, she ignored his extended hand. Before she could walk past him, he caught her upper arm and pulled her close.

Duchess clutched her purse and resisted the urge to melt against Muhsin's wide chest. She allowed him to hold her until they were inside the elevator. There, she wrenched her arm out of his grasp.

"Whatever you think is going to happen tonight, isn't," she assured him, retreating to the opposite side of the elevator.

Muhsin gnawed the inside of his jaw and tried to control his smoldering temper. Unable to resist his basest urges, he moved to close the small distance between them. When Duchess stood firm and raised her chin in defiance, he stopped. He'd never get her back if he lost control now, he realized. His lashes fluttered as he fought a heated battle with his emotions. Thankfully, the elevator made a quick ascent to the penthouse. There, they retreated to their respective rooms. Their doors slammed simultaneously.

Chapter 12

Duchess was ready to scream when the morning of the Jamaica trip finally arrived. She and Muhsin had been walking on eggshells since dinner two nights earlier. To her relief, he was usually gone each morning before she woke. Still, they spent the evenings together at his apartment. The tension there was so thick, it was almost palpable.

Muhsin felt guilt-ridden whenever he looked at Duchess. The tired, drawn look on her lovely face spoke volumes. He knew she had been humiliated, used and, most of all, deceived. He had no idea how to make any of it up to her, but he would die before giving up.

That morning, they boarded the jet silently. Duchess chose her place on one of the armchairs near the window. Muhsin took the chair opposite. They ignored the cozy sofa.

"Mr. Vuyani? Ms. Carver? May I bring either of you anything to eat or drink?" The flight attendant broke the silence with her cheery voice.

Duchess managed a smile, and then nodded. "Hazelnut coffee, if you have it," she said.

The attendant nodded before smiling at Muhsin.

"I'll have the same," he said.

When the smiling blonde nodded and exited the cabin, Duchess uttered a short, cynical laugh.

Muhsin's deep brown eyes narrowed slightly. "What's so funny?" he asked.

"I'll keep it to myself," Duchess said. She smoothed her hands across the sleeves of her silver silk blouse and looked out the window.

Muhsin seemed determined to strike up a conversation. "I could use a laugh."

"It's not funny. I assure you."

"I'd still like to know."

At that time, the captain's voice sounded over the cabin speakers. Conversation was stifled as the captain announced the particulars concerning the flight and instructed everyone to fasten their seatbelts.

Duchess closed her eyes as they began their ascent. Once the jet was airborne, the attendant returned with the coffee.

"So, are you going to elaborate?" Muhsin asked when he and Duchess were left alone.

"I was just thinking or . . . remembering," she sighed, adding cream and sugar to her coffee.

"Remembering?" Muhsin prompted, intrigued by the tone of her voice.

Duchess sipped the savory hazelnut brew and took her time responding. "I was remembering the ride we shared in this very jet."

Muhsin lowered his gaze and concentrated on stirring his coffee. His thoughts also drifted back to that time.

"I guess that was all part of your master plan, too?"

"Uh-uh," Muhsin quickly denied. He set the cup aside and moved off his chair. He knelt before Duchess, again triggering memories of that first meeting.

She wanted to look away, but couldn't ignore his warm eyes.

"That was a chance meeting, Duchess. I told you that and it was true. I swear it to you," he whispered as he knelt before her. "Once I saw you and the state you were in, I couldn't walk away."

"Why didn't you just tell me who you were?" Duchess queried, leaning slightly forward. "Why'd you have to play this game?"

"Do you remember how you felt about me then?" Muhsin threw back, his long brows drawing close. "If I'd told you who I really was, you'd probably have slapped my face and I never would've gotten anywhere with you."

"And look at us now," Duchess pointed out, a sad smirk tugging at her mouth.

The reality of it all drained Muhsin of further discussion and he moved back to his seat. The remainder of the trip passed in silence.

Valet service was just one of the many features available at Quincy's Montego Bay Inn. The establishment resembled a small castle, but it was no less enchanting than a big one.

Water flowed on three sides of the property and reflected beneath vibrant skies that seemed almost close enough to touch.

Duchess heard her name the moment she stepped from the limo. She placed one hand across her brow to shield her eyes against the sun. In seconds, she saw Quincy approaching the car. The man appeared even more lively and gregarious than he'd been several months ago.

"My girl, you are too lovely! You know that, right?" Quincy said, pulling Duchess into a warm hug.

Duchess could only laugh in response. She clung to the boisterous older man, taking comfort in his embrace.

"Boy," Quincy said to his nephew in a dry, disapproving tone.

Muhsin hadn't expected his uncle to acknowledge

him at all. He only nodded in response and watched Quincy turn back to Duchess and escort her into the cozy establishment.

"This all looks so relaxing," Duchess said, her eyes wide as she stared up at the high ceilings, tall columns and polished cream and beige checkerboard floors.

Quincy smiled, pride shining in his brown eyes. "It's relaxing, but running this place is a mutha."

Duchess's laughter lilted through the lobby as she allowed Quincy to escort her to the hall of elevators.

"I hope your room will be suitable," Quincy said as they waited for the bellman to unlock the door and carry the bags inside.

Duchess wanted to kiss Quincy's cheek when she realized she would have a room of her own. "This is perfect," she whispered, stepping into the softly lit gold and cocoa suite. The atmosphere was so cozy and inviting, she felt she could've enjoyed the entire trip from that location.

"You settle in and freshen up. We'll all have lunch in three hours," Quincy announced, pulling the door closed behind him and Muhsin. Outside in the white-washed hallway, his sweet smile faded. "You should be knocked upside the head for what you're putting that girl through. She looks like she hasn't slept in days," he said, eyeing his nephew coldly.

Muhsin raised both hands in defense. "I promise you, Q, I feel lower than dirt for what I did to her."

"Whatever," Quincy muttered, clearly unconvinced. "I'm sure millions of dollars could soften any blow."

"I don't give a damn about the money," Muhsin said, his gaze never wavering. "I'd sign it all over to you now if you asked me to. Duchess is all I want."

Quincy's eyes narrowed and he appeared more than

a little shocked. "A Vuyani giving away money? You *must* love her."

Muhsin closed his eyes briefly. "I do. I swear I do and I don't know how to make her believe me."

Quincy leaned against the doorjamb and watched the bellman place bags in Muhsin's room. "Have you talked to her?" he asked.

Muhsin tipped the bellman, then flopped down into one of the brown velvet armchairs. "Every time we start to talk, she'll say something that cuts me to the bone. She's hurt, I know it, but I can't make myself keep talking once she does it."

"Good for her."

Muhsin ran both hands over his head. "Uncle, can you just tell me what to do?"

"Keep talking to her, boy. Keep talking until she believes in you again. And it wouldn't hurt to tear up that agreement either," Quincy suggested slyly. He rubbed his nephew's head, then left the young man alone.

Duchess relaxed in the lounge next to the bedroom window. She enjoyed the enticing view and the cool breeze that set the floor-length cream curtains billowing. A storm appeared to be rolling in, but the overcast conditions only enhanced the rich green, orange, red and yellow hues of the environment.

She groaned when a knock sounded on the front door. Reluctantly, she pulled herself from the lounge and strolled to the living room.

Muhsin waited in the hall, his hands pushed into the deep pockets of his saggy black shorts. His brown eyes danced at the sight of Duchess looking so cool and lovely in a comfortably stylish white tennis dress and low-slung sandals. Slowly the light left his eyes and he leaned against the doorjamb.

"I didn't come to interrupt you," he began, frowning

down at himself. "I only wanted to tell you I'm sorry. Very sorry." He looked directly into her eyes. "I know you're hurting. I'm hurt, too. It hurts me every time I look at you and see what I put you through with this foolishness."

"Muhsin—"

"Duchess, just let me finish, please," he whispered, raising his hand for silence. "I know this may sound corny, but I was actually starting to believe I could change. In your eyes, I saw the man I wanted to be."

Duchess felt her lashes grow wet and spiky as tears filled her eyes.

"I'm determined to have you forgive me," he said, pushing himself away from the door. "If you can't, then I surely couldn't blame you."

Duchess clutched the door in a death grip. She ached to run to him when he walked away. Instead, she stood there and watched him stroll down the hall.

Dr. Henry Booker chuckled and teased Muhsin about his upcoming nuptials. "I must've read your name five times when I got the invite. You are absolutely the last brotha I thought would ever get married."

Muhsin chuckled as he reclined in a lounging chair. "Hen, you're hurtin' me."

"Hell, Blaze, can you blame me? Are you forgetting all the women who fall at your damn feet? Your fianceé must be somethin' else."

"That and more, man. That's why I'm calling."

"What's up?"

"She's got a friend with a nasty habit."

"Mmm . . ." Henry replied, understanding perfectly. He operated a private rehab clinic in Albany, New York. The place was top-notch and exclusive. It was known and respected for providing tough, unyielding care. "Well, you know her friend would be in good hands."

"I know." Muhsin prayed he wasn't overstepping his boundaries. Still, he knew Duchess was in over her head. She had no idea how much more serious Jaliel's problem could become if greater measures weren't taken. Besides, stepping in to offer some assistance was the least he could do. After all, he'd known Jaliel far longer than Duchess realized. "Henry, have someone there send me some literature on the clinic. This guy needs help."

"Will do," Henry promised. He spoke a bit longer with his friend before the call ended.

Quincy's handsome face reflected pure dismay as he eyed the inviting chef's salad before Duchess. "Sweet girl," he said, "you're killing me here. I insist that you order more than that."

Duchess shook her head. "I'm fine with salad, really."

Quincy rolled his eyes. "You eat like a bird."

"That's far from true, but I'm willing to take your advice here. What do you suggest I order?"

"It's about time," Quincy sang, pulling the menu from Duchess's fingers. By the time he was done ordering, there was enough for at least five people.

Duchess had little time to discuss the lunch menu. The reggae trio onstage was beginning their next set. Moments later, Quincy had pulled her to the dance floor.

Muhsin arrived for lunch some time later. It didn't take long for him to spot the couple twirling around the dance floor. In fact, everyone was on their feet, clapping and cheering for Quincy and Duchess.

As Muhsin looked on, he cursed himself for conniving such an angel. He watched her with his uncle only a moment longer and then waved toward one of the waitresses.

"Yes, Mr. Vuyani?"

Muhsin scratched his brow. "Could I have a phone over here, please?" he asked, smiling at the petite round-faced beauty.

"No problem, sir, and could I bring you anything else?" she asked, more than happy to wait on the handsome man.

"A Red Stripe and whatever they ordered," Muhsin replied, nodding toward Duchess and Quincy.

When the band finished their set, the dance partners took their bows and prepared to head out of the spotlight. The audience had other ideas. Along with the employees, they urged the band to play another song and begged Duchess and Quincy to give them another dance. The couple and the band happily obliged.

Muhsin wasted no time dialing Roland's number. After three rings, he grew impatient.

"Come on, Ro," he whispered, smiling when the connection was made.

"Huh?"

"Roland, it's Blaze."

"Huh?"

"Roland, wake up, man."

Roland yawned. "Man, what the hell . . ." He groaned, running a hand across his face. "Where are you now?"

"Jamaica. Listen, I need you to wake up and get on something for me."

Roland yawned again. "Shoot," he instructed.

"I need the document Duchess and I signed. I need you to express mail it to me here."

"What the hell is goin' on, man?" Roland asked, now wide awake.

Muhsin chuckled. "I want you to mail it to me so I can tear it up."

"Tear it up? You really want to do this, Blaze?"

"I really want to do it."

"She might not believe it's for real, you know?" Roland said, pushing himself up in bed.

"That's why I want you to draw up an amendment or something overriding what we signed."

"You're sure about this?"

"Never been more sure about anything."

Roland massaged his bald head and realized he was witnessing a metamorphosis in his friend. "I'll get right on it first thing," he said. "Where am I sending this?"

Duchess couldn't believe she was out of breath when Quincy seemed not to have broken a sweat. The waitress returned to the table just as they reclaimed their seats. In minutes, the wide round table was filled with fresh-broiled, grilled and golden-fried seafood. Everyone loaded their plates and prepared to indulge in the delicious feast.

"Uncle, what's goin' on outside with all the builders?"

Quincy slapped his forehead when he heard the question. "Lordy, I almost forgot!"

Duchess's eyes narrowed. "What is it, Quincy?"

"The party I told you two about, the costume ball—it's tonight."

"Tonight?" Duchess cried, laying her palm alongside her face. "I don't have a thing to wear."

Quincy shook his head and covered her hand with his larger one. "No need to worry, sweet. We have a lovely boutique that's been stocked with all sorts of outfits for the festivities. We even cater to gentlemen," he added, sending a pointed look in his nephew's direction.

Muhsin's shoulders rose beneath the deep purple T-shirt he wore. "I don't know if I'll be there."

Duchess winced at the twinge of disappointment she

felt at his words. When he caught her staring, she looked away.

Quincy's annual Masquerade by the Sea was in full swing when Duchess arrived. Of course, she was decked out in stunning glamour. Her trip to the inn's boutique proved more than successful. She wore an ankle-length creation that shimmered with gold beads trimming the high choke collar, fitted bodice and the train that flowed behind the ankle-length straight skirt. A matching head-band covered her forehead and half her face. She caught the attention of every man there. Unfortunately, she was only looking for one man in particular.

Quincy found Duchess standing at the ballroom entrance. He rushed over and treated himself to a hug.

"The most beautiful woman here," he declared, pressing a kiss to her cheek before leaning away to admire her attire.

"How did you know it was me?" Duchess asked, her voice almost drowned out by the upbeat pulsing reggae.

Quincy, who wore no mask, rolled his eyes in pretend disgust. "I never forget a woman," he told her, then winked suggestively.

Duchess smiled at his teasing, but the questioning look in her eyes could not be masked.

"I haven't seen that boy, either," Quincy said, reading her mind.

"Well, he didn't say he'd be here."

"Well, we aren't going to stand here and mope," Quincy said. He was determined to wipe the sadness from her face. "Let's dance." He pulled her into the grand candlelit room.

Fruity mixed drinks, delectable hors d'oeuvres and lilting island music set the scene for the party. Duchess indulged in a thick, creamy piña colada while enjoying the view from one of the balconies skirting the ballroom. The cool breeze and the thundering waves against the beach were an intoxicating combination. Duchess was halfway through the delicious drink when suddenly she knew she wasn't alone.

Muhsin stood behind her, his handsome face partially covered. The black mask with wine-colored trim was most effective in hiding the set look clouding his features.

"You changed your mind," Duchess whispered. She was breathless and unnerved by the man's quiet presence.

"I'm glad I did," he replied after another moment of silence. Slowly his eyes trailed the radiant gown before a pained look flashed in their cocoa depths.

Duchess clutched her glass a bit tighter when he leaned close. She wanted to melt when his raspy voice touched her ears.

"Duchess, do you think . . ." Muhsin silenced the question and turned his head away.

Concerned, Duchess moved even closer and pressed her hand against his chest. "Finish."

Muhsin couldn't bring himself to say anything more. Instead he pulled the mask away from his face, his other hand closing around Duchess's waist to bring her closer.

The glass Duchess held slid to the balcony's brick floor with a shatter. The sound went ignored as her fingers curled around the lapels of Muhsin's black tuxedo. She met his kiss eagerly, her tongue tracing the even ridge of white teeth before delving farther.

"Duchess . . ." He moaned, dropping his mask to encircle her tiny waist with his arms. His fingers caressed her bare spine like a musician strumming the strings of a guitar.

Duchess arched herself into his hard, warm body and

slid her fingers through his luxurious red hair. She
heard his low growl and shivered in response to the soft,
savage sound. Faintly she heard her name being shouted
in the distance. She squeezed her eyes shut and tried to
drown out the interruption.

Unfortunately, the crowd would not be ignored. The
guests were eager to have their host and his beautiful
dance partner entertain them. When Duchess heard
Quincy's bellowing voice, she extracted her fingers
from Muhsin's hair and pressed her hands against his
shoulders.

"I better get in there," she told him. Her body trembled beneath his fingers in response to the passion
smoldering in his eyes.

Muhsin nodded, but it took a moment before he loosened his hold around Duchess's waist. When she walked
back into the party, he leaned against the balcony railing
and watched her go.

The ball was incredible; a mixture of fun and romance
danced through the air. It was no surprise that Quincy's
soiree was hailed as one of the biggest social events of
the year. Inn patrons and locals alike raved over the lavish decorations, food and music.

After she and Quincy favored the audience with three
high energy dances, Duchess surrendered to the weariness washing over her. She realized Muhsin had excused
himself from the party some time ago and she decided
to do the same.

The heavy wind and looming clouds delivered rain
that only seemed to add something magical to the already glorious evening. Duchess took a slow stroll to her
room, but bypassed the door when she approached it.
Instead, she headed to Muhsin's door. Several moments
passed as she debated whether or not to follow her desire. Choosing to give in, she rapped the doorknocker

softly. Some seconds passed before she decided he wasn't there.

She had taken only one step backward when the door opened. Duchess caught her bottom lip between her teeth and watched him with wide, innocent eyes. He appeared as uncertain as she, standing barefoot wearing only his trousers, and with his white shirt unbuttoned and hanging outside his pants.

Duchess held her breath as her striking hazel stare slid from his handsome face to gaze wantonly at his wide, exposed chest and rigid abdomen. She took one step toward him just as he reached out to haul her hand against his body.

Their lips met in a devastating kiss, almost frightening in its intensity. Muhsin's deep moans held a tinge of helplessness as his big hands rose to massage her neck. Duchess pushed the door closed before slipping her arms around his lean waist. Her seeking hands found their way beneath his shirt and she grazed his sleek, caramel-toned skin beneath her long nails.

They moved through the suite, kissing passionately. Muhsin's hands rose to Duchess's hair and he went about removing the pins that held the elaborate coiffure in place atop her head. He whispered soft, raspy words of appraisal as his fingers became covered with sleek, silky strands.

Duchess's fingers were splayed across Muhsin's back. She gasped each time the chiseled muscles flexed and rippled. Muhsin kissed her as they moved into the depths of the suite. He made a brief stop by the nightstand in the bedroom, slipping something into his trouser pocket before urging her to move on. Duchess was so engulfed by the pleasure of holding him, she didn't realize they had moved to the terrace. When the cool breeze and droplets of water touched her skin, she pulled away and looked to-

ward the sky. Her lashes fluttered closed when she felt his
mouth along her throat. His tongue traced the pulse beat-
ing there. She shivered against the water on her skin and
the electricity his kiss produced.

Muhsin removed her gown with expert care and
tossed it inside the room. His shirt was plastered to his
wide torso. Duchess peppered his handsome face with
tiny kisses. Her lips caressed the long line of his brows,
his deep-set eyes, the length of his nose and curve of his
jaw. She peeled the soaked shirt from his back, then
went to work on the trousers.

Meanwhile, Muhsin had undone her garter clasp and
was peeling the stockings down her long legs. He let her
finish with his trousers and knelt before her as the pants
fell around his ankles. Duchess felt her knees weaken as
his hands glided over her legs. His mouth touched every
inch of bare skin as he eased the hose farther down. Her
heels and hose removed, he focused his touch on her
thighs. Duchess threw her head back, her mouth opening and closing as she savored the rain pelting her face.

Muhsin's lips touched the middle of the wispy gold
lace panties and he smiled when Duchess's entire body
jerked in response. His huge hands closed around her
lush cinnamon-brown thighs and held her in place. He
nudged the underwear with his nose, tugging aside the
wet garment using his strong teeth.

Duchess caught her lower lip between her teeth
when she felt Muhsin's tongue slip inside her panties.
As he thrust into the part of her that ached for his attention, she begged him not to stop. Muhsin pleasured
her relentlessly and without shame. His tongue delved
deeper every time, forcing Duchess's cries to grow
louder with every stroke. When she thought she could
stand no more, he pulled her down before him.
Duchess cupped his face in her hands and kissed him.

She moaned while suckling the taste of her body on his tongue.

In one easy, fluid movement, Muhsin stood, taking her with him. He carried her to one of the cushioned lounges on the terrace. He reached for his trousers, extracting the condom packet he'd pushed into his pocket when they'd stopped earlier in the bedroom. After settling back and putting the protection in place, he made her straddle his lap. Duchess leaned forward and pressed rain-drenched kisses to his neck and chest. Muhsin gripped her hips and settled her down over his throbbing masculinity. He felt her body stiffen when his wide length filled her completely. Then the inner walls relaxed and she was moving over him in reckless abandon.

The storm raged with increasing fervor, but the enthusiastic lovers hardly noticed. Muhsin's sensuous deep gaze was narrowed as he worshiped the beauty above him. His hands closed over her breasts, squeezing and fondling as he enjoyed the moistness of her feminity.

Duchess's hair hung like wet, black ribbons covering her face and body. She resembled some wild, sensual creature as her hips rotated and bounced over the magnificent male beneath her.

Their loud cries were muffled amid the thunder and rain. Of course, the exquisite climax lost none of its intensity. Muhsin held Duchess in a tight, possessive hold as his satisfaction rushed forth. Duchess quivered above him, grinding her hips against his to savor the moment as long as possible. Muhsin pulled her close and cuddled her against his chest. They shared a deep, lazy kiss as the rain and wind swirled around their bodies.

A tiny purring sound rose from Duchess's throat the next morning. She lifted her head off the pillow and braced herself on her elbows. She was sprawled on her stomach, alone in the middle of Muhsin's bed. *Just as well,* she thought, in no mood for heavy conversation on the heels of such an explosive night. She eased from the dark satin covers and slipped back into her gown. It took no time for her to shower and dress once she returned to her own room. She changed into a comfortable red sundress and strappy low-heeled sandals before heading out for breakfast.

The beach was as lovely as it had been the day before. Remnants of the storm were practically nonexistent. Duchess ventured out to the dining room veranda and chose a table with an umbrella. It was the perfect spot to enjoy the serene view.

"May I bring you anything, ma'am?"

Duchess smiled up at the tall, dark waiter. "A cup of your berry tea and a menu," she said.

"Very good, Miss," the young man replied, his shoulder-length dreads swinging merrily when he walked away.

The clash of the deep blue water against the surf caught Duchess's attention once again. The sound of the waves reminded her of the night before and she smiled at the scandalous memories filling her head.

"Excuse me, Ms. Carver?"

Duchess held her hand over her eyes and smiled at the man who had approached her table. He was tall with a smooth brown complexion and sparkling dark eyes. His wide grin revealed a perfect set of capped teeth.

"Sheldon Mitchell," he announced, offering his hand.

Duchess obliged. "I guess you already know me?"

Sheldon nodded. "I only wanted to come over and compliment you on your performance last night."

"My . . . performance?" Duchess replied, beginning to wonder how private her rendezvous on the terrace with Muhsin had been.

"Yes, you and Quincy brought the house down."

Duchess was both relieved and amused as she laughed. "Oh, yes! You caught that, huh?"

"Everyone did."

Duchess and her admirer were still discussing the party when the waiter returned with tea and a menu. She looked up to thank him and caught a glimpse of Muhsin across the veranda.

"Excuse me, Sheldon. I see my breakfast partner coming this way."

Sheldon glanced across his shoulder and smiled. "He's a lucky man," he replied, turning to shake Duchess's hand again. "I only wanted to tell you how much I enjoyed the dancing. It was one of the best parts of the evening."

Duchess placed her other hand over his. "I appreciate that."

Sheldon walked away just as Muhsin reached the table.

"Hope I didn't interrupt anything," he said, pushing one hand into the pocket of his saggy khaki shorts.

Duchess shook her head. "That was just someone who wanted to compliment my dance with Quincy."

Muhsin chuckled. "I agree. You two make quite a pair."

"It's your uncle with all that energy," Duchess declared.

"Nah, you held your own. I caught a few minutes of the performance before I left."

Silence settled between them as memories of the party surfaced. After a moment, Duchess cleared her throat and sent Muhsin a questioning stare.

"_____ _ight," she began, "you were going to tell me ____ ___ _hey called me to dance. We, um, didn't ___"

_____ers along his hairline and recalled his unease from the night before. "Do you ever think you could forgive me?" he asked finally.

Duchess couldn't help but smile at the uncharacteristic look of uncertainty on Muhsin's handsome face. It was very appealing. Leaning forward, she pressed her hand against his cheek and looked directly into his eyes.

"I don't think we should be getting into this right now, do you?" she whispered, and smiled when Muhsin closed his eyes and pressed a kiss to her palm.

He watched her intently for the longest time. His rich, vibrant gaze studied every inch of her face and her dark hair whipping around her in wild disarray. "I don't think I'm ready to hear your answer anyway," he admitted, grimacing at the faint sound of his voice. "How could you forgive me so soon after . . . I put you through something so cruel?"

Duchess massaged the back of his neck, her fingers playing in his close-cut hair. "You could have been much more cruel. True, you could've found a better way to . . . win my affections, but I believe you regret what happened," she said, though part of her wondered if her feelings were a result of the closeness they had shared the night before.

"Damn right, I regret it," Muhsin said. "I'm determined to show you I mean that."

Duchess shook her head, sending him a knowing look. "I already said I believe you regret what happened. There's no need for any more theatrics, I assure you."

"I want you with me, Duchess. I want you with me because you want to be, not because you have to be."

Duchess traced the curve of his mouth with the tip of her thumbnail. "Muhsin, please, can we just not talk about this right—"

"I know, I know. I won't push an

"Thank you." Duchess sigh

unshed tears.

need to tell you."

"What?"

"I love you."

"What?"

you and I wanted to say that long before you

w you felt."

laughter followed his words. "But there's something I

"Sorry I upset you," Muhsin whispered, though soft

s up with you coming and going like the wind?"

ath his arm.

ss asked, not pleased by his sudden reappearance.

e pallet—plate in one hand and a folder

d behind her and frowned. Muhsin

placed the plate and

huge crab leg of the

ing a long sliver of her

of triumph lifted from her

ncy for his tutelage.

glow on the

t to the

the

whi

at the airpo

to know you, a chance to fa

anything to make it r

wanted

AlTonya Washington

"Long before?" Duchess asked, her eyes riveted on his

"The...

wanted you...

day. Once her plate was prepared, she headed o...

beach. A late evening sunset cast an ethereal...

already magnificent setting.

Duchess sat on a burgundy pallet an...

between her legs. She selected a...

cracked it skillfully before remo...

succulent meat. A tiny gasp...

mouth as she thanked Q...

"Good job."

Duchess glance...

stood next to th...

tucked bene...

"What...

Duch...

...usin uttered a soft cu... from the sand. "I grew up knowing ho... much your dad and mine disliked each other."

before

"Because of your mother?" Duchess said, watching him nod.

"I'm sure your father was deeply in love with your mother, but he never forgot what Trent Vuyani did to get my mother by his side."

Duchess stood slowly, spreading her hands in confusion. "We've been through this already. I know all this."

"But what you *don't* know is how much your dad wanted to make mine pay for it," Muhsin said, pushing his hands into his pockets as he watched her. "When Vuyani experienced that rough period, my father swore your dad was to blame."

"My father?" Duchess whispered in disbelief. "That can't be. How?"

"Did he ever tell you about a company called Phaley's?"

Duchess shook her head.

"Vuyani and Carver were both in the running for that account. It could've singlehandedly restored Vuyani to success. Somehow your father got that account. Trent was sure he'd done something underhanded and vowed to make Jerome Carver pay for it."

Agitated and confused, Duchess shook her head. "What does all this have to do with what's happening between us? I assume you're going into all this ancient history for a reason?"

"It wasn't hard for my father's battles to become *my* battles," Muhsin confessed, folding his arms across his chest as he stared down at the white sand. "When he became ill and they said he wouldn't make it, I was mad at the world and anyone who'd ever done or said a thing against him. But, like my father, I also didn't need a reason to be ruthless," he added with a self-loathing smirk and took a few steps toward the waves crossing the sand. "Of course, the upset with Carver was forgotten until you contacted me about wanting to buy that building. I decided Carver Design Group would make a nice addition to Vuyani, and being that it was experiencing trouble, it would be even easier to acquire."

Duchess took a few steps toward him. "This is why you wanted controlling interest?" she asked.

He nodded, partially turned toward her. "It is."

"But you didn't get it."

"Not from you."

The spine-kissing shiver returned and Duchess wasn't so sure she wanted an answer to her next question. "What exactly are you trying to tell me?"

Muhsin turned to face her more fully. "I'm sure it's been brought to your attention. This issue of shares being sold?" he said, noticing the gradual widening of her eyes. "Vuyani went after your shareholders. We played on their worries about the company's troubles. With all our holdings, it was easy to mask who the shares were really being sold to."

Duchess began to pace the sand deliberately, in deep thought. "But I held sixty-five percent in total," she reminded him.

"You're forgetting the sixteen percent I requested as part of the building's sale."

"Forty-nine percent. Still not controlling interest," she countered.

Muhsin felt sick inside. Explaining his plan in detail brought a clarity he'd not seen before. How could he ever expect her to understand why, when he could scarcely understand it himself?

"Muhsin?" Duchess called in an attempt to shake him from his thoughtful state.

"You're forgetting Jaliel," he said softly.

Duchess went completely still. "Jaliel," she repeated in a flat, lifeless tone. "What about Jaliel?"

Muhsin retained eye contact, though he winced as her

gaze turned colder. "We discovered his drug problem long ago. To sustain it, he turned to gambling and only succeeded in acquiring more debt. He was happy to sell once the offer was made."

"But sell what? Jaliel didn't have—" She stopped herself, realization mingling with the disbelief still clouding her eyes.

Muhsin was nodding. "Yeah, we discovered the five shares he held. Part of his signing bonus when he went to work for your dad."

Duchess massaged her temples as though it pained her to think. "How could you use that? Use him?"

"I didn't know him," Muhsin said, rolling his eyes over how pathetic an excuse it was.

"Would it have mattered if you *had* known him?" Duchess whispered, her gaze growing blurred. "You could've stopped this long ago—long before I signed those papers," she breathed, squeezing her eyes shut to prevent the shed of unwanted tears. "You could have stopped this at any time and you didn't."

"Duchess—"

"What?" she whispered, raising her hands in a gesture of defeat.

Muhsin had no words, none good enough to justify what he'd done. Looking into her eyes, he could see her shock and disbelief being replaced by something else. He had prepared himself to see hatred filling her lovely eyes. Nothing prepared him for the hurt he saw instead.

Betrayal was a feeling difficult to stomach under any circumstance. When the betrayer happened to be the one you loved, the one you thought loved you, it was a pain like no other, Duchess thought. Standing before Muhsin, her mind barely registered the cool water curling around her feet between her toes as it rushed the sand in mounds of creamy foam. After all he'd told her, only one word filled her mind: love. He said he did, but could he even be capable of such an emotion? Her heart said, *Forgive this*. Her mind said, *Let him go*. A choice between the two was not forthcoming. Without another word, she turned and ran. It was the only choice she seemed able to make.

Chapter 13

Muhsin wasn't surprised when Duchess left Jamaica. He knew she needed time. But when one week passed, then another, he began to worry. His instinct told him she'd run to the only place she felt safe, the only place left that she felt was truly her own. From his office, he placed the call to Philadelphia that he'd put off for weeks.

"This is Gretchen Caron."

"She's at her father's place, isn't she, Gretchen?"

"Muhsin?" Gretchen whispered, shocked to hear the low, raspy voice grating through her line.

"Isn't she, Gretchen?" he repeated.

"Muhsin . . ." Gretchen sighed, running one hand through her short curls. "I don't know if I should. She trusts me."

"I know that," Muhsin assured her. "But know this: I won't stop calling until you tell me. I mean it, Gretchen. Even if I have to come out there."

"Can't you just give her a little time?"

Muhsin squeezed his eyes shut and rubbed his fingers through his bright hair out of sheer frustration. "I only want to know if we can move past this or . . . if it's too much to forgive. If she tells me there's no chance for us, I'll accept it and that's the truth. I owe her that much at least."

"Muhsin, I know—"

"No, you don't know," he whispered. "I love her. I've done horrible things and what's bothering her is my fault. I admit that, but I have to know if there's the smallest chance. I have to hear her tell me either way."

Though she didn't know Muhsin Vuyani well, Gretchen had no doubt the man was deeply in love with her best friend. Still, she had an obligation to keep Duchess's confidence. "Look, I'm sorry, Muhsin. I really can't tell you anything. I'm sorry. Good-bye."

Muhsin pulled the phone away from his ear when he heard the disconnecting click. He placed the receiver gently on its cradle and tapped his fingers against the number pad. A moment later, he pushed everything from the desk and slammed his fist down hard against its walnut surface.

Gretchen dialed out again the moment she hung up with Muhsin. Duchess had retreated to her father's home in the suburbs. Gretchen prayed she was still there.

"Yes?"

"Lord, Dutch, you sound like death!"

Duchess massaged her tired eyes and grimaced. "Thank you very much."

Gretchen closed her eyes. "Honey, I'm sorry. I just hate seeing you like this."

"I know."

"Um, I had a call from Muhsin a little while ago," Gret said, hoping the news would improve her friend's mood.

Silence greeted the news. Duchess felt her heart flutter at the mention of Muhsin's name but quickly dismissed the sensation.

"He really wants to find you."

"You didn't tell him anything?"

"No, Lord, no. Dutch, I do know how to keep a secret, you know. Honey, he misses you and wants to make things right. He said—"

"I don't want to know."

"Duchess—"

"Gret, please," she urged, the tears that had been pressuring her eyes now bursting forth. Her sobs rose softly. Gradually, they gained volume.

Gretchen massaged the bridge of her nose and cursed herself for upsetting her friend. She hung up the phone without saying good-bye.

Duchess stared at the cell phone perched on its charger stand. It had been ringing on and off for the last hour. Every call was from Muhsin and she didn't know how much longer she could keep herself from answering.

"Time to get rid of this thing," she said, padding barefoot across the bedroom to snatch the cell from her bureau. This time the number on the faceplate wasn't Muhsin's.

"Jaliel?" she said once the phone was pressed against her ear.

"Duchess, thank God."

"Where are you? What—"

"Dutch, wait, listen. I—I need money."

"Where are you?"

"I'm all right, don't worry."

But Duchess did worry. It was easy to tell Jaliel wasn't "all right," as he'd proclaimed. His voice sounded shaky and hollow and he coughed frequently. "How much do you need?" she heard herself asking.

"How much can you spare?" he asked with an uneasy laugh.

"Jaliel . . . does this have anything to do with Shaunnessy Wright?"

"Duchess, no, hell no. I swear. I haven't seen him since that night."

Duchess's heart went out to her friend. Hearing his distress, knowing how desperate his situation was, tore away at her. Still, she steeled herself against going completely soft. "Why not sell your shares? They'd bring you a comfortable amount," she asked.

Silence.

"Jaliel?"

There was a heavy sigh over the line and then a shudder as though he was crying. "I never meant to take you through this, Dutch. I got a lot to answer for and you're the last person I should be asking for help."

"Jaliel—"

"No, Dutch, it's not your responsibility and I'm sorry for everything."

"Jaliel, wait!" Duchess cried, fearing he would end the call and do something foolish. "Just wait. I'll send you the money."

"Duchess, don't—"

"Jaliel, stop, please. I want you to promise me something."

"Anything."

"Get help, *please*. Rehab, a support group, time off— anything. Just please don't do this to yourself anymore."

Silence.

Duchess closed her eyes and told herself he'd heard her. "Now," she said, "should I put this in your checking account or—"

"No, it's closed. Just wire it to me, I'll get it."

Duchess closed her eyes and sat on her bed. "When will I see you?"

Jaliel hesitated. "I'll be in touch," he said finally.

Swallowing past the sobs in her throat, she nodded. "I'll send money right away. I love you, please be careful."

Jaliel sniffed and cleared his throat. "I love you, too, Dutch. Thank you."

The connection ended, yet Duchess continued to hold the phone against her ear.

"You really didn't think the conversation was over just because you started crying on me, did you?" Gretchen asked when she arrived on the doorstep of the Carver estate two afternoons later.

Duchess offered no response. She left the door open, though, and headed back into the house. All the drapes and blinds had been drawn for most of the week. The peaceful silence that filled the large home was almost eerie.

"You look awful," Gretchen blurted out, following her friend into the house. "I can't believe you let yourself go like this because of a man. I don't care how fine he is."

When Duchess turned, her eyes glistened with tears. "He says he loves me. Everything should be fine, but it's not. Why is that, Gret?"

The simple admission softened Gretchen's heart. "Come here," she ordered, pulling Duchess into a tight embrace. After a while, they pulled apart and Gretchen smoothed Duchess's long hair back across her shoulders. "Have you eaten?" she asked. "Or showered, for that matter?" She laughed when she saw Duchess smile. "Come on." She turned Duchess toward the grand black-carpeted staircase that branched off to opposite wings of the house.

Upstairs, Gretchen washed Duchess's hair. Then she ran a hot bubble bath and let her soak in the beige claw-foot tub while she prepared a light supper. Afterward, she laid out a pink T-shirt and white cotton pajama bottoms before helping Duchess from the tub. Gretchen let her dress while she went back downstairs to prepare hot tea.

"So, what's going on?" Gretchen asked later in Duchess's bedroom, where they were enjoying the herbal brew.

"All I know is that I'm scared."

"Of Muhsin?" Gretchen squeaked.

Duchess swirled the lemon slice in her cup. "Of giving my heart to him and never really knowing why he didn't stop this and if it's all still a game to him."

"Honey . . ."

"I know what this started as, but he says it was all a plan to get me to fall in love with him. When he said he loved me and then told me about the stock, I suddenly wondered who the man was I was falling in love with? Was he real or was it just part of the scheme?" she asked, her stare wide with apprehension.

Gretchen set her cup aside, then scooted closer to Duchess on the bed. "I don't think it was part of the scheme and I don't believe you do either. I think Muhsin was more than content to do his father's bidding, but he never counted on falling in love with you. I think when he finally admitted that to himself, things had gone way too far."

Duchess shook her head. "But why couldn't he just tell me all this back then? The situation may have been far gone, but not nearly as much as it is now."

Gretchen hated the desperation she saw in Duchess's eyes. "Sweetie, I'm sorry, but these are answers I don't have. To get them, you'll have to talk to Muhsin."

"I know," Duchess whispered, managing a smile as she reached for Gretchen's hand. "I love you for being here, though."

"Where else would I be?" Gretchen whispered before pressing a kiss to Duchess's cheek. "Right now, though, I'm gonna get out of here and let you rest and eat your dinner."

"So you're leaving me here alone to eat your cooking?"

Duchess said, mock suspicion coloring her words. "Don't you think I need someone on standby . . . just in case?"

Gretchen giggled. "Girl, hush!" she ordered, pulling Duchess close for another hug.

Arm in arm, Gretchen and Duchess strolled toward the front of the house.

"Be careful in this rain," Duchess cautioned, pulling her friend into another tight hug. "The forecast says they're expecting conditions to worsen, and this road from the house tends to flood quickly."

"Get some rest," Gretchen said soothingly, knowing Duchess's rambling had virtually nothing to do with the afternoon's weather conditions. "Stop worrying," she finished, then headed out the door.

The road leading from the Carver estate was growing deep with water just as Duchess had predicted. Still, the yellow cab made a valiant trek up the curving lane. The treacherous journey was of little consequence to the cabbie, who'd been promised a fifty-dollar tip for the trip.

Let her be there, Muhsin prayed, unconsciously clasping his hands as he held them against his forehead.

The cab jerked to a halt right at the front door and Muhsin squinted past the rain-streamed windows toward the house. Other than the automatic track and flood-lights surrounding the grounds, he couldn't determine whether anyone was there.

"You want me to wait, man?" the driver asked.

"No need," Muhsin said, seeing the door opening.

Duchess tilted her head and frowned at the cab. When she saw its passenger, her expression cleared and she held on to the door for support. She noted that Muhsin's features appeared sharper and more guarded. To Duchess, he had never looked more incredible. She steeled herself against melting before him. She was about to ask what he was doing there, but he brushed past her and into the house. Then she noticed the suitcase.

"What is this?" she asked, her voice seeming to echo in the large foyer.

"Close the door," he ordered, then walked over and slammed it shut himself.

"What are you doing?" Duchess asked again, this time clenching her fists.

Muhsin jerked out of his heavy navy-blue bomber jacket. "How long did you expect me to stay away?" he asked, his deep cocoa gaze pensive and unwavering.

Duchess's eyes flickered toward the black leather suitcase he'd brought in. Muhsin smiled at the question in her eyes.

"Don't worry, I came here straight from the airport. I won't be staying," he promised.

Duchess simply turned to walk away.

"I'll go as soon as we talk," he added, bracing himself for her anger when she halted her steps and turned around.

Her eyes were narrowed and probing. "Talk about what? A simple business arrangement that was actually a plan to manipulate my feelings, or about how you continued to flat-out lie to me when you knew how I felt about you?"

Muhsin watched her stomp out of the foyer. He ran one hand through his wavy, damp auburn hair and followed her into the kitchen.

Duchess began preparing a plate of the steamed mixed vegetables, rice pilaf and warm rolls. Muhsin took a plate from the wooden dish rack and helped himself as well.

They ate in silence for several minutes before Duchess set her fork down and watched Muhsin suspiciously. "Why are you doing this?"

Muhsin continued to eat as he answered. "You know I love you. I told you that many times and I meant it. I screwed up—worse than that, I betrayed you, and, call me a fool, but I still think we have a chance and I pray you're thinking the same."

Duchess held her hands clenched so tightly, her nails almost pierced her palms. Her appetite disappeared and she left the table. Muhsin pushed his plate aside, then leaned back and closed his eyes.

Later, after Muhsin had toured the entire house, he walked toward a shallow light that cast a peaceful yet solemn effect upon the home. He found Duchess upstairs in her darkened bed chamber. She was leaning against one of the open French doors, watching the rain pelt the balcony railing. Long, white, gauzy drapes billowed about her slender form.

Duchess closed her eyes when she sensed Muhsin's presence in the room. Her nostrils flared when the scent of his crisp cologne drifted beneath her nose. Muhsin crossed his arms over his chest and leaned against the opposite French door. They stood in silence for the longest time, listening to the wind and rain mingling with the soft thunder in the distance.

"I've learned a lot in the time I've known you," Muhsin said, finally breaking the silence, his gaze still focused straight ahead, "and I've acquired a wealth of patience. When you're ready to talk, I'll be right here." Without another word, he left the bedroom.

Duchess was up early the next morning. She'd been unable to sleep with Muhsin in the house. She hoped he hadn't awakened, and decided to head downstairs. She passed the den on her way to the kitchen and stopped. One of the twenty-four-hour sports channels was still broadcasting, but Muhsin was asleep.

She tiptoed into the room and stole a moment to watch

him, smiling when his soft snores reached her ears. Slowly, she reached out to trail her slender fingers over his hair and face. The caress stopped when she brushed the curve of his mouth. She shook her head, then clicked off the TV and left the room.

In the kitchen, she prepared coffee and flipped on the TV. The day's top story was the weather. Rain was in the forecast for the rest of the week. Some areas could even expect flash floods. That day was set to be the last one for fair travel.

"Oh, no," Duchess said, groaning and remembering the suitcase Muhsin had brought with him. "He's got to leave before the storm gets worse." If he stayed, she'd never be able to resist him.

Muhsin walked into the kitchen while Duchess was adding cream to her coffee. He peered around her, his hand resting on her hip. "There enough for me?"

Duchess nodded and was about to move aside when Muhsin's grip tightened. His long lashes closed over his eyes as he inhaled the soft, airy fragrance that always clung to her skin.

"I miss you so much. I want you with me always," he whispered in her ear.

Duchess's lashes fluttered and she wanted to melt into his hard frame. Finding the will to resist, she jerked away. "Muhsin, you've got to get out of here before lunch."

He grimaced and reached for a mug. "After we talk."

"We don't have time for that now," she snapped, panic coming to her face. "I'm sorry if this isn't working out the way you hoped, but you cannot stay here. I want you to leave. I mean it!"

Fascinated by her mood, Muhsin leaned against the counter and watched her. "What's goin' on?"

Duchess saw no need to hide the truth. "The storm's

getting worse. You could be stuck here if you don't go today."

"Rained in, huh?" Muhsin remarked while filling his mug to the brim. "Well, it's not the most romantic way I'd like to spend my time with you, but it'll do."

Duchess slumped against the counter. "Can't you just let me go?"

"No," he said. "I've waited too long to have you to lose you now."

There was no anger on Duchess's face when she looked up at him. "What kind of game are you playing this time?" she asked and was struck by the hurt look that flashed on his handsome face.

He raised his hands. "No games, I swear. If I was playing games, I'd never have told you everything in Jamaica."

Duchess whipped her terry-cloth robe around her body and sent him a scathing look. "Taking my company and using one of my dearest friends to do it. Admit it, when you told me you hoped to change, to be the *best* man on the *inside,* that was all a lie, wasn't it?"

Muhsin set his jaw in a grim line. The muscle there twitched frantically as he watched her leave the kitchen. Why couldn't he just accept that it was over? *Because,* he silently admitted, *she is worth the fight. She is most definitely worth it.* "Stay cool, man," he whispered to himself. "She'll come to you. She has to."

Muhsin thought Jerome Carver's home was breathtaking. Still, he cursed its size and would've preferred something a bit cozier. After the episode in the kitchen with Duchess, he'd called for a car. He was promptly informed that all roads in the vicinity of the estate had been closed due to flooding. Muhsin couldn't decide if being stranded there was a blessing or a curse. He and Duchess had roamed the mansion for hours without seeing each other once. Around four P.M., he decided to get some work done and went into the huge library he'd located during his tour the day before. He had already decided on the perfect spot to settle down and spent close to ten minutes selecting books from the towering bookcases. He saw Duchess across the room just as he was about to settle in and begin his work.

"I'll leave," she said.

"Stop," he said, just as she moved off the long blue and green sectional sofa. "I think the room is big enough for the both of us, hmm?"

Duchess hesitated before resuming her spot on the sofa. She pulled a heavy mauve sweater over the green halter top she sported and tried to continue her reading. Unfortunately, her eyes were riveted on Muhsin.

"I called for a car. All the roads in the area are flooded," he said, feeling her watching him. "Looks like I'm here for the duration." He finally looked up at her.

"What do you think this is going to accomplish?" she asked softly.

Muhsin heard her clearly. "I'm not here to accomplish anything." He set his work aside. "I've already come clean and I want to make this right. All I can do is wait for you to come around."

"Why do you think I need to come around?" Duchess said, the honest admission setting her on edge.

Muhsin's grin was confidence personified. "Because you love me."

"A mistake."

"You don't believe that."

"You have no idea what that company means to me," she said softly, shaking her head. "To you it was just an acquisition, just a thing to soothe your need for revenge for the moment. You took and you took and you kept taking. I told you I loved you and still, no change." She shoved her book to the floor when she moved off the sofa. "And you think *I* need to come around?" she questioned pointedly before walking from the room.

"Damn," Muhsin cursed, berating himself for goading her. *Let her be,* a voice warned. He didn't listen.

He found her perched on the edge of her bed. She was facing the open French doors, where the rain pelted loudly against the balcony furnishings. Still, he could hear her sobs and went to her. Duchess averted her face when she felt the bed give beneath his weight.

"Muhsin—"

"Shh . . . I only want to be near you," he said soothingly, brushing his nose across her cheek.

Duchess needed the same and more. She turned, her lips seeking his. When his tongue thrust deeply, possessively inside her mouth, she whimpered and brought her hands to his face. She traced the sleek line of his long brows and the length of his nose. Her tongue dueled with his, stroking the even ridge of his teeth. Muhsin's brows drew close as he lost himself in the sweet kiss and the feel of her touch. Gradually, his fingers ventured beneath her sweater and he groaned at the feel of her silken skin underneath. Duchess rubbed herself against the pronounced bulge pressed against Muhsin's sweatpants. He broke the kiss and stared down at her for a moment. What he saw in her eyes encouraged him to go on. He pulled the sweater over her head and went to work on the fastening of her jeans. Shortly afterward, she was nude and Muhsin vowed that if he could have her just once, he would not take her again until things were resolved between them.

The wind and the rain's constant pelting against the windows took them back to the steamy night in Jamaica where they made love amid a violent storm. A shiver of decadence raced through Duchess when she rubbed against Muhsin's still-clothed form. Her fingers splayed through his hair and across the back of his neck while she placed tiny kisses along the strong line of his jaw.

Muhsin dipped his head and tugged her earlobe between his teeth. He suckled the soft flesh as his fingers charted a path down Duchess's hip and thigh. Again, she arched against him as his thumb brushed the highly sensitive flesh of her femininity.

"Muhsin, please . . ." She moaned, eager to feel him stroke her there.

He didn't disappoint her. His fingers sank into a wealth of creaminess and he pleasured her until her soft cries became screams. Duchess felt him move away and her eyes snapped open. She saw him easing down the length of her body, dropping wet, openmouthed kisses to the curve of her breasts, the slope of her hips and tops of her thighs. His massive hands curled around her there and he parted her legs. For a moment, he simply absorbed her scent, then his tongue traced her most intimate possession.

Duchess slid her hands through her long hair as he enjoyed the exquisite treat. Her legs trembled when his tongue invaded her body to pleasure her. Each thrust was deeper and slower. He eased his hands beneath her buttocks and lifted her closer to his mouth.

Duchess grew orgasmic, but Muhsin continued. He stroked her shamelessly as she quivered and gasped. He withdrew and pulled the T-shirt and sweats from his body. Without the barrier of clothes between them, that sweet friction was more intense. He retrieved his leather valise from the nightstand and took out a condom. With protection in place, he draped one of Duchess's shapely legs across his shoulder and sank his rigid arousal past the soft flesh that ached for more attention.

They found a mutual rhythm, their hips rocking in perfect accord. Again, Muhsin's hands slipped beneath Duchess's bottom to draw her closer. The increased penetration drew a sharp cry of pleasure from her lips.

The encounter, erotic with a sweet wildness they both craved, lasted for hours.

Delicious smells of breakfast coaxed Duchess from her sleep. She was wrapping the sheet around her body when Muhsin walked into the room.

"Hungry?" he asked, smiling when she nodded. "Come on."

Duchess noticed that a table for two had been set near the balcony.

While Muhsin poured the flavorful hazelnut blend coffee, Duchess looked outside. The rain was coming down in sheets and showed no signs of stopping. Duchess chose her place at the table and watched as Muhsin prepared her plate. There were sliced cantaloupe and honeydew melons, fluffy cheese omelettes and lightly buttered toast. Her hazel eyes slid across his powerful hands and onto his wide chest and chiseled abdomen. The black cotton pajama bottoms hung low on his lean hips. When he turned around to set a plate before her, she gasped.

"What?" he asked, his gaze snapping to her face.

Duchess swallowed and shook her head. "Nothing. I—nothing."

Muhsin pressed his fists against the table and frowned. "What?" he insisted.

"You—your back, I—I'm sorry," she whispered.

Muhsin went to the huge polished oak dresser and turned. In the mirror, he saw a multitude of scratches crossing his back. Pure male arrogance and cockiness were blatant in the grin that appeared on his face. "I'll heal. I'm glad you enjoyed yourself," he said, soberly coming to kneel beside her. "We just needed each other, that's all." He wanted her to understand that the situation was still unsettled. He stood, pressing a kiss to her mouth and smiling when he felt her kiss him back.

After breakfast, Muhsin took the dishes downstairs, but Duchess made no attempt to leave the room. Instead, she changed into a pair of jean shorts and an orange T-shirt. She chose a few movies and made a cozy pallet in the bedroom's living area. By the time Muhsin returned, she was already settled on the floor watching the first film.

"What's this?" he asked, reclining on the sofa.

"*Final Diagnosis,*" she replied, flipping her long hair across her shoulders as she switched positions on the floor.

Muhsin watched the beginning credits roll. "What's it about?"

"It's a psychological thriller about a psychiatrist who falls in love with his patient's married sister," she replied slowly, sounding a bit unenthused by the plot.

"Come here," Muhsin called, hearing the weariness in her voice.

Duchess didn't resist and moved to lean on his legs. Rain pelted the windows and the movie played while he stroked her hair.

"Did Gretchen tell you I called?"

Duchess nodded against his knee as she replied, "I was scared. I didn't want to talk to you." Muhsin's hand stilled and he smarted as though he'd been slapped. "Scared? You think I'd ever hurt you?"

"Not physically hurt me," she clarified, "but hurt me just the same."

"Duchess, I don't—"

"Muhsin, wait," Duchess insisted, sitting up as she spoke.

"When I saw the lengths you went to just to woo me and then . . . everything with the stock . . . I got scared."

"Why?" Muhsin whispered, his face clouded by confusion. "You deserve to feel every bit of what you're feeling and I deserve to hear about it."

Duchess shook her head. "I don't know. Maybe it was the fact that you could be so cold and calculating, all in the name of love. It started to make me feel like a prize, a thing you were trying to win, not love."

"Duchess, I meant it when I said I was through scheming. I meant *everything* I said to you on that beach."

"I believe you did," Duchess said. "I just . . ." *I just want to know why. Why you let this go on when you knew how I felt? Do I really want to know?* Unable to answer those questions or pose them to Muhsin, she groaned and held her head in her hands.

"Shh . . ." Muhsin said, pulling her back against his leg. He continued to stroke her hair and they spent the rest of the afternoon watching movies.

Later that evening, Muhsin woke and lifted his head off the sofa. Duchess had fallen asleep with her head on his knee. He smiled, then flipped off the TV and lifted her into his arms. He placed her on the bed and was about to leave when she called his name. He settled in next to her and pulled her into a spooning embrace.

When Duchess awoke a few hours later, Muhsin was looking right at her.

"Hungry?" he asked.

She smiled. "Definitely."

"Wanna help me make dinner?" he asked, already scooting off the bed.

Duchess followed. "What'd you have in mind?"

"Remember when I told you about my recipe for stir-fry with herb marinade?"

Duchess's hands stilled on the loose ponytail she was

fixing. "Yeah, I remember," she said softly, thinking how that evening seemed to take place a lifetime ago.

In the kitchen, they worked in silence. Duchess chopped vegetables while Muhsin selected the herbs needed for the marinade. In the midst of their preparations, he pushed a folder before her.

"What's this?" Duchess asked, opening the long, silver folder.

Muhsin focused on separating herbs. "Something I wanted to give you in Jamaica," was all he said before he left Duchess to sort out the rest on her own.

Her frown deepened when she recognized the document they had signed months earlier. She pulled it from the folder and waved it in the air.

Muhsin set aside his plate of herbs and wiped his hands. He took the document from her fingers and ripped it in half.

"What's this supposed to mean?" Duchess asked when he handed her the torn papers.

"I don't want that damned annex between us."

Duchess's eyes narrowed. "The annex?"

"The arrangement can't stand as it is. I can't even hope to work this out with you as long as we have that contract hanging around."

Duchess looked down at the counter. "I appreciate the gesture, Muhsin," she began, reluctant to continue, "but I'm sure this isn't your only copy."

Silence followed the observation, and then Muhsin began to laugh. Duchess turned to him with wide eyes. "I'm sorry. I shouldn't have said that," she said, thinking he was too humiliated to do anything other than laugh.

Muhsin ran one hand across his face. "I'd think something was wrong if you *hadn't* said that."

"So?"

"Look in the other side of the folder," he instructed.

Duchess did as he asked and found another document inside. Her eyes scanned the page and she realized he was overriding the original agreement. Also included was a document transferring ownership of the fifty-one shares of stock back to the Carver Design Group.

"We can sign the originals with Roland when we get back to Chicago. I simply wanted you to see this beforehand."

Mouth agape, Duchess could only stare at the papers for a few moments. "Why did you do this?"

"Because I love you. Like I said before, no tricks, no games and no contracts," he said, turning away when the ringing of the phone pierced the room.

Duchess was slow to set aside the papers. Finally, she answered the phone. "Duchess Carver," she said.

"Duchess, it's Roland."

"Hi, Roland, you're looking for Muhsin, I assume? Hold on," she said before the man could say another word.

Muhsin left Duchess in the kitchen and took the call in the den.

"Hey, man, sorry I bounced without telling you anything," he told Roland.

"Oh, I figured you were somewhere in Philly. Duchess doesn't sound quite like herself," Roland noted.

Muhsin grunted, massaging the bridge of his nose. "That's an understatement."

"How's she doing?"

"It's a mess. She doesn't trust me. Thinks my being here is part of another scheme."

"Damn."

"Hell, Ro, I can't blame her. After all the mess I put her through, I'm surprised she didn't call the cops when I showed up on her doorstep. If she doesn't believe I'm for real after getting rid of those documents . . . I don't know."

"So what will you do if she tells you it's over?"

Muhsin didn't want to think about that, but knew it was a valid question. "I won't do anything to get her back. As much as I love her and want her in my life, I'll let her go before I play another game with her."

The dinner was a success: stir-fried vegetables in a crushed herb marinade, soft cheese biscuits and fresh salad. The scratch of the utensils against the dishes, the grandfather clock ticking away the minutes and the rain falling outside were the only sounds in the air.

"Whew, that was good, if I do say so myself," Muhsin said, boasting and rubbing his stomach with both hands. "I don't know about you, but I'm stuffed."

Duchess smiled and set her empty plate aside. "Yes, it was good. I couldn't eat another bite."

Muhsin pushed his chair back and stood. "I'll clean up in here," he offered.

Duchess waved her hand. "I'll get it, don't worry."

"You sure?" he asked, one hand pressed against the front of his hunter-green T-shirt.

"Mmm-hmm. I'll be up in a minute."

Muhsin watched her a moment longer, but offered no further argument.

Much later that night, Muhsin was in bed going over a draft for the proposal he'd been working on. He was so engrossed with work, he didn't notice the door opening. Several seconds passed before he caught movement from the corner of his eye. He looked up and saw Duchess standing a few feet from the king-size bed.

"You all right?" he whispered, watching her nod. His deep-set eyes slid from her face to her attire. She looked incredible in the lavender see-through nightie with her long hair wound into a loose ball atop her head. Muhsin felt like a little boy viewing something he knew he shouldn't. Somehow, he managed to keep his composure.

Duchess approached the bed and removed the books

and pads from the gray satin comforter. Then she strolled to the head of the bed and pulled the papers from Muhsin's loose grip. She let them fall to the floor.

"Duchess . . ." he managed to say when she straddled his lap.

"Why?" she whispered simply. Her expression was a picture of uneasy anticipation.

Muhsin shook his head, completely confused by her question.

Duchess bowed her head for a moment before looking back into his eyes. "Why wouldn't you tell me the entire story before things went so far? When I told you I loved you, didn't that mean anything?"

"It meant everything," Muhsin assured her in a fierce tone. "Duchess, I never thought I'd hear you say those words. When you did, I was ready to say them, too. Then I thought about everything I'd done and I knew there was no way you could still feel the same once you discovered that."

"So why didn't you just tell me everything then?"

"Because I was selfish," he answered without hesitation. "I know that now. Maybe I knew it all along and just couldn't admit it. I wanted to keep you and I believed you'd run if I was totally honest."

Duchess pressed her lips together and took a deep breath. "What made you decide to tell me? This never had to come out."

Muhsin's smile reflected no humor. "I found that I didn't just want to *keep* you. I wanted to love you and I wanted you to love me in return. That couldn't happen without my being honest. Regardless of the consequences, if I couldn't tell you the truth, then I truly was incapable of loving you. I wasn't lying when I said I wanted to be a better man," he confessed. His hands roamed her thighs with subtle possessiveness. "I only want to hear you tell me that there's a chance for us. It's the only reason I came here. If you say there's no hope, I'll hate it like hell, but I'll accept it."

Duchess offered no response and cupped his face in her hands before pressing a soft kiss to his mouth.

"Duchess," Muhsin said in soft protest even as his hands settled on her thighs.

"You won't have to accept that," she spoke against his mouth before deepening the kiss. Her tongue thrust softly and repeatedly into the dark cavern of his mouth.

"Duchess, wait. . . ." he said, this time curling his hands around her wrists. It was some time before he attempted to pull her away, however. Her womanhood nudging his arousal sent a shudder through him. When she slipped her fingers into the waistband of his sleep pants, he jerked her away.

"Do you know what you're doing?" he asked, his low voice rough with love and desire.

Duchess leaned close. "I know."

Muhsin held her away. "Are you sure? I don't think I can stop if you change your mind halfway through."

"I won't do that," she promised, smiling when he began to pull her close. She settled more snuggly into his lap and favored his neck and collarbone with quick kisses.

Muhsin let go of his reservations and gave in. He allowed Duchess to take the lead and rested his head back against the carved design in the cherry-wood headboard. Duchess dropped kisses on his chest, her tongue reaching out to flick the tiny male nipples. She traced the muscles defined in his abdomen, her nose nudging his navel when she inched down. Muhsin sighed when he felt her against the front of his pants. Duchess smiled at the satisfaction on his handsome face and continued her sensuous assault on his manhood. She pulled the snaps loose and let her lips trace the powerful length of his maleness. The sound of Muhsin whispering her name urged her to continue. She added her tongue to the caress, thoroughly acquainting herself with the most sensitive area of his anatomy.

Muhsin's fingers disappeared in her dark hair as he held her head close to his body. Duchess's surprising skill left him weak and more aroused. His long lashes fluttered and he opened his eyes to find her pulling the gown over her head. His hands went to her breasts and his mouth followed shortly after. Duchess threw her head back and massaged his shoulders while his lips and tongue feasted on her erect nipples. Gently, she put protection in place, then settled herself over his throbbing hardness and eased down.

Muhsin grunted when he felt her sheath his body. He took more of her breast into his mouth as he thrust into her femininity.

Duchess rocked her hips in wild abandon for several minutes, crying out shamelessly as a powerful wave of sensation enveloped her. She begged that he not let the moment end too soon, realizing she was approaching her powerful climax.

"Why? Why now?" Muhsin asked when they lounged in bed later that night.

Duchess outlined a hard pectoral with the tip of her nail. "I didn't want to lose you either. I do love you, Muhsin. So much."

Unable to respond, Muhsin closed his eyes and offered a prayer of thanks.

"I was too afraid to tell you how I felt," Duchess said. "This whole thing was supposed to be business, and then . . . I break my own rule and fall in love with you. Then I found out what was really going on and I wanted to hate you when all the time I was really angry with myself for falling in love with a fantasy."

"Duchess, I—"

"Muhsin, listen," she whispered, raising one hand. "Yes, I hurt. I hated you all over again. I knew I couldn't go on hating you, but I didn't know if I could, if I should trust you, trust myself. I believe your feelings are sincere, and when all is said and done, I guess your scheme was foolproof after all."

Muhsin rubbed both hands over his close-cut auburn hair and grimaced. "Scheme. That word is always gonna be there, huh?"

Duchess shrugged. "I'm afraid so. I'd like to try moving past it, though. I'd like to try moving past all of it."

"So would I."

A moment or two passed in silence. Then Duchess stretched like a lazy cat. "So what now?" she purred, favoring the man next to her with a sultry stare.

Muhsin grinned, his deep dimples appearing. "Well, I don't know about you, but I'm all talked out."

"So?"

"So," he said, pulling Duchess across his body. "I predict we won't be getting out of bed for a couple of days."

Duchess giggled. "Only a couple?" she asked, trailing her mouth across his jaw.

Muhsin nuzzled her cheek. "We got a wedding to plan, remember? That is, if you still want me?" he asked, looking up into her face, his warm gaze expectant.

Duchess hugged him tightly. "I want you. Always. I love you."

"I love you, too."

They sealed the words with the sweetest kiss and spent the rest of the week in passionate splendor.

Chapter 14

Back in Chicago, Duchess laughed as she and Ophelia conversed by phone that morning. For the last fifteen minutes, the two young women had tried unsuccessfully to settle on their agenda for the day.

"Well, why don't we just have lunch first and then we can go to the dressmaker's afterward?" Duchess suggested.

"Spoken like a woman whose stomach doesn't expand every time she eats," Ophelia retorted.

Duchess burst into laughter. "Girl, you're crazy!"

"What?" Ophelia cried, pretending to be offended. "I'm serious."

"Please, Ophelia. I mean, what size do you wear, anyway? A size negative-one?"

Ophelia giggled. "I knew there was a reason why I liked you."

"So, it's finally settled. We'll meet at the Chop House at noon sharp," Duchess said, marking a check in her calendar next to her notation to confirm lunch with Ophelia. "I'll be stopping by the florist's as soon as I get out of here."

"You need me to go there with you?"

"Nah," Duchess drawled, tucking a loose tendril of hair behind her ear. "I can handle it. I've already chosen the flowers for the ceremony but I'm not sure about the ones for my bouquet and for you and Gret. Really, it's just a lot of last-minute stuff."

"Well, all right, if you say so. I'll see you at the restaurant."

"Noon sharp," Duchess said before ending the call. She set the green cordless on the burgundy-tiled kitchen counter and checked her day calendar. It was seven-thirty A.M. and she had a full schedule.

Muhsin and Duchess had returned to Chicago a week earlier. Since then, Duchess had been in the process of planning their wedding. Everyone marveled at the headway she'd made undertaking such a heavy task.

"And I'm not done yet," she whispered, thumbing through the black organizer. Her gaze narrowed when the book opened to the phone directory. Jaliel Norris's name stood out like a beacon and she traced the letters with her index finger.

Duchess closed her eyes and pictured Jaliel in her mind. She had not spoken with him since the day he'd called for money. She had no idea whether he was alive or dead. Movement in the kitchen's arched doorway caught her attention and she looked up. Muhsin stood, leaning against the doorjamb. A happy smile came to her face as she admired the cut and fit of the stylish mocha suit he wore. The trousers flattered his long legs and toned thighs. The coat was perfectly tailored to fit his wide chest and back.

"How long have you been standing there?" she asked.

Muhsin pushed himself from the door and strolled into the kitchen with his hands pushed into his trousers' deep pockets. "I've been standing there long enough to hear that you're running in too many crazy directions planning our wedding," he told her, pulling his hands from his pockets and easing them around her waist.

Duchess wound her arms around his neck when he

lifted her against his chest and placed her on the round red oak kitchen table. "I'm enjoying myself," she assured him.

Muhsin loosened the thick belt around her pink and blue terry-cloth robe. "You sure?" he asked, pulling the robe apart. "'Cause I know plenty of people in the business of planning these things," he said, going to work on the flimsy ties at the bodice of her gown.

"Baby, the last thing I want is some stuffy event. I want a fun wedding," she said, gasping when his middle finger slipped inside her gown to stroke the curve of her breasts.

"Fun, huh?" he replied, lowering his face to the side of her neck.

Duchess raised her head to give his lips more room to roam. "Uh-huh. I want something where people can let down their hair and have a good time. I want my own personal touch on this thing because I plan on getting married just once . . . for life."

Muhsin gathered her in his arms and pressed his forehead against hers. "For life, huh?"

"Does that scare you?" Duchess asked, pressing a quick kiss to his mouth.

Muhsin toyed with the ponytail bouncing down her back. "Scared of spending my life with you? Never," he assured her and then took advantage of her barely clothed state.

Duchess let him pull the robe from her shoulders. His hands coursed over her thighs and he parted her legs.

"Muhsin . . ." Duchess said in a warning tone. He ignored her, of course, and slipped his fingers inside the crotch of her panties. "Muhsin, no. Sweetie, you've got to go." She sat up on the table.

"In case you forgot, I'm the boss."

"Yeah, but you've got people waiting on you," she reminded him.

"They can wait," he growled against her breasts.

"Well, I can't. Besides, we're meeting for dinner tonight and I want to have everything done by then."

Muhsin groaned and frowned when he pulled away from her. "You only get one chance a week to resist me. Next time, I carry you off to bed."

"Deal," Duchess whispered, giggling when he gnawed her neck.

When Muhsin was gone, she turned back to the directory and found the page with Jaliel's name.

As planned, Duchess and Ophelia met for lunch at the popular Chinese café, the Chop House. Of course, they barely tasted anything from the inviting Pu Pu Platter they'd ordered. Talk of the wedding was their primary interest.

"I can't believe you've made so much progress planning this thing, Dutch. You make me feel like a complete wimp."

Duchess laughed and slapped Ophelia's hand. "What the hell are you talkin' about?"

"Girl, I'm serious. It takes a special person to plan something so tedious," Ophelia said, fiddling with the ruffled neckline of her pearl-blue silk blouse. "There are so many details."

"I won't disagree with you there." Duchess sighed, recalling how hectic her morning had been.

"I mean, Tan and I had a very small affair, but I 'bout went crazy getting all the arrangements together."

Duchess crossed her arms over the bodice of her long-sleeved olive-green cotton dress. A thoughtful expression came to her lovely face. "You know, Oph, Muhsin and I have had so many upsets during our relationship, this is the first thing that's been truly wonderful. I guess I want to thoroughly enjoy every moment of it. Besides, it's nice to be caught up in something so beautiful."

"So did you decide on your bouquet?"

Duchess leaned forward, bracing her elbow on the small round table. "I decided on mine and Muhsin's birth flowers."

Ophelia pressed her hand to her chest. "Oh, Duchess, that's so beautiful."

"Thanks. Before I toss it, I'm gonna take one of each flower for our wedding album."

Ophelia sighed. "I love it. So everything went all right with the caterers, too?"

"Mmm-hmm. Now after my final fitting and getting you and Gretchen taken care of, I'm home free. I have her measurements and she said whatever you liked, she'd go with."

"It's a good thing you don't have a long line of bridesmaids."

"Honey, I couldn't have stood it."

Suddenly Ophelia laughed. "I can't believe Muhsin decided on two best men!"

Duchess chuckled. "Well, Roland and Tan are his two best friends. Hush, Oph, I think it's sweet."

"So what about the music? I know Muhsin had a say about that."

Duchess took a sip of her raspberry tea and nodded. "You know him so well. We decided to have a string quartet perform at the ceremony, and Muhsin doesn't know it yet, but I'd like to arrange for Regina Belle to sing. Muhsin loves her."

"Duchess," Ophelia breathed, undoubtedly impressed.

Just then a cell phone rang. Both women checked their bags.

Duchess waved her hand. "It's mine," she announced, clicking the TALK button. "This is Duchess."

"Hey, sweetie, it's me."

"Hey, Gret, thanks for returning my call. Is everything all right back there?"

"Oh, the business is fine. It's the people who work for you that are making me want to scream."

Duchess laughed. "What's the problem?"

"Girl, everyone wants to work in the annex. They say the office space there is more conducive for creativity."

"Oh, Lord." Duchess sighed. "Oh well, at least everyone is eager to work."

"Hmph."

"Anyway, um, about the reason I called . . ."

"Oh, yeah, somethin' about Jaliel."

"Yeah, I tried calling him this morning but the operator said the number wasn't in service. Do you know if it's changed? She said she had no further information on it."

Gretchen closed her eyes and uttered a muffled curse. She had hoped to keep the situation with Jaliel hidden from Duchess until after the wedding. Now she realized she had no choice but to go into it.

"Gret?"

"Dutch, Jaliel didn't come back after his leave. Now he's lost his condo and I've got no idea where he is."

"Oh, no," Duchess said. "I'd hoped he'd decided to just take some extra time to relax. I had no idea he'd had a relapse." She decided against telling Gretchen about the money she'd sent Jaliel weeks earlier.

"Well . . . maybe he's checked himself in somewhere."

"But you don't believe that, do you?" Duchess asked, taking Gretchen's silence as confirmation. "Listen, I'll, um, I'll talk to you later," she said, suddenly too aggravated to continue the discussion.

"Problems?" Ophelia asked, not liking Duchess's troubled expression.

"Ophelia, I think I need to go check on a friend."

* * *

Muhsin glanced up from his menu just in time to see Duchess arrive in the restaurant's dining room. His intense stare narrowed as he leaned back to watch her being escorted by the host. He couldn't help but notice the attention she drew. That didn't bother him. He could certainly understand her effect on the opposite sex. After all, she had captured his heart the first time he saw her.

"Sorry I'm late," Duchess whispered, going right to Muhsin's arms when he stood. She kissed his mouth and began to pull away when his hold tightened on her arms.

"What's the matter?" he whispered, smoothing his large hands across the clinging fabric of the dress she wore.

Duchess was surprised that he could detect something she'd tried carefully to hide. Still, she denied anything was wrong with a quick shake of her head. "I'm fine."

Muhsin didn't force the subject, but continued to watch her closely.

"I talked to the deejay for the reception," Duchess said as she set her purse aside and picked up the menu. "I told him what we wanted, but he still suggested we both come in sometime in the next couple of days to select some stuff. He wants to make sure he plays our favorites."

Muhsin was interested and nodded. "Sounds good. I want to make sure he's got a good selection of old-school and a few new joints thrown in. Nothing corny or too sappy."

"And what can I get for you folks this evening?"

Duchess and Muhsin glanced up at the waiter, and then scanned their menus.

"Um, I'll have the shrimp bisque with the sourdough rolls and a house salad—vinaigrette dressing."

"And to drink, ma'am?"

"White wine."

"And for you, sir?"

"I'll take the same, but throw in a side of fettuccine for me."

The waiter jotted down the orders and smiled. "Very good. I'll be right back with your drinks."

"So, anyway, if you have some time tomorrow, we can—"

"Duchess, I don't want to hear another word about the wedding until you tell me what's got you so upset."

Duchess brought her hand to her forehead and massaged the dull ache forming there. "The closer we come to the wedding, I've been thinking about Jaliel a lot more. I really want him to be there, but no one seems to know where he is. I'm worried."

The dimple flashed in Muhsin's cheek when his jaw tightened. He wanted nothing to cloud what was supposed to be a happy time. Duchess had been through too much already. "Have you called everyone you can think of?"

Duchess nodded. "I even called Gretchen, who hasn't talked to him since they had a falling out. She told me he quit and I found out they wouldn't renew his lease for the condo because of his arrest and that whole mess."

Muhsin massaged his jaw. "That is strange," he admitted.

Duchess fiddled with her silverware, the heavy fringe of her lashes shielding her gaze. "If it wouldn't bother you too much, I'd like to go back to Philly just to make sure he's all right."

Muhsin smiled at the way she phrased the softly spoken question. He knew she would go whether or not he approved. "I have no problem with it, but I'm coming with you."

"Maybe you should stay in the car," Muhsin suggested when he parked the rented Explorer outside the Philly club where they'd had the run-in with Jaliel and his drug supplier.

Duchess shoved her purse beneath the seat. "You know I can't **do** that," she told him, smoothing back her hair into a ponytail. "Besides, do you really want me out here alone?"

Muhsin realized her point. "Don't leave my side," he ordered, leaving the SUV.

Dressed in sagging jeans, rugged hiking boots and sweatshirts, the gorgeous couple drew no real attention when they entered the club. The bartender, however, recognized them right away.

"We didn't come to start any trouble," Muhsin explained.

The man waved his hand. "Please, brotha, you deserve a special table and free drinks after the favor you did us."

Duchess propped her elbow on the bar. "Favor?"

"Shaunnessy Wright hasn't been back in here since that night," the man said.

"Has Jaliel Norris been back?" Duchess asked.

The bartender grimaced. "Unfortunately."

"Unfortunately?"

"Miss, your friend is a drug addict," the bartender replied in a blunt tone, though he watched Duchess through sympathetic eyes. "Maybe he started off on the easy stuff, but he's graduated to some killer chemicals. The way he looks, he won't be around much longer."

"Well, has he come in tonight?" Duchess asked, trying to dismiss the man's black prediction.

The bartender glanced at Muhsin, then shook his head. "But he could show up anytime."

Duchess felt her phone vibrate in her back pocket and turned to answer it. While she was occupied, the man motioned to Muhsin.

"Man, Norris is here in the back. I didn't think the sistah could take seeing him like he is."

Muhsin nodded. "Thanks, man. Keep her occupied," he said, glancing toward Duchess before he went off in the direction the bartender had instructed. He found Jaliel easily since there was no one around him. He took a closer look and almost grew nauseous by the man's appearance. He agreed with the bartender's feeling. Muhsin was about to walk away when Jaliel looked up and recognized him.

"Vuyani!" he called, moving from his table.

Muhsin grimaced at the smell of urine and liquor reeking from Jaliel's clothes. "Norris," he replied.

"Man, what you doin' in here?" he questioned, incessantly fidgeting as he tried to decide between keeping his hands in his pockets or on his hips.

The man was definitely on something, Muhsin noted coolly, eyeing the jittery motions with a knowing gaze. "Just passing through," he answered finally. "What're you doing up in here?"

Jaliel shrugged twice. "Just passin' through, too, I guess. Times been rough, you know? I'm out of work right now."

"Mmm . . . and whose fault is that?"

Jaliel uttered a short, uneasy laugh. "Man, how's Duchess doin'? I really miss her."

Muhsin decided to come clean. "She's here in town," he said, pulling a piece of paper from his wallet. "I want you to go to this hotel. There will be a room there in your name. There will be a change of clothes there. Use the shower. Put on the clothes. Duchess wants to see you. I'll be bringing her by sometime tomorrow morning. I want you decent."

Jaliel took the slip of paper and held it reverently. "Thank you, man. Thank you. I just need a chance to get back on my feet."

"Save it, Norris. I'm doin' this for Duchess. I got the feeling she believes she can save you."

"Thanks, man," he said, then tapped Muhsin's shoulder when he was about to walk away. "Could you spare a few bills, my man? For toothpaste and stuff?"

Muhsin knew what the money was for, but he handed Jaliel a fifty-dollar bill anyway. "You be there in the morning. Don't make me come looking for you, Norris."

Duchess was ending another call when Muhsin returned.

"You ready?" he asked.

"Mmm-hmm. Listen, some friends of mine who live here in town want to throw us a dinner party tomorrow night to celebrate our wedding. They may not be able to make it to Chicago."

"Sounds good," Muhsin replied absently, helping her off the bar stool.

Duchess turned. "Wait. Shouldn't we tell the bartender how he can reach us in case Jaliel shows up?"

"Already taken care of," Muhsin muttered.

When he and Duchess returned to her condo, Muhsin stayed downstairs to arrange the accommodations across town for Jaliel. When he went to the bedroom, Duchess had soft music playing and the lights were low. She was enjoying the view of the city from the balcony.

"Aren't you cold?" he asked, folding her in his strong embrace.

Duchess snuggled back into the embrace. "Mmm . . . I was," she cooed.

"What are you doing out here?" he asked, rubbing his hands over her gown's chiffon robe.

Duchess closed her eyes. "I was thinking about Jaliel. I just can't believe this is happening to him. You know, he was always the responsible one, the big-brother type keeping me and Gret in line. I mean, he wasn't a saint, but drugs . . . All I've ever known him to do was a little weed."

"A lot of times, that's how it starts," Muhsin noted, pressing his cheek against her hair.

"But he wasn't a chain-smoker or anything like that."

"Doesn't always matter, baby."

"Well, I don't care. I'll do anything to get him back on his feet."

"Such as?" Muhsin asked.

"I'd get him back to work, for one," Duchess said. "That's probably what he needs. Something to keep him occupied. Then I'd get him back in his condo—whatever he needs. I can't just turn my back on him. Surely that would send him completely over the edge and I can't handle knowing he's out there with nowhere to go, no food, no money."

Muhsin turned Duchess around to face him. "Baby, that sounds really admirable. You're a true friend, but you don't seem to realize that all this stuff you want to do for him will do more harm than good."

"Excuse me?"

"Baby, all you're doing is helping him continue his habit."

Duchess's hazel gaze grew stormy. "I don't want him on this stuff, Muhsin! That's why I—"

Muhsin's eyes narrowed. "Why you what?"

Duchess wouldn't meet his stare. "It was only a few dollars."

"A few dollars for what?"

Sighing, Duchess stepped out of Muhsin's embrace

and walked closer to the balcony railing. "He called a couple of weeks after I got back from Jamaica. He sounded so desperate . . . I wired him some money. I was just so worried about him being out there with nothing. I know I made a mistake, but I just want back the friend I miss so much."

"I know, honey, I know, but situations like this call for tough love. Jaliel doesn't need material things. He'll just piss 'em away on crack or whatever will get him high. He needs help, Duchess, and he needs it from a place he can't just leave until he's kicked this thing."

Duchess tried to shake off his hold. "You make it sound like he needs to be in jail."

Muhsin shrugged. "He obviously can't do it on his own."

"But to throw someone away just because they have a problem—it's cruel."

"It's a cruel habit, Duchess."

"You don't know Jaliel," she snapped, her eyes watery with tears. "I've known him all my life and I won't just turn my back on him."

Muhsin cursed when he heard Duchess crying. "Baby, shh, stop this," he said, pulling her close. When the sobs grew heavier, he picked her up and carried her to bed. Without removing his clothes, he settled in behind her and held her close as he rocked her to sleep.

Shaunnessy Wright's permanent scowl appeared to darken as he waited for Jaliel to finish his second coughing spell.

"I'm through with your sorry ass, Norris," he all but snarled into the phone.

"Shaunnessy, man, wait, wait," Jaliel whispered, raising one hand in the air while he held the receiver pressed to his ear with the other. "Man, I promise you, I got the money for the stuff. I'm stayin' at the Carlyle, man. See? I'm gettin' my stuff together."

"Man, why don't you call somebody else?"

Jaliel uttered a quick, nervous laugh. "Come on, man. You the only one I know who can get me what I need. I been a loyal customer."

"Loyal customer, huh?" Shaunnessy repeated, gesturing to one of his associates in the room. "All right, Norris, I'll send somebody over there in a while." He clicked off the phone in the midst of Jaliel's litany of thank yous. He looked up at the man standing near his desk and handed him Jaliel's address. "I think it's time to write off one loyal customer."

Jaliel checked his appearance in the mirror. He looked terrible, but several times better than he had earlier. The doorbell sounded and he went to pull open the door for Duchess and Muhsin.

Duchess was shocked when she saw Jaliel. His handsome, chocolate-toned face now seemed gaunt and ashen. His teeth appeared yellow and rotting in some places. Still, she managed a smile when he pulled her into a tight hug. Arm in arm, they walked into the hotel room. Muhsin followed, but remained in the background.

"Jaliel," Duchess whispered as she smoothed her hands across her bell-bottomed jeans and took a seat on the sofa. "Where have you been? I've been so worried."

Jaliel rubbed his hand across Duchess's back. "Traveling. I just needed to get away for a while."

Duchess tensed at the lie. "Gretchen said you'd quit your job?"

"Damnit!" Jaliel snapped. "I told her I was taking that leave of absence, but you know she's been wanting me out of there for a long time."

"That's not true. We care about you and want to help you."

Jaliel glanced at Muhsin, then leaned closer to Duchess. "All I really need is a loan, just a few hundred. 'Til I get back on my feet."

Duchess pressed her hand against his rough cheek. "Honey, don't you miss work and your friends?"

"Them jackasses?" Jaliel hissed, turning his face away. "They don't give a damn. The bastards all turned on me."

Duchess folded her arms across the snug burgundy sweater she sported. "You're wrong, Jaliel. And to prove it, I'm inviting you to a dinner party Missy and James are throwing for me and Muhsin at their condo tonight."

Muhsin groaned inwardly at the invite. He closed his eyes and prayed Jaliel would decline.

"You really want me there, Dutch?"

"Would I be asking otherwise?"

Jaliel nodded and squeezed her hand. "I'll be there."

"You promise?" Duchess asked, already writing down the address and phone number to their friend's home.

Jaliel slipped the information inside his pocket. "I promise."

Duchess took that as a sign that all hope was not lost for her friend. She cupped his face in her hands. "After tonight, we'll talk about getting you back on your feet."

At least twenty people filled the posh condo of Missy and James Harvey. The dinner party for Duchess and Muhsin was lovely and energetic. The dinner was served buffet style with all sorts of delectable entrées and desserts. Besides the impressive spread, there was dancing and the sharing of memories about old times. When someone mentioned Jaliel, Duchess announced that he should be there any minute.

Gretchen approached Muhsin as he filled a plate from the buffet.

"Is he really coming?"

Muhsin helped himself to a heaping spoonful of macaroni casserole. "He promised Duchess."

"Hmph."

"What?" Muhsin asked, glancing at Gretchen.

"After all these months? Now he wants to get back in the social scene?"

Muhsin ate his food while they talked. "I got the feeling he really wanted to be here."

"Oh, yeah? How'd he seem when y'all left him?"

"He seemed grateful when Duchess mentioned getting him help, but it's hard to say if he meant it."

"That's interesting," Gretchen noted. "I mean, we haven't been around each other much but I know he's been using. Heavy. Everybody here knows."

"Have you told Duchess how bad it is?"

Gretchen frowned. "Honey, Duchess is in denial about how bad it is. She knows everything, but she doesn't want to believe it. She thinks she can save Jaliel or something."

"Yeah, I know." Muhsin sighed, a frown darkening his attractive features. He heard someone call Duchess's name and watched as she ran across the room to take the phone away from the hostess. He watched her take the call. When her expression changed from expectancy to confusion, he went to her.

Duchess smoothed a shaking hand across the chignon she wore. "What are you saying? I don't—"

"What's wrong?"

Duchess pulled the phone from her ear and shrugged. "It's someone telling me Jaliel's had a heart attack or something, I—"

Muhsin took the phone. "This is Muhsin Vuyani, I'm Ms. Carver's fiancé."

"Uh, yes, sir," the young woman said, clearing her throat before she continued. "We got this number from Mr. Norris's pocket when they brought him in."

"Brought him in?"

"Hotel housekeeping found Mr. Norris passed out in his bathroom. He's had a heart attack, sir. We believe it was brought on by a drug overdose."

Gretchen followed Muhsin and Duchess to the hospital. They waited almost an hour and a half before the doctor was free to speak with them.

"Mr. Norris was very lucky. If they had gotten him here five minutes later, he wouldn't have made it. He won't make it the next time this happens," the doctor stated grimly.

"Will he be all right, though?" Duchess asked, rubbing her hands across her arms, left bare by the spaghetti straps of her maroon gown.

"For now," he replied. "Your friend has a drug problem, and whoever is supplying the drugs is dealing poison. I mean that literally."

Muhsin stepped forward. "Wait a minute. You mean someone sold him some bad stuff?"

"That's exactly what I mean."

"Jesus," Gretchen whispered, shaking her head.

"Can we see him?"

The doctor smiled at Duchess. "He's resting now. Perhaps in the morning?" he offered, his green eyes sparkling in a friendly manner.

Duchess nodded and watched the doctor leave. When he was gone, she rubbed her eyes and yawned. Muhsin retrieved her cashmere wrap from a chair and placed it across her shoulders. "Gretchen, would you take her back home and then come back here when you're done?" he added when Duchess had walked on ahead.

Gretchen's dark eyes narrowed. "Come back?" she whispered.

"I'll explain later."

Dr. Henry Booker asked his secretary to hold all calls while he spoke with Muhsin.

"I was wondering if I'd hear from you again, Blaze," Henry said as he spoke into the speakerphone. "I take it you received all the information on the clinic?"

"Yeah, thanks, Hen. I got it."

"Has your fiancée's friend found the help he needs?"

Muhsin sighed on the other end of the line. "Not exactly, which is why I'm calling."

Henry sat straighter in his desk chair. "I'm listening."

"This guy won't come willingly."

"Mmm . . . now I see why you called."

"Can we get him in without his consent?"

Henry sighed. "It can be tricky. I will at least need a family member or close friend to sign for him and I'll need the doctor to sign the necessary papers confirming the problem."

"I'll get right on it," Muhsin said.

"And I'll fax the paperwork as soon as I speak with the attending physician."

"Thanks, Henry."

"Just get him here. He'll get the best help possible."

Muhsin clicked off the cell phone and closed his eyes. "Lord, please don't let her hate me for this."

Duchess got a late start the next morning. She took a cab to the hospital so she wouldn't disturb Muhsin, who had returned late the night before and was still asleep. When she arrived at the hospital, Gretchen was already there.

"How's Jaliel?" Duchess asked when Gretchen left the nurses' station. "Where's the doctor? I want to go in and see him."

"Dutch, wait," Gretchen said. "Jaliel's gone."

Duchess ran both hands through her long, loose hair. "Gone? What do you mean, gone? Is he—"

"No, no he—he's . . . They've taken him to a facility. Someplace where he can get help."

"What do you mean, a facility? Where is he?"

Gretchen clasped her hands together and stepped closer to Duchess. "Honey, Muhsin thought it would be best for Jaliel. He knows—"

"Muhsin thought?"

"Honey, please don't get upset."

"Where's Jaliel?" Duchess whispered, placing one hand on her hips and bowing her head.

"Muhsin has a friend, a doctor who runs a clinic, a rehab clinic in Albany, New York. Jaliel can get real help there, Dutch."

"Can I see him?"

Gretchen nodded. "Muhsin wants to take you. It's a good place, Dutch. I've read over all the literature and Jaliel—"

"Gret, stop," Duchess whispered, waving her hand once. Closing her eyes, she leaned against the wall.

"Sweetie?" Gretchen said softly, smoothing her hand across the tan suede jacket Duchess wore over a jean jumper.

"I need to get out of here," Duchess said.

Gretchen pulled her friend close. "We'll go to my place. You can think, give yourself some time to get used to this."

Duchess nodded and they left the hospital. Taking a cab, Duchess followed Gretchen back to her apartment. The two spent the better part of the day reminiscing over their friend and happier times. Duchess spoke with Henry Booker and was content that Jaliel would receive top care. She and Gretchen enjoyed tea in the kitchen, where they spoke with the doctor via speakerphone. They were each given a chance to ask questions and voice concerns regarding their friend. Duchess had tried to reach Muhsin by phone, but was unsuccessful. She decided to head back to her condo later, knowing he was probably climbing the walls because he hadn't seen her for most of the day. For now, she'd stay with Gretchen and try to relax.

"Is she here?" Muhsin asked when Gretchen answered her door a little later. A flash of relief raced through his body when she nodded.

"Come in."

Muhsin kept on his beige overcoat and followed Gretchen to the kitchen. Duchess was there, leaning against the kitchen island with a mug of tea in her hands. He pushed his hands into the pockets of his hunter-green trousers and slowly approached her. Uncertainty clouded his handsome face.

"I didn't know how else to handle it," he said, the moment her eyes connected with his.

Duchess set her mug aside and listened.

"Jaliel needs good help, Duchess," he continued, bracing one hand against the oak island. "He needs to be in a place he can't just leave when he gets frustrated, and he needs to go without seeing you. Because, like it or not, you're a crutch for him and as long as he knows he can fall back on you, he'll never get better." Muhsin felt his heart pound faster when she continued to stare at him. "Duchess, if you hate me for this, I—"

"Come here," she called, extending her hand. When he took it, she pulled him close and stood on her toes to press a kiss to his cheek.

Muhsin blinked. "Are we still okay?"

Duchess raked her fingers through his soft, auburn curls. "We're better than okay," she assured him. "Thank you. Thank you for helping my friend. You were right, I was doing more harm than good."

Muhsin pulled her tight against him and squeezed his eyes shut. "I was afraid you'd hate me all over again for stepping in and handling this."

Duchess pressed a kiss into his neck. "Hate you?" she whispered. "I love you even more. Jaliel needed someone objective in his corner. I know you did it for me, but it was for Jaliel's benefit. Now it's up to him to make the most of this chance."

Muhsin pulled back and smiled. "I thought I was making another mistake."

Duchess traced the cleft in his chin and the curve of his sensuous mouth. "Mr. Vuyani, you may not know this, but even us independent sistahs need a little help every now and then."

"I can't wait to make you mine," he said, cupping her face in his hands.

"I'm already yours," she said, turning her face into his hand and pressing the softest kiss to his palm.

Chapter 15

Duchess gave a languid stretch and snuggled deeper into the covers of the decadently beautiful, canopied bed. *Today is my wedding day,* she silently chanted and took time to reminisce over the journey to that moment. At last she decided she'd much rather get started making new memories and whipped back the covers. A soft knock sounded on the room door just as her toes curled into the carpet.

"Duchess?"

"Muhsin?" she whispered, hearing the familiar raspy voice of her husband-to-be. "Muhsin, what are you doing?" She giggled as she strolled across the room.

"I'm waiting for you to open the door," he replied and twisted the knob for emphasis.

Again, Duchess giggled. "I can't."

"Why not?"

"It's bad luck for you to see me before the wedding. You know that."

"Bad luck? After what we've just been through? You can't be serious!"

"That's exactly my point. We should be the last people trying to tempt fate."

"I see." Muhsin groaned even as a sly smile crossed his mouth. "Just one kiss?"

"Ha!"

"What?" he whined, pretending to be offended. "You don't think I'd settle for that?"

"Have you ever?" Duchess challenged, leaning against the door as she thoroughly enjoyed their playful banter.

"This is torture," he said, trailing his finger around the doorknob. "I couldn't sleep a wink without you."

The quiet raspiness of his voice warmed Duchess from head to toe. "Liar," she teased softly, being deliberately coy.

Muhsin grinned in response. "We won't have this door between us much longer, you know."

"Oooh, is that a warning?" Duchess asked, giggling again over the playful threat.

"Damn right."

"Muhsin Vuyani! Get away from that door this minute!"

"Ophelia?" Muhsin and Duchess spoke in unison.

Ophelia interrupted the rendezvous with all the subtlety of a battering ram. Tan, Isaiah, Roland, Tia and Gretchen were right at her heels.

"Come on, man, breakfast awaits," Roland called, clapping Muhsin's shoulder.

"Damn, can't I even talk to her?" Muhsin complained, his voice alive with humor.

"Not when you're trying to persuade her to be naughty," Gretchen scolded, waving her hands to shoo him away from the door.

"Come on, Moose," Tan urged, standing between his friend and the door.

"Yeah, 'cause beggin' won't work," Isaiah assured him as he waved the guys toward the stairway.

"Yeah, save the begging for tonight," Roland teased mercilessly, joining in when everyone laughed.

On the other side of the door, Duchess's stomach ached from laughter. She could hear Muhsin still complaining even as his voice faded down the hall.

"All right, Dutch, you can open up now, the coast is clear," Gretchen announced.

"What's all this?" Duchess gasped, finding Gretchen, Tia and Ophelia standing in the hallway. Before them was a tea cart filled with delectable pastries, cheeses, fruits, juices and, of course, tea.

"For the bride," Tia announced, leading Duchess to the armchair next to the sliding glass doors that led to a private terrace.

The ladies prepared a plate filled with sinful treats for Duchess. Then they helped themselves.

"Happy?" Gretchen asked when she'd taken the chair next to her best friend.

Duchess closed her eyes and savored a sugar-laced strawberry. "Mmm, frighteningly happy. Is that good?"

"It's *very* good," Gretchen agreed lazily, then reached out to pat Duchess's cheek. "And *very* deserved."

Grabbing Gretchen's hand, Duchess kissed her cheek.

"All the best, Blaze," Isaiah said, raising his juice glass in a mock toast.

Muhsin raised his own glass in response. "Thanks, man. I never thought this would be me, you know?"

Isaiah nodded, grinning when he glanced across the kitchen, where Tan and Roland stood, arguing over how the eggs should be prepared. "You've come a long way, kid."

"And I've done a lot of wrong along the way."

"Blaze . . ." Isaiah began, shaking his head to ward off the turn in conversation.

Muhsin wouldn't let the moment slip away. "I don't know if I ever told you, man: I'm sorry. You didn't deserve that, neither did Tia. She really loves you and I apologize for coming between the two of you because I envied what you had and couldn't find a way to make it happen for myself."

Isaiah's eyes narrowed and he nodded once, knowing Muhsin spoke the truth. In the midst of a firm handshake, they shared a hug.

The wedding was nothing like they had planned. Instead of a huge event with all of Chicago society in attendance, the gathering at Muhsin's estate was smaller, more intimate and, in everyone's opinion, far more memorable. Duchess was the image of a fairy princess in a handstitched gown of the finest satin and silk. The long chiffon sleeves were flared at her wrists and partially shielded her hands from view. Muhsin was equally impressive in a white tux, complete with a tailored three-quarter-length jacket. His gaze was unwavering as he watched his bride make her way down the long, flower-lined aisle past their six guests in attendance.

The ceremony was presided over by the minister who had married Duchess's parents, and who was more than happy to do the honors. The vows were taken beneath the gazebo that was practically hidden behind the massive trunks of the splendid oaks that dotted the spacious landscape. The chilly onset of another late autumn evening provided a nippy breeze that settled in just as the minister presented Muhsin and Duchess Vuyani as husband and wife.

Later, Duchess experienced a pang of sadness when she spoke with Jaliel during the reception, also held at the estate. Jaliel wished his friend every happiness; Duchess wished he could have been there for her special day, but it was enough to know that he was safe and making great progress toward recovery at the clinic.

The newlyweds agreed that Duchess would spend one week a month in Philadelphia to oversee matters at the Carver Design Group. The buzz about the company had become favorable with talk of the new annex. Once again, the client list was growing and, unbeknownst to anyone, Duchess had already been toying with the idea of expanding into the Midwest. Chicago, to be more specific.

Happiness grew over the announcement that Isaiah and Tia's nuptials would be held within the next year. Gretchen, the maid of honor, and Roland, who served as one of the best men, had arrived arm in arm for the wedding. They had been virtually inseparable for most of the day. Of course, they were the target of several teasing remarks by the other three couples. Still, the two remained very secretive and would only admit to enjoying one another's company and nothing more. Not to be outdone, Tan and Ophelia shared the biggest surprise when they announced the expected arrival of their first child in the spring.

During their first dance as husband and wife, Duchess trailed her nose along the strong line of her husband's jaw. "What are you thinking?" she whispered.

Muhsin fixed his warm cocoa stare on his wife's face. "Thinking about how much I love you," he said and dropped a kiss to the tip of her nose.

"Aww . . ." Duchess gushed before her expression sobered in a playful manner. "I expect that to be a constant thought in your mind, Mister Vuyani."

He pressed his forehead to hers. "No problem."

"So what else are you thinking? Seriously?"

Muhsin looked out over the group and smiled. "I never thought this was important to me."

"What?" Duchess asked softly, brushing the back of her hand across his cheek.

"Love. Real love," he said, looking back at her and leaning close to kiss her cheek. "Friends, *good* friends," he added, looking back out over the loving couples that joined them on the dance floor. "This is what matters. What makes it all worth it."

"And you truly believe it was all worth it?" Duchess asked, tilting her head back to look directly into his eyes.

"Most definitely," he responded promptly. "Every painful, dramatic, heart-wrenching moment of it." He laughed when Duchess slapped his shoulder. "Seriously," he continued, once his own laughter had quieted, "many things could have been handled differently, but I don't know if I'd be the man I am right now if we hadn't gone through all the frustration."

"The man you are right now," Duchess repeated softly. "A better man inside?"

Muhsin nodded. "I'd like to think so. I hope you think so, too."

Duchess shook her head, a skeptical look in her eyes. "No, I don't think so. I *know* so."

Muhsin's smile returned and he buried his handsome face against her neck, hugging her tightly. "Mmm . . . my wife," he whispered in a tone of complete male satisfaction.

"As it should be," she whispered back, just as their lips melded into the sweetest kiss.

The wedding guests responded to the newlyweds' display of affection with heavy applause and hearty cheers for a happy life.

Epilogue

Muhsin and Duchess lounged in bed in the Canadian mountains after an enthusiastic session of lovemaking. They lay on their sides and stared out at the steady fall of snow from the huge paned window.

"Did you and Quincy plan this?" Duchess asked, snuggling close against her husband's chest.

He kissed her shoulder. "Hell, no. The man hated my guts after what I did."

Duchess closed her eyes. "You're exaggerating."

"Maybe a little. But he didn't like what I did one bit."

"Well," she said, staring around at the cozy cabin lit by a blazing fireplace, "he must have forgiven you to send us to this incredible place for our honeymoon."

"He did it for you, but I don't mind benefiting," Muhsin admitted before he began to nibble her shoulder.

"Speaking of benefiting," Duchess said, "there's still the issue of thirty million dollars gathering dust."

"And it'll continue to do so until those two are ready to assume control of it."

Duchess frowned. "What two?"

Muhsin inhaled deeply and smiled. "The thirty million has been split into two trusts. One for Tan and Oph's son or daughter when he or she reaches twenty-one."

"Muhsin," Duchess breathed, "that's wonderful. And the other trust?"

Muhsin slipped his hands around her waist and effortlessly pulled her astride his body. "The other is for our child. Who, if I'm not mistaken, has yet to be conceived but will be in the very near future."

Duchess's light eyes narrowed seductively. "You're sure of this?"

"Quite sure. Of course, I'll need your cooperation."

Duchess settled herself more securely against her husband. "And you shall have it, Mr. Vuyani."

"I love you," he said, searching her eyes with his. "I'll tell you that every day."

"I love you," Duchess spoke against his mouth. "Always."

Muffled laughter rose in the cozy room when they pulled the covers above their heads. Outside, the snow raged with renewed vigor.

Dear Readers,

Love Scheme was an enjoyable story to create. I hope that you all were entertained, intrigued, outraged and delighted. Duchess and Muhsin's story held several twists and revelations. Still, the topic I wanted to explore most was the element of change and its effect on the characters in the story. Capturing the essence of these changes and how it served to deepen the relationship between the hero and heroine was especially important to me. I hope you all agree that this love scheme resulted in real love.

As always, your thoughts and opinions on my work are truly appreciated. E-mail me: altonya@writeme.com

Peace and blessings,
AlTonya R. Washington

About the Author

AlTonya Washington is a South Carolina native. She's been a fan of the romance genre since age thirteen and embarked upon a writing career in 1994. *Love Scheme* is her fourth contemporary romance.

BOOK YOUR PLACE ON OUR WEBSITE AND MAKE THE ARABESQUE ROMANCE CONNECTION!

We've created a customized website just for our very special Arabesque readers, where you can get the inside scoop on everything that's going on with Arabesque romance novels.

When you come online, you'll have the exciting opportunity to:

- View covers of upcoming books

- Learn about our future publishing schedule (listed by publication month and author)

- Find out when your favorite authors will be visiting a city near you

- Search for and order backlist books

- Check out author bios and background information

- Send e-mail to your favorite authors

- Join us in weekly chats with authors, readers and other guests

- Get writing guidelines

- AND MUCH MORE!

Visit our website at
http://www.arabesquebooks.com